■   ■   ■   ■

The kidnap victim. The female
operative. The diamond king. The
beautiful terrorist. He had been
pulled into their lives and their
struggle. They had gained power over
his life and his expectations. In a
very real way they had become a
threat to his very existence, but
there would be no escape from them.
Not until the game was finished.
Not until it was played to the end.

END GAME

END GAME

JAMES UNDERWOOD

WARNER BOOKS

A Warner Communications Company

WARNER BOOKS EDITION

Copyright © 1987 by James Underwood

Cover art by Edwin Herder

Warner Books, Inc.
666 Fifth Avenue
New York, N.Y. 10103

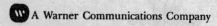 A Warner Communications Company

Printed in the United States of America

First Printing: February, 1987

10 9 8 7 6 5 4 3 2 1

**For Carol,
whose faith made it possible**

"Perhaps it is all a matter of limits; beyond those limits, the rules of control no longer apply."

PROLOGUE

The snows had been heavy throughout the Schleswig-Holstein. From Hamburg to the northern border of Germany, it lay white and pristine beneath the forests. Only a few of the roads that wound through the region had been cleared, the others lay hidden from the early light under a frozen blanket.

Deep in the shadows, obscured from the road that passed but twenty yards to the east, a man knelt by the trunk of a great pine. He was dressed in the white snow suit of an infantryman on winter manoeuvres; white parka, white gloves, white hood. He cradled a rifle in his arms and watched the road with the intensity of man bent on his task. He did not move, or make a sound. He sat silently in the cold, passively watching the empty road before him.

From a distance, the sound of a car slowly making its way along the road grew in clarity and strength. The engine labored then occasionally raced, as its wheels abruptly lost traction and then, just as abruptly, regained it.

Cautiously, the man in the shadows looked around himself. The road to the north was clear for the kilometer or so that he could see, before it circled back to the east toward the sea and the Keil Bay. There were no reflections or signs of movement from the surrounding woods. It was deathly still, as if the very air were frozen beyond its ability to move.

The man exhaled heavily. Then, purposefully, he raised the rifle to his shoulder and looked through its telescopic sight once again.

The range would be fifty yards, he told himself. As the car approached from the south, the sun would be on his left shoulder. It would be an easy shot. For a distance of two kilometers to the south the road could be seen clearly; there would be plenty of time. He would be able to watch his target approach with no chance for a surprise. Gradually, the man lowered his rifle and replaced his glove. Casually, he watched the frost from his breath dissipate into nothingness.

When the dark gray Mercedes finally came into view, it almost startled the man. Quickly, he positioned the rifle and peered through the scope. The face of the driver came clearly into focus the moment he did so, the cross hairs of the sight almost perfectly centered on the man's forehead. Patiently, the rifleman waited for the range to decrease to the appointed distance.

It was a matter of mechanics now. All that had to be done was to wait, take aim, pull the trigger, and then retrace his steps along the path he had broken in the darkness. The battered Volkswagen van he had left just over the ridge to his west would be waiting for him. A change of clothes, a drink from a flask of hot coffee and he would be on his way to cross into Denmark and safety.

Just a few seconds more and it would be done.

He removed the glove from his right hand, letting it fall to the snow by his thigh. Carefully he gripped the stock of the rifle. It felt cold to his touch. As the Mercedes came into range, he brought his finger into contact with the trigger, took a deep breath and steadied himself.

"Well, one more for God, country, and George Long," the man said aloud and pulled the trigger.

The sharp crack of the rifle shot shattered the silent morning. Its report echoed in the stillness then faded. The rifleman watched coldly through the telescopic sight as the Mercedes drifted to the left side of the road and stalled on the frozen berm, its windshield burst. Slowly, he stood and stretched himself. Then, suddenly tired and very cold, he started forward to check the accuracy of his shot.

The sound of a woman's scream stopped him short.

He watched as the passenger door of the Mercedes came partway open. Apparently jammed against the snowbank, it began to move back and forth in a frenzy. He could see her silhouette through the cracked remnants of glass. He had not seen her before. Perhaps she had been slumped over in her seat, her head in the lap of the driver?

The man hesitated, clutched his rifle, then stepped back into the shadows. Methodically he readied himself for a second shot. It was unfortunate, but it was the only answer, the expected remedy. As he assumed a firing position, he centered the Mercedes in the scope's field of vision.

The door continued to thump frantically against the frozen crust that held it. Its beating was almost rhythmic. Finally two pale bare hands thrust out and then a blond head. She wriggled. Like an animal caught in a steel trap, she tried to force her body free, and the sounds of her sobs and moans reached the man in the shadows. He could see the bright red splotches and streaks of blood on her. He could read the fear and horror in her face, the wild-eyed panic, as if she knew what was to befall her, and at that moment something stirred deep within the man. He paused. With his prey held perfectly in the sights of his weapon, he froze. Then, with a tremble that shook him to his spine, he lowered the rifle. What does it matter? he thought. What the Hell does it matter?

He continued to watch her struggle for several moments.

Then he stood and turned his back. Quietly and slowly at first, so he would not attract her attention, he began to make his way away from the scene. But the vision of the young woman failed to clear from his mind, and the sounds of her struggling carried all too audibly in the cold air. With each new scream he trembled more violently. Suddenly, he was running. The branches tore at him as he lunged up the slope. A cascade of dislodged snow fell about him like a shroud of ashes as he went.

"It's very simple, John. You blew it." George Long stood at the window as he spoke. His hands were clasped loosely behind his back as he surveyed the Danish coastline from the safe house's vantage point. "You did practically everything wrong."

John Pfifer sat in a straight-backed chair in the middle of the room. He faced the dying embers of a fire in a stone fireplace and watched the delicate fingers of smoke meander upward toward the flue. Slowly he turned to the ample man at the window and studied him coldly. He was a round-shouldered little bastard, he thought. Round-shouldered, thin haired, and as cold-blooded as a hungry bear. He also held the power in his stubby little fingers to snuff out his life without so much as a question having to be answered.

"Yes, you're right. I blew it. I should have killed the girl, but I didn't. I won't lie to you. I won't give you that satisfaction. So, what now? Now that I've fallen from grace. Am I to be classified as unsalvageable? Have my replacement ready, do you? Perhaps I'd make a good trial run for him."

Long turned quickly and spoke, making no attempt to disguise the anger in his voice.

"Don't taunt me! If it weren't for me, you'd be dead at this moment. The first car on the scene of your little fiasco was a patrol car. The authorities knew about the whole thing within an hour. And, as you should know, the Germans don't take kindly to messy little operations on their home turf. For

Christ's sake, man, they found your rifle not half a mile from the very spot. They had the gall to ask me to identify it!''

''And did you?''

''What do you think?''

''My question still stands. What now?''

''We're going to have to bury you for a while. Not literally, as attractive as that sounds at the moment. You'll be checked into a hospital in the States, a company hospital. I want to know what kind of physical condition you're in. I want to know if you've lost your mind completely or if there is some way we can relieve your 'stress,' let's call it.''

''And then, if they can't prop me up?''

''Pray they can, John Pfifer. Pray they can.''

Long walked briskly from the room. The last glimpse Pfifer got of his face revealed how truly angry he was. His cheeks were flushed, jaw set, eyes hard. It was a rare show of emotion from an otherwise unreadable countenance. Pfifer realized, perhaps for the first time, how important he must have been to Long.

Now, things would be different.

To break under pressure was the worst thing a contract agent could do. It branded him as unreliable. There was no reason or excuse that could be given to explain it away. He had broken. His usefulness would be severely limited from now on.

Pfifer continued to watch the fire. The smoke grew more delicate, the embers more gray. In his mind he suddenly saw beyond the fire, and what he saw caused him to grow cold.

CHAPTER
One

Martin Stein slept, but not soundly. The faint creak of footsteps making their way to the side of the bed woke him, and when he opened his eyes he saw her there, the pale light from the window bathing her in its glow, her faint nude whiteness and the partial light making her appear almost like an apparition, somehow not real, not flesh at all.

But she was flesh, and warmth, and a badly needed release, and he smiled and allowed himself a long look as she bent low over him and gently shook his shoulder.

"Martin, are you awake?"

"Yes."

"It's time."

Playfully he reached out for her, but she stepped back quickly and avoided his hand. When she spoke again her voice had an admonishing edge to it.

"It's almost twelve."

His smile gone, Martin Stein pushed the blanket away and sat up. Suddenly, he felt foolish. She had asked him for his help, and he had made a promise, a promise that he now regretted, but that was beside the point. He had committed himself.

"Gretchen, you're a beautiful girl, but you can be a real pain sometimes. Do you realize that?"

"I'm sorry, but we'll have to hurry as it is. It's quite foggy." Her voice softened to a conciliatory purr, her usually subtle German accent thickening perceptibly. He loved that voice, and the cool blue eyes that now pleaded with him. But stubbornly, he resisted them for a moment.

"That's just wonderful. Where are my clothes?" he said as sharply as he could manage.

"They were mostly on the floor," she answered, a hint of laughter in her voice, "but I collected them."

With that, Gretchen pulled a neatly folded stack of clothes from the dresser drawer behind her and laid them beside him on the bed.

"You've been a busy girl," he said as he reached out for his trousers and began to dress.

"We will be busier before this night is through. Can you hurry?"

They did not turn on the light. They dressed in the half-light. They spoke softly when they did speak, and when they had donned their warm dark clothing, they stepped out into the hallway and closed the door quietly behind them.

"Just a second," Gretchen whispered and touched his arm, "I forgot something."

Before he could speak, she left him standing alone in the darkness and went back into the room. He heard a drawer open and then close, and then quickly, she was beside him again.

"Let's go," she said and immediately turned away.

Martin, not bothering to question her, simply shook his head and followed her down the hallway to the stairwell.

Outside, the streetlights were haloed in the fog, their

milky glow making only a shallow penetration into the translucent night. Tenement houses stood along each side of the old cobblestone street. Three stories each, shoulder to shoulder, and cloaked in a century of soot and grime, their little dark windows stared inquiringly, but blindly, out into the opaqueness.

There was no traffic; it was still. The only sounds were those their footsteps made as they moved along. Occasionally, furtively, Gretchen looked back over her shoulder, and Martin, noticing her anxiety, took his opportunity to make a show of telling her to relax, even though he was far from being able to relax himself.

"You parked the car around the next block?" she asked, ignoring his attempt to reassure her.

"Yes, I did as you asked. But I still think you're carrying this whole thing a bit too far."

"I don't think so," she snapped, the edge back in her voice.

"Fine," he said and looked straight ahead. "Whatever makes you happy."

They continued down the street at a brisk pace. His uncertainty getting the better of him, Martin began to turn with Gretchen to look behind them, and once, for an instant, he thought he saw something in the shadows of an entryway. It was a hint of movement, nothing more, but it unsettled him. Would it be possible for someone to be following them? And if so why?

"Did you see that?" he asked.

"No," Gretchen answered but at the same time noticeably increased her pace.

"I guess your overworked imagination must be contagious, then."

As he spoke, she gave him a stern look. It struck him as funny. He was beginning to laugh when they turned the corner, but then he cut his laugh short as he spotted his car and saw a man standing beside it. Gretchen saw him as well and stopped abruptly.

Instinctively, he took her by the arm, and together they hesitated.

He had not realized how nervous he had become. Now he was aware of his pulse as it raced. He wondered if she could tell, if she was as alarmed as he. And as he strained to see in the dim light, he was confused as to what to do.

The man was dressed in a long, soiled overcoat. Beneath his floppy hat his face was dark and shadowed with stubble. He did not notice them, but began to rock back and forth, silent and oblivious, bracing himself with his buttocks against the passenger's side of Martin's white Austin Mini.

But then, as they stood and watched the man, the faint smell of wine reached them in the damp air. Relieved, and at the same time repulsed, Martin glanced at Gretchen and then stepped forward.

"Here! You! Get your bloody ass off of my car!" Martin shouted with more confidence than he felt.

The man, startled by Martin's sudden outburst, stood bolt upright, staggered stiffly forward a few feet, and then leaned against a brick wall. As he did, a brown paper bag fell from his hand and its contents shattered onto the pavement. Crumpling limply beside it, he muttered, "Bloody Hell, Bloody Hell," over and over again.

Martin approached the slumped figure and stopped in front of him for a second, but the stench of stale wine and filth assaulted his already uneasy stomach and he hastily turned away and waved for Gretchen.

"Come on now! Quickly!" he shouted at her.

As Gretchen stopped beside him, he fumbled for his car keys and hoped she did not see the way his hands trembled. Turning his back to the drunken man, he opened the door for her, then hurried around the car to get in behind the wheel. In a few seconds, they were away.

Neither spoke as they drove; Martin steered cautiously

through the fog, Gretchen seemingly lost in her thoughts. Their eyes met from time to time, but each looked quickly away.

Finally, the silence became unbearable for Martin, and he felt compelled to ask the same questions he had asked her before.

"You're sure this will be the end of it?" he asked.

"Yes, I'm sure."

She had answered quickly, as if she had anticipated his question. It made him angry.

"I don't know how you could be so stupid in the first place."

"I told you. I needed money. I had no choice."

She had told him. She was a foreign student. She had lost her part-time job. An acquaintance had made what seemed a simple proposition. All she had to do was pick up a small package from a ship and deliver it to a man parked in a van on a major London street. It had worked very well several times, she said. Apparently it had been incident-free. But the risk, if unfulfilled, had still been there.

"All you had to do was ask me. I would have taken care of you," Martin said, his tone still biting.

"I didn't know you that well when I first got involved."

"And now?"

"Now it's different, of course."

Martin smiled briefly, then fought it off.

"These are dangerous men," he said. "They may not like it when you tell them you're finished with their little scheme. I don't know why you feel you have to see them again. I don't know why you have to go through the routine again at all. It seems like the absolute height of stupidity."

"I gave my word," Gretchen answered weakly.

"Yes, and it seems we all get ourselves in trouble by giving our word, don't we?"

Martin shifted in his seat. He blinked his eyes at the

brightness of an oncoming car; one of the few they had passed.

"If you don't want to help me . . ." Gretchen started to say.

Martin's anger began to rise again. He cut her off in midsentence. "I said I'll help you. If I let you go out there alone tonight, I might not get you back. I don't have to like it, do I?"

"No, I suppose not. I appreciate it though; you know that, don't you?"

"As a matter of fact, I do," he said and smiled at her, finally allowing the warmth back into his voice.

She smiled at him in return, but the strain was evident in her expression. "We'll be there soon," she said.

Martin pressed on. The wet cobblestones gleamed in the wash of his headlamps. As he came to each turn, he glanced over at Gretchen, and she nodded to assure him he was on course.

It was amazing, he thought, how she could know her way around London as well as she did. He had lived there all his life and did not know the maze of streets as well. He did notice her counting to herself as they went, and it puzzled him vaguely. Perhaps that was how she did it, by memorizing the number of blocks in each direction, but why would she do it that way?

She was a paradox to him; at once both helpless and extremely self-reliant. She had escaped, somehow, from East Germany, only to run into trouble over something as simple as losing her job.

It was her helplessness that appealed most to him, though. She made him feel more competent than he had ever managed to on his own. She had made it very easy indeed, in many ways, for him to express his manhood. If he could only get through tonight. . . .

"I've been meaning to ask you something," Gretchen said suddenly.

Martin glanced at her for an instant, then back at the road.

"You've never explained it," she began, "and if you don't want to talk about it now, I'll understand. But, when we first met, you seemed to be very close to your father, and very interested in his diamond business. Now, for the past month I think, you never even mention him. Have you had some disagreement, some argument? It's not over me, is it? Because I'm not Jewish?"

Martin flexed his hands on the steering wheel. Because she was not Jewish? He wished he could laugh, but the truth of it hurt him too deeply to allow it.

Painfully he considered it. First the strange meeting with the American; the sturdy little man who had told him secrets held close for half a lifetime, who had told him things that had surprised him and had made him more proud of his father than he had ever been before in his life. He could hardly believe.

Then, in cruel counterpoint, the second edge of the truth, the sharper edge that had cut him to his soul.

The photographs. A portrait of soldiers before a banner of black on white against a field of red. Who had left them on the seat of his car to find, to stare at in disbelief and then dismay? He had burned them in the fireplace of his father's study when he returned home to move out. And he had to move. He had to distance himself from the obscenity of it, the sudden vile shock of the deeper secret his father lived with, the very fact of which he could not force himself to form into words.

How could he tell her these things? How could he tell anyone? He dared not even think of it himself too deeply or too long.

Because she was not Jewish? A macabre irony.

"It has nothing to do with you. I don't want you to think that for a moment, but it's something I can't talk about. It's something I try not to even think about."

"I wish you could. It might make it better. It can't be as horrible as you think."

"I can't begin to explain, and I do not wish to be questioned further about it."

Martin drove faster now. The little Austin's tires pattered and shuddered over the pavement. He saw Gretchen studying him out of the corner of his eye. He marveled at the beauty of her. What did she see in him? She had come into his life so quickly and so easily. He was almost afraid to analyze it, for fear he would discover it was some cruel joke, some fluke that would disappear just as quickly and mysteriously as it had come. He did not know if he actually loved her, or if she actually loved him, but he did know that he could not bear to lose her. Not now, not until he could regain his grasp, find his new direction. No, he could not bear to lose her; he would not be with her tonight if he could.

Gretchen was asking him a question. It forced him back to consciousness.

"I'm sorry. What did you say?"

"I asked if your sister was still home from America?"

"Yes, she is."

"It must be exciting, going to school over there."

"I don't know, she was talking like she wouldn't go back. I'm not sure I know exactly why."

"I'd like to meet her sometime."

"You'd like her. She's a bit headstrong at times, a lot like you," Martin paused for effect, "but she's all right. And she's been more like a mother to me than a sister."

Gretchen smiled. Martin exhaled a long breath, silently grateful for the change of subject. She seemed to have a talent for that; knowing when she shouldn't press him further. It made him feel a bit played on from time to time, but some would call it sensitivity, wouldn't they?

As they neared the Thames they could smell the river, sense its dampness and proximity, but they could not see it.

Even as they passed over it on the Tower bridge, they could not see it clearly. The lights that shone from above the ancient structures served only to illuminate the blank wall of fog around them and deepen the shadows. They were aware of little more than a black void beneath them.

Martin peered out of his window and grimaced.

"How are we going to find our way in that muck?"

"We will, you'll see," Gretchen reassured him. "Perhaps it won't be as bad on the water."

"It looks pretty unlikely to me, love."

"Let's at least try. I want this over with tonight."

Dubious and annoyed, he had seen a gracious way out, only to have her deny him. "If you insist," he said sharply, then strained to see their turnoff.

The parking area of Saint Katherine's Dock was nearly empty. An old van was parked under a security lamp. It was a delivery van, but with its signs crudely painted over. Martin looked at the van hard for a moment and then glanced at Gretchen. She pointed toward the opposite end of the lot and he nodded.

"We're both getting paranoid you know," he said as he shut off the engine. "And I'm more of a bloody fool than I ever thought possible."

Gretchen looked at him silently for a moment. The little car's exhaust popped and tinged as it began to cool down.

"Lead on," Martin finally said.

As she got out of the car, she pulled the hood of her jacket over her head, hiding her long blond hair. When she started off, Martin fell into step slightly behind her.

In the fog and darkness it wasn't difficult for Martin to imagine Saint Katherine's as it once had been. With the boutiques and shops and artists' studios closed, and scarcely a light showing, the old brick buildings looked, in silhouette, like the old warehouses that they were built to be. There was, of course, the marina in the midst of its quadrangle—the pleasure boats did look somewhat out of place—and the hotel built at the entrance gave the final lie to the illusion. Nonetheless, if you chose to see only what you wanted, it did look very much like it once must have. The dock, the river, the dark edifice of the Tower of London in the distance.

"I wonder if you can see over into the grounds of the Tower of London from the top of that hotel?" Martin asked.

Gretchen turned to look at him, a quizzical look on her face. "I have no idea."

"That's where they'll put us if we get caught tonight, you know."

"They don't put people in the Tower anymore; even I know that."

"Maybe they'll make an exception in our case. Special consideration for extraordinary stupidity."

Gretchen let his sarcasm go unanswered and continued to walk.

During the day at Saint Katherine's throngs of tourists crowded into the shops and choked the walkways, but now the old dock slept peacefully in the fog. Only a few lights still glimmered from the hotel. The dock and marina were in darkness. The scent of the Thames lay heavy in the air as the boats in the marina creaked and groaned at their moorings.

Gretchen walked briskly now, as if she knew exactly where she was going. She seemed anxious, but directed, nervous, but well rehearsed. She led the way around, beyond the dock's ancient lock to a ladder that disappeared over the edge of the wharf. When Martin stopped beside her, he could hear her breathing clearly quickened and excited.

There was a small boat tied to the bottom of the ladder; its stubby foredeck and low windshield drenched by the wet air. Martin felt less than enthusiastic, but Gretchen climbed quickly down the ladder into the boat's open cockpit and pulled the canvas covers off of the control panel. He followed her tentatively, the boat rocking as he stepped on board and crossed to sit on a wet vinyl seat. Past him the river was almost completely hidden in the mist.

"Just look out there, will you?" he said. "It's impossible."

Gretchen looked at him as if he had said nothing. "Why don't you drive? I'll untie us. Once we're moving, it should be better."

He studied her. She seemed determined, suddenly resolute. Martin hesitated. He glanced back up the ladder to the wharf above and then back at her. She stood quietly waiting.

"I wish I knew why this is so important to you," he said, more to himself than to her.

"Please, I can't do it alone."

He took a deep breath and then let it out. He was tense, and more uneasy than he liked to admit to himself. He tried to make light of it.

"Oh, what the hell," he said and moved to the driver's seat.

At the boat's wheel, Martin looked at the control panel for a moment. Gretchen had already put the ignition key in place. Briefly he wondered if that was what she had almost forgotten in her room. He muttered to himself then turned the key to the start position. The engine came to life on the first attempt. As the engine idled, Gretchen began to untie the lines.

Untied and under way they left the dim light of Saint Katherine's and plunged into the murk. The river was black and cold under their hull, the fog on the main channel thicker and wetter, if anything. They could see only a few yards in front of them as they crept forward, and Martin once again looked at Gretchen and shook his head pensively.

"This is insane," he said.

"Steer back toward the bank. We can follow it."

"You'd better start thinking of ways you can warm me up after this is over, girl."

Gretchen gave a nervous laugh, then looked away from him. He failed to catch her expression. Gradually he eased the wheel over and they arced back toward the edge of the river, the echoes of their engine's exhaust becoming louder and more distinct as they approached.

Downriver, in midchannel, a group of freighters were anchored. Formless in the fog, leviathans, asleep and almost invisible, they were but a huge darkness on the river, all apparently idle and lifeless. But in the bowels of one of these freighters, valves were being turned, boilers prodded to life, and the hot stench of human sweat mixed with the fumes of fuel oil. Above decks, men moved carefully about in the darkness, as they prepared for getting under way, and, all the while, no one showed a light or made an unnecessary noise.

A ladder with a small landing had been lowered over the side of the freighter. On the landing, two men stood bundled against the night, the black waters of the Thames lapping inches from their feet. One of the men was tall and angular, his features hard and lined by the wind and sea. He wore the dark topcoat and cap of a sea captain, and stood as if at attention, arms to his sides, head straight forward, his mouth pulled taut into a line, a noncommittal line that was neither frown nor smile.

The second man was stocky and much shorter than the first. His face was round and fleshy behind a close-cropped beard. Almond-colored skin showed at his cheeks and forehead. He stood relaxed, as a man stands when he feels he is in control. Dressed in field-green fatigues and jacket, he held a coffee cup casually in his right hand, while with his left he adjusted the angle of the fur cap he wore on his bullish head.

"Your agent is late," the captain said in a detached tone.

The bearded one shrugged. "Not so very late."

"How can you even be sure she'll find us in this?"

The bearded one laughed and flung his cold coffee into the river. "She will find us, Captain. When she is near, we will hear her engine and turn on the spotlight over this landing.''

"That will be dangerous."

"Who will see us on a night like this?"

"For our sake, let us hope no one does."

As they stood on the landing and looked into the darkness, they could hear faint machinery noises behind the black bulge of hull at their back, and they could smell the rancid odor of stack gas from the freighter's funnel. Directly in front of them a second freighter lay dead-still and dark, except for dim anchor lights.

"You don't like me very much, do you?" the bearded one suddenly asked.

"I do not like the risk to my ship, that is all."

"Is not ten million dollars in diamonds worth a little risk? Apparently the KGB believes that it is."

"You should have waited for better weather. You do not understand how dangerous it is to navigate the Thames in fog. The smallest of miscalculations . . ."

"It is you who fail to understand. It is precisely this weather that makes tonight perfect for our purposes. Who could follow my agent on a night such as this? Who would be prepared?"

The captain stared back in stony silence.

"You've navigated this river many times before. Besides, you have radar, have you not?"

"We have radar."

"So what is it you do not like? Don't tell me you disapprove of extorting a little money from a rich Jew? Don't tell me that offends your sensibilities? If so perhaps Moscow should be informed? Perhaps you need to have your instructions clarified?"

"I understand my instructions."

"See that you do, Captain. See that you do."

Suddenly the bearded one laughed, but then as his laughter echoed back to him from the side of the freighter moored near them, he fell silent, and together they continued to wait.

Martin Stein and Gretchen steered their boat between the silent hulks. The cold steel mammoths seemed like dark ghosts, close yet shrouded. Martin grasped the boat's wheel more tightly and looked blindly forward.

"Are you sure you can find the right ship?" he asked.

"Yes," Gretchen answered, covering the lie in her voice. "Just keep going."

The fog engulfed them. They moved concealed within its obscuring folds, blending invisibly into the mist, as they left the cluster of ships and moved farther downriver. Then, for several minutes, there was a sensation of total emptiness. The fog became too thick to see even a few feet forward. Martin glanced nervously at Gretchen and started to move the throttle back a notch.

"No," Gretchen blurted. "Don't slow down. We're late already. Listen. If there are no echoes, there can't be anything in front of us."

Gretchen's voice was not as calm as it had been before. Martin sensed it. Strangely, it gave him fresh confidence of his own. He pressed the throttle a bit farther forward than it had been before, then smiled, pleased with himself.

Gretchen looked as if she were about to object, but almost instantly the fog cleared away completely, creating a pocket in front of them. She relaxed, then tensed again, as the unmistakeable odor of stack gas reached them. It was strong, and it was close.

"There," Gretchen said and pointed forward.

Ahead, a group of freighters began to take form. Martin studied them and thought he could tell which one of the freighters had fired its boilers. There was a slight disturbance of the fog over its superstructure; a billowing.

"Is that the one?" he asked.

"I believe so."

"Are you sure?"

"A kiss for luck?"

"Why not?"

Martin leaned near her, pushed the hood from her head and watched her hair tumble about her shoulders. She smiled at him in a way she had smiled only at special times. Then softly she said his name and reached out for him, placing her hand behind his neck.

As he came close to her and touched his lips to hers, he felt a quick, sharp prick at the base of his skull. Confused, he pulled back from her, then gradually a different sort of fog began to close in on him, and he was not confused anymore. Suddenly, he realized there was no package to be picked up from the freighter and no man waiting in a van on a London street. He began having trouble moving his hands and feet, and before he slipped completely from consciousness, he realized that he had been deceived, terribly deceived, first by his father, and now by the woman he thought he loved.

They had not seen the lone watcher standing on the bridge wing of the nearby freighter. Gretchen had not seen him. Neither man on the landing had seen him. Only the captain of the ship he stood on knew he was there that night and had been there for the previous two nights. A man dressed in dark clothing, his face smeared with soot, his ultrasensitive microphone, his infrared camera, there to watch as Gretchen's boat came under the umbrella of light over the landing, there to record and photograph.

But as the men on the landing climbed aboard the freighter dragging Martin Stein's limp body with them, and as the small boat turned away, back into the fog, before the eerie clanking of the freighter's anchor chain could be heard as it was wrenched up by its capstan, the watcher was signaling frantically to his control on the waterfront, and the lights were already beginning to flash on the telephones in a building at One Grosvenor Square as a duty officer was dialing his emergency number.

Long before the freighter slipped away into the darkness, events were beginning to engage that would move the cogs in a distant and deadly clandestine mechanism.

CHAPTER
Two

In a westward flood of color, the restless Atlantic began to change her hue from black to sapphire as morning came upon the rocky New England coast. The peaks of evergreened mountains felt the first red and gold wash of sunrise, and hungry seagulls began to circle overhead in the freshened currents of the morning sky.

Concealed in the convoluted coastline, a small island lay protected in a maze of narrow inlets and green promontories. Except for the shallow cove it held in its granite grasp, it was the same as a thousand other islands in the region; almost invisible in its similarity.

But sheltered from casual view by a shroud of pine and fir, an old sloop lay at anchor in the island's cove. She was plank-hulled and weathered; even the once bold, block letters on her transom faded beyond recognition. But she was sturdy yet, and her generous beam and thick timbers suggested strongly that she could still ride out the worst of coastal gales.

Within the sloop's cabin, John Pfifer sat at a small table and drank hot coffee from a pewter mug. He was a slender but muscular man, his dark hair and full beard slightly streaked with gray. He wore faded jeans and a dark blue, roll-neck sweater, held his hot mug gently and sipped the bitter brew. Occasionally, he glanced through the porthole beside him and looked out at the narrow inlet to the cove. He studied it stoically, as would a man who expects no visitors.

Around him, in the carefully fashioned shelves and lockers of the cabin, Pfifer had stowed his few possessions. Books in German, Polish, and Russian and a library of cassettes occupied a long shelf on the starboard side. Back issues of European magazines and newspapers lay about here and there. A hand-carved chess set, game in progress, rested on a platform attached to the forward bulkhead. Above it, an old chronometer hung from a brass screw, ticking in the hollow silence.

Pfifer glanced at the old clock, put his mug down firmly on the table, then got up and moved to a small low cabinet.

The cabinet, like the rest of the old sloop, was put together like a fine old puzzle, every joint and panel mated flush and smooth. Pfifer had to marvel at it, at both its complexity and its simplicity. It had been built with purpose and with care for it to endure, which it had.

He knelt to open the cabinet doors.

Inside, a cruder hand had hacked away the shelves and some of the internal bracing to install a radio. Pfifer snapped on the power switch, adjusted the receiver's frequency, then stood up. In a few seconds, the speaker began to hiss and crackle with air noise.

He looked down at the gray face of the radio; its cherry-red power light, its black plastic knobs and dials. He looked and he waited. After fifteen minutes, he bent down and snapped it off, a look of concern briefly crossing his face.

Then, with a sigh of resignation, he turned and mounted the steps that led out of the cabin and onto the sloop's afterdeck.

The morning light that met him as he emerged was strong, and the woods that surrounded the cove alive with the early morning routines of the birds and small animals that lived in its shadows. At intervals, the sounds of their calls to one another and the rustle of their movements reached him. He stood still, listened, and took in the heavy, sweet smell of the pine boughs and sea air.

It was clear and there was a fresh breeze. About the decks of the sloop the rigging had been cleared and made ready for a morning sail. Lines were coiled neatly, the sails stripped of their canvas covers. But instead of hauling in his heavy stern and bow anchors, Pfifer stood motionless on the deck and looked south. He knew there would be no sailing today.

The radio, by its silence, had brought him the one message he wanted least to hear. It was a summons; silent, but distinct. He could only wonder where they would send him this time, and who would die. Perhaps this time it would be him.

The woods gave a rushing sound as the breeze shifted. At the same time, a hint of airplane engine noise drifted in. Pfifer shook his head from side to side as he recognized its familiar cadence, then wiped his hands on his jeans absentmindedly before he began to retow the lines and gear that he had only moments ago laid carefully out. As he worked, the sound of the airplane became clearer and stronger. By degrees, the sounds of the peaceful woods were drowned out by it.

Suddenly, over a ridge to the south, a single-engined amphibian burst into view. It was just above the treetops and its white wings and bulbous fuselage stood out starkly against the deep-green backdrop. Pfifer got just a glimpse of it before it sank from sight on its way toward a landing in the channel. He knew it was safely down only when the pitch of its engine dropped off.

As the amphibian, a Lake Buccaneer, taxied through the inlet, Pfifer recognized a familiar face at the controls. The man waved to him, Pfifer waved back. It was Harry Fisher, of course. They wouldn't send a stranger to him, not in seclusion, especially not now.

Harry Fisher manoeuvred his craft carefully past the sloop's stern and then revved its engine to give enough thrust to power up on the sandy shelf that sloped into the cove on its east side. When he was firmly beached, he shut down.

Pfifer watched stoically as the plane's canopy popped open, and Fisher eased himself out. It was Harry all right; bearded, slightly less than average height, a good twenty pounds overweight, and he wore the only attire Pfifer had ever seen him wear—plaid shirt, faded jeans, bright orange hunter's cap. It seemed to be the uniform of the outdoorsman in these parts. Dressed as he was, and with his folksy demeanor, Harry blended right in with his surroundings. No one would easily guess what his true function was. It would seem too absurd.

He was a sharp little man, indeed, though. Nothing of substance escaped his keen sense of observation. Inconspicuous himself, Harry made an excellent watcher of men.

Harry stood beside his plane and gave Pfifer a wave. When he spoke it was with a friendly and a familiar tone. "Where's your canoe, John?" he asked. "You didn't sink it, did you?"

Pfifer laughed. "It's off to your right, behind those trees."

Harry nodded and then disappeared into the foliage. In a moment he returned dragging an aluminum canoe behind him. He launched it into the cove and covered the short distance in a few efficient strokes. Pfifer handed him a line as he coasted alongside.

"What did you do, swim back aboard?" Harry asked.

"As a matter of fact, I did."

"I don't know how you can stand it. Water must be ice cold this time of year."

"I was going sailing. You know how I dislike dragging that thing along behind me. Besides, the water isn't as bad as you might think."

Harry grunted at Pfifer's last comment.

"So, what brings you up here this morning?"

"It's called employment."

"I was afraid of that."

"I'm sorry, John."

What little of the morning's high spirits that Pfifer had left within him vanished. They were replaced by an expectant and unwelcome anticipation.

"Give me your hand," Pfifer said in a monotone as he leaned over the rail.

Harry groaned as Pfifer helped him aboard. The two men stood and looked at each other for a few seconds before either spoke. Now the silence in the cove was deeper than it had been before, as if the creatures of the forest were waiting to see if the interruption was over before they went back to their routines.

"I knew you'd be up when you missed your regular broadcast," Pfifer finally said. "Can you tell me what's going on?"

"I really don't know much about it, John. All I know is that I'm supposed to get you to Boston as quickly as I can. That's why I didn't radio you that I was coming. They had me flying at first light so I could land here as early as possible."

"Well, I knew they wouldn't leave me up here forever. All the same, I wish they'd let me stay longer."

Harry straightened his cap self-consciously and looked away. "Well, let's get this old girl buttoned up and go."

"Fine, I've about got it done anyway."

They moved about the sloop and closed her hatches, replaced her sail covers and tucked everything back into its appropriate locker. Then, Pfifer went below and came back up with a single leather suitcase. He handed it down to Harry, who had climbed back down into the canoe. In a moment, they were moving back across the cove toward the plane.

"So how's the air charter business been doing lately?" Pfifer asked between strokes of his paddle.

"Better than the company would like, I think."

"Interferes with your accessibility, I suppose."

"Something like that."

It figured. The agency was like that. They would have selected Harry because he was a good pilot and familiar with the area. They would have invested in a good cover for him, not expecting that his charter business would flourish.

The nose of the canoe touched the beach with a granular scrape. Harry stepped out quickly and gave a hard pull. Pfifer stepped out beside him.

"Throw your bag in the cockpit, and I'll go put the canoe back where you had it," Harry said.

Pfifer stowed his case. Then, he turned and looked back at the cove. It was a tranquil picture. He stared long and hard at it, so he could remember it, so he could come back to it in his mind when he had the need. All too soon, he sensed Harry back by his side.

"How long have I been up here, Harry?"

"Six months, give or take."

"Seems a lot longer than that."

Harry studied him as if trying to make up his mind. Trying to formulate the final entry in his report? Pfifer wondered if Harry was a friend, or if he was just another one of George Long's soldiers. Clever in his deception, measured in his responses. For his own peace of mind, Pfifer decided to think of Harry as a friend. Whether it had been merely a charade or not.

"Let's go now, John," Harry said softly.

They turned the plane by hand and got in. Then, with a firm tug, Harry closed the canopy and started through his preflight checks. He went down his instruments methodically before he turned over the single Lycoming engine above their heads. When he finally hit the switch, it sputtered, then caught. After a few seconds, he brought it up to speed and eased them into the water.

They passed close by the stern of the sloop on their way out of the cove, then aimed for the narrow inlet. At the mouth of the inlet the plane's wing-tips practically touched the lower limbs of the trees, but they slipped through unscathed. Once out into the open channel, Harry nudged the throttle forward and picked up speed.

"The wind's been kind of changeable today," Pfifer said, raising his voice above the steady drone of the engine.

"I noticed," Harry said. "We'll give it a good long run."

They taxied as far up the channel as they could before they turned upwind. Then Harry paused, studied his instruments for a moment more and surveyed the distance in front of them. Pfifer knew he needed at least eleven hundred feet of clear water to take off in when conditions were ideal, and Harry had mentioned, more than once, that the sharply rising promontories in this particular channel never offered much of a safety margin. Today, the concern was plainly readable in Harry's face.

"What are you waiting for?" Pfifer asked.

Harry glanced at him but said nothing. Then he abruptly pushed the throttle full open.

The plane lunged forward, clumsy at first, rocking back and forth, dipping one wing float and then the other in a peculiar waddling motion. As the speed built up, the small waves in the channel slapped the bottom of the hull-shaped fuselage, and a fine spray billowed behind.

As they gained speed, the little plane became less and

less like a small boat and more like an airplane in its dynamics. It steadied up, became more stable.

Harry glanced at the airspeed indicator and began to pull back on the stick. Gradually the plane lifted itself free from the grasp of the water and rose. Looking ahead, Pfifer gauged the rapidly diminishing distance between them and the shoreline of trees. One particularly tall tree loomed directly in their path. Pfifer concentrated on that tree and attempted to shut everything else out of his mind.

Harry pulled back on the wheel. The plane struggled fractionally higher, then they were over the treetops. Two solid thuds jarred them just as they cleared. Harry held them in a steep climb for several more seconds before he leveled out.

"Dents in my goddamned airplane, I hope you know!" Harry shouted.

"What's that they say about an inch being as good as a mile?" Pfifer asked as calmly as he could.

"I don't know, but whoever said it was an idiot!"

They both laughed, then Harry looked down at his wristwatch and frowned. As he looked up, Pfifer made a circling motion with his index finger, and Harry nodded, understanding Pfifer's request. He put the plane into a turn.

They would take one last look, whether they had the time or not.

Pfifer watched closely, but as they passed over the cove, he could get only a brief glimpse of the sloop. Then it was lost from sight, obscured by the thick greenery. He could only wonder how Harry had managed to find the island in the first place, let alone chart his way back. Obviously, there were things about the wilderness he had not learned and possibly never would.

Harry completed his circle and then turned south again. He throttled back the engine to cruising speed and steadied up on the proper bearing.

One green ridge, followed by a blue inlet, followed by

endless others, slipped by beneath. Pfifer closed his eyes and allowed his head to fall back against his seat. When he awoke he would be back in the life he had wanted to forget, the old habits reactivated, the old instincts called upon again. But for now, briefly, he could sleep. With luck, he would not dream.

But he did dream, and those dreams were populated with ghosts. Faces, shadows, some clear, some indistinct. Some from the very fringes of his memory; faces and forms of men he barely knew. They came to force the tranquility from his sleep, to sharpen the edges of his fear, for they were the faces of his dead, and they beckoned him.

His dream became a white-hot maelstrom; a protracted and dizzy blur. He fought for his breath as it dragged him to its depths. As he descended, the whiteness became blackness, the blackness suffocating.

Suddenly, a hand shook him.

"Damn, John. Are you all right?"

It was Harry's face he saw first as he opened his eyes. He sat up, put a hand to his own face, felt the perspiration.

"I'm fine," Pfifer said, with perhaps a bit too much emphasis.

"You must have been having quite a dream, if that's what it was. Are you sure you're all right?"

"It was just that, Harry, a dream, nothing more."

Harry nodded, then turned his attention to his instruments and his compass. Pfifer, now wide awake, looked blankly out the window. Below, houses and villages dotted the clearings along a gray road, but in his mind Pfifer saw something quite different. It was a scene that had replayed itself many times, and as Pfifer studied the graceful twists and bends of that road, he reluctantly welcomed it once again. It would bring him anger, and through anger, strength. He would need that strength to draw from in the days ahead. He would need it more now than ever before because now he was weary. Not physically weary but, more dangerously, weary in spirit. He would need to remember what had sparked that initial inner flame. He would need to remember it and hope it would be enough to see him through. For when the flame died out, he would surely die with it.

He would have to go back to the beginning. In the beginning it had seemed so simple, so clear.

A young boy held his father's hand to keep from being separated in the crowd. Around them people were laughing, smiling; many carried packages. Their long coats seemed like dark drapes to the little boy, his father's hand firm and reassuring. They progressed through the confusion, their destination a mystery to the child. All he knew was his father's hand and the crush of the crowd. But that was enough. A child trusts his father blindly. The father is so great and seemingly so wise. It is natural to trust him, to depend on his strength.

Then, suddenly, there was a loud noise, and then screaming. The young boy was thrown to the ground as the crowd around him fell about like great trees toppled and in one horrible explosion. It was chaos, but the child understood only one thing; he no longer had hold of his father's hand.

He got to his knees and looked for his father, but what he saw bore no resemblance to anything or anyone he knew. It was a horror beyond horror. It made an indelible picture in the child's mind. A picture that would haunt him for a lifetime.

It had been a mindless terrorist act, one that the child would never understand or accept, not even as he grew older, gained experience. Simply one of so many car bombs to be detonated on the streets of London, it was the one of primary relevance to the child. That the victims of its terrible blast weren't selected by any other method than pure chance did nothing to ease the pain, the damage, nothing to rectify the shock and the loss.

And what was equally difficult for the young man, as he grew up, was to accept the fact that no one could be found and held responsible. No one could be brought to justice, no one person available as the single point of focus for his hate. And, because there was no channel into which the hate could be directed, it was natural that hate would grow, that it would rise as water rises behind a dam, and that finally that dam would give way. It was all that could have been expected to happen, or so the child told himself as he grew into a man.

In time, he became a self-sufficient man, outwardly needing no one. He neither attracted nor sought out many friends, and so he was called aloof, cold, a loner. Perhaps he was simply afraid to form attachments with other people, afraid to face the vulnerability of it, the potential for pain. For whatever reasons, he stood apart from other men. He went his own way. He was "different."

He did distinguish himself as a student of foreign languages. Concentrating his energies as few men do, he developed his talent to an impressive degree, and it was this talent that attracted the attention of the recruiters; those discreet hunters of new players for the game.

They dangled the bait briefly, but he did not fit the mold they had in mind. He was not a social animal. He did not mix. He did not possess the charm and wit that made an effective spy. His uses were perceived as too limited for regular service with the Company. He was quickly dropped as an active candidate, but his records were kept on file. Perhaps later, he was told.

When he graduated, he was drafted into the army, and because of his language skill was made an interpreter. It was George Long who found him not long after, stationed in Germany.

Long came looking for a talented interpreter who would take a risk for the right reason. Pfifer listened to his proposition, agreed, and the arrangements were made with Pfifer's command.

Before he knew the extent of his commitment, he had handed his very future over to George Long. It look a period of years before the truth of his situation came fully to light.

At first he was given a small apartment in Berlin, a one-room affair. From his window he could see the people scurry about their business, taste the sights and sounds of the great city. In the coffeehouses and cafes, he took pleasure in listening for the different dialects and at guessing their origins, and as time passed, he became quite good at it, finding it easy to catch the subtle differences. With little practice he went on to the next step and became proficient at imitating each dialect. Very soon, he could go among most any group and blend in convincingly. It became an enthralling pastime.

While in Berlin, he received other training: advanced firearms, disguise, codes, and secret writing techniques. He learned how to follow someone unnoticed, and how to spot a tail and lose him. He had a talent for the basic fieldcraft, quickly becoming expert. And the better he became, the more his training intensified. Quickly, it became hard work. And then George Long his ever-present taskmaster.

It was Pfifer's talent with language, though, that fascinated Long the most. He encouraged Pfifer to hone his skill to the extreme, telling him that it would give him mobility after the fact. It would save him time and time again if he could perfect it. Mimicry; it was as much a gift as a skill, and Pfifer had the gift. It could be put to good use. It was the one disguise that could be used immediately and effectively.

And so Pfifer applied himself, partly because he believed Long and partly because he enjoyed the challenge. If he had known where it would lead him, the nature of the bond he was forming, perhaps he would have felt differently. But nonetheless, he set himself brilliantly at the task. In one year he could pass himself off as a German in a room full of

Germans, a Pole among Poles, and perhaps most flawlessly
a Russian. In two years he could place himself within a
dialect of each language. He could be a Berliner, or a
Bavarian, an East German from the north or south. Soon
Long told him he was ready for his first field assignment.

When they called for him, he had been ready for over an
hour. He'd paced back and forth in his small apartment until
he thought he could stand it no more. The anxiety had built
to the point that he either had to do something or burst. At
the sound of the car below in the street he almost bolted to
the door. At George Long's knock, he abruptly opened it.

Long stood in the hallway, his coat pulled about him
loosely. He looked at Pfifer and smiled coolly.

"You look a bit nervous, John. Relax."

"I'm fine, are we ready to go?"

"Yes, it's a short ride. I'll go over the situation once
more on the way over. There's very little for you to do,
actually; all we need is for you to listen to this fellow and
tell us if you think he is legitimate. We'll do the rest."

"I understand."

Long nodded and then turned. Pfifer followed him down
the hall.

When they reached the street, Long guided Pfifer to the
rear seat of a white Mercedes sedan, and then got in after
him. Pfifer got a brief look at the driver and at the other
man in the front passenger's seat, but neither man made a
distinct impression. They were like so many of George's
soldiers, average in every way.

"Okay, Frank," Long said, and immediately they were
off.

In a moment, Long laid something heavy in Pfifer's lap.
Anticipating his question, he said simply, "Just in case,"
and smiled as Pfifer hefted the thirty-eight caliber revolver.

"Just in case of what?"

"Sometimes these things are a setup. We have to be

sensible and at least assume that we could be walking into a dangerous, or at least potentially dangerous, situation.''

Pfifer nodded and tried to look nonchalant.

''Just stay toward the back, and keep your eyes and ears open.''

They made their way to an industrial section. Rows of dark warehouses lined the narrow streets. Littered alleys made intersections and divisions between them. Pfifer studied their impassive facades and fought back the urge to tell Long to turn back, that he had changed his mind.

This would be no exercise. The man they would be meeting would be one of the ''opposition,'' a possible defector, if they were lucky. If they weren't lucky, they would be heading into a trap. The possibilities rattled around Pfifer's head like broken tumblers in a lock.

What if it were a trap? What would he be required to do?

They arrived all too soon. At Long's signal the driver dimmed his lights for the final block. When they came to a stop, they were in front of an old brick warehouse. To Pfifer, it looked no different from the other structures they had passed. But this one contained danger, and a proving ground for a fledgling agent.

They stood beside the car in a close group. Long spoke softly.

''Frank, you and Jack will go in first. If it looks all right, signal us and we'll move in.'' Long looked at Pfifer. ''John, just stay near me.''

Pfifer tried to acknowledge his instructions, but found his mouth too dry to speak. Silently he watched the two agents move away toward the warehouse door, and in a moment they disappeared inside. The front door squeaked faintly as they closed it behind them.

Turning, Pfifer looked at Long and was surprised to find Long staring at him, almost studying him.

''Are you all right?''

''Sure.''

"It's too late to turn back at this point."

"I'll be fine, really."

The warehouse door opened, Frank stepped out and waved them on. In unison, Long and Pfifer stepped forward. Pfifer unconsciously handled the revolver in his pocket. It felt damp to his touch.

They entered a small office. It was tiny; Pfifer had somehow expected that he would be entering a large factory. Instead, it was barely ten feet square. On the back wall, two windows, one on each side of a smudged door, opened out into the main building. Beyond, it was totally dark. Pfifer began to feel extremely ill at ease. His instincts were telling him that he should know what was lurking in the darkness. He turned to Long and shook his head. Long met him with a hard look.

"Where is he?" Long asked the one named Frank.

A single bulb burned overhead. Pfifer caught just a quick look on Frank's face. It was a troubled look; out of place, unexpected. When Pfifer saw it, he realized that his anticipation must have been shared.

"Jack said it was okay. He went to get him."

Long nodded, his face an unreadable mask.

In the next instant, chaos exploded. Both windows of the little office burst in on them, and a shotgun blast pinned Frank to the wall.

Without thinking, Pfifer dove for the floor. When he landed he found he had withdrawn his revolver and had thrust it in front of him. Methodically he squeezed the trigger three times into each window. Behind him he heard George Long calling his name. Then there was silence.

Pfifer was bleeding from the bits of glass lying shattered on the floor. They made a crunching sound as he backed out of the room on his hands and knees. Outside, he looked up and saw Long leaning against the grimy brick wall.

"We need to get out of here, and very quickly," Long said.

"Frank?"

"He's dead."

Pfifer let Long help him to his feet. When he stood, he still clutched the revolver, damp now with his blood instead of nervous perspiration. But he was calm. He followed Long to the car, got in beside him and laid the revolver on the floor between his feet. He had the presence of mind to look around them to try to spot any activity spawned in response to the commotion.

"It looks like we're all clear, George," he said in a perfectly level tone of voice.

George Long just nodded, and drove them away.

CHAPTER
Three

Harry put the Lake Buccaneer neatly down onto the runway at Boston's Logan International Airport. The small amphibian touched wheels smoothly and then rocked gently as he braked. Then, after he made his final call to the tower, he glanced at Pfifer before beginning to taxi toward the general aviation hangars. Pfifer met his gaze coolly.

"My instructions are to drop you off at that hangar over there," Harry said and pointed straight ahead of them. "A man wearing a red scarf will meet you inside and take you to your briefing."

"You'll be heading right back then?"

"Yeah, right after I refuel."

Harry taxied to within fifty yards of the hangar and stopped. In a second, no longer, the hangar doors began to open. As they opened, a man dressed in a dark topcoat and wearing a red scarf around his neck became visible.

"That's him," Harry said.

"Looks like it."

The man strained to push the reluctant doors fully open, then motioned them forward.

Harry nudged the throttle, and they began to roll toward the open door.

"Too bad about the chess game," Pfifer said offhandedly.

"Why's that?"

"You were about to win it."

Harry continued to stare straight ahead.

"I wonder what George would have to say about our unauthorized radio traffic?" Pfifer asked.

"Oh, I told him about it. I didn't want him thinking we had developed some sort of secret code." Harry shot a quick sidelong glance at Pfifer as he spoke, then added, when he noted Pfifer's expression change, "I didn't want him suspicious of either one of us."

Pfifer shook his head. "Don't worry about it."

They disappeared into the shadows. Inside, the hangar was empty except for a light green Dodge sedan parked at the opposite end. Harry came to a stop, shut off his engine, and popped open the canopy. As he and Pfifer climbed stiffly out of the small cockpit, the agent came to meet them.

"Mister Pfifer?"

Pfifer stared at him blankly for a moment, then turned his back and rested his suitcase from the plane. When he turned around, the agent was offering his hand to Harry.

"Mister Fisher?"

"Who else?" Harry answered, curtly ignoring the man's hand. "And I suppose you're in a hurry?"

"Silly question, Harry," Pfifer interrupted. "You know they always are."

Harry and Pfifer looked at each other for a moment, then they grasped each other's hand in a firm but brief handshake.

"So I was about to win one for a change, you say?"

"No doubt about it."

"Well, I'll be damned."

"See you around," Pfifer said.

"Sure."

Pfifer looked at the agent, and motioned for him to lead on.

The agent did not look at Pfifer as he drove. He watched the traffic, glanced in his rearview mirror, shifted his weight in his seat. He seemed to want to ignore his passenger, not acknowledge him, not involve himself in conversation. Pfifer wondered what the man had been told about him. George Long could be supremely intimidating at times. He had learned that firsthand.

Pfifer was finding it difficult to assimilate. The noise and the color and the activity assaulted him from all sides. He was glad his nonconversant charge was the one driving. It gave him time to look, to think, to deal with his mounting tension. What would George Long have to say? What new little adventure would he have in mind? What would be the consequences for him? Of all the possibilities he could imagine, none aroused anything but mild dread.

As they approached the tollgates for the Callahan Tunnel, leading off of Logan's promontory, the traffic slowed and closed in around them. When their turn came, the agent dropped exact change into the tollgate basket and they plunged ahead. The sound of the traffic roared and echoed as they dove into the enclosed space, and Pfifer thought for a moment of the tons of water they passed beneath and found himself looking at the flat gray concrete and white tile walls with more than casual interest.

When they emerged from the fluorescent glare of the tunnel, back into the natural light, the agent made a left turn and wove briskly in and out through the jumble of traffic. The Dodge bucketed and banged over potholes and patches in the road. Pfifer noticed that the agent's hands showed white at the knuckles.

They made a series of turns, crossed over a short elevated

bridge, then slowed to pick their way through an industrial zone. Suddenly they were surrounded by intense activity: tractor-trailer rigs loaded and unloaded to their left and right, workmen milled about. The agent pointed a nervous finger ahead.

"It's the next warehouse," he said.

It was an old brick and metal structure, with most of its windows boarded up. The corrugated sheet metal of its three ground-level truck doors was battered and rust streaked. Pfifer judged it obsolete enough for the Company to own. As they approached, the agent picked up a hand-held radio and spoke into it. He spoke softly, only a single word: Pisces. A moment later someone began to haul open the door.

The agent drove into the warehouse and stopped. As he did, the door crashed closed behind them and abruptly chopped off the outside light. Pfifer allowed his eyes to adjust to the dimness for a moment before he got out of the car.

There were skylights at intervals in the roof of the warehouse. They made pools of light on the bare concrete floor. In one such pool of light, two men in white medical coats stood beside a beige van. They talked in whispers to George Long, but as Pfifer slammed his door shut, Long cut off the conversation and walked toward him.

"It's been a while, John," Long said and stopped a few feet away. "How have you been?"

Pfifer stared back at Long. He had not changed, no fatter, no grayer, and still that tacitly threatening manner. Still that certain discordant vibration about him that kept you from trusting him too quickly.

"As well as can be expected, I suppose. How about you, George?"

"I don't seem to be getting any younger."

"I know what you mean."

Long stood and looked at him silently for a moment. It

made Pfifer uneasy. He knew Long too well. Even his small talk would have some purpose, some secondary value. And of course, they had not spoken since Pfifer's problem in Germany. Pfifer still did not know exactly where he stood—with Long, or with the Agency.

"Suppose you tell me what you have on your mind, George," Pfifer began. "Then we can go from there."

Long nodded. "Fair enough," he said, and then, "Follow me."

Long walked to the rear of the warehouse and opened a door. A shaft of light fanned out from it and sharply divided the darkness in the building. Pfifer caught up to him as he stepped through and out onto a loading dock. It was bright outside, and the sunlight glancing strongly off of the bare concrete caused Pfifer to squint hard for several moments.

"I'm not going to pull any punches with you," Long said coldly. "You are on tenuous ground. Your little fiasco in Germany came very close to ending both of our careers. Now, you may have an opportunity to redeem yourself."

Pfifer looked past Long; beyond, he could see Boston Harbor. Further away he could see the long gray runways of the airport. He took a deep breath and looked back at Long. "Go on."

Long stood there in the cold, his coat wrapped loosely around himself, his expression hard; impassive.

"Number one; absolutely no variation in my instructions will be allowed. None. Number two; once the operation has begun, you will stay in daily contact using the methods I specify and no others. Do you understand so far?"

"I understand, George."

"This will take some time to explain. There is more than just one situation to deal with. I have a written brief and some photographs. I'll get them."

With that, Long left Pfifer on the loading dock and returned to the warehouse. In a moment, he was back with a large manila folder.

"You will read this in its entirety before you leave. Study the photographs, the names, and so forth. To begin with I'll outline the important points.

"Last night, in London, a group of terrorists kidnapped a young man. His name is Martin Stein. We need the situation resolved."

"Is he one of ours?"

"No, but his father is connected. The details of that are in the brief."

"Doesn't sound like my line of work."

"Let me go on. There's more to this than just another terrorist kidnapping. The son has details, damaging details about his father's activities. It's information the KGB would be very interested in. Information they're not going to get, if we can help it.

"Howard Stein is the father's name. He's a diamond cutter by trade. A very successful diamond cutter. His cutting house handles millions in diamonds every month. But that's beside the point. Howard Stein fulfills a very useful function for the Agency. Namely, he funnels diamonds into East Germany to support one of the few remaining networks we have there."

"And the son's been briefed on all of this?"

"Howard Stein is an old man, and not a healthy one. We were grooming the son to take his place."

"Bad timing, I'd say."

Long looked back at Pfifer, his face showing no emotion. "You have some reading," he said and passed Pfifer the envelope.

Pfifer took the envelope and then folded his arms in front of himself. He looked out into the harbor once again. In the distance, a tug churned hastily along, leaving a wake of cold white lace behind her as she sent. Pfifer watched as the black breath of her diesel engines stained the blueness of the sky.

"Suppose I can't get him out in one piece? What then?"

"The primary goal is to bring the problem to a conclusion. You will be supplied whatever you need."

Pfifer turned his attention back to Long. The Central Intelligence Agency had chosen this man well. His capacity for brutality was endless. Whatever ended the situation with the least amount of damage to the Agency, Long would authorize without the slightest trepidation. Pfifer shuddered at his own fate so unavoidably in this man's hands.

"What are your thoughts on the matter?" Long asked.

"Morally or practically?"

"That's a strange question, coming from you. I don't recall you bringing it up before."

"Perhaps I should have, but don't worry, George, I'll do what you ask. I don't have much choice, do I?"

Long smoothed back an errant strand of his thinning hair. He stared blankly back at Pfifer. Pfifer had no trouble understanding the answer to his question.

No. He had no choice. When he stepped across the line dividing him from the normal world, when he surrendered himself to Long's control, he had relinquished choice. He had become dependent on the Agency for support, for the very elements of his survival; food, money, safe shelter. Without the Agency, he would be a fugitive in fact. A hunted man with no assets and the overpowering presence of the CIA at his heels.

"Again, what are your thoughts on the matter?"

"What can you tell me about the kidnapping itself? What are the time frames, the ransom? I assume they have asked for one."

"Yes, they've demanded ten million dollars in cut diamonds, to be available for delivery within forty-eight hours. Twelve hours of which are gone."

Pfifer exhaled a deep breath.

"They haven't specified a method of delivery as of yet. But you won't be concerned with that. We'll handle anything that pertains to the ransom, from London."

"Where do I start looking? Do you have any ideas at all?"

"We know exactly where Martin Stein is."

Pfifer stiffened.

"He was taken aboard a freighter moored in the Thames. The freighter, *The Baltic Merchant*, is of Polish registry and was under surveillance. We got lucky, it happens."

"I wouldn't call it luck, George. It sounds like this was done right under your nose, and you couldn't stop it?"

"It's not that simple."

"I would hope not."

"The freighter, as I said, is of Polish registry, probably meaning it was co-opted for the operation by the KGB to begin with. The only safe thing to do is to assume these terrorists are controlled by Moscow.

"So we can't go in with our guns blazing and let the Russians know that Stein's son is that important to us. If they look too closely at Howard Stein, there's a good chance they will connect him with us, and then with his activities. They could all too easily end up burning the entire network."

"Aren't you forgetting something? Won't these terrorists interrogate their hostage, just as a matter of course, to see if there are any bonuses to be had?"

"That's why we're moving as quickly as we are. We know that Martin was drugged heavily, and we're banking on the drugs making it unproductive for them to question him for a while, but I do have to tell you this, given his personality profile, under even mild interrogation, we feel Martin is likely to talk."

"Where's the freighter now?"

"At the moment, Rotterdam."

"Is there any way you can think of that we might be able to anticipate the freighter's movement? And, do you have any information at all about the situation aboard the freighter; personnel, blueprints, where they might have Martin Stein aboard?"

"What I have is all in the file. Before you read it, though, I want the medical men to look you over. There are still some questions left over from your hospital stay."

"I'm fine, they gave me a mild tranquilizer for a while. I haven't taken them for over a month now."

Long frowned.

"Whatever these doctors prescribe, you will take without variation. Is that clear? I want your physical condition completely under control."

Pfifer shrugged. "Whatever you say."

They went back inside. Pfifer walked to the van and submitted unenthusiastically to an examination. In ten minutes, he had been cursorily gone over and had a small amount of blood taken. Neither medic spoke to him, beyond telling him to remove his sweater or take a deep breath. He gave them low marks for their bedside manner. When they had finished with him, he pulled on his sweater and looked toward Long.

Long placed a chair directly under one of the skylights and motioned to Pfifer.

It was always a delicate balance, the fine line between what an agent needed to know if he were to be able to do his job, and what he should not be told for the sake of the security of the larger operation. But as Pfifer read Howard Stein's file, he became uneasy. It was far too complete. It was as if Long wanted him to know everything. It was puzzling, and it was troubling. It raised suspicion. But Pfifer would not ask Long about it. Long would have his reasons. It would be best if he simply studied the information, and made a mental note to be extremely careful in how he proceeded.

Stein had immigrated from Germany near the end of the Second World War. According to the file, he had gained some success early on, and it had multiplied rapidly over a forty-year span. Currently he was considered one of the most eminent and unreproachable processors of raw diamonds. His financial situation indicated that the terrorist kidnappers had chosen their target well. Stein could apparently afford to lose the ten million in diamonds far more than risk his clients' confidence through the publicity of a messy ordeal with police and press. The quieter the situation could be handled, the better for the elder Stein.

There were three in the Stein family. Langley had supplied photographs and short biographies of each. Rachel was the elder of the two children, twenty-six, eighteen months older than her brother. She was reportedly doing postgraduate work at the Massachusetts Institute of Technology in Boston. Currently, though, she was visiting her father in their London home. Pfifer looked at her picture for a few seconds. Plain, he thought; not unattractive, just plain. Straight dark hair, slender. Nothing remarkable.

Martin's photographs were more extensive, as they should have been, given the situation. He was an intense looking young man. His eyes dark and piercing, a permanent pout on almost effeminate features. He was slender like his sister, but his slenderness somehow gave the impression of fragility. He was anything but an imposing figure. With him, in one photograph, was a striking looking blond girl. They looked rather out of place with one another.

His biography listed a succession of different schools, and noted a proclivity for political activity with several obscure fringe groups. From what Pfifer could see, Martin Stein was a restless young man born at the feet of a great fortune, but somehow erratic, as if he were overwhelmed by it all. From the file, Pfifer questioned the initial wisdom of entrusting him with his father's secrets. With luck, Martin Stein would find the strength to endure his ordeal.

Howard Stein was represented by a single photograph. It was a studio portrait, the kind done for lobby walls. It looked vaguely retouched, slightly less than totally true to life. Pfifer studied Stein's photograph the longest of all.

Stein was an old man, older than Pfifer had expected. He had a proud square jaw, and, even though his face was deeply lined with wrinkles, it still radiated a certain strength, and something else, something disturbing but intractable.

"How are you coming?"

Pfifer looked up from the file and saw Long standing at the edge of the shadows.

"I'll be a few more minutes," he said.

Long retreated.

The details of the kidnapping were outlined next. Pfifer went through them hurriedly. When he had finished, he folded the file and laid it on his lap.

"George?"

"Yes?" Long answered from the darkness.

"According to this, the girl that took Martin to the freighter was followed after she delivered him. Is she still under surveillance?"

"Yes, as a matter of fact, we believe she's the one making the ransom demands and terms known to Stein."

"Then, I believe, she's the place to begin. I think it's safe to assume that the freighter won't just sit in Rotterdam and wait on us. They're bound to move fairly often to maintain their security. Why else would they choose a ship to hide their hostage? This woman may give us an idea or two about where the freighter is scheduled to be next."

Long came forward and stood beside Pfifer. He nodded his head slightly.

"That's exactly what I thought. By the time you're in London, I'll have the exact location and setup. If there's any way you can make contact without blowing our security I'll put you in. Now, there are some other points that need to be made."

Long began to talk at length about the methods they would use to communicate with one another. They discussed drops and phone numbers to call. Several were new. Pfifer questioned this, but Long waved him off. All he would say was that he had his reasons for the changes in procedure and that Pfifer must comply.

"Your code name for this assignment will be 'Pisces.' Use of that code name will get you cleared directly to me. Remember, you will have one control—me. I will not delegate anyone to give you instructions or receive your reports. If you are contacted in the field by anyone, all I want you to do is identify them, if you can, and report it to me. Is that clear?"

"Perfectly."

"One last thing." Long reached into his coat pocket and withdrew a vial of capsules. "The medics have prescribed something for you. Take one of these things now, and continue taking them until the bottle is empty. The instructions are on the label."

"Your concern for me is touching, George."

"Just remember what I said. Do exactly as I tell you on this one. Check in at Heathrow after you've cleared customs. I'll give you further instructions then."

As he took the vial of capsules, Pfifer looked at Long's rotund little face. He was met with an almost perfectly empty expression.

CHAPTER
Four

The beach near the cottage was empty. The afternoon sun, filtered pale by a slate-gray haze, bore down on its wind-blown ripples, as a troubled sea rolled low breakers onto a sepia-brown shoreline. The air was filled with the sound of those breakers and the smell of the sea.

In the cottage, Gretchen Templin sat and looked out a bay window. She had not slept. She was still too excited and too anxious.

She knew the next few days ahead would require her to be alert and clear of mind. But she could not force herself to relax. Instead, she had sat by the little window throughout the night, and when morning had come she had looked out onto the empty beach and watched it grow more starkly barren as the shadows receded.

The first part of her assignment had gone as planned. Juan had given her a reassuring embrace and told her so himself. She had done extremely well, he had said. He had every confidence that she would continue to perform equally as well in the next few days. Only she did not feel particularly confident at this moment, for she knew something the others did not.

She knew that after they had lifted Martin Stein's limp body out of the boat, after the brightness of the landing had gone dark, when she had turned her boat back into the fog, she had almost panicked. She had come perilously close to running away.

Suddenly, as the darkness closed in around her, she realized that she was alone, completely alone. The full weight of her responsibilities fell upon her and seemed to draw the very breath from her chest.

And her fear made her overcautious. For much of the distance back up river, she little more than idled the boat's engine. Tentatively, she groped through the fog, straining to see where she was going. Several times she became disoriented and lost track of her position, and when she finally found her way back to Saint Katherine's Dock, her heart throbbed so hard her temples hurt and tears streaked her face.

At Saint Katherine's, as she tied up the boat, she thought she saw people watching her from the dark windows of the shops. The shadows seemed alive with movement. When she reached Martin's car, she was shivering, but happily, the little Austin started quickly and carried her away from what she tried to tell herself were most probably imagined dangers.

From the docks, she did not return to her tenement. She drove the circuitous route that she had rehearsed to the safe house, the little cottage by the sea, and there she sat down quietly by the telephone, made one call to establish that she was at her post, and then a second to Howard Stein.

Stein's reaction to her call surprised her. There were no hysterics as she had anticipated. He was calm, cool, measured. It was as if he was the one in control of the situation and not her, as if a long contemplated nightmare had finally arrived, unwelcome, but expected. It unnerved her; his stark Aryan abruptness. Where was his fear? Without fear, how could she hope to control him? How could they hope to succeed? She had expected him to ask for some proof that they had indeed kidnapped Martin. He did not. She had expected difficulty getting him to agree to the ransom amount and to the timetable. He acquiesced immediately. It all went so perfectly; too perfectly.

Now, many separate plans would be put in motion. The group responsible for actually picking up the ransom would be making its final preparations. Stein would be doing what he needed to do to gather the diamonds. In a few hours, Juan would be checking in from Rotterdam. But for her, the waiting would begin. Except for the final call to Stein, she would be merely the conduit between the teams; a relayer of messages, left to do battle with the alteration between fear and boredom.

When she had had Martin to contend with, she could at least see her goal directly. She understood what she was supposed to do. The risk was tractable, manageable. Now, so much would be out of her hands. Now, she would be faced with the horrors of waiting without knowing exactly what was taking place.

And so, for now, still dressed in the dark clothes she had worn the night before, Gretchen continued to man her solitary vigil.

Behind the cottage, in tall thick salt grass that covered the hills, Orin Brady lifted binoculars to his eyes. A radio was strapped to his belt, and earphones covered his ears under his camouflage hat. And even though he wore thick thermals under his camouflage jacket and trousers, the unremitting dampness had penetrated him to his core. He had been lying in the grass for several hours now. The small of his back ached. His knees and elbows stung each time he moved. He was uncomfortable, and he felt exposed. It would be very difficult for anyone to see him from the cottage, he told himself. But still, he wished the grass was twice as tall and twice as thick as it was.

Orin lowered the binoculars, looked at his watch, and thought about the two other agents in the damp basement of another cottage a half mile down the beach: Josh, the technician, with his own set of earphones on, monitoring the cottage's telephone line and methodically scanning for radio transmissions, and Freddy, the marksman, his rifle propped against the wall behind him, relaxing while he waited for his next turn on the hill, probably reading some magazine.

They would all get their fill of this one, Orin thought. Already it had the earmarks of a protracted situation. God only knew how long they would be stuck out there in the waist-high bracken, waiting for something to happen. And damn the English weather; with hope, as the day wore on, the sun might manage to burn its way through the overcast. If not, they would all have pneumonia before they were finished.

Abruptly, Josh's voice sounded in his ears.

"Orin, pull back. Pat McKintosh is here. He wants to talk with you. Freddy's on his way down now."

"Right, Josh. On my way," he answered and immediately began to ease himself around.

When Orin reached the crest of the hill, he stood carefully and let the blood redistribute itself in his body. He was quite a bit stiffer than he had realized. He laughed at himself because of it, but was glad that his men could not see him.

For an instant the breeze picked up, and its cold gusty breath sent a shiver through him. He swore loudly, then looked quickly around but his immediate area was quite devoid of any activity. The cottage was completely obscured from view below. The channel and a long strip of beach lay desolate.

In anticipation, Orin looked to his left. Soon a lanky figure with a shock of red hair came into view, making his way along a footpath. When he came into the open, he too was wearing camouflage.

"Where the hell is your hat, Freddy?" Orin called out. "You look like a lit match without it."

"Sorry, I got booted out pretty quick. I guess I forgot it."

"Well, you better wear mine, then."

Freddy stopped beside him and watched silently as Orin removed the radio and handed it over along with the hat and binoculars.

"What kind of mood is the old man in?" Orin asked.

"He's still hot."

"He's been hot all night. I'd better go see what he wants."

"Has anything been happening down there?" Freddy asked and peered over the edge of the hill.

"Absolutely nothing. So just keep your eyes open and let us know if she makes a move. I should be back in a couple of hours to relieve you."

"You should get some rest, Orin. You've hardly let any of us share the misery."

"I feel responsible."

"There was nothing you could do."

"Right," Orin said and waved Freddy off.

Freddy was probably right; there had been little opportunity to do anything during the kidnapping but watch. He had certainly risked his life, as he had followed Martin's fleeting car through the fog, lights dowsed, peering intently at its dim taillights. He had almost been seen as it was, and he had no idea that Gretchen would have a boat waiting. But still it bothered him. No matter how brilliant he had been in following Gretchen to the safe house, the fact remained that he had let the kidnapping take place. His assignment of quiet security for Martin Stein had been botched.

Orin watched until Freddy disappeared into the tall growth, then he turned and began to walk. The footpath was deep and narrow and ancient. He thought fleetingly about the countless other men whose footsteps he tread upon, then turned his mind to the present.

McKintosh had been hot, all right. Orin had never seen the man so upset in the two years he had worked for him. The Chief of London Station had generally been praised for his cool head under most circumstances, but this business had really rattled him. Orin wished he had not been the one that had been charged with keeping an eye on Martin Stein that night. He thanked God that he at least had been able to follow Gretchen to the safe house. If he had blown that, the situation would be hopeless.

Why did McKintosh want him now? It had been hours since there had been any new activity to report. In fact, the girl had not moved from the cottage. There had been no calls either in or out, since the wiretap had been established, and, as near as they could tell, she had made no radio broadcast. She had simply been quiet, waiting, but waiting for what?

The path wound about a gentle knoll. A stone cottage stood just beyond, beside it a wooden shed where they had hidden away their car. Orin looked up and swore under his breath when he saw a bright yellow Rover parked boldly in front. It was an uncharacteristic lapse for his boss. Any other time, he would have parked away from a surveillance post and walked in.

Orin increased his pace.

When he reached the cottage, he pushed the rough plank door open and went quickly in. It was dank and cold inside. Sheets covered the furniture. In the main room, a braided rug had been thrown back, exposing a trapdoor that led to the basement. As he approached it, Orin stopped as he heard the sound of someone mounting the steps.

"Is that you, Orin?" Pat McKintosh called out in his high nasal voice.

"Yes sir," Orin answered.

McKintosh emerged into the room. He was a thin man,

and his thinness made him appear taller than his six feet. His pale complexion looked even whiter than usual to Orin. There was a tightness to his expression, and tired puffiness under his eyes as well. McKintosh paused at the top of the stairs and returned Orin's gaze.

"If you want a current report, sir, I'm afraid there hasn't been any change in the situation for some time now."

"Thank you Orin, but that's not why I'm here. We've been in contact with Langley, as you realize, most of the night. They've decided to send us some help, someone from Special Operations."

McKintosh lowered his voice and took a step closer.

"He'll be arriving later today. Also, they want to attempt to put a man inside the cottage for a look around."

Orin did nothing to mask the look of incredulousness that came onto his face.

"Pardon me for saying so, sir, but that's crazy. There's no way he'll be able to get into that cottage without her spotting him. Let alone have a chance to look around. They'll blow our surveillance."

"Langley seems confident their man can pull it off. We'll have to let him have his go, whether we like it or not. I've been told he'll be arriving separately. I'll have him brought straight here. Your instructions are to simply watch the cottage as you have been, and to offer no assistance or interference."

"No assistance or interference?"

"That's verbatim."

Orin shook his head silently. Somehow this new situation made him angry. What did Langley think, that they were incompetents?

McKintosh hesitated, seemed to come to a decision, then continued. "I know the man they're sending. One of them, at any rate. His name is George Long. He can be dangerous."

Orin looked up.

"Dangerous in what way?"

McKintosh hesitated again, then spoke in almost a whisper.

"Dangerous to your career, and to mine. His recommendations to Langley may have a great deal of weight on how our problem is perceived."

"You mean who gets the blame for it."

"Yes."

Orin stared at McKintosh. Suddenly he realized that McKintosh was frightened. He wondered why. Surely his mistake wouldn't destroy McKintosh's career, not with his record. What was it that McKintosh wasn't telling him?

"You've done a good job for me, Orin. I've appreciated it more than you know. But there's something I have to ask you to do. I have friends in the agency that are telling me that Long may be looking for more than just a way to help us. Too many people know about this Stein kidnapping; too many for what should be a very limited operation. A lot of questions are being asked."

"Why should that concern us?"

"If you knew a little more about Company politics, you wouldn't have to ask that question. Take my word for it, Long is trouble."

"What do you want me to do?"

"There's no reason to tell Long anything beyond what Langley has told him. I know it may be hard to understand, especially since he has supposedly been sent to help us, but I don't want you to discuss anything you've been doing on the Stein assignment. If he has questions, refer him to me."

Orin looked steadily at McKintosh for a moment before he answered. It was a matter of loyalty, he supposed. Loyalty and perhaps self-preservation, even though he did not like himself for thinking in those terms.

"You're right, I don't understand, but I'll do as you ask."

McKintosh relaxed perceptibly. "Good, thank you. I'll see that my report of your surveillance makes it clear you weren't negligent in any way. And, of course, you weren't."

"Don't think you have to do that," Orin said abruptly. "I'm not looking to make any kind of trade here."

McKintosh noted Orin's anger and adjusted his tack quickly.

"Of course not, Orin. I didn't mean to insinuate that we were. You obviously realize that you'll be protecting yourself as well as me. We'll leave it at that."

"Fine. Now, when does this hotshot second-story man arrive?"

"We'll let you know when he's picked up at the airport. After you've been alerted, you will take no action against anyone approaching the cottage. That's clear, isn't it?"

"Perfectly."

"Make sure your men are informed."

"I will."

McKintosh attempted a brief smile. Orin stared blankly back at him.

"I'd better get back to London before too many people begin to wonder where I am."

"Have a good drive back. I noticed your car is parked conveniently enough."

"Yes, I know. Sorry about that."

"No problem, I guess."

After a furtive glance back toward the basement, McKintosh stepped briskly by Orin and then continued out of the cottage. Seconds later, Orin heard the Rover start up, then drive away.

"Damn!" Orin said and began to rub his elbows and then his knees. The absolute gall of the man! What kind of trouble was he in? What kind of trouble were they both in? Orin shook his head and then started for the basement stairs.

The basement was in darkness, except for one dim bulb over a table set against the south wall. Josh, mustached and spectacled, prematurely bald, sat at the table in a wooden chair. He sat hunched over, leaning forward. The band of his earphones divided his shiny scalp. He made a perfect picture of concentration. As Orin approached him he held up his hand in a cautioning gesture.

"She's moving," he said.

"Where?"

"Just out on the beach."

"Anyone else around?"

"No."

"Well, there will be soon enough."

CHAPTER
Five

Pfifer approached London in darkness. Ahead, through the airliner's window, he could see the city's lights spread out in a flickering spiderweb of complex strands. Most of the passengers around him slept. Only a few reading lights interrupted the darkness of the cabin.

He glanced at the luminous dial of his wristwatch, and then he stretched as much as he could without disturbing the passenger next to him. It was late, past twelve. He was tired.

The flight had been bumpy most of the way from Boston. But then, he had never learned to sleep on commercial airplanes even on the smoothest of flights. Anyway, it had given him the opportunity to think about the possibilities of his assignment in relative security for a few hours. Once in London, he would be plunged into the game headfirst. He would either have to go on directly to Rotterdam or follow up on Gretchen Templin, depending on what that situation was. In either case, his day would be much longer before he got any rest. The Agency would get its money's worth out of him on this one. George Long would see to that.

But he had been allowed his period of refuge. There had at least been that. The six months of seclusion had given him a chance to revive, a chance to think beyond the immediate need to survive. He knew he might not enjoy that luxury again. Today, tomorrow, the next day perhaps; this was all he could reasonably conceive of as his future. At least his six months of inactivity had given him the time to reflect on the past, to sum up what he had gained and what he had lost. In the past seven years, he had been afforded only brief moments to consider such things. Now that he had been given that chance, he wondered if it would make any difference.

It was a matter of rhythms. It had never occurred to him before. The things he had done had set a rhythm to his life that had carried him along, from to event to event, in an endless, seemingly unbreakable chain. No matter what he did, the chain lengthened, the rhythm continued. He had no reason to expect it would not continue to the end; his end.

The stewardesses, who had been preparing the cabin for landing, were called to their seats for final descent. The lights blinked on over most of the passengers' seats, and people began to shift and move in anticipation. Pfifer brought his seat upright, tightened his seatbelt and then looked back out the window.

It was a flawless ending to a rough flight. The airliner touched down with only the faintest of bumps as the tires met the runway. A short roll under moderate braking brought them under control for the taxi to the terminal. Then, once at the terminal, the engines were quickly cut, and the bustle of people, packages and coats replaced the whine of jets as the dominant sound in the aircraft. Pfifer unsnapped his seatbelt, but then waited for some of the confusion to clear before he got up.

The man seated next to Pfifer got up immediately. Briskly he bulled his way into the crush of people in the aisle. Pfifer watched him pushing ahead, ignoring the objections of those around him, and in a few minutes, he had melted well into the stream. Pfifer smiled and wondered if the man, who had been silent throughout the long flight, was perhaps in a hurry to get to a telephone. If that were the case, something told Pfifer, George Long would know that he had arrived safely in London even before he checked in himself. It was just the sort of thing George Long would do. At all times, he was thorough to the point of predictability.

Slowly Pfifer slipped out of his seat and eased into the stream.

Customs was perfunctory. But then Pfifer was far too much the professional to travel with anything that would raise an official's eyebrow. He had only a single suitcase and nothing out of the ordinary, save his little vial of pills clearly marked as a prescription. Routinely he was on his way with a fresh English stamp in his passport.

He moved off with the general flow, easily now, without feeling conspicuous. Casually he watched for an available telephone. Then, finding one, he fished for the proper coins and dialed the number from memory. As he waited for his call to go through he was glad to notice he had become accustomed to the noise and commotion of people around him again, the color and activity having a less dazzling effect.

Then the phone was answered on the third ring by a soft, feminine voice.

"American Embassy," she said.

"This is Pisces," Pfifer said.

"Yes, we've been expecting your call. Wait please, while we patch you through."

Pfifer acknowledged her and then watched the excited

procession of people moving by him. Each with a place to go, he supposed, someone waiting for each of them. Only a brief time elapsed before he recognized Long's voice on the line. There was background noise; Pfifer assumed that he had been patched through to Long's aircraft, still en route.

"John, listen carefully. Look for a heavyset fellow driving a gray Jaguar just outside the main terminal. His name is Joe Bryant. He will take you where you want to go, and he'll have some items that you will find necessary. After you are finished with your task, proceed on your own; repeat, on your own. Understand?"

Pfifer acknowledged by repeating Bryant's name and the description of his car.

"Good, signal next when you are in Rotterdam."

The line went dead.

Pfifer replaced the phone easily in its cradle and made a quick visual sweep. Failing to notice anyone taking special interest in him, he moved off directly to the main exit.

He only had to wait a moment at the curb before a gray Jaguar pulled to a stop in front of him. Pfifer approached it carefully and stooped by the passenger door.

"My name's Joe Bryant," the driver said with some urgency. "I have some instructions for you from George Long. If you don't mind, we'll talk as we drive. We've got some ground to cover."

The driver was a paunchy little man with a fleshy face. His cheeks sagged, his eyes looked permanently sad. Like an old hound, Pfifer thought and wondered how friendly this old hound would be.

"That's fine with me," Pfifer answered as he put his suitcase into the backseat and climbed in beside Bryant.

Bryant put the Jaguar into gear and quickly pulled away.

He inserted them expertly into the traffic and then immediately began to talk.

"We were able to follow the girl. She ended up in a small cottage in Essex. We believe she made the ransom call from there. Long wants you to get inside and find out what you can. He said you'd know what to look for."

"What can you tell me about the cottage and its immediate surroundings?"

"It's right on the beach. There aren't many other structures near it. Plenty of tall grass though; that should give you enough cover.

"It's a small cottage; frame construction, four rooms on the ground floor. There's an attic with windows at each end. If she has a radio, it's probably up there. We're monitoring for her broadcasts, and we do have a phone tap. There's no basement. A narrow lane leads down to the place from the road. It's dirt and it sort of winds down and around to the cottage. As I said, there aren't many houses in the area."

Bryant glanced at Pfifer for a moment and then added, "We have a man in the tall grass on the hill between the cottage and the road. He has binoculars and a two-way radio. We've all had instructions not to interfere. Do you have any other questions?"

"Did Long supply me with anything useful?"

"It's in the glove box in front of you."

Pfifer leaned forward and opened the wooden door of the Jaguar's glove box. Inside he found a metal cylinder. He lifted it out, looked at it briefly and then slipped it into his coat pocket.

"You seem to know pretty much what's going on. Do you know if the freighter is still in Rotterdam?"

"Yes, it's still sitting right there; also we haven't had any new communication with the kidnappers. We've all just been waiting for the delivery instructions."

"How long will it take us to get to the cottage?"

"About an hour, if the traffic doesn't get any worse."

"Good. Unless there's something else you have to tell me, I'm going to try and catch a nap."

"There is something," Bryant paused, "just between you and me."

Something in the tone of Bryant's voice sounded a warning in Pfifer's subconscious. He tried to read Bryant's face but could not. It remained the same sad-faced mask.

"I'm listening."

"I've been with the old man for a long time. Perhaps too long. I've watched both of the kids grow up. What I'm trying to say is, none of us know exactly what your instructions are pertaining to Martin. The old man and his son haven't been on the best of terms lately, but he loves him, and he wants him back alive. Do you understand what I'm saying, what I'm asking? If you could give me an indication, off of the record, it would be meaningful to them; to me."

Silence fell between them; a darkness. Bryant drove on, his expression unchanged, as he waited for Pfifer's answer.

Perhaps Bryant had been on his assignment too long, Pfifer thought. It was apparent that he was more concerned about the Steins than he was about himself. If Pfifer told George Long what Bryant had asked him to do, namely break security, Bryant would be on his way home at the first opportunity. Pfifer was uncomfortable with the prospect of holding whatever remained of this tired old agent's career in his hands. He wished he could tell him something that would ease his consternation, but the words Bryant wanted to hear would be a lie.

"Any indication, as you put it, would have to come from George Long," Pfifer began. "And just to make sure we understand each other, don't read anything either into or out of the response I'm giving you."

"I understand," Bryant said, without so much as a glance at Pfifer.

Pfifer wondered if he did.

Pfifer sank in his seat and closed his eyes against the glow of the oncoming headlights. He still could not sleep, but at least he could preempt any game of cat and mouse with Bryant. He could not tell the man what he wanted to hear, that he would rescue Martin Stein, that he would not consider any other solution to the problem. He did not even know if he could get to Stein. Just catching up to the freighter would not help him. What he needed was some planning time, some anticipation. He had to know where they were going and as much as he could about what their plans were. He had to be able to put himself securely in the freighter's path. At the moment, he was just chasing shadows.

One thing, of course, was certain. For all of George Long's careful effort to give Pfifer a thorough briefing in this case, it was a given that he had not told Pfifer everything. Long would not do such a thing. He did not think that way. There had to be a side game in progress. There always had been before. Nothing had happened to change that basic method of operation. Whether Pfifer would learn about Long's parallel project or not remained to be seen, but its existence was fundamental. Pfifer would bet his life on it.

Hopefully, someone at Langley was keeping track of all the odds and ends of the puzzle. Pfifer could not worry about it. It was a realm too far removed from his own. He would and should be concerned with one thing at a time, and first would be the kidnappers' safe house. If he was successful there, he would worry about Rotterdam.

Occasionally the Jaguar would hit a particularly deep rut, or a brighter light than usual would glare into the car, or a sharp unexpected sound would cause Pfifer to involuntarily open his eyes for a second. He got glimpses of the countryside; the dark-green hedgerows, scattered farmhouses, ancient old stone pubs. Each brief look became a sort of mental snapshot. As he closed his eyes again, it took a short time for each image to fade and his line of thought to return.

It would be dangerous to alert the kidnappers to the fact they were under surveillance. If they even suspected that they were being monitored, they might roll up their whole operation immediately, kill Martin Stein and disappear. For that reason, the safe house would have to be penetrated with great care. To be detected would make Stein's death a foregone conclusion. Pfifer would just as soon not see the boy killed, if it was not absolutely necessary. Even Long would have to agree that it would be preferable to bring him home alive.

It would still be dark when they reached the safe house; with luck Gretchen might even be asleep. That would make things so much easier. But Pfifer had learned that things are seldom easy. If you expected to survive, you would do so on the strength of your planning. There was never a substitute for knowing what lay around the next bend in the road, or what was hidden along the way. He would have to make his breaks beforehand. If he did not, he would fail.

Hopefully the safe house would contain some clue. There might be a schedule, a list of telephone numbers, a codebook; something that would tell him where the freighter was expected to be and when. If Gretchen was to communicate with the freighter, she would have to have something. If she had written it down, kept a record of some sort, perhaps he could find it. If she had committed it to memory only, his efforts would be wasted, the risk taken for nothing.

The telephone tap and the radio monitoring would, of course, tell the listeners when the kidnappers communicated, and could possibly even supply good information, if the codes were broken in time. But still Pfifer would have to rely on the CIA to relay the information to him, and he would have to surface repeatedly for updates. No, what he needed was to know, exactly, from the start, where he could intercept his target. His primary advantage, if he had one, would be his ability to move quickly and independently. That could not be compromised, if he hoped to succeed or, indeed, survive.

Pfifer had finally dozed off, but he did not sleep long before Bryant shook him gently by the shoulder.

"We're almost there. A half mile from here the lane goes off at about a forty-five-degree angle. I'll drop you here and tap my brakes just as I pass. That should spot it for you."

"It's the only cottage on the lane?" Pfifer asked, now fully awake.

"Yes, and it's right at the end. There's a little less than fifty yards of open ground between the cover of the grass and the cottage, so be careful."

Bryant pulled the Jaguar to the side of the road and stopped. Pfifer got out quickly.

"I'll come back by in an hour. If you're here, I'll pick you up and take you where you want to go. If you miss me, wait another hour and look for a white Ford Escort with a redheaded kid driving it. Got it?"

"Right."

Pfifer tapped on the car's roof and stepped back. Bryant looked at him hard, then drove away. He'd be upset when Pfifer didn't show, Pfifer knew, but it couldn't be helped. Long had made a special point.

Pfifer began to walk along the side of the road. He kept his attention divided between his footing and the Jaguar's taillights. When he saw them flash, he marked the spot for reference. Bryant moved around a bend and out of sight shortly afterward.

It was quiet, the first real quiet he had experienced since he had left the island and the old sloop. He walked at an easy pace, glad to be out of the car. The night air was heavy with moisture. The gentlest of breezes stirred.

The dirt lane was nearly overgrown when he came upon it, but there were signs that a car had passed over it recently. Tire tread imprints were clear in the damp earth, even in the dull moonlight. Pfifer glanced around, then stepped briskly forward. It was impossible to know if he was being observed, but at least the tall grass hid him immediately. If anyone was watching him, he would have been there one moment and then simply gone the next.

Bryant had mentioned that the lane wound down to the cottage. It did. It snaked down a gentle slope toward the beach and the sea, so narrow that even the smallest of cars would have to force the thick grass back with its fenders as it drove. Pfifer walked along the grassy crown of the lane, between the wheel ruts, trying to leave as few deep footprints as possible. When he rounded a last turn the lane leveled out, the grass tapered off in height, and Pfifer found himself on the edge of the beach.

He paused and looked behind him. The hill was dark and still. He knew a man must be up there somewhere watching him, but after a fruitless scrutiny, he turned back around, took several deep breaths and tried to focus his concentration. The thought of a silent spectator did little to comfort him. He supposed it didn't matter, though. What did matter was what happened in the next few minutes.

The cottage was perhaps only forty-five yards away. Bryant had been quite accurate in his estimate. There was also no cover, just as he had warned. He would have to cross the open beach exposed. If anyone happened to look out of the cottage as he crossed, he would undoubtedly be seen. They would have to be blind to miss him.

The cottage's windows were draped, but faint light showed at the separations—so much for the possibility that Gretchen would be sleeping. Pfifer steeled himself, checked his pocket to make sure he still had the cylinder, and stepped slowly out onto the beach. It occurred to him, as he trudged through the soft sand, that the entire operation could come to a very abrupt end at this point. As he considered that possibility, he had genuinely mixed emotions, but the thought of Martin Stein, in the hands of his kidnappers, forced him forward.

When he reached the cottage, he stopped by the rear door and listened. There was no sound from within to tell him where Gretchen might be. He hesitated before he proceeded.

The cottage was made of clapboards, weathered, warped, and paintless. The rear door showed signs of recent repair. A fresh piece of plywood adorned it, probably held it together. Pfifer suspected it would squeak loudly if he tried to open it. After he exhaled a long quiet breath, he began to move around the cottage in a clockwise direction.

A small car had been parked near the cottage and covered with a tarpaulin. Pfifer stepped over the stones that had been used to hold it down and continued to circle around to the front. Still he heard no sound from inside.

The front of the cottage had a large picture window that faced the sea. Its drapes were drawn back and a shaft of gold light fanned out from it onto the sand. Pfifer stood at the window and peered into the cottage. The front room held an old overstuffed platform rocker that faced the window, a couch, a low coffee table, and in one corner a desk with a bright lamp. On the back wall a door opened into a narrow hallway. Two small bedrooms and a kitchen, Pfifer supposed, probably adjoined that hallway, but where was Gretchen?

He had to pass in front of the window in full view of the room in order to reach the front door. He had decided to try it and had taken the first step when he heard a foot fall on the wooden floor of the cottage. Quickly he stepped back, hopefully in time to keep from being seen. With his heart beating clearly in his ears, he stood and waited for some reaction from inside.

He heard more footsteps, then the scrape of a chair. Slowly he eased himself into a position where he could see.

A small blond girl sat at the desk with her back to the window. She leaned forward and rested her elbows on the desktop and gently rubbed her temples with her fingertips. Her long hair glistened in the bright light. A dark green towel was draped over one shoulder; her bare skin looked pale in contrast to it.

Silently, breathlessly, with the soft sand and the distant roar of the surf to mask the sound of his movement, Pfifer slipped across the front of the cottage and paused.

The front door of the cottage was hung in an upper and lower section; Dutch doors. The upper section stood open to the night. Pfifer stood to one side and listened. Still there was no indication that he had been detected.

He removed the cylinder from his pocket and held it in his hand. It was about two inches in diameter. The general shape was much like that of a common flashlight, but only six or seven inches long. Recessed into the cylinder, to prevent its accidental actuation, there was a press button. At each end of the cylinder a small opening.

The gas contained in the cylinder was not lethal, but it would, upon inhalation, completely incapacitate for a period of between ten and fifteen minutes, depending on the size and weight of the subject. The beauty of the gas was that it would completely dissipate to an ineffectual level within sixty seconds. The drawback was that the gas was designed to be used in a confined space. In this situation, Pfifer would have to place the cylinder close to Gretchen, or it might not put her out.

Pfifer peered carefully through the door. Gretchen still sat at the desk. The distance between them was twelve feet, no more. Pfifer looked at the floor; it was covered partially by a threadbare oriental rug. There was a clear line between them. The platform rocker was well to the left, the couch to the

right against the wall. He had two choices; he could carefully pitch the cylinder onto the couch and hope that the
distance would not be too great for the gas to work, or he
could roll the cylinder across the floor under Gretchen's
chair. If the gas worked properly, Gretchen would simply
feel sleepy. She would think that she had dozed off for a
moment. If Pfifer was fortunate enough not to alert her, he
would be able to thoroughly search the cottage, and Gretchen
would be none the wiser. Pfifer needed time to look for the
information he was after. It was essential for him to know
where the freighter was to go. He had no choice but to take
the risk.

Pfifer held his breath, leaned over the bottom half of the
door, and with one fluid motion pressed the button on the
cylinder and rolled it toward Gretchen. If Gretchen turned
around now, she would see him standing at the door. If the
cylinder overshot the rug, it would roll under the desk and
perhaps strike the wall. Gretchen would be alerted, suspicious before passing out. In either case, he would have
failed. With a cold fascination, he watched as the cylinder
progressed.

The cylinder was designed to release its gas slowly. It
made a very faint sound as it rolled across the flat low nap
of the rug, not unlike the rustle of a cotton curtain caught by
a sudden draft.

For a moment, it looked as if the cylinder were going to
overshoot. Pfifer started to withdraw from the doorway.
Then he noticed that the fringe of the rug was slightly
thicker than the rest, that its binding might provide a soft
stop for the cylinder to come to rest against. He watched,
amazed, as the cylinder did that very thing.

The gas continued to escape almost noiselessly from the
cylinder. Pfifer could only hope that enough of it would
reach Gretchen to be effective. It would either work or it
wouldn't, he told himself.

Suddenly, he could hold his breath no longer. He stood back from the door and moved into the shadows.

He looked at the empty beach. He could see the sudden lace of the breakers as they tumbled onto the sand in the pewter moonlight. Beyond, the English Channel appeared black and endless in its expanse. He stood there, studied the scene, and drew several breaths of the chill air deep into his lungs. Momentarily he glanced at his wristwatch then returned to the doorway.

Gretchen had folded her arms in front of her and had put her head down carefully on them. She sat motionless, relaxed. Pfifer opened the door and went in. She did not stir. He approached the desk and looked into Gretchen's face. She looked tranquil and innocent. Her breath came in long regular motions. The gas had apparently done its work.

The towel flung over her shoulder did little to conceal her from the waist up. Little droplets of water still clung to her from her efforts to refresh herself. The jeans she wore were faded, her feet were bare. Pfifer guessed her age to be less than twenty. She was a very beautiful girl, he thought, beautiful and damned. Somehow it made him angry, and then suddenly sad.

Pfifer bent down and retrieved the cylinder from under Gretchen's desk and then stood back from her. Now there was only the search of the cottage to think of, and what little time he had for that was soullessly slipping away.

There was a list of handwritten numbers on a pad by the telephone. Beside the numbers were dates. Pfifer took a page from the back of the pad and copied down everything in order and arrangement. He put his copy in his pocket and then replaced the pad and pencil in the exact spot he had found them. Quickly and methodically, he then began to go through the rest of the cottage.

He found a lift-up panel in the hall ceiling that led to the attic, found the radio that Bryant had suspected, and beside the radio he found what appeared to be a list of frequencies and times. He copied a portion of its contents, checked his watch, then swore softly. Carefully, and now more quietly, he retraced his steps and replaced everything he had disturbed.

As he entered the front room, he looked at Gretchen. She still slept peacefully at the desk, but she had turned her head somewhat. At some point, the gas-induced sleep had probably become natural sleep. Now, Pfifer knew, at any time, it would be quite possible for her to wake up.

As quietly as he could, he crossed the room and went out the front door. Carefully he latched it behind him. Then, once outside, he moved off down the beach, counting on the rising breeze to cover his footprints in the sand.

CHAPTER
Six

Bryant took the basement steps slowly. He had a particular way of negotiating them; turned slightly sideways, right foot, then left, one at a time. It was his back. When it was cold and damp it always stiffened up. He cursed it and grimaced with the pain, knowing if he stayed in the basement for very long it would only get worse.

"Hi, Joe," Josh called to him as Bryant reached the basement floor. Josh hadn't turned around. He still sat at the table with his back to the steps, facing the whitewashed wall.

"How did you know for sure it was me?" Bryant asked, slightly curt in his tone of voice.

"Freddy wouldn't have let anyone else by. Besides. . . ."

"Never mind. You young upstarts always think you have all the answers. What's going on? How's our man doing?"

"Orin just called. He's gone."

"Gone? I just dropped him off twenty minutes ago." Bryant moved closer to the table. The light fell across his chest. It accentuated his puffy body. "I'd better get out there and pick him up. He did get in, didn't he?"

"Orin said he did. He was in the house twelve minutes. There was no sign of commotion. He's apparently done it."

"Apparently."

"Orin said something funny, though. He didn't come back up the same way he went down. He went down the beach."

"Down the beach? What the hell?"

"That's what Orin said."

"Who knows what he may be doing out there now? Special Ops hasn't told us a thing, those bastards."

The bitterness in Bryant's voice caused Josh to turn around and look at him.

"It is all the same company, isn't it Joe?"

"Sometimes I wonder. . . ."

Josh held his hand up abruptly.

"It's Orin again. He says the lights went out. He thinks she's gone to bed!"

"Does he see any sign of our man at all?"

Josh worked his microphone. Bryant waited impatiently.

"No," Josh finally said.

"Damn!"

The time passed slowly. Bryant waited thirty minutes, could wait no longer, then left.

He drove slowly along the road; too slowly; it was conspicuous and he knew it. He came to a complete stop at the turnoff, but Pfifer was not there. He was tempted to get out and walk a short distance down the dirt lane, but he thought better of it. Angrily, he got back up to speed and drove toward London.

Ordinarily, Joe Bryant would not have gone near the American Embassy, but tonight was a very special situation. Bryant was the one that worked directly with Howard Stein. Stein knew Bryant and had, over the years, grown accustomed to communicating with the Agency through him. It was important that Bryant stay near the center of things. Stein had insisted on it.

Bryant parked his car three blocks from Grosvenor Square and walked. He was somewhat out of breath when he reached the embassy's side door, and he was grateful someone opened up immediately. As it was, it turned out to be Pat McKintosh himself.

"How did it go?" McKintosh asked, without formality, as he bolted the door shut.

"He got in. There was no sign of trouble. But he hasn't been picked up yet. We don't know where the hell he is."

They were standing in a hallway. The light was dim, but Bryant could see McKintosh clearly enough to recognize his troubled expression, and when McKintosh spoke, it was obvious he chose his words carefully.

"Did you learn anything interesting from him?"

"No."

"I see. Did he learn anything interesting from you?"

"What, exactly, do you mean by that?" Bryant asked, letting his anger begin to show at the inference.

"Nothing, I suppose."

"Go ahead and say it, you have something on your mind."

McKintosh met his gaze for a second. They stared hard at each other before McKintosh finally spoke.

"Nothing Joe, except I wonder sometimes whether you remember who you work for—the Agency, or Howard Stein."

"I work for you, but I am concerned about him. I would hope that you are too."

"Of course."

McKintosh broke it off and turned down the hallway. Bryant fell into step behind in a strained silence.

"We've put a man in the house, you probably should know," McKintosh said over his shoulder.

"How's the old man doing?"

"As well as can be expected I suppose. Listen, Rachel is here. You'll have to take her home. The sooner the better. George Long from Special Ops is here as well. I'd like to keep those two apart if I can."

"Rachel! What's she doing here?"

"She wasn't satisfied with her briefing." McKintosh's tone sharpened. "That one's got a mind of her own. See if you can calm her down on the way home."

"I'll do what I can."

They came to a heavy door; McKintosh produced a key and opened it carefully, Bryant stepped through to allow him to close it behind them.

The room they entered was comfortably furnished, if utilitarian, in its decor. There was a couch, several upholstered chairs, and desk with a telephone rowed with pushbuttons for a number of different lines. George Long sat expressionless behind the desk, Rachel Stein on the couch facing him.

Sitting in a rigid posture with her arms folded tightly in front of her, Rachel wore a trim gray suit, plain blouse, little makeup. Her hair was dark brown, shoulder length and combed straight. The combined effect of her conservative dress was to make her look older than her twenty-six years. She looked up sternly as McKintosh and Bryant came into the room, but brightened as Bryant caught her glance.

"Rachel?" Bryant said and approached her.

"Uncle Joe."

"You shouldn't be here, you know that."

"I had to come. No one's telling me anything." Rachel gave a sharp nod at McKintosh. "They're still not."

"We've told you everything we can, at this point," McKintosh said in defense of himself. "Now you must go home with Joe. Your father needs you with him."

"What father needs most is his son back!"

McKintosh frowned.

George Long shifted his weight in his chair; it caught the

attention of everyone in the room, as perhaps it was designed to. Then he smiled and spoke softly.

"Before Mr. Bryant leaves, perhaps he can give us a report on what has happened tonight so far? Was my man successful, for instance?"

Bryant looked at Rachel and then at McKintosh.

"That would be fine. Go ahead, Joe," McKintosh said.

Bryant gave a carefully edited summation of the night's events. Long smiled faintly as he finished.

"Thank you Mr. Bryant. By the way, don't expect your man Freddy to pick him up either. I'm sure John is a long way away by now. That in itself tells me he got at least part of what he was after." Long paused and looked at Rachel. "Now perhaps the young lady has had a few of her questions answered as well?"

"Yes, and I thank you," Rachel said and got up.

"Can I take you home now?" Bryant asked.

"Yes, please."

Long said his polite good-byes, and as they turned to leave, McKintosh followed stoically to let them out the side door. He said nothing as Rachel and Bryant went out into the night, but simply closed the outer door securely.

Once outside the embassy, Bryant and Rachel fell into step. But Rachel walked more quickly than Bryant would have liked. Each of her footsteps clicked defiantly forward, forcing him to press to keep up. Abruptly, Bryant reached out and caught Rachel by the arm.

The street was empty. Only the odd light shone from a window here and there.

"Slow down a little, girl," Bryant said. "I've already put some miles in tonight."

"I'm sorry Joe, but the way this thing is being handled has made me really mad." Rachel shook her head. "Under the circumstances, you wouldn't think I would have to come begging for information."

"Listen to me for a minute, will you? You're still new at

all this. Even George Long has limits on his access to information. You can't expect to be told absolutely everything; it's far too dangerous."

"I still don't like it. I feel like a spectator. I should be doing something to help. Martin is my brother."

"Yes, and you should keep something in mind. The same thing that has happened to Martin could very easily happen to you."

"Don't try and frighten me. McKintosh has already been through that whole routine. I can take care of myself."

"Don't talk like a fool! Think what the risks are!"

Bryant released Rachel's arm and they began to walk again. In a few minutes, they came to a corner. A streetlight glowed overhead. Rachel stopped and turned around.

"I don't mean to make you angry, Uncle Joe. Please try and understand. My father's health isn't good. Another year or two and I won't have him. If my brother's killed, I'll be all alone. It frightens me."

"You'll always have me to look after you."

"I know, and I appreciate what you've done for us. Martin, and me, and my father. Just tell me what's happening. Not knowing is the worst of all."

"Let's keep walking." Bryant took her arm again, this time gently. As they stepped off the curb together, out of habit and reflex, he looked to see if they were being followed, but the sidewalk was clear behind them.

Rachel was family to Bryant; the family he never had. But he still had the presence of mind to realize he was the worst possible person they could have chosen as her control. That she was too close to him, knew him far too well, and could read him like a child reads a parent. What could he tell her? What should he tell her? These were the very last of decisions he should have been asked to make. He could not help but be torn between his instinct to protect her and his duty to keep her under control.

But still he had to tell her something, and with the hope

she could not unravel more than would be good for her to know.

"If I were to tell you more," he began, "it would be a serious breach of security. They could hang me out to dry, and well they should. Even though I may have already blown it . . ."

Rachel gave him a hard look. "What do you mean?"

Bryant paused to consider his answer.

"What do you mean, Uncle Joe?"

"The agent that I took to the safe house—I made an attempt to question him, but I believe he learned more from me than I did from him. From what I told him, he has to have made the connection between the Agency and your father, if in fact he didn't already know."

"Why is that so important?"

"If he's picked up, if these terrorists question him, it would be more detrimental than questioning Martin. They might well realize that what they are dealing with is more than just a kidnapping. All it does is increase the risk, further jeopardize the network."

"Thank God at least Martin doesn't know. He's always been such a reactionary. And this latest blowup between him and my father. I wish I knew what that was all about."

Bryant took a deep breath. He looked away from her and then back. "I'm afraid I don't know what the problem is either, Rachel. When he came home that day he didn't speak to me or his father. He just got his things together and moved out. All I know is that he was deeply disturbed by something. What? Who knows. It's hard to understand."

"And that's not the only thing that's hard to understand, Joe. If I'm supposed to continue my father's activities, why haven't I been allowed to tell him that I've been briefed?"

"In time, Rachel. He will tell you when he's ready. In the meantime, it's far better not to worry him."

"I don't know, Joe. He's kept his secret for so long. Sometimes I feel as if I barely know him. Old acquaintances will turn up at the office every now and then. People that obviously know him well. People that he's never mentioned to us before. For as long as I can remember, he would take short trips and be gone for a day or two with no explanation. I know now that they weren't all just business trips. What else is there that he hasn't told us? When am I going to get the opportunity to learn? What if he never tells me on his own?''

The more Rachel talked the more uncomfortable Bryant became. He tried to hold back uneasiness in his voice as he spoke, but he did a poor job of it.

"He's had to keep secrets; too many people are at risk."

"I know, but the point is the Agency told me about the network, not my father. For twenty-five years he hasn't shared his secret. Why should he choose to share it with me now?''

"He knows he's not immortal, Rachel. None of us are. Eventually, he's going to tell you the whole story, and it will be far better if he believes that you learned it from him. If he knew the Agency went behind his back to recruit you, it would cause unnecessary turmoil."

"Unnecessary turmoil wouldn't be the word, but then at least everything would be out in the open."

A small van passed them headed in the opposite direction. They both looked up as it passed. Then, as quickly as it had appeared, it disappeared, turning down a side street.

"What did you find out from this agent? Long called him John. What was he like?''

Bryant tried not to react to her question. Rachel folded her arms in front of herself and looked at him hard.

"What's wrong?" Rachel asked.

"Nothing."

"I don't believe you."

"Stop pressing me Rachel."

"Then tell me something!"

They walked on in silence. Now Bryant walked more

quickly, Rachel lagged behind. They covered the remaining block and found Bryant's car. In a moment, they were inside and driving away.

"I'm going to keep on pressing, you know that, don't you?" Rachel said as Bryant brought the Jaguar up to speed.

"Yes, I'm afraid I do."

"Please, then, at least tell me about this man you met tonight, Long's agent."

"You think my telling you about him will make you feel better?" Anger revealed itself in Bryant's voice as he spoke. "You'd like me to tell you that he's a regular James Bond type, wouldn't you? Well, no such luck. I didn't like the man. He was cold, detached. I've seen that look on other men. Too many other men."

Rachel sat quietly. She did not move. Bryant's anger mounted. He knew she was waiting for an explanation.

"Okay. You want to know what I think? I believe he's a contract agent. Probably an assassin."

"An assassin? What for? What are you saying?"

"I'm not saying anything, and don't jump to any conclusions."

"How can I not? You've just told me they've sent an assassin after my brother. What am I supposed to think?"

"Don't think, just keep doing what you are told."

"Why would the Agency want to kill Martin? What would it accomplish?"

"I'm not sure. There may be something we're not aware of, but it's dangerous to draw a conclusion on the little we know."

"You've come to a conclusion, though, haven't you?"

Bryant stared back at her blankly.

"Don't lie to me, Joe. You owe me the truth, if nothing else."

"You want the truth? I don't know what the truth is anymore. Things just aren't as simple as they were once.

The whole damn world has gotten too damn complex for me. Don't come to me for the truth.''

"If I can't get the truth from you, then who can I? Who was there to help put things back together after my mother died? Who has always been there when any of us needed anything?"

"It's been my job."

"No, it's been more than that. You care for us. You care for us all. Don't try and hide it. You're just as concerned for Martin personally as anyone of us. I believe that."

Bryant shook his head and grappled for the right words to tell her; words that would ease the pain when the time came. Perhaps those words did not exist, but he had to try, for much of what Rachel said was true. He did care.

"Whatever you say, whatever you think, whatever you believe, it doesn't change anything. Understand? Whatever happens is out of your hands. Can't you see that? This whole thing is more involved than just Martin. It's more involved than any of us. It went beyond that twenty-five years ago. It's just gone way beyond our control. We can't call it back now, even if we wanted to."

"Would you want to?" Rachel asked, lowering her voice.

"I'm not sure. I'm honestly not sure. We've done a lot of good, but suddenly the price is turning out to be higher than we expected."

A pair of headlights caught Bryant's eye in the rearview mirror. He swore under his breath and wondered how long they had been following. He had let himself get too involved in the conversation to pay proper attention to his basic tradecraft. He squinted into the brightness to try and see how many men were in the car behind them.

He had to make a decision; if he took evasive action, he might lose them, but they would know who he was anyway—they had had more than enough time to read his plates. If he continued to the Stein house, he would expose Rachel. They just might not know who she was at the moment. He vacillated, not knowing what to do.

"Rachel, were you followed to the embassy?"

"I doubt it. I was at my very best; very careful."

"I wish I could say the same thing."

Rachel looked quickly behind them.

"How long have they been there?" she asked.

"That's the problem. I'm not sure."

"You're not sure about much tonight, are you?"

"I guess you're right."

"There's an entrance to the underground just ahead; shall we split?"

"Suppose there's more than one of them?"

"No problem." Rachel was very cool now; she tapped her purse. "I brought company."

"That's very un-British of you. What all did they teach you in America?"

"Lots of things. Don't miss the entrance."

"Okay, but you take the car, I'll be the decoy."

"I can handle it."

"You probably can, but humor me this once."

"You're in charge."

"You seem to remember that only when it suits you. Ready?"

"Ready."

It was neat and quick. Bryant pulled to the curb. Rachel slid over as he stepped out. In an instant, Bryant disappeared down the entrance to the underground and Rachel accelerated hard away. They did it as smoothly as if they had done it a hundred times. Bryant would marvel at it later.

A Mercedes sedan skidded to a stop at the entrance seconds later. The driver's side door opened and a man got out, but as he looked between the dark entrance to the tube and the fleeting taillights of the Jaguar, he could not choose between the two, and after a string of mumbled oaths he got back into the car. By that time the Jaguar had made a turn and had slipped out of sight.

Rachel drove rapidly. She took the side streets. She doubled back twice. She constantly checked her rearview mirror. The man in the Mercedes would have had to be very good, indeed, to have caught up with her. Only after she felt she was safe did she head straight for home, and only then did her thoughts turn to Joe Bryant.

He would be all right, she told herself. He would easily lose whoever attempted to follow him. Twenty-odd years of living in London had given him a remarkably complete knowledge of the city, and his experience would see him through. When she got home, she would hide the Jaguar in the garage for him to pick up later. Poor Joe, he wouldn't get much sleep tonight. But then, that couldn't be helped.

She drove past large houses, each dark and quiet, surrounded by green lawns and hedgerows or stone fences. No one followed her on the road. Ahead she saw the familiar stone fence and iron gates to the Stein estate. They had always reminded her of ramparts to a fortress. In fact, she had considered them as such in her childhood games. The memory brought a brief smile to her face, until she remembered the stakes in the real game at hand.

She stopped at the entrance to the drive and got out. Finding the heavy gate had been left unlocked, she pushed both halves of it back firmly and listened as they came to rest with a deep clang against the stone. Then with a quick brush of her hands to remove the wet rust from her palms, she got back into the Jaguar and drove it forward toward the house.

It was an old, stone house, large, and partly covered with vines. Tall oaks surrounded it and cast their black shadows about the grounds. Rachel followed the drive as it circled to the left and stopped at a detached carriage house. Then, checking to make sure the Jaguar would fit in the close space, she eased it in and shut off the engine. For a moment, she sat in the dark and quiet.

Finally she opened the door to get out, but as the interior light came on she saw the leather suitcase lying on the back seat. She hesitated, until her curiosity got the better of her, then reached back between the Jaguar's front bucket seats and turned the case around so she could open it.

She was expecting some cute security tricks with wires or rods, but the case opened easily, and when she began to go through the contents they were mostly unremarkable; the normal things a man travels with. But when she reached a zippered pouch at the bottom of the case and opened it, she was surprised to discover a current passport and a plastic vial of pills, labeled with a prescription and half full. She dropped the vial back into the pouch at first, but then picked it out again, and looked closely at the faint lettering on the label. Temporarily, she put the vial in her coat pocket. Then, with some anticipation, she opened the passport.

He looked differently than she had imagined. But then she was not sure exactly what she was expecting. A villainous sneer perhaps? Scars, or a marred complexion? He was none of that. He was almost handsome; this bearded assassin, the man Bryant believed might be charged with the convenience murder of her brother. But what could she tell from a photograph? She put the passport in her inside coat pocket and got out of the car. She would look this man over in better light. Bryant probably had no idea the man's passport had been left behind, anyway.

She found her way through the shadows to the rear door, let herself in quietly, and stood in the dark kitchen. But then, suddenly, a beam of light flashed in her face, blinding her.

"Miss Stein?" a man holding a flashlight said. "Where is Joe Bryant? Isn't he with you?"

"My God, you scared me half to death!"

"Sorry, but I'm not supposed to be here. I couldn't

exactly advertise my presence by leaving a light on, could I?''

"Damn McKintosh and his security!"

"I'm only following my orders."

"I know."

"Like I said, I'm sorry."

"Then would you mind shutting off your torch?"

"Of course." The light went out.

"We were followed, we had to split up; take evasive action, I believe it's called." Rachel paused to blink her eyes, trying to make the blind spots go away. "Now, if you don't mind, I'm going upstairs. How is my father?"

"He's finally gone to sleep."

"Good, he needs it badly. Good night."

"Good night."

Rachel moved past the agent, into the hall, and then to the staircase. In a moment was in her room with her door closed.

She sat on her bed and turned on the lamp beside it, pulled out Pfifer's passport and studied it closely. If she could only meet him, she thought, find out more about him, determine if he was an even greater threat to her brother than the kidnappers.

She studied his photograph. She would not forget his face.

Joe Bryant could see the reflection of his face in the glass door of the telephone booth. He alternately watched the empty street and inspected his dark stubble. McKintosh at last answered the phone.

"This is McKintosh," he said, not at all happily.

"This is Joe, we picked up a tail somewhere near the embassy. We had to split, I believe we lost him."

McKintosh uttered an uncharacteristic four-letter word.

"She took the car, she should be safe by now."

"I'll call and find out. How could you be so careless?"

Bryant let the question pass.

"I'll have to tell Long. He won't be impressed with our efficiency. He insisted on seeing our surveillance post as it is."

"I'll need a lift."

"Right. Where are you?"

Bryant told him.

"I'll have someone there in fifteen minutes."

"Thanks."

Bryant hung up and continued to look at the empty street. There was no sign of morning yet. It was just dark and damp and cold.

CHAPTER
Seven

The rumble of a heavy lorry and the burst of its strong beams came over Pfifer's shoulder as he walked along the side of the road. He turned and hailed the driver and was pleased to hear the huge truck immediately begin to slow. It was a cold night, and he had a long journey ahead of him. He needed something to break his way.

He had already wasted too much time finding a ride. Whatever Long's reasons were for him to break off contact with the London group, Pfifer hoped they were good ones. At the moment, he was simply impatient; eager to get on with it.

It would have been so much easier to let Bryant drop him near some sort of public transportation or perhaps even take him into London. As it was, he would have to hustle in order to make Rotterdam by morning. There would be no rest, no time to think, he would have to move and improvise and mostly move.

The truck ground to a halt. Its driver leaned out of the

window. Pfifer, partially blinded by the truck's lights, squinted to make out his face.

"You've picked a good night for it, guv'ner," the driver said.

"Yes, and I could stand a ride."

"Jump aboard, I've been on the road for twenty hours now; I could stand someone to talk to."

"Fair enough," Pfifer said then moved around the cab and climbed in.

The driver was a stocky man, clean-shaven with streaks of gold dental work in his smile. He worked the lorry's gears, throttle, and clutch with a grace born of long practice. He moved the rig off smoothly, and then true to his word, began to talk.

"Beautiful night, ain't it, guv'ner?"

"That depends entirely on what a fellow has in mind."

"So true," the driver said and laughed. "My name's Brian. What's yours, mate?"

"John."

"Well, pleased to meet you. What put you out of the house at this hour?"

"Part design and part accident."

"Aye, sounds like a woman to me."

"Right."

"They're regular demons, they are. But God bless them. Love them all, wish I could. Love them all." Brian laughed again and glanced at Pfifer as he did. This man is no fool, Pfifer thought, and got the distinct feeling he had just been sized up.

"What are you hauling, Brian?" he asked in as friendly a tone as he could manage.

"Glue, barrels of glue."

Pfifer smiled.

"Aye, don't take it lightly, mate. 'Tis dangerous stuff 'tis. Why a mate of mine had himself a terrible time, he did. Laid his wagons right over on their sides, he did. Sticky mess it was, everything glued right there to the pavement and all, what?''

"I can see what you mean.''

Brian grunted as if to drive home his point. Pfifer looked out the window at the passing countryside. How many miles, he thought? How many hours? He tried to divide his mind between what he had learned in the safe house and what he had to do to reach London.

"Where are you from, mate?''

"America,'' said Pfifer, leaving his train of thought.

"That much I can tell; what part?''

"The Northeast. What about you?''

"Who, me? I been all over, mate. I hang me hat where ever I'm at, so to speak.''

"I could tell you were a man of the world.''

"Aye, you and me both, guv'ner. Men of the world on the road together. What could be more poetic? Right, guv'ner?''

"Right, mate,'' Pfifer said and then they both laughed.

As luck would have it, Brian took Pfifer within a few blocks of where he needed to go in London. When Pfifer stepped down from the cab onto the dark street, Brian gave him a good-natured wave and then pulled away. Pfifer watched as he did, and when the big rig was out of sight he began to walk.

The station was nearly empty, empty enough for Pfifer to be noticed easily. As he reached the bottom of the steps, leading from the street down into the terminal, he was immediately aware of that, and it made him uneasy. The best cover was a large and active crowd, the worst a thin and bored one. You could lose yourself so easily in a large crowd, you could practically pull it around you like a blanket, and if someone was attempting to follow you, they would often give themselves away, as they jostled to keep up with you. But bored people had nothing to do but watch you and remember you, and you could never tell if their interest in you was professional or casual. If someone was watching for you, you had no way to avoid them.

Pfifer turned to his right and walked slowly to the men's room. Once inside, he made sure that he was alone and then began to inspect the trash bins. It was one of George's favorite drops. A trash bin, filled to overflowing with the most disgusting refuse, certain to be avoided by everyone. Everyone, that is, except the recipient of the drop.

Pfifer took the fullest of the two containers and turned it upside down. Along with an avalanche of unmentionables, a canvas bag dropped to the floor. Quickly, Pfifer scooped up the mess and then proceeded to a stall, carrying the canvas bag.

Long had been his usual efficient self. The contents of the bag included a plain blue business suit, shirt, tie, shoes and black leather briefcase. A small pouch with shaving gear was in the briefcase, along with some general clutter just to make things seem normal. Pfifer was surprised, though, to open the new passport Long had provided and see it was a perfect duplicate of his own. Long apparently wasn't taking any chances he would run into an official at Heathrow that might remember him, traveling under a different name, and become suspicious. Good old George Long, Pfifer thought, he really knew his business. Without looking, Pfifer knew that there would be an envelope in the inside pocket of the suit coat and that in it he would find plane tickets, train tickets, and money sufficient for his purposes.

Pfifer checked his watch and then hurriedly began to dress.

Rotterdam customs officials gave the bearded man in the dark blue suit only a cursory glance as he passed through. Pfifer appeared to be just another business traveler on a late flight, perhaps with an early-morning meeting. He seemed to move with a purpose to his step, carried only a briefcase, no luggage. All in all, nothing unusual.

One man did take special notice of him, though. A man

sitting in the arrival area engrossed in a newspaper, a newspaper he had read from front to back eleven times. Pfifer spotted the man, perhaps because he was expecting him to be there. He even spotted the pay telephone the man would probably use to call London and report his arrival. But Pfifer simply ignored him and went to find a cab.

The cab driver knew the hotel his passenger asked him about and wondered why such a well dressed man would want to stay in that part of town, but never mind, the tip might be better if the questions were kept to a minimum. He let his passenger sit undisturbed as he made his way from the airport. Only occasionally did he even glance at the bearded face in his rearview mirror.

Pfifer now had the basic information he needed to begin to formulate a plan. The CIA had told him the freighter had sailed from London on Wednesday morning, shortly after five o'clock. Ten hours later, it had moored in Rotterdam. They had told him exactly where. According to the numbers dates and times he had copied from Gretchen's pad, the freighter would sail from Rotterdam no earlier than twenty-four hours from its arrival. That time coincided with the deadline given to Howard Stein. The kidnappers would evidently want to know if the diamonds had been gotten together for them and if the delivery instructions had been agreed to, all prior to disembarking.

The leader of the kidnapper's group, the terrorist Juan, would present a constantly moving quarry for Pfifer. He was either smart or getting very good advice. But now Pfifer had the edge he had needed, the freighter's itinerary. According to the information Pfifer had found at the cottage, the destinations would be Rotterdam, then Hamburg, then around Denmark into the Baltic, the final destination more than likely being a communist-controlled port in Poland or East Germany.

The communications would be by telephone in Rotterdam, telephone again in Hamburg, and then by radio from that point on. All the communications would be initiated by Gretchen and timed in such a way that, even if her phone was tapped and her radio transmissions monitored, the freighter would have sailed safely back into international waters before any listeners would have had time to reach it.

Juan evidently had limited faith in Gretchen. He had designed safeguards so that even if she had been successfully tailed and watched, which it turned out she had been, he would still be in the clear. Pfifer had to admit it was a brilliant plan, even down to the ransom. Cut diamonds would be difficult to mark for identification later, but of course, they would be easily negotiable wherever the kidnappers wished.

What he needed now was to get close to the freighter. He needed to know what security measures had been taken and how many men Juan had under his control. He needed to assess the possible ways he could board the freighter without detection and, in fact, if it could be done at all. He could not afford to underestimate Juan. He would have to assume him a formidable adversary.

His initial move would be to approach the freighter in broad daylight, dressed as a common seaman. He would look for some excuse to go aboard, if he could. Anything he could see or find out from the crew might help him. His final plan would generate from what he learned.

The hotel he had asked the cab driver to take him to was within easy walking distance of the wharf where the freighter was moored. Also, George Long would have a cache for him there; the clothes he would need and a firearm just for good measure. With luck, Pfifer would be able to get some rest as well. But first, he would have to report in.

Pfifer leaned forward. When he spoke it startled the driver for an instant.

"I've got a call to make. Stop at the first booth you see, will you?"

In less than a block the driver pulled to the side of the street and let Pfifer out.

There was a light rain falling. Pfifer stepped quickly into the booth and dialed a number. When the phone was answered he said three words, "Pisces, Rotterdam, clear," then hung up. He was back in the cab again and they were on their way in less than a minute.

"Your destination is about four blocks from here, sir," the driver said. Pfifer acknowledged him and settled back into his seat.

There was activity in the street as Pfifer got out of the cab and paid his fare. The neon lights from the bars glared into the darkness. Loud music blared. Groups moved along in both directions, most drifting from one open door to the next, sampling the smoke and din, oblivious to the drizzle.

As Pfifer's cab pulled away, an English sailor staggered by with a girl under each arm. Zigging and zagging the width of the sidewalk, the girls carried him more than accompanied him. Occasionally one or the other would swear and complain of his weight or his capricious course, and in the shadows someone laughed, and the sound of footsteps shuffled off.

Pfifer watched them pass, then crossed the narrow walkway and entered the hotel.

Past the smudged doors into the lobby, it was much as he had remembered it. Mustier perhaps, the gold floral pattern of the carpet more threadbare, the long purple drapes more frayed. Yes, it was much the same, a tattered harlot past her prime, but not past her function.

Pfifer had stayed in this place and countless others like it, for it was the charter of such places to be blind and deaf, to remember nothing, recognize no one, pay no attention to detail. And of course no one made reservations for this hotel. As long as the proper amount of currency changed hands, in any season, there would always be a vacancy. Here Pfifer would be allowed his anonymity and after his few hours stay could disappear again, knowing that he had left no trace.

The night man slouched in his chair behind the desk, as all night men do, in a state of only semiconsciousness. This particular one, however, had trained himself to wake at the sound of soft footsteps on matted carpet. He opened his eyes and automatically lifted a key from the dusty grid of pigeonholes behind him as Pfifer approached.

"Sir, a room?" he grunted from folds of fat festooned from his jowls, his voice as thick as his appearance.

"The Royal Suite perhaps?" Pfifer answered in sharp, curt German.

"Sorry, sir, but the Royal Family is using it tonight," the night man said and then made a yellow smile at his joke.

"Anything you have left then. I'll be out in the morning. I'll pay you now."

"That is our policy."

Pfifer took the register and the pen that were offered and wrote with the proper amount of illegibility. The keys were dutifully slid across to him as he counted out the deutsche marks.

"Second floor, straight down the hall to your left," the night man said and dropped Pfifer's money in a drawer.

Then Pfifer heard the main door of the hotel groan open behind him. Resisting the urge to turn around, instead, he used the expression of the night man as a sort of human mirror. The man's glassy expression assured him that the two people who had entered were nothing out of the ordinary. Relieved, Pfifer picked up his keys and moved toward the staircase, waiting until he gained the second floor landing before he allowed himself a direct look below.

The man was about fifty, thuggish in manner. The girl was young, middle teens, heavily made-up. Pfifer watched the quick exchange of money and keys and then turned and went down the hall.

The room was simply furnished: a swaybacked mattress on a metal bed frame, a washbasin with an empty pitcher, a straight-backed chair with a stained cloth seat. There was one window, painted shut. Pfifer put his briefcase on the bed, took off his coat and folded it over the back of the chair, then glanced at his watch and listened as the sound of footsteps moved past his door.

He would have to wait for a while, then he would go down the hall to a heating vent near the common bathroom. The grill would be loose, George Long's little gift on the other side. After the cache was retrieved, Pfifer might lie down for an hour, but not until then. Until then he would fight to focus his mind and keep his thoughts from wandering.

Pfifer paced back and forth in the small room. It had begun to rain more heavily outside. He could hear the splatter of water as it streamed from the hotel's gutters and fell to the dark alley below his window. In the distance, the wail of a siren grew louder as it approached.

CHAPTER
Eight

The blast of steam whistles, the sounds of heavy cargo cranes, and the shouts of men reached Captain Nicoli Lubelski as he stood in the morning light by the forward bridge window of his ship, the *Baltic Merchant*. He had watched the procedure his men now performed below countless times. He knew by heart the sequence, the very cadence, of the work, but still it held him. Still it fascinated him, the act of delicate and precise loading by crane. Each time the steel tentacle of cable with its hooks and turnbuckles dipped down into the heart of the ship, Lubelski could visualize the practiced movements of his crew securing the pallet according to plan. He could anticipate to the instant when the cable would grow slack and begin to retract upward. This he knew, for as a young seaman, he had worked by the hour in the holds of ships, he had become hard and strong and sure, handling pallets and cables and gear.

And men, most of all, Lubelski had learned to handle men. In his years on merchant ships, Lubelski had learned to read his men to a great degree. He had learned to spot the dangerous ones, the reckless ones. He had learned to spot the drinkers and, to a point, the ones that he would lose during a voyage; the ones that would try to defect. Knowing his men and their breaking points had enabled him to gauge how hard he could push and what he could ask and expect. His Russian masters had appreciated this acuity, and he had appreciated continuing in the role he loved: captain of his ship.

Lubelski's bloodlines straddled the ancient conflict. Half Polish and half Russian, he neither hated the Russians nor particularly loved the Poles. What he loved was his ship, and being captain of her. He would tolerate much, bear quiet obedience, if it meant he could remain master of his ship. If his masters had been Polish instead of Russian, he would be no more or less concerned. Lubelski's life was the sea and specifically his ship. He would say that he was a practical man and not a political man; that made survival easier. After all, the world might one day grow tired of the communists, but it would always have need of its sea captains.

Lubelski was alone on his bridge. The port and starboard doors were open, leading out to the bridge wings on either side. The smell of the Rhine drifted in on the cross-draft. The sky was blue between dark patches of clouds and the decks were still wet and slippery from an earlier shower. Behind him he heard the door that led up from below decks open and he sensed the presence of the man who joined him. Involuntarily, he stiffened.

"Captain," Juan said, "I see you pay close attention to your business."

Lubelski turned and faced him. Several thoughts occurred to him as he looked at the stocky terrorist. The pervading thought though was that he would be glad when he was rid of him. He steeled himself to be patient.

"As do you," he said.

"You still have some hostility toward me, Captain. That is bad. We should be friends, you and I."

"I have no bad feelings for you. It must be your imagination. Sometimes when a man is not used to being cooped up on a ship?"

Juan looked quietly at Lubelski, his eyes unwavering.

"I appreciate your concern, Captain," Juan said and smiled. "All my men will be glad when we can get off this ship. As will some of your crew, no doubt."

"Your security measures have interfered with some of the normal functions of the crew; that is all, I assure you."

"I shall accept your assurances."

The two men stood slightly apart, their eyes locked in a steady stare. Lubelski folded his arms across his chest and smiled back at Juan.

"And how is our passenger this morning? Still unconscious?"

"Unfortunately."

"Even more unfortunate if he remains comatose, I should think. Perhaps you should have given your agent better training with the drugs she uses."

Juan grimaced, his eyes narrowed. Lubelski sensed that his anger was close to expressing itself.

"We should be ready to sail by the time you requested," Lubelski said, changing his tack. "My men are making good progress with the cargo."

"That's good, Captain, very good. I will want to sail, as you put it, whether you have all of your cargo stowed or not. You realize that of course?"

"I realize that we must not do anything that would appear to be unusual, and that leaving cargo would create many questions."

Juan took a deep breath before he answered.

"In that case then, you must make sure that we are ready. The responsibility is yours."

"Of course."

"Good morning, Captain."

Juan turned and left the bridge. The ominous tone in his

parting remark caused Lubelski to laugh inwardly. Juan was no doubt deadly serious, but on the *Baltic Merchant* he would have to do more than talk in a rough tone to command this captain's respect. Lubelski would not be manipulated that easily. Still, the lowliest vermin could sometimes cause a most dangerous bite. Lubelski cogitated, then turned back toward the window.

The work continued. More and more crates and pallets mounted in the ship's holds. Lubelski made an approving wave to one of his lead seamen, when the man turned and looked up at the bridge. Then he checked the time by the chronometer behind the chart table and calculated that they would be complete well before Juan's three o'clock deadline. Perhaps that was best. Another confrontation with Juan would do no good. If all continued as planned, they would leave no cargo stranded on a Rotterdam wharf and Juan would be convinced that his word had been heeded and, for the moment, be placated. That would be a good day's work, indeed.

Lubelski felt the need for a breath of fresh air and stepped to the bridge wing. Below him, one of Juan's men stood joint watch with a crewman over the ship's gangway. Suddenly, the two men turned and looked at something on the wharf. Whatever had attracted their attention was close to the side of the ship. Lubelski attempted to follow what he judged to be their line of sight, but to no avail. His curiosity piqued, he made for a descending ladder to investigate.

The two men who stood watch over the freighter's gangway were laughing when Lubelski arrived. When he asked them what they found so humorous, they pointed to a ragged-looking seaman staggering up the wharf. The seaman lurched from object to object, using what he could for support as he came. His clothing looked soiled and wrinkled, even from their distance. Lubelski shook his head in embarrassment for the man.

"He must have had quite a night," a crewman said as they watched the rumpled seaman approach.

"Quite a night," Juan's man echoed.

The seaman made unsteady progress until he reached the bottom of the gangway, then he stopped and called up to them. He spoke a slurred Polish. It surprised them.

"What's he saying, Carl?" Lubelski asked his crewman.

"I can't understand him either, Captain."

"He's probably still drunk. Go down and tell him to get away from the ship before he is crushed by the machinery."

"Yes, sir."

The crewman named Carl and Juan's man both went down the gangway. When they reached the bottom, Carl began to talk to the seaman.

"You must get away from the ship, my friend, before you are hurt. You are in no condition."

"Thank you, but my ship, where is my ship?" the seaman spoke more clearly.

"And what is the name of your ship?" Carl asked.

"The *Baltic Star*."

Carl shook his head and frowned. Juan's man held a blank expression.

"What's his problem?" he asked Carl.

"His ship sailed yesterday, it was on this wharf just before we arrived, according to the crane operators. This poor devil must have lost track of an entire day."

"Then I would say he has a problem, for sure."

"Yes, and look at him. He's in a bad way, still."

The seaman leaned against the railing of the gangway and rested his head on his arms. He stood slumped, feet planted wide apart. For several minutes he did not move. Carl looked up at his captain with a plaintive gesture. Lubelski nodded and began to descend the steps. When he stopped beside them, Carl told him the seaman's story.

"Take him to the bridge," Lubelski said. "Call down for some coffee. I will alert the radio room to try and contact his ship."

As Lubelski spoke, Juan's man became suddenly alarmed.

"I'm sorry, Captain, but I have strict instructions. No one unauthorized is allowed to board."

"Let me remind you that I am the captain of this ship," Lubelski said, his tone biting.

Juan's man wavered in his determination for a moment, then his jaw set hard and his hand went to his sidearm.

"No, Captain, I must insist. I have no choice in the matter."

Lubelski tried to control his anger.

"Captain," the raggedy seaman said, raising his head. "I appreciate what you are trying to do for me, but I wish to cause you no trouble. I will feel better in a few hours. I will have time to catch my ship in Hamburg."

"Give me your name. I can at least radio for you once we are underway."

"No, Captain, please. All I ask is that you allow me to stand here for a few moments to catch my breath."

Lubelski shook his head as he looked at the pathetic figure in front of him. "Very well," he said. "I will have some coffee sent down to you."

"That would be good."

Lubelski turned to reboard his ship. Juan's man stood in his way.

"If you do not move yourself," Lubelski said coldly, "you will find your Cuban ass floating in the Rhine."

Juan's man stepped quickly aside and then followed Lubelski up the gangway a few steps behind. Carl smiled and remained at the gangway's foot.

"Your captain seems like a good man," the seaman said in a soft voice.

"He is a fair man," Carl said, slightly embarrassed. "You were a fool to miss your ship."

"Yes, you are right enough, but you must have at least come close to doing the same thing yourself at some time."

"Haven't we all?" Carl said and smiled.

"You have a fine ship. Where is your home?"

"I'm much like my captain; my ship is my home."

"Yes, and it seems you have uninvited guests in your home. Hopefully not for long?"

"No, not for long."

The two exchanged knowing glances.

The seaman, like all seaman, was curious about the ship. Together they passed the time talking about the generalities. Where was it that the crew was berthed aboard? Was it as small and cramped as his own ship? Did the *Baltic Merchant* often carry passengers as it apparently did now? The seaman seemed interested in anything Carl wanted to say. Each time Carl would fall silent he would nudge him along with another question. Carefully, the seaman listened, and, as unobtrusively as he could, he studied what he could see of the freighter.

The coffee arrived via a mess cook dressed in a streaked white uniform. It seemed to revive the seaman. His speech became clearer still. He stood straighter. In a few more minutes, he would be ready to leave. He would just walk across the wharf and sit on those crates for a while. Then he would be on his way. Carl took his empty cup and watched him go, only slightly uncomfortable about all that he had told the seaman. After all, he was a countryman, the dialect was unmistakable. He was probably from the same area of Poland as himself. Carl now wished he had asked.

In the shadows of the bridge, a stocky figure raised his binoculars and watched as the seaman crossed to the crates. He adjusted the focus and studied him carefully.

It was only a few hours now until Gretchen's call would come. Juan wanted to make sure that the drunken seaman was just what he appeared to be. If there was any doubt, then Juan would make sure that the seaman got free passage to Hamburg, or at least partway. He turned and called for the captain with the ship's phone. Before he got a reply, the door from below decks opened and Lubelski appeared on the bridge.

"I'm right here," Lubelski said, still irritated. "What was it you wanted?"

"I want you to simply follow my instructions, Captain. Nothing else. Now, tell me, who was that man you were so anxious to invite aboard?"

"He was a simple Polish seaman who was unfortunate enough to get himself drunk and miss his ship. I offered him the courtesy of some coffee and communications with his ship. It's a common thing to do."

"Perhaps, Captain. But not on this voyage. Do you understand?" Juan raised his binoculars. "How do you know that he was what you say he was?"

"I have been judging men, especially seamen, for twenty years. This man had the look and the language of a seaman. A Polish seaman at that."

"Tell me something, Captain. Do you ever recall making a mistake in your judgments of men?"

Lubelski paused and then answered, "Of course, occasionally."

"Occasionally?" Juan dropped the binoculars to his chest. "Do you know what it would mean if I made such a mistake, even once?"

Lubelski was silent.

"It might very well mean my death and the death of my men. It would certainly cause serious difficulty. What I am saying, Captain, is that I cannot afford mistakes. Any mistakes."

"I understand."

"I wonder if you do, Captain? I wonder if you do?" Juan raised the binoculars to his eyes again and swore. The ragged seaman was gone.

Pfifer carefully picked his way back up the wharf. The confusion of men and equipment and cargo made it easy for him to disappear. As he went, he became less and less the drunk seaman and quickened his step.

Martin Stein was still alive, of that much Pfifer was sure. It made sense. It was far too early in the game for Juan to discard his trump card. Stein would be too valuable if Juan ran into trouble. Even though Pfifer saw no sign of Stein, he was sure of his presence.

Also, Juan, and not the captain, was firmly in control of the *Baltic Merchant*. It had been fairly easy to spot the odd extra men moving about the freighter's decks or standing idle away from the main activity. On a freighter the *Baltic Merchant*'s size, there would be seldom any unoccupied hands during the loading of cargo and stores. Even the untrained were normally put to use. No, the extra men had to belong to Juan. They were his own private security force, separate from the rest of the crew, undoubtedly directed by him personally.

Pfifer would have to give more thought to his planning. It would be difficult, if not impossible, for him to get on the freighter with so many eyes and ears available to detect him. It would be unlikely he would ever get off alive even if he did. He would have liked to have made it to the bridge with the captain. Then he would have at least been able to familiarize himself with part of the ship's interior, but that was not to be.

According to Gretchen's note pad, the freighter's next port of call would be Hamburg. Pfifer would have to have a completed plan by its arrival there if he was to have any chance of success, because after Hamburg the freighter would continue to steam up the western coast of Denmark. It might or might not stop at another port before it turned east and then south again to make the run through the shattered puzzle of Danish islands that would separate it, at that point, from the Baltic Sea and the safety of the Russian Fleet. Once the freighter was in the Baltic, Pfifer had to face the fact that Martin Stein would be lost.

Pfifer shook his head pensively. George Long must have understood the complexity of this problem. Why had he thrown him into it with so little backup and without at least the framework of a plan? What was Long thinking about? What was Long doing that Pfifer hadn't been told?

A warehouse stood at the end of the wharf. Along the warehouse wall, facing Pfifer, were three telephone booths. Pfifer felt for the slip of paper in his pocket and went toward them. He had checked every phone booth he had seen in the immediate area of the freighter. The number he had been looking for had been the middle of these three. He checked the number again just to be sure.

He perhaps should have left for Hamburg that moment, but it was important to know if Gretchen was adhering to her schedule. If she were, then someone from the freighter would appear at the booth just prior to casting off. Pfifer had to wait. He had to know whether or not he was still working with good information. He could not wait on the wharf, though. It was too likely someone would become curious about him and begin to ask questions; questions he had no answers for. There was also the possibility that Juan would be patrolling the general area; another reason to disappear for a while. There would be no call from Gretchen for several hours, at any rate.

The warehouse was a two-story structure. Pfifer looked at it carefully. If he could gain entrance to the second floor, or the roof, he might be able to watch the booths without being in plain sight. He would have to return with enough time to find a willing door or window. With one last look, he moved off.

CHAPTER
Nine

"Find him," Juan said as he stood before the six men he had summoned to his cabin. "Look in every alley, every bar, and every hole—but find him. If he is what the captain believes, it shouldn't be difficult.

"Once you have him, I want him brought back here. Tell him we have contacted his ship and his captain wishes us to take him to Hamburg. If he resists, use whatever force is necessary. I, unlike Captain Lubelski, do not believe he is a simple seaman, so be careful. Expect resistance.

"I have selected you six because you are the ones who remember seeing this man. Make no mistakes."

A young man in the group gave a nervous laugh at Juan's last comment. He cut it off abruptly when he met Juan's stare. Self-consciously, he looked down at the deck.

Juan stared at each of them in turn, searching their faces for the resolve he hoped they shared. He had full confidence in only one of them, Miguel. Miguel stared back coolly. He had already proved his worth by bringing Martin Stein to

Juan's attention in the first place. He, among them all, was the most reliable.

"If there are no questions, return here no later than two-thirty. We sail at three."

The men shuffled dutifully out of Juan's cabin. The last one out closed the door behind him softly. Juan smiled to himself, then frowned and turned to his porthole.

In a few minutes, Juan saw his search party cross the gangway and begin to work its way up the wharf. They went in twos, just as he had instructed them. When they reached the end of the wharf, each pair struck out in a different direction. Juan continued to watch them until they were out of sight.

If the mysterious seaman managed to elude his men, then he would have no choice but to draw a dangerous conclusion. He pondered his alternatives as he surveyed the activity before him, and the frown on his face took a deeper set.

Perhaps Lubelski was right. It would be far better if he were. If the ragged seaman was no more than he appeared, things would continue smoothly forward, the ten million dollars' worth of diamonds would continue to move closer. He would have finally proven himself to his Russian benefactors, once those cold white stones fell into their hands. Yes, it would be far better if Lubelski was right, but was he? How could he be so sure, and, if the stranded seaman was not what he appeared to be, then who was he? What were the possibilities?

Local authorities or any number of intelligence organizations could conceivably have an interest in the freighter; it did sail under a communist flag. This was, perhaps, the most feasible possibility, not to mention the least dangerous. It would mean that Stein's whereabouts were still secret, the security still intact. If this was the case, the plan was still workable. They would be safe enough once back on the open sea.

If this seaman was in some way connected to Stein, though, entirely new questions would be in order, entirely new dangers would have to be considered. Howard Stein might have turned to a number of people for help: the British police, the British intelligence service, the Israelis. The list could be lengthened, complications expanded, with little imagination.

Juan clasped his hands behind his back and began to pace back and forth in his cabin. His face and any expression was masked by his beard. He stared ahead as he walked, his eyes focused somewhere beyond the small confines of his small cubicle.

There was only one safe assumption he could make. He knew this, but he approached it with dread. How could he be sure? If his men were unsuccessful in finding the seaman, who would know the answer? Suddenly, he stopped short.

In a few quick steps, Juan was out of his cabin and into the passageway. He moved swiftly down its narrow length past a row of cabin doors. He stopped at the last one and knocked firmly.

"Yes?" answered a voice from inside.

Juan identified himself, and immediately the door was opened, and a khaki-clad man, wearing a green, billed cap, stepped back from the doorway to let him enter.

The cabin's single porthole was blacked out. In the dim light, Juan could barely make out the shape of the young man on the bunk. He felt for the light switch on the bulkhead beside him and snapped it on.

"Go find the doctor, Raul," he said sharply. "Tell him to come here. I want to see him immediately."

Raul blinked from the sudden brightness, acknowledged Juan, then left. After he had gone, Juan sat down on the chair beside the bunk.

Martin Stein lay on his back, his arms limp and straight alongside his body. Juan could see the faint red needle marks on them in a neat pattern. Studying his lax face, Juan wondered if now it were possible for the young man to even dream. His guess would have been that he could not.

Soon the sound of hurried footsteps echoed from the passageway, and a stooped, frail man, with only a wisp of white hair on his head and with deep lines and wrinkles in his face, came through the door. When he saw Juan he attempted to stand straighter and he smoothed the yellowed white coat he wore with his brown spotted hands.

"You asked for me?"

"Yes, I want you to bring him around. I have some questions to ask him. How soon can you have him coherent?"

The old doctor looked from the stern face of Juan to the placid face of Martin Stein and back again.

"If he can be brought around," he began, choosing his words with caution, "it would take me several hours. I cannot make a guarantee even then that he will be completely awake, or that . . ."

"I understand," Juan said, interrupting. "Begin now. Call me when he is ready. I will be with Lubelski."

Juan turned his back on the doctor and withdrew down the passageway. Once through a side door and on to the main deck, he paused at the rail. The fresh air bathed him but did little to relieve his tension. He looked down the wharf. Beyond the towering cranes, the black-hulled merchants and gray warehouses, somewhere in the jumble of the city in the distance, a stranger held the answer to a vital question. He must find him. If not, the uncertainty would only grow, his confidence only erode. He must find him!

Pfifer would not have chosen this particular bar if it were not for its close proximity to the wharf. First, it was too small and too quiet. Second, it had no back entrance. At least the proprietor was appropriately disinterested in him. He had taken Pfifer's money, served him, and then ignored him.

Pfifer sat in a booth at the back of the bar. The men's room door was to his right, a clear view of the front door available to him when he peered around the partition between his booth and the next. Periodically he could hear the shuffle of footsteps as people passed by the open door and then the rustle of newsprint as the proprietor leafed through a paper on the bar.

He should have been hungry; he had missed a couple of meals, but the stale sandwich and the warm beer sat untouched before him on the rough planks of the table. Perhaps it was the peculiar nervousness he felt, subtle but real; like the smell of rain on the air just before it begins to fall. Perhaps that nervousness was instinct at work, instinct he could not simply ignore. For whatever reason, he sensed a certain immediacy that told him danger would manifest itself, and soon.

His instinct had signaled him several times before. He had never tried to analyze or question it; his practice had been to simply allow it to put him on his guard, simply acknowledge the threat as real. This time as before, without knowing quite why, he needed his sense of foreboding and began to think about the weapon he had left behind in his hotel room.

Just then, the spill of light through the bar's entrance was obscured twice. It caught Pfifer's attention. He sat quietly and listened as one of the men spoke softly to the proprietor. The proprietor's reply must have been only a nod or a gesture.

Pfifer rose carefully, staggered a little for effect and glanced at the bar. The two men were looking in his direction as he did.

He knew who they were; it was in their attitude. They were wide-eyed, alert, inquisitive, slightly tense. They were the hunters, and they had been told their prey was dangerous. Pfifer ignored them and turned toward the men's room.

With a clumsy shove he went in. Then, once inside, he steeled himself and waited.

There was no exit, not even a window. There was a sink against the back wall, to the right a stall with a battered door, on the left a urinal. The door into the men's room opened right to left, so a man entering would tend to look to his right first. Pfifer studied the layout for a moment, then, with a reluctant look at the soiled floor, he slipped his shoes off and crossed to the stall.

He positioned his shoes so that they would be partially visible from the entrance door. Then he took a few sheets of tissue, folded them into a wad, and used them to jam the stall door shut from the outside. Prepared, but not satisfied, he went to the front wall and stood so he would be to the left of whoever entered.

They might come one at a time or together. He might be quick enough to handle one but probably not both. All he could do now, though, was to wait with his back to the cold wall and wonder if he still had it in him to kill. He leaned back and listened to the steady surge of his pulse in his ears and tried to control his breathing.

The one who came through the door first was inexperienced. When he saw the closed door of the stall and the toes of Pfifer's shoes, he moved forward immediately, letting the door close behind him. Pfifer's approach was both quick and lethal. A violent chop at the base of the man's skull, and he slumped to the damp floor.

Hastily, Pfifer stripped the man's gun from his hand, thrust it into his belt, then dragged him into the stall and propped him up on the stool. For an instant, his and the dead man's eyes met, and Pfifer felt his stomach begin to turn and averted his face. Quickly, he backed out of the stall, closed the door and returned to the wall.

Pfifer pulled the gun from his belt and looked at it. He recognized it as a Nagant, 7.62mm. Unsilenced as it was, it would make a loud enough noise to be heard for blocks. He hefted the Russian-made weapon in his hand and waited.

The second man was patient. He must have realized it was taking far too long for his companion to emerge. Pfifer was stuck. If he tried to escape through the bar, he would be easy to pick off. The second man could be hiding in one of the booths, or behind the bar, or perhaps just outside the door. Even if he was lucky enough to spot him in time to get off a shot, it would be a miracle if he wasn't hit himself in the exchange; sobering thoughts.

It took nearly twenty minutes for the second man's curiosity to get the better of him. He called out at first, "Renaldo, are you all right?" Then let several more minutes pass in silence.

Pfifer continued to wait, holding the Nagant firmly in his grasp.

The door began to move slightly. Slowly it eased open, a fraction of an inch at a time, as gently as it could be done. Then it stopped moving. Pfifer guessed that only a sliver of an opening could be available for the man to look through. He held his breath and waited for the man to appear.

The safest thing to do would be to put a bullet through the door. But there was the noise to think about and the crowd it would draw. Plus, Pfifer had work to do on the wharf; the last thing he needed was a legion of frantic policemen combing the neighborhood for him. No, Pfifer had to wait it out. The proprietor might return at any moment—if he had been lucky enough to be bribed and not otherwise disposed of. That would be problem enough.

Abruptly, the door was flung open and the second man leaped through, gun in hand. It startled Pfifer, but he had already decided what he was going to do and simply reacted. With all of his strength, he brought the Nagant down on the man's head and crushed his skull.

The man fell heavily to the floor face first, his gun clattering down beside him without going off. Pfifer closed his eyes for a moment, swallowed hard and then wiped the perspiration from his brow. Cautiously he stooped and checked for a pulse. There was none.

The second man was larger, heavier. It took some effort to deposit him in the arms of his comrade. Pfifer was feeling quite light-headed by the time he had accomplished it and closed the stall door. He slipped his shoes on and left the men's room, this time genuinely unsteady. He hoped there were no more of Juan's men waiting for him.

The bar was still empty. The proprietor nowhere to be seen. On his way out, Pfifer pulled the front door shut and turned the open sign around to read CLOSED. Then, cradling the Nagant under his light jacket, he walked toward his hotel. There was a light rain falling, but he did not feel it.

CHAPTER
Ten

Juan and Lubelski stood alone on the bridge wing of the freighter. Juan stood erect, his hands at his sides, eyes straight ahead, as he stared down the wharf. Lubelski stood with his elbows propped on the hardwood railing and studied him carefully.

"Two of your men have not returned," Lubelski said, more as a statement of fact than as a question.

"No," Juan answered curtly.

"They were men you trust not to simply take this opportunity to leave your company?"

Juan turned and glared at Lubelski.

"They didn't bolt, if that's what you're trying to imply. They must have run into difficulty."

"And what will you do now?"

"We will sail on time, whether they have returned or not. I have decided to leave a man behind, my most reliable man, to find this seaman and deal with him."

117

"I suspect your man will deal with him in one particular fashion, no matter what the truth of the situation is."

Juan smiled, "You begin to understand."

Lubelski turned and looked onto the bridge. Preparations for getting under way were well along. Hatches were closed, crewmen were on station, the freighter's power plant primed and ready. He wished he were as confident in Juan as he was in the men of his crew. He turned back to Juan as the little Cuban continued.

"It is apparent we are dealing with a man of some experience. As soon as we are under way, we will question anyone who remembers seeing our visitor, collect whatever information can be had and contact the center in Moscow. This man's description will probably fit a hundred different men from a hundred different intelligence services, but it is an effort we will make just the same."

"As you wish."

"Yes, and of course there is young Martin. A thorough questioning of him would now seem to be of paramount importance. If your illustrious doctor can manage to bring him back to consciousness?"

"He is still working on him."

"I see," Juan said coldly. "If he fails, tell the good doctor I will take great pleasure in working on him."

Lubelski shook his head and fought to control his temper. What was it about this twisted little man that inspired such loyalty from his men, such trust from Moscow? Whatever it was, it escaped him.

But someone in the Kremlin saw promise in Juan's plan beyond Lubelski's doubts and objections. The target was Kremlin-approved, the method was Kremlin-approved, the use of Lubelski's vessel likewise approved. It was fully and entirely approved by the Kremlin and by the KGB. Of course, what this meant to Lubelski was, if the mission failed, it would be entirely his fault and no one else's. It would all be somehow blamed on him for lack of cooperation or some other mindless accusation. Such was the system.

Lubelski pushed himself from the railing, the look of distaste clear on his face. "I have some transmissions to get ready," he said and started to walk away.

"Wait, there is something I want you to do first. We are about to receive an important telephone call. You will take it for me."

"Is there some reason?" Lubelski asked, surprised and suddenly wary.

"Let us say that I am simply letting you participate in a more active way." Juan smiled as he spoke, but there was no smile in his voice.

"Won't your agent in England be expecting to talk to you personally?"

"She will give her report as long as you have the correct identifier. It will be a very short report. She will not be alarmed by the use of a go-between."

"Fine, then." Lubelski turned and started his descent to the gangway.

"You do not wish to do this, Captain?"

"Do I have a choice?"

"No, Captain. You do not."

Lubelski continued his descent.

As he stepped off the *Baltic Merchant* onto the wharf, Lubelski glanced back over his shoulder. Juan still stood alone on the bridge wing and stared down the wharf, but now with the hard lines of apprehension in his expression. Lubelski was not surprised. Perhaps it was because he had seen so many men like Juan run their course. And Juan would run his course, with little variation from the norm. It was just a matter of time and usefulness before he would meet his fate head-on. Lubelski could afford to be patient. He could afford to tolerate the uneasy collaboration among himself and Juan and Moscow. He could even allow himself to be manipulated by the little bearded terrorist within safe limits. In fact, if Juan had some perception of control, it might even make things easier.

But he disliked the man, and it took all of his self-control not to show it more openly than he did. He would have to work on that; it was unprofessional of him.

Lubelski neared the phone booths. As he checked his watch, his thoughts turned to the slender young woman who would be counting the minutes with him until she obediently placed her call. He thought of her and then, strangely, thought of his home and wondered, wistfully, if he would ever see it again.

From where Pfifer sat, he could see the length of the wharf. Even in the afternoon, the level of activity was high. The cargo vessels moored along each side belched black smoke. Cranes picked up pallets and crates from the almost incomprehensible melange below them. And beyond, barges and tugs crowded by in the brackish Rhine.

It had not been difficult for him to break into the warehouse. Even though it had been some time since he had worked with lock picks, the old tumblers and pins had been loose and cooperative in a side door, and he had found his way easily to a second-floor window just above the telephone booths. He had pulled up a crate to sit on and then patiently watched and waited. As the minutes passed he unconsciously tapped the crate beneath him with his heels.

The wharf and the booths below went from sunlight to shadow as clouds passed overhead. Suddenly, Pfifer saw someone leave the *Baltic Merchant*. When the man neared, he recognized him as the captain. Lubelski disappeared behind one obstruction and then another as he progressed. Pfifer watched him carefully, until he reached the booths.

In a moment the phone began to ring. Pfifer counted each ring and watched Lubelski's reaction; he seemed to be counting as well. Each ring brought Pfifer's level of tension more sharply into focus. He released a deep breath as Lubelski finally answered.

Pfifer had planned to stay right where he was. There was no reason for him to move, no reason for him to risk being seen by another one of Juan's men. Ideally he would be able to watch the freighter get under way from this safe vantage point, and then leave for Hamburg. But, as Lubelski talked below, Pfifer took his eyes from him and looked back along the wharf, and from a position roughly halfway between the *Baltic Merchant* and the warehouse, in the shadow cast by the huge, steel, base structure of the crane over her head, Pfifer saw a woman dressed in gray. She appeared to be watching Lubelski.

Pfifer swore under his breath when he recognized her. This was the last place Rachel Stein should be at this moment, but there she was. The distance between them wasn't great enough for him to doubt her identity. It provided an unexpected and unneeded new problem.

Assumptions were always dangerous, but Pfifer had to make a decision as to what to do. He had to assume that if he stayed clear, it was likely that Rachel would follow Lubelski back to the freighter. And that, unless she was extremely proficient, Juan's men would be able to pick her up. Then the kidnappers would have double the bargaining power and Pfifer no chance at all to succeed.

Damn! How had she managed to slip away from her protection in London? What was Long thinking about? Why hadn't he been warned?

Below him, Lubelski hung up and began to return to the freighter. He walked quickly, but not conspicuously so. An occasional, subtle look from side to side was all there was to suggest that he might be slightly more interested in what was going on around him than normal.

Pfifer had brought his briefcase with him from the hotel. Quickly he picked it up from the floor and opened it. He withdrew a pistol, wrapped in an oily cloth inside, and took a second to inspect it. It was his weapon of preference: a silenced Luger, 9mm. George Long usually had a mind for such details. Pfifer had only been mildly surprised when he had pulled it from the vent in the hotel. Satisfied, he verified its clip was full, shoved it in his belt at the small of his back and got up. Carefully he pulled his light jacket over it and hoped the weapon did not show.

When he looked back out through the window, he swore again. Rachel was gone. Pfifer looked carefully, but he could not spot her.

The freighter appeared to be in the final stages before getting under way. The crew was in the process of singling up: reducing the number of lines holding the ship to the wharf. Two of the men were working near the gangway, ready to pull it aboard. Chances were, all of Juan's men were now on board. They were probably only waiting for Lubelski to return before they actually cast off. Pfifer reflected for a few seconds, then made his way quickly down through the warehouse to the wharf.

He moved briskly away from the warehouse to one side of the wharf, keeping his eyes on Lubelski. If the captain turned and looked behind him, Pfifer would want to anticipate him and step out of his field of vision—any crate or piece of equipment would do for a shield. At the same time, he needed to find Rachel again. If he could, he would try to manoeuver her out of the way until the freighter was gone.

Lubelski continued along the wharf without breaking his stride. Pfifer was just beginning to relax when he heard light footsteps behind him and felt the press of something cold and hard in his side.

He turned, but not quickly enough.

"Mr. Pfifer, stop right where you are, please."

Pfifer stopped, then slowly completed his turn to face Rachel Stein.

She looked younger than her photograph. Same straight brown hair, same unremarkable face, but somehow different. She held a small automatic tightly in her hand and stared at him with a slightly wide-eyed expression. She was tense, but she was in control of herself.

"In here," Rachel said and backed into a space between two large crates. Pfifer moved forward until she told him to stop.

"That should get us out of sight," she said.

"I could have saved my effort."

"What do you mean by that?" she asked, flushed but steady.

"You obviously can take care of yourself."

The *Baltic Merchant*'s whistle screamed as the freighter pulled away from the wharf under her own power. Rachel was startled by the sudden blast, but she collected herself immediately.

"I believe they're under way now," Pfifer said. "You can relax."

"Just stay where you are."

"I wouldn't recommend it."

Pfifer turned and gestured down the wharf. A crane began to move toward them on its tracks. A burly longshoreman held the end of its heavy cable by the shackle and walked along with it. He seemed to be watching them with some interest.

"You might be right," Rachel said.

"You can put your gun away as well."

"Not quite yet, thank you. Give me your arm."

Pfifer held out his arm for her. She hooked her left arm through his right and then pressed the muzzle of her pistol against his side with her right hand. When she urged him forward it looked as if he were escorting her from the wharf. In addition, it prevented him from making any quick movements, for if he did he would most certainly be shot.

"Just go nice and slow. You wouldn't want me to slip, would you, now?" she said softly.

"Absolutely not."

Rachel smiled at the longshoreman as they walked past. He tipped his hardhat to her and smiled back. Pfifer continued to walk in step with her at a measured pace.

"Very good, Mr. Pfifer," she said when they had gotten beyond the longshoreman's hearing range. "Now, just keep going. My car is parked not too far from here. We can talk."

"If you want to talk, I've opened a way into the warehouse at the end of the wharf. It's closer, and it's out of sight."

Rachel thought for a moment. Then she gave him a hard look and pressed her automatic a bit more firmly into his side.

"Okay, but don't do anything we'll both regret."

"You're in complete control."

"Yes, and it's going to stay that way."

When they reached the warehouse Rachel released Pfifer's arm and allowed him to push open the door. He led her up a narrow staircase to the second floor and stopped by the window.

"Sit on that crate, and put your hands behind your head," Rachel said.

Pfifer did as he was told.

"What did you want to talk about?" he asked.

Rachel ignored his question and took a look out of the window. "You could have seen me from here," she said and then looked back at Pfifer.

"I did see you, Rachel."

She seemed surprised at the sound of her name, but in a second it passed, her composure returning.

"You've been briefed, of course, that's how you know my name."

"I've been briefed, but I must have missed something. Suppose you tell me what you're doing here?"

"That's simple. I've come to stop you from killing my brother. You see, I've been briefed as well."

Pfifer paused for a few seconds and looked at Rachel. She seemed quite calm. He wondered what she actually knew and what she had simply guessed. She had obviously had some training, but by whom was the question. Maybe there were surprises all around. He decided to probe to see what she would tell him.

"What makes you think that's what I'm here to do?"

"I have reliable information."

"I see. Well, just for the record, I'm trying to get your brother off of that freighter, not kill him. I could have already done that."

"When? How? I don't believe you." Her sudden concern betrayed her.

"One little limpet mine clamped to the right place on that freighter's hull, with a timer to set it off, would take care of the whole group. You can believe that."

Rachel's eyes widened, she fought back a tremble.

"You haven't done that, have you?"

"If I have, you're too late, aren't you?"

Rachel's fear turned to anger rapidly. "Answer my question, damn it!"

"You're an absolutely charming girl," Pfifer said, noticing her grip tighten on the automatic. "Did you know that?"

"And you're going to be absolutely dead, if you don't tell me what I want to know."

Pfifer shifted his weight on the crate and stretched himself. He wondered just how far could he push her.

"Don't think that I won't kill you," she said, rapidly becoming impatient. "I know exactly what kind of man you are, and it wouldn't bother me a bit."

"Spoken like a true soldier. Is that what you are Rachel, just someone's soldier? Whose?"

"That's none of your business."

"I'd say it is, right at the moment."

"You have ten seconds to answer my question."

Pfifer remained silent. As the seconds ticked off Rachel became more and more exasperated.

"Okay," she said, her voice almost hoarse. "If you can't be frightened off, perhaps you can be bought. What would it take to call you off? Name your figure."

"You don't want your brother rescued?"

"I don't want my brother killed! At least there's some chance his kidnappers will set him free."

"If you leave your brother in their hands, he's as good as dead. As far as calling me off, you may have already done that. I'll have to check with London. If you found me, Lord knows who else can."

"I found you because I had the right information."

"Joe Bryant?"

Rachel shook her head, but she averted her eyes as she did.

"Bryant is a foolish man. He hasn't done you any favor, or your brother. All he's done is make things worse; complicate the situation."

"Joe had nothing to do with this. It was my idea."

"I see."

"No, you probably don't see. But it doesn't matter."

"So what next?"

Rachel's glance fell to the briefcase at Pfifer's feet.

"What do you have in there?"

"A change of clothes, some documents, that's all."

"Show me, but do it very slowly."

Pfifer reached down and picked up the case. Holding it where Rachel could see it clearly, he worked the latches and opened it. He was suddenly sorry he had left the Nagant in the cache in the hotel. If she found it in his briefcase, perhaps her search for his weapon would end there. And he knew that was what she was doing. Someone had spent some time with her on the fundamentals. He wondered if she would grasp the significance of the oily cloth that was inside.

Rachel looked closely at the briefcase and then back at Pfifer.

"Where is it?" she asked.

"Where is what?"

"Your gun. You wouldn't be here without one."

Rachel's automatic was aligned perfectly on him. He could tell it was cocked, and he could only assume the safety was off. She had been too good so far to make a stupid mistake like that. Pfifer was fairly sure she would not kill him in cold blood, but any sudden movement on his part might tip the scales, cause her to pull the trigger. He stalled for a moment, then put the briefcase down carefully on the crate beside him.

"You don't answer questions very well, do you? Suppose you stand up and turn around, and keep your hands behind your head."

Pfifer stood slowly.

"You'll find my gun in my belt, at the small of my back. I have no other weapons."

As he turned, Rachel moved closer and quickly pulled the Luger from his belt. He watched her over his shoulder; she did it with her left hand while being careful not to let the automatic in her right hand veer from its target. She was actually quite good, he thought. Her only mistake so far had been in not searching him when they first reached the warehouse.

"There," Pfifer said. "Now we both feel better."

"Not quite. Stand still. If you move . . ."

Pfifer stood with his hands behind his head. Rachel frisked him thoroughly. When she was satisfied she stepped back.

"Now I feel better," she said.

"You thought I lied to you?"

"Suspicious is better than dead."

"Good for you."

"Let's go."

Pfifer turned around. Rachel was trying to put the Luger in the waistband of her skirt, but no matter where she put it, it made an obvious bulge on her trim body. Finally she buttoned her jacket over it in front.

"You look like a regular gun moll."

"Move," she said, motioning him forward.

Pfifer picked his briefcase up and led the way. Once they got outside, Rachel took his arm in the same way she had before.

"My car is only a block from here," Rachel said, casting a glance around.

"And where will we be going, if you don't mind me asking?"

"Amsterdam."

They continued to walk. Rachel matched his stride, but at each step the muzzle of her automatic pressed into Pfifer's side. He found it hard to think about anything else. When they came to the end of the block, Rachel stopped, looked behind them and then motioned him down a side street. They passed by a row of parked cars until they came to a blue Ford Escort. There Rachel stopped again.

"You'll drive."

"Sorry, my license is expired."

"That's the least of your worries. Now get in."

They got in the car. Rachel removed the Luger from her skirt, pushed it under the seat, then produced the car keys from her jacket pocket. Pfifer took the keys and stared at her for a moment.

"What are you looking at?" she asked coldly.

"I'm wondering about that, myself," Pfifer answered, then started the car.

CHAPTER
Eleven

Orin was back on his hill. Periodically he raised his binoculars to his eyes and gave the beach a quick sweep to the limits of his field of vision. It was clear and empty.

That was more than he could say for his present state of mind. Things had become far more complicated than he could have possibly imagined. What little control they had gained over the situation had suddenly been denied. Rachel had disappeared, McKintosh's final reserves of composure had disappeared with her. It no longer was a matter concerning the loss of Martin Stein. It was a matter of losing the whole operation. The loss of Rachel meant the loss of Stein's cooperation. Orin could see the full weight of responsibility moving in his direction. They would be looking for a scapegoat now, and he would be it. Orin began to feel sick to his stomach. What could he do?

He had gone over it in his mind countless times. He could not have known what Gretchen had planned. How could he? What more could they ask? He could not swim after them in the fog. It was a miracle he had managed to follow Gretchen to the safe house.

But that wouldn't be enough. Not now. Orin shook his head and tried to turn his mind back to the task at hand. His future might be in doubt, but he still had a job to do, and he would do it as well as he could.

Gretchen had finally shown a sign of life. She had made calls. Josh had caught them and put them on tape. Apparently she did not know about Rachel yet. No one had made mention of it to her, as far as they could tell. There had been a short call to a number in London, a single code word. Then the call to Rotterdam, and again a short coded message, totally meaningless to them. It was maddening. They were helplessly watching the kidnappers proceed with their plan unhampered, even though every word they said was being intercepted, if not understood. And if George Long's man was making any progress, none of them had been informed. Damn them all anyway.

It had gotten quiet again then. After Gretchen's brief flurry of activity she had made no other calls. Orin wondered if her role was now completed. If now she would simply remain in the safe house until her comrades gave her the signal to leave. They had no way of knowing what she would do next, or when. Obviously others would be picking up the ransom, whoever they were, wherever they were. For Orin and Josh and Freddy the time might pass slowly now, very slowly, but it was certain that a lot would be going on elsewhere.

Orin moved slightly, trying to get more comfortable in the little indentation he had made in the soft ground. When he raised the binoculars to his eyes again he saw the rear door of the cottage swing open. He focused quickly and lay very still.

Gretchen stood in the doorway and seemed to be looking directly at him. Unconsciously he tried to settle down more deeply into the thick growth. He kept telling himself that she could not possibly know he was there; nonetheless, his body began to tighten with anxiety as he held the binoculars firmly to his eyes.

She had changed her clothes. She wore a thin white pullover sweater that clung to her in the light breeze and jeans that were faded and snug. A few errant strands of blond hair played over her face; she casually pushed them back with her hand.

Apparently satisfied with her inspection of the hill, Gretchen stepped outside into the sunlight and walked around the cottage to the spot where Martin Stein's car had been hidden. Carefully she checked the tarpaulin that covered it and repositioned several of the securing stones she had used. When she was finished she stood and looked out toward the open beach. Suddenly, perhaps impulsively, she strode around the corner of the cottage out of Orin's view.

Orin radioed Josh.

"Josh, it looks like she's going for another walk. I may have to shift position to keep her in sight. If we lose contact for a few minutes, don't get excited."

"Right Orin, watch yourself," Josh acknowledged.

Orin laid his radio in the grass and got up. He let the binoculars dangle from his neck on their straps and took a deep breath.

There was a chance that Gretchen would just keep walking this time. It would be simple for her to go down the beach and turn up on one of the hundreds of pathways. There could be a car waiting. Orin couldn't take the risk. He would have to follow her as closely as he dared. If he lost her, they would lose what small connection they had. He had blown it once, he had no intention of doing it again.

He turned around and climbed the hill quickly. When he reached the top he caught his breath, then moved off to his left. The footpath paralleled the beach in a meandering fashion. The amount of cover it offered varied a great deal, but it was better than nothing, and as he saw it, his only alternative. If Gretchen noticed him he would have to improvise. Hopefully, she wouldn't.

He moved carefully but rapidly along the footpath, and in a few moments he saw her. As she walked slowly by the water's edge, she held her shoes loosely in her right hand and watched for the most comfortable footing. Ahead of her the beach narrowed, and the footpath converged with it. The salt grass tapered off thin and low. An open field spread out to the right.

Gretchen was no more than a hundred yards away when she turned and looked at him. He didn't have time to even make an effort to conceal himself. On pure impulse, he waved at her. Gretchen returned his wave and began to walk toward him. He watched with mixed emotions as she approached.

His mind raced. He tried frantically to think of a story that would explain his presence and the way he was dressed. People with innocent motives just didn't sneak around in the bracken dressed in camouflage. What could he tell her? What would work?

"Hello," she said when she reached him. There was no trace of apprehension in her voice or in her expression as she spoke.

Orin smiled, at a loss for words.

"Did I interrupt your bird-watching?"

"Bird-watching? Oh no, not at all. I wasn't having much luck, anyway. I'm afraid I'm not much good at it yet." Orin hoped she didn't sense the waver in his voice. He stared at her for a long moment. She began to smile at him.

"You're an American, aren't you?"

"Yes."

"What is your name?"

"Orin." He gripped his binoculars, he could feel his hands begin to perspire. She just continued to look at him and smile. He could not help thinking how beautiful she was.

"Am I making you uncomfortable?" she asked.

"Well, I do feel a little foolish."

"The English take their bird-watching very seriously, you know."

"Yes, I know. I thought I'd try it just to see what it's like."

"I always thought there were other things more interesting to look at than birds."

"Now that you mention it, you're probably right."

"You're very nice. Would you like to walk with me for a while?"

Orin hesitated. The smile faded from Gretchen's face.

"I'm sorry. Am I too forward?"

"No, not at all," he said and tried to smile as naturally as he could.

Gretchen turned, took a few steps and then stopped and waited for him to catch up to her. When he stopped beside her she very casually and warmly took his hand in hers.

"Let's walk near the water. The sand is firmer there," she said.

Orin matched her steps and let her keep hold of his hand. At the water's edge they turned right and moved slowly along.

"You weren't watching birds, were you?" she asked, not changing her friendly tone.

"No; how did you know?"

"The look on your face when I walked toward you."

"I'm afraid, then, I'm not any better at watching girls than I am at watching birds."

"That's all right. I didn't mind you watching me." She squeezed his hand slightly. "I'm glad we met. I needed someone to talk to."

He looked into her face for a moment. She returned his look openly and unwavering. Her cool blue eyes matched the cool blue of the sea.

"Are you staying near here?" she asked.

"Not too far from here. Why do you ask?"

"I was just curious."

"You're a beautiful girl, but I imagine you know that."

Gretchen smiled at him, then looked quickly away.

"I'm not being too forward for you now, am I?" he asked.

"No. A woman likes to be told she is attractive. Providing it comes from someone she thinks she might like."

They had gone down the beach some distance when Gretchen stopped and looked out toward the English Channel. Her blond hair moved gently in the breeze. Orin found himself staring at her.

He felt as though the sand were being gradually pulled from beneath his feet, as if he were someone standing in the surf as the waves receded. He could hear his pulse throb clearly in his ears. Suddenly, he took her by the shoulders, turned her to him and then kissed her. She leaned against him without struggle, let him kiss her a second time, then pushed him gently away.

"I'm sorry," he stammered. "I just went completely over the edge, I guess." Self-consciously, he stood back from her.

"I have to go back now."

"I understand."

"It's not that, but please don't follow me. I can't explain."

He felt an intense coldness in the pit of his stomach. He chided himself for acting like a schoolboy. Gretchen began to walk away from him.

"Orin?" she said over her shoulder. "I still think you're very nice."

"I'm glad for that," he called after her.

"I may walk this way tomorrow. Would you be here if I did?"

"I don't know."

Gretchen stopped and turned.

"It would please me very much," she said.

Orin just looked at her. Finally she turned her back to him and continued to walk away.

The sun reflected sharply off of the sea. The sand felt

warm beneath his feet. He could hear the soft thunder of waves close by and feel a fine mist from their spray. It took him several moments to remember who he was and what he was and what he had to do. When Gretchen was out of sight, he walked back to the footpath and began to try to find his way back.

Orin had barely reached his position when his radio sounded. "Orin, we have a visitor that wants to talk with you. Do you hear me?"

"Yes, Josh. I just made it back. Send Freddy down."

"He's already on his way."

"Right."

What now, Orin thought? Why had Josh referred to a visitor without identifying him. What was going on? The whole situation seemed to be coming apart at the seams. Almost carelessly, Orin climbed up the hill. What would he tell them about Gretchen? What did he have to tell them? Strangely it didn't seem to matter.

Orin met Freddy halfway back to the cottage. The concern was plain on Freddy's face when he saw his boss away from his post, but he said nothing, and Orin offered him no explanation. They exchanged glances and equipment without a word, then Orin continued along the footpath.

There were no cars parked outside the cottage. Orin entered without knocking but stopped short just inside when he saw a small but heavyset figure standing in front of the fireplace. The man turned and looked at him casually, with an expression of only mild interest, but, Orin suspected, great acuity.

"You are, of course, Orin Brady," the man said.

"Yes, and you are?"

"George Long."

Orin nodded. The man turned back toward the fireplace.

Orin looked Long over. He noted the damp sand on his shoes and the slightly flushed appearance of his cheeks. So this was George Long. He was disappointed. This thick little man looked anything but ominous to him. He looked more like a winded old man than a dangerous enforcer of Langley's will. The only thing that disturbed him was the damp sand on those shiny black shoes.

"I expected that you would be with Pat McKintosh."

"McKintosh was detained in London. I understand he is making a direct report to the assistant director . . . . You've no doubt been informed about Rachel . . . For the moment you may consider me in charge."

"I see. I suppose this is about Rachel?"

"You would do well to suppose nothing and do your job."

Orin stiffened.

"Do you have anything to report?"

"No."

"No? I understand you were away from your position for some time. Yet you have nothing to report?" Long faced Orin and gave him a stern look. Orin reacted to it more strongly than he expected. An uneasiness began to grow within him. Those sandy shoes—he had to ask the question.

"She took a walk down the beach, that's all. I followed her. There were no outside contacts. If you don't mind, did you come in from the north or the south?"

"Would it make a difference?"

Orin hesitated. What if Long had seen him on the beach with Gretchen? What would happen if Long caught him in a lie?

"I only wondered if you saw any activity that I should know about. That's all. We don't have enough manpower to patrol the area extensively."

Long smiled faintly, then his expression went blank again.

"There is one item of information that you may find useful. Rachel has been spotted in Rotterdam. She is now in the company of my agent."

"I'm glad. We were all worried about her."

"I didn't say that she was safe. That remains to be seen. Now, I have a few questions to put to you and I want you to give me the most candid answers you are capable of. Do you understand? There is more at stake than you know."

"I will cooperate, of course."

Long held his hands out to the cold hearth. It made an indelible picture in Orin's mind and it unnerved him. There was something symbolic in the way he did it. Almost as if he could see a flame that was not there, feel its heat.

"What do you know about Rachel Stein?"

"Not much, really. She's been in the United States for the last few years. We've only seen her during her visits from college. What exactly are you trying to find out?"

"Have you ever been assigned to keep her under surveillance?"

"No."

"That's interesting; McKintosh told me that you had been from time to time."

Orin shook his head. McKintosh would have said no such thing. Was Long attempting to lay a trap for him? Why? What was Long probing for, trying to find out?

"It isn't true. Bryant has been keeping an eye on her almost exclusively for as long as I have been involved."

Long looked steadily at Orin. He showed his subtle smile once again before continuing.

"You are a loyal man, but not a liar? Is that right?"

Orin's emotions began to oscillate between a growing anger and an underlying fear.

"What do you think Rachel is guilty of?"

"A better question would be, what is she capable of, and while we're at it we might ask who could be helping her?"

CHAPTER
Twelve

When they were clear of Rotterdam, they took the super-highway west. For miles the landscape was a mirrored puzzle of glass hothouses punctuated with small green fields. Then, before they reached Delft and the Hague, they turned north. A deep canal paralleled their route to the left as they made the turn. A stand of poplars on the far bank cast shadows and reflections on the water.

Rachel was quiet. She seemed to divide her attention between Pfifer and the road ahead. She held her automatic precisely aimed at all times. She showed no sign of any lapse of concentration that he could take advantage of. Pfifer was patient, but time was slipping away. He had to find a way to regain control, and he had to find it fast.

"I take it you have friends in Amsterdam?" he asked.

"Yes."

"And I can safely assume they aren't CIA, can't I?"

"Don't worry, Mr. Pfifer. You'll be properly taken care of," Rachel said and then rubbed her eyes.

"You've had a long night, haven't you?"

"Yes, but don't think for a moment that I will fall asleep on you."

"It would be impolite."

"It would also be stupid. Now be quiet and drive. Can't you go any faster?"

"If you'd been looking, you would have noticed that every so often there have been traffic cameras mounted on top of the light poles. Clever people, the Dutch. If you speed, the camera takes your picture, and in a few days you get a nice note from the police."

Rachel looked to see if Pfifer was telling her the truth.

"Then don't speed," she said.

"I wasn't. It might make an interesting picture, though. Interesting enough to end your career with the CIA."

"I'm not too concerned with that at the moment. Now, please, just drive."

Pfifer decided to press.

"You've been to school in America, haven't you?"

Rachel tried to ignore his question.

"Even if I hadn't read it in your file, which I did, you don't quite have the accent you should. You've jumbled some of your pronunciations. What school were you in?"

Rachel sighed.

"Let me see if I can remember. Oh, yes, M.I.T. That was it, wasn't it? Now, let's see, what was your major?"

"Chemistry!" Rachel shouted. "What difference does it make? Do you have to talk?"

"Chemistry. Very impressive. That should help you with your cloak and dagger work, shouldn't it?"

"I'm beginning to tire of this new tactic of yours."

"Massachusetts Institute of Technology. Postgraduate work?"

"How did you ever guess?" Rachel asked sarcastically.

"You're too old to be a freshman and too smart to have been held back."

"If that was a compliment, I didn't like it much."

"Is that where they recruited you? M.I.T.?"

"That is none of your business."

"How did they do it? Let's face it, the British and certainly the Israelis should have been first in line. Why the CIA? Or perhaps the CIA just thinks it's in front of the line?"

"I don't see what any of this conversation can accomplish. As of now, you are out of the picture. You're going to be put under wraps until this whole thing is over. Do you understand that? You must."

"I know I have a job to do, Rachel, and the only way you will stop me from doing it is to kill me. Are you prepared to do that?"

"If I have to pick between my brother's life and yours, yes."

"Suppose you're wrong? Suppose the furthest thing from my mind is to kill your brother? Suppose what I've been telling you is true, that all I want to do is get Martin off of that freighter? Are you ready to take the responsibility?"

"I've told you. I have reliable information that what you plan to do is to kill Martin. You're wasting your time trying to fool me into thinking otherwise."

"You're dangerous, Rachel. You and every little overzealous misguided fool like you. You're dangerous to yourself, and you're dangerous to everyone around you. Wake up. Look around. Don't believe every lie you're told. If you don't start thinking for yourself, you'll lose everything important."

Rachel started to become truly angry.

"The last thing I need from you is a lecture."

"Maybe it's just what you do need. Obviously your father never took the time to tell you the real facts of life."

"I've had it! Now listen to me closely. We will not talk about my father, the CIA, my school, or anything else. Get the picture? Shut up and drive!"

Rachel allowed the aim of her automatic to go slightly

wide as she shouted. Pfifer saw it and reacted instantly. Reaching out, he grasped her wrist, squeezed it as hard as he could, then leaned to his right, pinning her against the passenger door.

Rachel screamed and pulled the trigger of the little automatic twice. The sound was sharp and deafening in the small car. The windshield shattered, sending shards of glass back over them. Frantically, she tried to strike him with her left elbow and with her feet. Pfifer took her blows until he could pull the car to the side of the road and stop. Then he tore the gun from her grasp and gave her a hard backhand to the jaw. She gave him a startled look, as she sagged into unconsciousness.

Pfifer sat there a moment. As he tried to collect his thoughts, he looked at Rachel and slowly began brushing bits of glass away from her eyes. He had stalled the car; the highway was clear in both directions. What next, he thought to himself. So far he had killed two men, and now he had pistol-whipped a young woman. What more would be required? His thoughts made his blood run cold. If it was within his power, he knew exactly who he would choose as his next target. But that would be tantamount to suicide, wouldn't it? They would find him for that one, he would never be free, and killing George Long wouldn't stop the madness. It would only give it more impetus. No, he would have to forgo that particular solution to his situation. Pfifer grimaced; it was the first time he had ever consciously thought of killing Long. What was happening to him?

He decided against tying and gagging her. The trunk of the Escort would be too small for her, anyway. Besides, someone would surely pass by and see him toppling her in. No, instead he straightened her in her seat, made sure her seatbelt was secured and let it go at that. He put her automatic in his left coat pocket so it would be as far away from her as possible.

About a third of the windshield had been blown away, but

the driver's side remained mostly intact. Rachel came to as Pfifer was carefully picking up as much of the shattered glass as he could from the seats and dash.

"There goes your deposit," Pfifer said when he noticed her eyes open. "Now, the ground rules are these; you make a move to get out of those seatbelts and I'm going to hit you again. You're not a particularly pretty girl, but you could look a lot worse, if you get my meaning."

"You bastard!"

"Verbal abuse is acceptable. In fact, indulge yourself. It might make you feel better."

"You son of a bitch, no man has ever hit me!"

"How many of them have you held at gunpoint?"

"I should have shot you when I had the chance."

"Be patient, the way my luck's going, you might get another opportunity."

Rachel stared at him coldly. Her body was tight with rage, her face flushed with color. Pfifer found it difficult to break his eyes away from her.

"What are you going to do now?"

"I thought you wanted to go to Amsterdam? That's fine with me. I have a few friends there myself. Amsterdam is such a versatile city, don't you think? Seems like the Dutch are among the world's best at playing both ends against the middle."

Rachel looked perplexed. "You're out of your mind. I hope those terrorists blow your brains out."

"We'd better get moving, before someone stops to see what our problem is. We wouldn't want anyone to be offended by your language, would we?"

Rachel raised her hand slowly and felt the line of her jaw. Pfifer could see it was starting to get puffy on her right side. He wondered if it was broken. He looked away from her as he started the car and moved back out onto the road.

"If any pieces of glass blow into your eyes, let me know.

We're only a few minutes from the city. The rest of the windshield should hold that far.''

"Your concern is touching.''

Pfifer had to smile.

"You certainly aren't short on spunk, or sarcasm, are you? Ever think of being frightened? Any normal person would.''

"Are you frightened?''

"All the time, Rachel. All the time.''

Pfifer drove. Rachel sulked in her seat. Neither spoke for several miles. The wind buffeted badly through the car, but Rachel offered no complaint.

The highway eventually crossed over the canal and stretched out to the north. Soon they passed a sign for the turnoff to Aalsmeer and, further along, the sign for Schiphol Airport. Pfifer turned to Rachel and spoke in a loud voice so she could hear above the roar of the air passing through the car.

"Rachel, if I were to take you to Schiphol and put you on a plane, would you go home and stay there?''

"No.''

"Well, at least you aren't a liar.''

"What do you plan to do with me, and with Martin?''

"I don't know what I'm going to do with you just yet. I need to put you into friendly hands before I can do anything else. That's about all I do know. As far as Martin is concerned, I thought you had your mind made up. What makes you doubt your 'reliable information' at this point?''

"I don't doubt it. I just wanted to hear what you would say.''

"I see. Well, you just go on thinking whatever you want. I really don't think I can change your mind, anyway.''

The sun was beginning to set as they reached Amsterdam. Pfifer picked his way carefully through the narrow streets. Often they came to canals and crossed short, arched bridges. In the canals, clusters of low barges and boats hugged the edges, dark and huddled. The canals themselves burned red and orange in the dying light. The lights glowed from the gabled row houses as they slipped past.

After they had penetrated deep into the city, Pfifer pulled to a stop at a corner and squinted through the windshield. Was it the right street? It had been a long time. He hesitated, then turned to the right. Quickly, they came to a bridge, crossed it and then turned right again. In three blocks Pfifer stopped and shut off the car.

"Put your hands behind your head, Rachel."

Rachel did as she was told. Pfifer reached beneath her seat and removed the Luger. Rachel looked at him with an astonished expression.

"You left that there?"

"You wouldn't have gotten to it in time. You can put your arms down now."

"Why have we stopped?"

"Because we've arrived. Stay put until I come around to your side."

Pfifer slipped the Luger into his belt and buttoned his coat. Then he got out of the car. As he did, the first thing that struck him was the quiet on the street. He could even hear the gentle lap of the water in the canal. Only in the distance could he hear voices and the sounds of traffic. It was too early for it to be so quiet. He looked around carefully, but saw nothing overtly wrong.

"Hurry up please. I need to take care of something," Rachel called from inside the car.

Pfifer went around and let her out. She stood shakily and tried to smooth her wrinkled clothes. He reached into the car and withdrew his briefcase as she preened.

"We have a short walk first."

"It had better be very short."

"It is."

He took hold of her arm and they moved off. A hundred yards ahead they came to a barge moored against the side of the canal. A dim light showed from inside its cabin. Pfifer pointed Rachel to a crude ladder leading down to its afterdeck.

"Are we expected?" Rachel asked as she stepped over the edge.

"Yes and no," Pfifer said, following her onto the barge.

Someone inside heard their voices and footsteps. A face appeared at a window. Pfifer saw only a brief double reflection, as if from spectacles, then the face disappeared. In a moment, the cabin door swung open and a large man dressed in denim work clothes appeared in the doorway. Pfifer recognized the low voice as the man spoke and felt an immediate sense of relief.

"I thought you were dead, John," he said. "Who's your friend?"

"She's my dear grandmother. Can't you see a family resemblance, Carl?"

"Come below," Carl said and moved quickly aside.

Once they were inside, Carl shut the cabin door heavily behind them and then motioned them into better light.

Carl had no electricity. A coal-oil lantern hung from a rafter by a chain. It threw its weak light on the odds and ends of the very tired-looking furniture that filled the cabin. His was one of the two thousand or so houseboats and conversions that clogged Amsterdam's canals; a symptom of that city's perennial housing shortage. It was unpretentious, and met his meager needs.

"Rachel, this is Carl Burge," Pfifer said. "She needs to check out your plumbing."

"Such as it is."

Carl pointed down a corridor. Rachel went ahead, carefully stepping around the clutter. Pfifer set his briefcase on the deck and then eased down onto a couch. Carl remained standing.

Carl was a physically powerful man. Barrel-chested, thick, but not fat. He dwarfed Pfifer as he stood over him. Pfifer thought back at the times he had seen that physical strength in action. As he studied Carl, though, he became increasingly aware of a tenseness about him that was unusual. He hoped that it was just his imagination.

"You're not overjoyed to see me. I can understand that," Pfifer said.

"I did think you were dead. I'm surprised, that's all."

"By rights, I should be dead. But as you can see, not yet."

"What brings you to Amsterdam?"

"An assignment."

"Still working for the same people?"

"That's a peculiar question, Carl. Perhaps I should ask you the same?"

Carl removed his glasses, carefully folded them and then placed them in his shirt pocket. He looked steadily at Pfifer with dark, sad eyes. There was anger in those eyes, Pfifer thought; anger and something else.

"Who is the woman?"

"A complication."

"They generally are."

"Yes, I suppose they are. Nonetheless, I need your help."

Carl shook his head from side to side.

"I cannot help you. I am no longer in the game."

"All I need is someone to take the woman to the American Embassy and a way into Germany, through the back door."

A long silence fell between them. Pfifer grew more and more uneasy as it progressed. Carl had been a reliable operative for as many years as he could remember. He and his brother, Samuel. They had been among the best. Active or retired, Pfifer couldn't imagine Carl not helping him. Unless perhaps he had been told not to.

"Have you heard from George Long lately?" Pfifer asked.

Carl shook his head again.

"If I were to help you, it would not be for George Long. In spite of him, maybe, but not for him."

"I don't understand. What's happened?"

Carl slumped to a chair. Pfifer saw the beads of sweat on his forehead as the light fell across him from the lantern overhead. He began to understand, but he still did not know the why.

"Would Samuel help me?"

"Samuel is dead."

Pfifer went numb.

"How?"

Carl stared back at Pfifer. "Does it matter how?"

"It might."

"It doesn't matter, believe me. It only matters that he is dead, and I am finished. You will be soon as well."

"Perhaps, but I'm not ready to give up quite yet."

Their conversation trailed off to silence again. Then Carl looked at Pfifer and shifted his weight in his chair. A look of uncertainty clouded his face. Pfifer felt for him, and the dilemma that he faced. Carl was a man that had once played loyalty above all else. It was painful to watch him grapple with his fear so plainly. Finally, he shook his head and frowned, accepting the inevitable.

"I can get you into Germany. The usual way, through Francine. I cannot help you with the woman. You will have to take her with you."

"I'd rather not take her to Francine."

"She is an uncooperative companion?"

"Yes."

"Then you have no choice but to take her. I cannot take responsibility for her at all."

"All right, agreed, but there is a car. A blue Ford up the street. The windshield is smashed. It needs to disappear."

"That will be easy."

"I appreciate it, Carl."

"If you do, then do me a favor. When you leave tonight, don't come back."

"Consider it done."

Carl seemed to relax a bit. He smiled and rubbed the palms of his hands on his knees. Neither Carl or Pfifer had noticed Rachel standing in the doorway. She chose that moment to come back into the room.

"Thank you, Carl."

Carl turned and acknowledged her.

"If you are hungry, there is some food. Only cheese and bread, I'm afraid, but help yourself. I must go out for a while."

"I am hungry, thanks again."

Carl got up, picked his jacket from a nearby chair, then turned to Pfifer.

"Stay inside until I return, John. I have been watched from time to time. In fact, if you had come a week from now, you would not have found me here. Too many people seemed to have learned how to find me."

"I understand."

Carl gave Rachel a courteous little bow and then left. They felt the barge move slightly and its mooring lines creak as he stepped off.

"Carl is an operative?" Rachel asked.

"Was an operative," he corrected her. "How long were you listening?"

"For a while."

"I'm not surprised to find that eavesdropping is right up your alley."

Rachel shrugged off his comment.

"Who is Francine?"

"She's into a slight variation of our line of work. You'll get the chance to meet her later tonight. You said you were hungry."

"Yes."

"Look behind you on the counter."

She turned her back to him and then moved to a crude wooden shelf attached to the cabin's port side. She found Carl's cheese and bread there and began to unwrap it.

"Carl appears to be a man who has lost his nerve," Rachel said matter of factly.

"You're quick to judge people, aren't you? Did you ever think to give someone the benefit of the doubt?"

"I've been told it doesn't pay."

"So, on top of everything else, you're a cynic?"

"You don't like me, do you?"

"No."

Rachel turned and looked at him. In the soft light she was almost pretty, Pfifer mused.

"I'm not a monster."

"I can understand your motivation. You love your brother. You've also got guts enough to try and do something to help him. You haven't done badly. Your only problem is that you're misguided, that's all."

"At least you're consistent. Do you want something to eat? Some wine? Perhaps you need one of your pills?"

Pfifer flinched. He'd forgotten about Long's stupid pills. He had taken the first few on schedule, but then he had left them behind. So that was how she recognized him. The pills and his passport had been left in Bryant's car.

"So you go through suitcases as well? You're an all-around talent, aren't you?"

Rachel flushed. "You go to hell."

Pfifer stood. Rachel held her ground defiantly.

"Want to hit me again? Will that make you feel better?"

"I'll feel better when I can get rid of you."

"Suit yourself." Rachel reached into her coat pocket and pulled out Pfifer's vial of pills. Then she dropped it to the deck and crushed them under her heel. She did it before he could stop her. Mistake. He had blown it by not searching her.

Rachel sat down across the room in an old, overstuffed

chair. She folded her arms in front of her, leaned her head back and closed her eyes. Pfifer knew she was too angry to be able to fall asleep so quickly, but she had cut off their conversation just as efficiently as if she had. More points for her, Pfifer thought, as he stooped to retrieve what was left of his medication.

The label from the crushed vial was all he could save; the rest was reduced to ruptured capsules and fine red-and-white granules. Pfifer made a mental note to try to obtain a refill at his first opportunity.

Pfifer sat back down on the couch. His eyes rested on Rachel, but his mind was on other things. He could hear the sounds of the city around him: traffic, a small outboard motor faint but approaching, the sound of a window being closed firmly against the intrusion of the night, the occasional creak of the barge against its mooring lines. Rachel didn't believe him; he didn't dare trust her. He thought about the few people left he could trust. It was a short list. Uneasily, he wondered if George Long should be on it.

CHAPTER
Thirteen

It was nine o'clock when Pfifer heard the van pull to a stop beside Carl's barge. It startled him; he had been dangerously close to sleep. Quickly, he looked at Rachel, curled up in her chair like a child in innocent and vulnerable repose, then carefully he rose and walked to her side.

"Rachel," he said as he leaned over her. "Wake up. There's someone outside."

Rachel sat upright, blinked her eyes and fought off a yawn. She shuddered when she realized where she was and remembered the events that surrounded her. For a moment, though, Pfifer saw past her hard defenses, and caught a glimpse of what lay just beyond.

"What did you say?" she asked, looking up at him.

"There's someone outside. They may be here to pick us up. It's possible they may be here for an entirely different reason. We'd better put ourselves in position."

"What do you want me to do?" Rachel asked, allowing the alarm to show in her voice.

"Just sit in this chair so whoever comes through the door will see you. I'll be behind the couch. Relax, and when they come through the door, smile."

"Smile?"

"Just do it."

Rachel nodded, grasped the arms of the chair, and riveted her eyes on the cabin door. Pfifer moved back around the couch and dropped down.

It was probably an unnecessary precaution, but Carl could have just as easily gone to an enemy as a friend and told them about him and Rachel. It would have been an easy setup, far too easy, and Pfifer was in no position to take the chance. His instincts forbade it.

The van's engine stopped. A single set of footsteps sounded on the ladder, and then on the deck of the barge. After a brief hesitation, there was a knock at the cabin door.

"Come in," Rachel said, her voice steady now, under control.

Good girl, Pfifer thought, and pushed the Luger's safety off.

Pfifer heard the door creak open and then close carefully. The instant he heard the lock click home, he came up from behind the couch and drew aim.

"Stay right where you are," Pfifer said.

He was an old man, bent and thin and wrinkled. He was dressed in paint-spattered green overalls and paint-spattered boots. He looked at the Luger Pfifer held on him with a cool detachment, as if he truly did not care, as if he were beyond fear.

"Are you John Pfifer?" the old man asked.

"I'm Pfifer."

"Carl Burge sent me to you. We should all go as quickly as possible. It's not safe for you here."

"Who are you? What's your name?"

"That doesn't matter." The old man glanced at Rachel and then back at Pfifer. "Come now. It's a long drive and I will need some time to rest when I return so I will be able to go to work.''

It was a mental flip of the coin. Something along the lines of heads you win tails you die. Could he trust this man? Could he trust Carl? Which way would the coin fall this time?

Pfifer motioned to Rachel, picked up his briefcase and stepped forward. The thought occurred to him that he was placing a great deal in the hands of a complete stranger. He wondered if Rachel was thinking those same thoughts. He wondered if he would be as brave in her position. He had his doubts.

"There is one thing Carl asked me to remind you, before I forget," the old man said.

"Yes, I can guess what it is. Tell him I will keep my word."

"Good," the old man said and then led the way for them.

Pfifer waited for Rachel, then stepped out behind her. He still held the Luger as they went forward single-file across the deck. As they mounted the ladder, he looked briefly at the canal behind them. It was black and bottomless in the moonlight, and the reflection of that naked orb shimmered on its surface. He took a deep breath, then continued up the ladder.

The neighborhood was far from asleep. Many lights were on in the narrow houses lining the canal on both sides. Pfifer watched for signs that they were causing special interest, but if someone were watching them there would be no sure way to know until it was too late.

The old man led them to a battered Volkswagen van, pulled open its side door and stepped out of the way so they could get in. Rachel climbed in first and sat on a box that had been placed as a crude seat. Pfifer followed her, and when he was seated beside her the old man slammed the door shut and went around to take the wheel. In a moment the van's engine rattled to life and they lurched forward.

There were no side windows in the van, only a small rear window covered with a tattered curtain. Pfifer swept it aside and looked out when they passed the spot where he had parked the Escort. It was gone. Satisfied, he sat down again beside Rachel and together they peered forward to watch the streets in front of them as the old man hurtled the van briskly through the narrow maze of the city.

"Why did you tell me to smile?" Rachel suddenly asked.

"A smile is a very arresting thing. Most people will pause, even if for just an instant, when someone smiles at them. We might have needed that extra instant very badly."

"I see," Rachel said and looked forward again.

The van drummed and roared inside. Rachel had spoken practically into Pfifer's ear so he could hear. He had answered the same way. The scent of her hair made him slightly uncomfortable, but in a moment his defenses were up again. He concentrated on the blur of signs, cars, and buildings that flashed by.

"I'm sorry I destroyed your medication. You made me very angry."

"Are you still angry?"

"Not necessarily."

They rounded a series of sharp curves. The van rocked back and forth, forcing them to lean hard against each other. Rachel ended up against Pfifer's side. She stayed there a moment, until she finally pushed herself away. Reflexively, Pfifer felt to see if her little automatic was still in his pocket.

"You still don't trust me, even in the slightest, do you?" Rachel asked, noticing his manoeuvre.

Pfifer met her stare, but said nothing.

"I thought not," she said, reading his expression.

They tried to ignore each other as much as possible, but the speed and frequency of the van's turns made it difficult. Eventually, they cleared the city and headed out across the level polders—the rich, reclaimed farmland a high percentage of the Netherlands consists of. The road, slightly elevated from the dark green expanse on either side, became straight and very smooth. The drone of the van became steady and monotonous.

Rachel had fallen asleep against him. He put his arm around her to keep her from falling forward as the van came to a stop. The old man cut his engine, then got out, slamming his door shut behind him. When he did, Rachel was jarred awake.

"We're here," Pfifer said and removed his arm.

"Where?"

"Francine's."

"Oh," she said and followed him shakily as he climbed from the van.

They were at a crossroads. There were gnarled trees clotted about the intersection, and a scatter of buildings. All was quiet and dark except for lights and the rattle of glasses and dishes from a tavern a few yards away.

"You know where you are?" the old man said as he walked around the front of the van.

"Yes," Pfifer answered. "You can leave if you like."

"That's what I'd planned on."

"Good luck, and thank you."

The old man looked at Pfifer for a second and then nodded toward Rachel. Without any further ceremony, he got back into his van and drove away. Pfifer and Rachel watched him disappear across the polders.

"A strange man," Rachel said.

"No, not as strange as you might think. Just another player. You'll meet a lot more before you're through."

Rachel paused, wiped the sleep from her eyes. Pfifer thought he noticed her shudder slightly.

"What now?" she asked.

"The tavern is Francine's. We're going inside. If I were

you I wouldn't say anything or try to get away. There's virtually no place for you to go, anyway."

"Understand something. I don't intend to try and get away from you. I don't intend for you to get away from me, either."

He looked at her for a second. She was tired, but none of the determination had faded from her expression. Pfifer shook his head.

"Well, fine. Let's go meet Francine, then."

"Lead on."

The tavern was old but impeccably kept. The flower boxes and trim were brightly painted in red, white and blue. Gay ruffled curtains adorned the spotless windows. Pfifer led Rachel through the front door. Inside, couples sat about, some in booths, some at tables near a fireplace. Pfifer ignored them and walked directly to a staircase rising to the tavern's second floor. Rachel followed as he began to climb them. They attracted only brief glances from a few of the patrons. Conversations continued unabated, the background noises undisturbed. Rachel hurried to keep pace. At the top of the stairs Pfifer turned to the left and knocked on a door.

When the door opened, a woman appeared. She looked about fifty, slightly plump. She wore a simple but elegant white gown and carried herself with an aristocratic presence. Pfifer stepped through the door without a word. Rachel followed at his heels.

"Well," Francine said. "John Pfifer, what brings you to our door this night?"

"I need your help. I need to get into Germany, she needs to come with me. I'm not sure who might be following us."

Francine studied them both for a bit, then smiled. It was a slightly mischievous smile. Then, suddenly, it was blotted out by other thoughts.

"I have talked to Carl. The arrangements have already been made. But there is something you should know first. Your people have begun to look for you and the girl. They are looking in Amsterdam now. Carl was questioned. I must ask you before we can continue, are you in some sort of trouble? Have you perhaps done something naughty for a change?''

Pfifer attempted a smile. She was a cautious woman. Her caution had undoubtedly saved her many times. He would have to be careful what he said.

"There has been some confusion. They're simply trying to straighten it up. When I check in, once we're in Germany, things will quiet down. Carl should have no problem. You have nothing to worry about.''

Francine's smile began to return.

"You've never lied to me before. I have no reason to expect that you are lying to me now. But nonetheless, we will have to be very careful. I must insist on that.''

"What do you have in mind?''

"You will see. If I am to trust you, you must trust me.''

Francine turned to Rachel.

"Now, dear, you look like you've already been through quite a lot for one day already. Come with me and we'll see what we can do to make you more comfortable.''

Francine took Rachel by the arm and led her from the room through a side door. She turned and smiled back at Pfifer before she closed the door behind her. It was a puzzling smile; Pfifer had never seen her smile quite like that before, not at him, at any rate. He stood there feeling somewhat miffed, not knowing exactly why. As he tried to relax, he cast his eyes about the fine old antiques and thick oriental rugs that furnished the suite. She was quite a woman, Francine. He considered her as he waited.

Francine had her secrets, no doubt. She also knew a number of others' secrets as well, and she held them like trump cards, playing them when the need arose. She was a master of walking that fine line between factions. It was why she had survived. It was why she would probably continue to survive. Pfifer wished he could be so sure of his own fate.

After a few minutes, Francine returned. She stopped in front of Pfifer, propped her hands on her hips and shook her head.

"You aren't pleased with me," Pfifer observed.

"That girl is frightened half out of her mind. What have you been doing to her?"

"I've been protecting myself from her mostly. And I doubt very seriously if she's very frightened. She's too young to know what real fear is."

"I can see that you know as little about women as most men."

"I don't claim to be an expert."

"Well, at least you aren't arrogant." Francine stepped closer to him and pulled on his beard. "That must come off. You will find shaving things in the bath through there, to your right. I will do what I can with Rachel. One of my girls must have something she can wear, and perhaps we can do a thing or two besides. It will be a rush job."

Francine made a brisk exit, not waiting for Pfifer's agreement. He knew, without her having to clarify it, that her authority would be absolute if he wanted her help. With some resolution, he turned and went toward the bath.

The bath had adjoining doors to both the sitting room and the bedroom. As Pfifer entered, he noticed the bedroom door was still open, and when he turned and looked through it he saw Rachel standing by the bed, dressed only in her slip. She folded her arms in front of her self-consciously when their eyes met. After several seconds, Pfifer pulled the door shut, but the image of her lingered as he found razor and soap, stripped to his waist, and methodically began to shave.

They might not have recognized each other. The change in their appearance was much more dramatic than Francine had led them to expect. As Rachel emerged from Francine's bedroom, she stopped short and stared at Pfifer, who in turn stared at her.

Rachel wore a rather snug-fitting pair of jeans and a pale peach-colored blouse with ruffles at her cuffs and collar. Her face was made, and they had curled her hair. Pfifer had to admit that the difference was astonishing. He also had to admit he liked what he saw.

Pfifer wore jeans as well, with a gray sweater and suede jacket. However, the greatest change was in his face. Clean-shaven, it was as if ten years of his age had been stripped away. He looked less stern, less intense. Only his cold gray eyes remained to give the keen observer his clue.

"Do I look that bad?" Rachel asked.

"Don't lie to the child, John. And stop staring," Francine said and laughed.

"Don't take this the wrong way, Rachel, but you look better than I thought you could look."

"I'll take that as a compliment," Rachel said and smiled, still unable to take her eyes from his face.

"I mean it as one."

"Well," Francine interrupted, "you two have very little time before you leave, and I have a few more things to attend to. So behave yourselves and I'll call for you when it's time." Francine laughed again softly and then turned and left the room.

Rachel took a tentative step toward Pfifer. Then she reached up to touch his face, but he intercepted her hand as she did and held it.

"You look much different without the beard, not so dark and foreboding."

"I'll take that as a compliment, and then we're even. What do you think of Francine?"

Rachel's smile faded. She looked away as she answered.

"I think she's a complicated lady. And I'm sure she must have an interesting story."

"Yes on both counts, but her story is hers to tell, not mine."

"What about your story, John Pfifer. Who are you and what are you all about? I'm trusting my life to you, and I know nothing about you."

"The less you know about me, the safer you are. And, coincidentally, the safer I am."

"So you'll just have to be a mystery man, is that it?"

"Yes, if you want to put it that way."

Rachel turned back toward him and met his gaze.

"You confuse me, do you know that?"

"No, I thought you were particularly unconfused in your ideas about me."

"Please, I don't want to argue with you just now."

"We might be safer arguing. Do you understand what I mean?"

"In more ways than you know."

Pfifer suddenly realized that he still held her hand. He let it go and took a step back from her.

"You're a quick study. Is this your new tactic? Come on to me in hopes I'll drop my guard?"

They stood and looked at each other, a certain tension building between them. Rachel's cheeks began to color; Pfifer expected her to become angry, but it passed and when she finally spoke, her voice was calm.

"How do you think Francine will get us into Germany?"

"We'll just have to wait and see. She's a very resourceful woman, and the favors people owe her are beyond accounting."

"Why don't we just go across normally? You don't think anyone could have followed us this far, do you?"

"Someone followed us to Carl Burge."

"You said Carl was a known operative. Francine said specifically that 'your people' had talked to him. That doesn't mean that we were followed from Rotterdam."

"You could be right, but it's always safer to assume the worst, and not just the easy or convenient."

"Is that another of your ground rules?"

"Yes."

"But no one knew we were headed for Amsterdam. Anyone from the freighter would have had to have a car waiting to follow us. That isn't likely, is it?"

"Except for one thing. You knew we would be heading for Amsterdam."

Suddenly, Rachel's anger began to get away from her.

"Who do you think I'm working for, the kidnappers? Are you crazy?"

"No, unfortunately for you I'm not. First of all, I happen to know how difficult it is to get a weapon of any kind through customs these days. You didn't seem to have a bit of trouble, did you?"

"For your information, I bought the gun after I got through customs. You've guessed I'm involved with the CIA, but you're off base thinking . . ."

Rachel was interrupted by the sound of a heavy truck. It seemed to stop in back of the tavern. Pfifer moved to the window to take a look.

He could not see the truck clearly; it was obscured by the trees. But he could make out its general outline. As he strained to see in the dim light he sensed Rachel close to him.

"What is it?" she asked.

"It looks like a semi: a tractor-trailer rig. If I had to make a guess, I'd say we're about to be shipped into Germany. That will be a first—for me, anyway."

Pfifer glanced down at Rachel. She looked suddenly unsure, subdued.

"It'll be okay," he said, wondering why he felt the need to buoy her spirits.

"It's not that," she said.

"What is it then?"

"Will you answer a question for me, without pulling any punches, or holding anything back?"

Pfifer hesitated before he answered her, surprised by her sudden shedding of armor, the genuine, plaintive tone in her voice and in her expression.

"I'd rather have no answer than a lie," she said softly.

"Then ask your question. If I answer it, it will be the truth, as I know it."

"Do you believe Martin is still alive?"

Pfifer took a deep breath. Beneath it all, there was one truth about Rachel. She cared for her brother. What she did she did because of that. He hoped the answer he was about to give her was indeed the truth.

"I believe he is, Rachel. I can't tell you exactly why, but my instinct tells me that this Juan is too cautious to have thrown away your brother's life. It's too valuable a bargaining chip. It wouldn't make any sense. Not yet."

Rachel fell against him gently. Then, quickly, she pulled back from him and turned away. Just as she did, Francine knocked at the door.

"We need to move quickly now," Francine said as she entered. "The driver is far off his normal route."

Francine carried a denim jacket in her hand. She gave it to Rachel, then, after a knowing look at Rachel's expression, she looked at Pfifer and gave him a stern and slightly sly glance.

"It may be somewhat cold, but it will be fine," she said.

"You're a devious woman, Francine," Pfifer said, "but lead on."

They followed Francine out of the room and down a second set of stairs that led to the rear of the tavern. When they reached the truck, the driver had already opened the double loading doors at the rear of the trailer. He was nowhere to be seen, but they could hear him working from somewhere in the midst of the trailer. The abrupt screech of nails being pulled from wood was clearly audible from within.

"Ja, this one should do the trick, Francy," the driver called from the shadows.

"Good, but hurry now. John, perhaps you could lend a hand?"

"Right," Pfifer answered and jumped up into the trailer.

The trailer was loaded with wood crates. None of the markings were easily readable in the dim light, but Pfifer recognized much of the load as machinery. He could not tell exactly what kind, other than it was heavy and smelled of oil and cosmoline. He climbed over the tops of the crates to the middle of the trailer, where he reached the driver.

The crate the driver had selected for them was about three feet wide and six feet long. Its top had been carefully removed and put to one side as the driver worked at emptying its contents.

"You pull this lot out, I hide it up forward," the driver said.

Immediately Pfifer began to grope in the crate and lift the heavy cast-iron pieces out. They were cold and greasy to the touch.

"What is this stuff, anyway?" he asked.

"Used machinery, mostly obsolete."

"That's appropriate."

"What?"

"Never mind."

Quickly the crate was empty. Pfifer turned and began to make his way out of the trailer. The driver followed him. When they reached the double doors they stopped. Francine and Rachel looked up at them from the ground.

"We're about ready," the driver said to Francine.

"I'll get the blanket and a light," Francine said and walked briskly back to the tavern. Rachel stood alone in the darkness for a few seconds, then stepped closer to the end of the trailer.

"You can climb in here if you want," Pfifer said.

"Sure."

Pfifer knelt and offered her his hand. She took it and let him help her up. Once inside, she stood beside him.

"Give your eyes a minute to adjust to the darkness before you try and go forward."

"Good idea."

Francine returned and handed up a thick blanket and a flashlight. Pfifer took them and then motioned for Rachel to follow him.

"Stay close, and watch your step."

The three of them went forward. Pfifer, Rachel, and the driver. When they reached the crate Pfifer folded the blanket into the bottom of the crate and stepped in. As he laid down Rachel hesitated.

"There's not much room," she said.

"There's enough."

"Go on now, missy. We're short on time. He'll behave himself," the driver urged.

Pfifer heard Rachel exhale a long nervous breath, then she stepped into the crate and laid down beside him. She had barely settled into position when the driver dropped the lid of the crate in place and began to nail it down. It was immediately pitch-dark in the crate. The hammering shook splinters and dust down on them and the blows rang in their ears. Then, with one final tap, the job was done. They listened as the driver climbed away from them and slammed the trailer doors shut.

They lay facing each other. Pfifer could feel Rachel's warm breath on his face, but he could not see her in the total darkness.

"Are you comfortable?" he asked.

"For now. How long do you think we will be in here?"

"It may be a couple of hours. The driver will have to backtrack for a distance so he can drive across the German border at his usual place. Once in Germany, he'll have to be careful where he stops and opens up. Sorry."

The truck's engine started. As it jerked forward the crates around them creaked and moved. Pfifer felt Rachel tense.

"Will we be safe in here?" she asked.

"We'll be safe enough, just relax. Try and sleep."

"Not likely."

"Suit yourself."

"Where exactly are we going, once we're in Germany?"

"Hamburg."

"That's the freighter's next destination?"

"Yes."

They listened to the noises in the trailer as the driver built up speed. The load shifted perceptibly each time he gained a higher gear. In a few minutes, though, the rig attained its cruising speed and everything stabilized. Soon, Pfifer sensed Rachel beginning to relax.

"Do you have a plan?" she asked.

Pfifer could not think of any reason not to tell her, at least within limits, what he had in mind. In fact, it might keep her calmer if she knew what to expect in the next few hours. He collected his thoughts carefully before he began.

"The first thing we'll need to do is find a cobbler."

"A what?"

"Someone to forge us new walking-around papers. You'll be in the country illegally, remember. No stamp on your passport."

"Oh."

"Then we'll find the nearest place we can catch a train to Hamburg. I'll hand you over to the right people, and then you'll be safe again."

Rachel shifted her position. She brushed against him as she did.

"Why don't you turn your back to me. It will give you more room," he suggested.

"Sorry, of course."

"Is that better?" he asked when she completed her turn.

"Put your arm around me. I'm cold."

Pfifer felt her reach back and take his arm. He chose not to resist her as she brought it around herself firmly. Then, for a long time, they lay quietly beside each other listening to the road noise, the steady hum of the tires on pavement, and the strained note of the truck's diesel engine. There was no way to know where they were or even in what direction they were headed. Neither could, or would, sleep.

"What will happen to me?" Rachel asked, breaking the silence.

"It's hard to say. You're not the usual case, are you?"

"Because of my father?"

"Exactly."

"How much do you know about my father?"

"A successful man. Up from nothing after the war. Donates a bunch of money to a worthy cause. A Company man. That's about all."

"You don't know the first thing about him, I can see that."

"He plays a high-risk game. I know that. I suspect you and your brother are being groomed to take his place when the time comes."

Rachel sighed.

"What's wrong?"

"It all seems so complicated all of a sudden. Yesterday it wasn't."

"Maybe you're just beginning to understand a few things. It's just not a clear-cut business. But one thing is certain—it will destroy you and it will destroy those around you, eventually."

"I wish I could tell you. Then you would understand. My father is a very brave man."

"I don't doubt that he is. But look at the price he's paying for it. Look at what he stands to lose, because of his noble bravery, if that's what it is; everything he loves."

Rachel stirred, in doing so she tightened her grip on Pfifer's arm.

"I know you won't talk about yourself, and I understand why, but answer this for me. If you feel the way you say you do, why do you continue to do what you do? You are obviously an agent of experience—why couldn't you just drop out of sight, retire? You must have other friends like Francine that could help you. Maybe friends that the Agency doesn't know about?"

It sounded so simple. It was the sort of question he would expect her to ask, though. She didn't know yet exactly who she was working for, or the terms of her employment. He wondered if she would believe him if he told her. Probably not. How could he expect her to? He wouldn't have believed it himself in the beginning. How could he tell her that this was a game that could only have one ultimate ending?

"Let me just say this, Rachel. It's hard to know for sure what the Agency knows and what it doesn't. It's a bit like a house of mirrors—when you see something, you can't really tell if it's real or not, not until it's too late. You don't make assumptions if you can help it."

"You're saying you're afraid to quit, aren't you?"

"I suppose so."

"Then why did you come after me on the wharf? Why did you take the chance? You could have just stayed where you were; I wouldn't have seen you. You would have been clear. Why did you take the chance?"

The truck began to slow.

"Be quiet for a few minutes. We may be getting close to the border."

Rachel tensed in his arms as the truck came to a full stop. They could hear voices, and the intermittent bark of a dog.

"Be very quiet now, no matter what happens," Pfifer said.

No sooner had Pfifer spoken than someone worked the latches on the trailer doors. As they creaked open, a pale light filtered into the crate through the cracks in its planking. Pfifer could clearly see Rachel next to him. She looked back at him, her eyes slightly wide with apprehension.

Suddenly, a stronger beam of light snapped on and began to probe the darkness in the trailer. Thin stripes of light penetrated the crate from time to time as the search continued. Pfifer began to grow uneasy. If they were discovered, both he and Rachel would be the guests of the German government for quite some time. George Long would be in no position to help them. He might, in fact, make matters worse. What if he charged Pfifer with kidnapping Rachel, to halve his loses, so to speak? That would be Long's style and it would probably work.

The light veered away and the trailer became dark again. Then there were more voices, a mild argument, the scrape and grunt of someone climbing into the trailer. Pfifer tensed involuntarily. Whoever was in charge wanted a more thorough look, it seemed. Hopefully, it would not be too thorough. Pfifer began to worry about the machinery parts they had displaced. Where had the driver hidden them? Would they be noticed? If anything looked suspicious, would they bring on the dog? The dog would find them instantly.

They were near the middle of the trailer. Several rows of crates were between them and the doors, but they clearly heard the footsteps of the man climbing through the cargo. As those footsteps neared, Pfifer suddenly realized that the man would have to pass directly over them to reach the front of the trailer. As a precaution, he put his hand to Rachel's face and closed it over her mouth. She attempted to shake his hand free for an instant, but then the man crossed over their crate and she lay quietly as dust fell into their faces and the weakened planks creaked inches above their heads.

The border guard worked his way as far forward as he could and then called out. There was nothing, he said, nothing at all; they had been mistaken. A second voice from outside the trailer grunted a terse reply. Then come out, and be quick about it, he said.

Immediately the border guard began his return climb. This time he was much faster, almost careless, obviously eager to remove himself from a dangerous situation. As he crossed over Pfifer and Rachel's crate he slipped and came down hard. A plank over their heads cracked in two. The guard's foot protruded partway into the crate.

It must have startled the border guard as much as Pfifer and Rachel, for he swore loudly, drowning out the sudden reflexive movement they made within the crate. The guard, oblivious to them, withdrew his foot and continued out of the trailer. When they heard the loading doors slam shut, Rachel went limp, and, Pfifer exhaled the long breath he had taken and held.

"That was close," Rachel whispered.

"I'd stay quiet for a while yet. We may have to sit here some time before we get moving again."

Rachel shifted her weight as he spoke.

"Stay still," he chided her.

"I'm getting stiff."

"So am I."

According to the luminous dial of Pfifer's watch, they waited half an hour before the truck began to move forward again. At first it was a series of short advances and then finally the rig ground steadily through the gears up to road speed.

"Now can I talk? And most of all, can I move?"

"You can get up and run around if you want."

"Not quite. This crate is getting smaller and smaller all the time. I thought for sure we were going to have that guard in with us as well."

"There would have been surprises all around, wouldn't there?"

Rachel laughed, her nervous tension finding a vent.

"Yes, I'm sure there would have been."

They continued along in their cramped little vessel, now awake and full of apprehension. Rachel's body felt taut to Pfifer, and her breath came shallow. Finally Rachel spoke, her voice betraying her uncertainty.

"We must be in Germany; why doesn't he stop?"

"Relax, he will soon. It has to be a place that is safe. He'll need time to break us out of here."

"Of course."

"Keep something in mind, though. You are now in Germany illegally. Your passport hasn't been stamped. If any official asks to see your papers, you're in big trouble."

"You said you could get new papers."

"Yes, but we still have to make the connection. There's going to be some ground to cover."

Rachel trembled.

"Are you cold?"

"No, scared."

"You're learning."

"Hold me?"

CHAPTER
Fourteen

The sudden silence woke them.

"We're not moving?" Rachel asked.

"No, we've stopped. Lay still."

Pfifer sensed his pulse rate begin to elevate. Soon, they would find out if they had made it safely into Germany, or if they had been neatly delivered to the opposition. It would be a cruel joke if they emerged from the trailer into the wrong hands.

Pfifer strained to reach the Luger at the small of his back.

"What are you doing?"

"Exercising my suspicious nature. Now be quiet. If anything goes wrong in the next few minutes, I want to be able to hear whatever I can."

The Luger was cold and reassuring in his hand. He grasped it firmly and listened. Directly, he heard the doors of the trailer open and the sounds of the driver climbing in.

There was nothing tentative in the driver's approach. He reached them quickly and began to remove the nails from the crate's lid. Pfifer and Rachel lay waiting as the driver's claw hammer bumped and banged above them.

"How are you in there?" the driver called out.

"We're fine," Pfifer answered.

The crate's lid was suddenly pulled away. Pfifer looked up into the driver's face. It was cast in shadows, but Pfifer could tell he was bearded, with deep lines at the corners of his eyes.

"I've bad news for you, I'm afraid," he said.

"Were we followed?" Pfifer asked as he stood carefully and then bent down to help Rachel.

"I'm not sure, but I believe so."

"That is bad news. How far back are they?"

"They laid back, just after I got onto this road. They must know there's no turnoff for the next several kilometers. You'll have to hurry. All you can do is go on foot, cut across the open ground. I'm sorry."

"Where are we?"

"We are a few kilometers north of Rheine, do you know it?"

Pfifer nodded.

"To the northwest there is a small village, Hopsten. You might find help there, transportation."

"Which direction will you be heading in?"

"Back to Rheine, if I'm stopped I'll simply tell them I made a bad turn."

Pfifer shook his head.

"No, continue to Hopsten. Wait for them to catch up to you there, then turn around. If you turn around now, they will know exactly where we are."

"As you say."

The driver led them out of the trailer. Once on the ground he hurriedly closed the trailer's doors and then went briskly to the cab of his tractor. He pulled away without so much as a glance backwards. Pfifer and Rachel watched him move off in the moonlight. The truck's exhaust belched black at each shift. The red running lights glowed brightly in the darkness.

"How do you feel?" Pfifer asked.

"Glad to be out of that crate."

"Well, I hope you're ready for some exercise."

"I get the distinct impression that we aren't going to Hopsten or back to Rheine."

"You guessed right. Now, come on. We have to get clear of the road as quickly as we can."

They trudged off into the darkness, Rachel following him obediently off the road and across an open field. Pfifer kept the pace up relentlessly for several minutes until they had crested a gentle knoll. There he stopped and waited for her to catch up to him. She was breathing heavily when she stopped beside him.

"Look there," he said, pointing to the road.

A dark-colored sedan moved down the road at a rapid speed. Its lights were out. Its driver was taking full use of the bright moonlight and the openness of the road to mask his presence. Pfifer smiled and shook his head.

"I guess that's our answer. Someone is going to great lengths to follow us. Any ideas who?"

"The kidnappers?"

"I don't believe so."

"Who do you think, then?"

"Perhaps someone we aren't aware of. A joker in our deck."

Pfifer turned and looked at Rachel. She looked genuinely troubled. He could tell she still hadn't completely regained her breath. Her chest rose and fell in deep movements beneath her denim jacket.

A joker in the deck, he had said. Now it was no longer just a suspicion—and it was someone other than Carl Burge, who simply wanted out of the game—and it certainly wasn't Francine, who would have far too much to lose if she had broken her rule of confidence. No, it was someone else, and although Pfifer had no idea who, he could only think that this particular joker had something to do with George Long.

But what could he do if for some reason Long had decided to shadow him? What could he do but continue with his assignment. Long would have his reasons. Pfifer only wished he knew what those reasons were.

"I wish you wouldn't look at me that way, it frightens me."

"Let's get moving again," Pfifer said, ignoring her remark. "Pace yourself, though, we have a long walk."

As Pfifer strode off, Rachel fell in behind him without a word. Hopefully, she would leave him with his thoughts. Hopefully, he could make some sense of the growing feeling of malaise that was beginning to come over him. Pfifer rubbed his stomach to ease a sudden discomfort, then slipped the Luger into his belt.

Long would know that Rachel had slipped her traces. He would guess correctly that she would come after him in Rotterdam. Long would have been concerned when Pfifer didn't check in on schedule. It was conceivable that Long would have alerted everyone he could to be on the lookout for them. But if that were true, why hadn't Carl Burge told him to contact Long? Why hadn't Carl told Francine? Didn't Long want him to know he was being watched? What difference did it make? It was confusing, and it didn't help Martin Stein.

Who did it help?

The morning came blue and clear, the German countryside green and pastoral as they walked along a narrow road a pace apart. They walked neither fast nor slow, but at the ponderous tread of the weary. Through the night they had rested only periodically, and now it had begun to show in them both plainly. As they reached a thin stand of oaks, Pfifer stopped, unconsciously pressing his hand against his stomach.

"Are you all right?" Rachel asked.

"Just fine."

"Where are we going, anyway?"

Pfifer studied her coolly. It felt so good just to stand still for a few minutes. A gust of wind rustled the dusty green leaves over their heads; as it died the pain in his abdomen eased.

"It's a very small village. I'd guess it to be no more than three kilometers further."

"Good. I could use some breakfast—and a bath!"

"We'll be able to find both there. And with luck, some papers."

"Your cobbler?"

"Exactly."

"Suddenly, I'm not as tired."

"We'll wait a few more minutes."

Rachel narrowed her eyes and looked at him hard. He marveled at how radiant she looked. All the excitement apparently agreed with her. He wondered how bad he looked to her.

"At least we know we aren't being followed anymore. We haven't seen a vehicle all night. We must have given them the slip, don't you think?" Rachel asked.

"We have for now."

"You need another shave."

"You've taken to looking pretty closely at me, haven't you?"

"What did you expect? After all, we have shared the same shipping crate. How many men can a girl expect to do that with in a lifetime?"

Pfifer shook his head.

"Rachel, I'm not sure how many men there are around that could handle you, shipping crate or no. But that's beside the point."

"And what is the point? When do you plan to tell me how you're going to go about getting my brother off that freight-

er? I'd have a lot more confidence in you, if you told me
what you have in mind."

As Rachel spoke, she stepped closer to him.

"Fair enough. I'm going to mine the freighter."

"You son of a bitch! You do plan to kill my brother!"

Rachel swung at him with all her strength. He caught her
by the wrist, doubled her arm back around her, and pulled
her close to him. She was immobilized, crushed hard up
against his chest.

"Listen, you little fool! Don't be so damned quick to
think the worst of me. I can't get onto the ship, not with
Juan's men crawling all over the thing. I'll have to use the
mines to force them to put him off."

"Oh," she said in a whisper.

"Now, are you ready to go, or what?"

Slowly he released her from his hold. When he could see
her face clearly she was flushed. She swallowed hard and
gave him what he thought was a rather strange look. Then,
unexpectedly, she stepped close to him again and kissed him
gently on the mouth. It surprised him.

"Francine is absolutely right," he said. "I apparently
don't know the first thing about women."

Rachel smiled faintly.

"I'll bet you could learn."

Pfifer turned away from her and began to walk, without
making any comment. Rachel sighed audibly and started
after him.

It was a sleepy little village; a mere crossroads in the midst
of the farmlands. Humble little cottages were clustered on
its outskirts, and only a few shops and a single inn occupied
the main intersection. Pfifer and Rachel found their way to
that inn and sat under its blue canvas awning at a table
adjacent to the street. All about them white flowers bloomed
from planters and pots. Only occasionally did someone pass
by on the walk. In the distance Pfifer could see the spire of

a stone church. The pervading silence surrounded them as they sat and waited for service.

"We must be their first customers of the day," Rachel said, fidgeting in her chair.

"Be patient. If my memory serves me correctly, the breakfast will be worth the wait."

"This 'cobbler,' is he near here?"

"Just around the corner. We'll see him right after we eat."

"Great, then we just have to get to a train, or will you want to rent another car?"

"No, the train."

Just then a portly waitress came out of the inn and approached them. She smiled as she stopped at their table and glanced from Pfifer to Rachel and back again. Pfifer acknowledged her cordial greeting and ordered for both of them. She smiled again, pirouetted, and then left them to their conversation.

"You speak German beautifully. Like a native."

"I thought you said you didn't speak the language?"

"Still testing me, aren't you? I don't speak German, but that doesn't mean I can't tell how comfortable you are speaking it. And besides, she certainly didn't have any trouble understanding you. By the way, what did you order? Weiss something?"

"Weisswurst, spiced sausage and veal. You'll eat it with sweet mustard, and you'll like it."

Rachel looked doubtful.

"Trust me, just this once."

"You make it difficult. I'm not a great fan of sausage."

"Ah, a flaw in your character?"

A car passed by slowly. It dampened Pfifer's meager attempt at levity. It was a dark gray sedan, two men in dark suits occupied its front seats. Pfifer tried not to stare at it. Rachel was quick to catch his change of mood.

"Problem?"

"It's always a possibility, but the worst thing we could do would be to bolt. Just relax."

"Do you ever relax?"

"Every now and then, and it gets me in trouble every time."

Breakfast arrived.

The waitress was all smiles and agility as she placed the various plates and condiments on the table before them. Pfifer wondered if their slightly wrinkled clothes and his now noticeable stubble had peaked her interest. If so, he guessed that they would probably be the topic of her gossip for the next several weeks. But that was no problem. Hopefully, in a few hours they would be on their way.

The waitress left them. Pfifer turned his attention to his sausages, but after a few bites he pushed his plate away.

"That's a terrible waste. These are delicious," Rachel said between mouthfuls.

"I'm glad you like them."

Rachel, in good spirits, looked up often to take in her surroundings, or look at Pfifer. He noticed the brightness in her eyes, and the high color in her cheeks. As he did, a curious longing stirred within him in surges, only to be pushed back again each time his thoughts returned to what lay ahead, each time the realities closed in around him.

They were still exposed. They might have evaded their immediate pursuers, but the chase was far from over, and Pfifer knew it.

If he were alone, he could virtually disappear, become a peasant, or any number of equally invisible characters. He could make himself almost impossible to follow. With Rachel, it was much more difficult. His options were limited, his flexibility reduced, the risk increased. Their best bet would be to keep moving, but it was just that, a bet. They would need luck. And luck was capricious at best.

When they had finished, the waitress came and took away

their dishes. Pfifer folded a few marks under an ashtray and then stood. Rachel stood with him.

"Let's go," Pfifer said, pushing his chair to one side.

The sun was high and bright when they stepped out onto the street. The air was still fresh and cool from the long night. Rachel took Pfifer's arm as they walked and a faint smile came naturally to her face. She followed his lead without question as he picked his way between buildings and stone walls.

"This is a beautiful place," she said.

"Yes, I suppose it is," he answered.

"How much farther?"

"We're here."

Pfifer stopped at the door of a shop. It appeared quite closed, but the door opened easily to his touch. As they entered a buzzer sounded from somewhere in the back of the building. The immediate shuffle of footsteps accompanied its sudden ring.

It was a simple print shop, dusty, cluttered, disorganized. The owner of the shop, when he approached, was a stooped little man, near seventy, with stained apron and eternally black hands. He feigned not to know Pfifer for a few brief moments.

"You can relax, Hans. She is a fellow wanderer, and she is my friend."

"Then I approve, but since when have you taken up with Jewish women?"

"Recently."

"Perhaps you will benefit?"

"That's a compliment for you, Rachel. If Hans would consent to speak in English, you would have heard it for yourself."

"I've already made up my mind to like this man, now he's made it easy," Rachel said warmly.

"Ah, a girl with some sensitivity," Hans said and winked boldly.

"Enough of that, old friend. I need you to exercise some of your artistry. The usual articles."

Pfifer pulled a wad of marks from his pocket and began to count. Hans watched him with a wry grin. Unconsciously, he wiped his hands on his apron as Pfifer counted.

"The same price?"

"Yes, and the same quality. How soon do you need them?"

"This morning."

"I see, and what nationality are you this time?"

"German; it's the easiest. Rachel, of course, will have to be English. When can you have them ready?"

"Three hours from now, but first I need photos."

"Fine, and afterward, if we could use your quarters to freshen up?"

"My house is your house as always."

Hans turned abruptly and led the way for them to the rear of the shop. Rachel followed close behind Pfifer as they went deeper into the jumbled shadows.

CHAPTER
Fifteen

Hans's living quarters consisted of one fairly large room directly over his shop. There was a toilet and tub complete with makeshift shower nozzle curtained off in one corner. The remaining space was open. A stairwell covered by a trapdoor dropped from the middle of the room leading to the shop. Around it, a bed, an old porcelain stove, a rough plank table, a small desk with a telephone, and a mismatched collection of chairs that were arranged in a semblance of order. It was all slightly dusty, and the smell of printer's ink permeated everything. It was just as Pfifer had remembered it: not glamorous, but apparently secure.

Pfifer sat at the desk in an old oak swivel chair, his hand resting on the receiver of Hans's telephone. He could hear the steady rush of Rachel's shower water as he looked out a nearby window at the village, now peaceful in the midmorning lull. Tentatively, he lifted the receiver to his ear, heard the steady drone of the dial tone, then replaced it.

It was a strong temptation he resisted; the temptation to

call Long and tell him where he was and bring him up to date. It was a strong urge to simply call in the cavalry, have them come to him and take Rachel off of his hands. But he dared not do it. Hans had one of the very few phones in the village. The ease with which it could be monitored precluded him from using it at all. The risk would just be too great.

At that moment, Rachel shut off the shower. Pfifer heard the swish of the plastic shower curtain being pushed open and soft footfalls as she stepped out of the tub.

Quickly, he picked up the receiver again, unscrewed the mouthpiece, removed the element inside and slipped it into his pocket. Then, just as he dropped the receiver back into its cradle, Rachel pushed aside the heavy partitioning curtain and stepped into the room.

"I suppose you've just called in?" Rachel asked, pulling her large blue towel more modestly around herself.

"No, as a matter of fact, I've decided to wait until we reach Hamburg." Pfifer paused and looked directly at Rachel. Beads of water tracked delicately down her legs. Her dark hair fell in damp ringlets over her shoulders, making them look starkly pale in contrast. "You look refreshed," he finally said, thinking things of an entirely different nature.

"Yes," Rachel said, coloring slightly, "you should try it yourself."

"Perhaps I will."

"Would you trust me not to run away, or send smoke signals to the enemy camp, or some other backhanded thing?"

Pfifer laughed.

"Why not?"

Rachel's eyes narrowed. There was a slight tilt to her head as she looked at him.

"Excuse me," Pfifer said as he moved past her and behind the curtain.

*   *   *

When Pfifer emerged from his shower, he saw Rachel sitting in the middle of Hans's bed. She had dressed. She sat with her knees pulled up in front of her, arms clasped around them. She frowned as their eyes met.

"You still don't trust me, do you?" she asked.

"What makes you say that?" Pfifer asked as he adjusted the position of the Luger in his belt.

"The door downstairs is locked. The telephone is dead."

"It never hurts to take precautions. You must know that by now."

"Damn you," she said softly.

"That probably happened a long time ago, Rachel."

"What now?" she asked coldly.

"Hans should have our papers ready soon. When he finishes, we'll find some transportation to the nearest train station."

"What happens in Hamburg?"

"We'll have to wait and see."

They heard the door open at the foot of the stairwell, and then the jangle of keys.

"Hello, hello?" Hans called out.

"Come on up," Pfifer said.

The stooped old printer came slowly up the stairs. When he reached the top he looked at Rachel and smiled.

"Ah, it has been a long time since I've had such a pretty girl in my bed."

Rachel laughed politely. Hans turned to Pfifer.

"Your papers are ready. You would want to leave immediately?"

"Yes, for the obvious reason," Pfifer answered.

Hans's expression darkened. He raised an admonishing finger to Pfifer's face.

"If you have brought trouble to my door, I shall not appreciate it," he said.

"Hopefully we haven't, but we do need to be on our way. Do you know someone who could take us to the train?"

Hans lowered his hand slowly and thought.

"I might know someone, but it will cost you money."

"That goes without saying."

"Very well then, I'll make a call. Perhaps it is time for me to expand my business a little."

Pfifer reached into his pocket and brought out the pilfered element to the telephone. He tossed it casually to Hans.

"You'll need this," he said. "And be as discreet as you can with what you say over the phone."

Hans hefted the element in his hand, looked hard at Rachel, and then back at Pfifer.

"You will wait for me downstairs," he said, his tone now charmless and cold.

"As you wish," Pfifer said and nodded to Rachel.

Rachel climbed out of the bed and followed Pfifer down the stairs. When they reached the bottom, Pfifer closed the door behind them and then led the way through the shadows to a front window. Quickly, he glanced outside at the empty street and then turned towards her.

"I think we've fallen from Hans's good graces," Rachel said, attempting a smile.

"He walks a fine line. You'll meet a lot of people just like him, if you stay in this business."

"Do you trust him?"

"Only so far as I understand his motivation."

"What is his motivation?"

"Money, and staying alive. Hopefully not in that specific order."

"That's not a very reassuring thing to say."

"It wasn't meant to be."

A moment of silence passed before they heard Hans begin to descend the stairs. They listened as he came down them at his ponderous cadence: one step at a time, each seemingly slower than the one preceding it.

"It is arranged," he said as he joined them at the window. "Now if you would care to inspect my work, you have only a half hour before you will be picked up."

"Of course," Pfifer said.

Hans took them to the back of the shop. Their papers lay under a bright lamp on a table. Pfifer picked them up and looked at them carefully.

"Excellent work, as always," he said. "We'll want the negatives to our photographs as well, as I am sure you have anticipated."

"My usual procedure."

"Where are we to be picked up?"

"There's a church down the street. An alley runs behind it. You will see the place to wait in safety. A bread van will pass slowly, its rear doors will be open. Just get in and close the doors. The driver will know where to take you. There is no need to speak to him or show yourselves. In fact, I suggest that you do not."

As the old man spoke, he withdrew curled photographic negatives from a drawer. He held them to the light for Pfifer to see and then placed them in a metal dish on the table. Producing a match from his apron pocket, he struck it and laid it against the film. Immediately the negatives burst into flames and reduced themselves to a charred smudge in the bottom of the dish.

"I believe we understand," Pfifer said as he watched the last of the flames die out.

"You will pay me now for this little extra service. Then you can take your papers and go."

Pfifer and Rachel found the old church with little trouble, and stepped out of sight into an alcove built in its rear wall. From the alcove they could see the length of a cobblestoned alley bordered by an alternation of old buildings and vine-covered walls. A stream of drainage water coursed between the moss-covered pavement stones at their feet as if outlining the cut of a jigsaw puzzle. They waited there quietly, each lost in his own thoughts.

Rachel was reticent. She had not spoken to Pfifer since

they had left the print shop. She seemed to be making an effort not to look at him, not to meet his gaze directly. Impassively she stared at the encrusted wall that was opposite them across the alley. Pfifer could sense a tenseness in her, a growing anxiety. He was about to speak to her and at least make an attempt to try to relax her, just as the sound of a truck echoed up the alley.

"Stay well back until the truck has passed," Pfifer warned. "If this is our ride, he's early."

Rachel glanced nervously at Pfifer, then took a step back. In a few seconds the truck went by. It was a flatbed, running empty. When it was gone the silence descended on them again.

Pfifer looked at his watch and then at Rachel.

"Are you all right?" he asked.

"Fine," she answered stiffly.

"Be patient, they'll be along in a minute."

Rachel nodded, then continued staring straight ahead.

The minutes went slowly by. From somewhere down the way they heard the squeak of a clothesline pulley. Erratically at first, then methodically, every few seconds the pulley squeaked.

"Life goes on, right?" Pfifer asked.

"I suppose so," Rachel answered, glancing at him.

The sound of another engine cut them short. Pfifer looked at his watch, then back at Rachel. He nodded. The truck came slowly, tentatively; the driver obviously looking for something.

"This could be our boy. Are you ready?"

The bread truck was a chalky white. Its red lettering was faded and chipped. Dents and scratches adorned it. Tediously it grumbled by them. Pfifer got a brief glimpse of the dark-skinned driver as it passed.

The right-hand rear door was open but the left door was shut, blocking their view into the back of the truck. Rachel started forward. Pfifer checked her with a strong grip on her arm.

"What's wrong?"

"Quiet. Wait."

The truck moved fifty yards past the church, then it stopped. The driver revved his engine impatiently. Pfifer peered around the corner of the alcove to take a look.

The right side of the truck seemed to be filled with loaves of bread on racks. Everything looked normal enough, but Pfifer stayed where he was. Casually he pulled the Luger from his belt and checked its clip. Rachel caught her breath as he did.

The bread truck idled sedately, its low exhaust note reverberating down the alley. Pfifer continued to wait. Rachel fidgeted nervously behind him.

He had almost convinced himself he was being overcautious, when the left door of the truck began to open and two men stepped out. One carried a shotgun, the other clutched a revolver. Both were dressed in dark suits.

Pfifer looked at Rachel for a moment, then carefully around the inside of the alcove. A heavy timber door was at its rear, probably leading into the church, but it had been solid to his touch when he had tried it earlier. It would take far too much time to break it down at this point. Pfifer swore to himself and then pulled Rachel behind him.

"Get down low. Stay quiet and don't move," he said, his voice cold and deliberate.

Rachel complied immediately. Pfifer raised the Luger to the ready and waited.

He would have to step out into the alley. He had no choice. If the man with the shotgun fired into the alcove, Rachel would certainly be struck by its spray of shot. There would be no escape from it.

Carefully, Pfifer listened for their footsteps, but the sound of the truck's engine muffled them. He took a deep breath, closed his eyes for an instant, opened them, then stepped forward. His mind was blank, imageless. On his face he wore a smile, a smile to greet the devil with.

It took two quick, clean shots from the Luger. Two hiss thumps, and the men crumpled. Their unfired weapons clattered to the smooth cold stones beside them as they fell. The driver, apparently watching in his mirror, accelerated violently away, disgorging his load of bread and racks as he went.

Sensing Rachel at his side, Pfifer lowered the Luger and looked at her. She was white, eyes wide, mouth slightly open. Pfifer knew the look. She did not know whether to scream or cry. The sudden, and ultimate, realization, the nearness of death, had paralyzed her.

"We must move quickly now," he told her and took her arm.

Rachel froze. The look she gave him told him she was as afraid of him now as the lifeless forms before her. She tried to speak but no words came. Pfifer began to walk. He pulled her along stiffly with him. Gradually she moved with less reluctance.

He replaced the Luger at the small of his back and looked circumspectly about them. Then, suddenly, they heard screaming behind them. It carried clearly down the alley, high-pitched and hysterical. Quickly Pfifer turned them into the first narrow passageway that looked like it might take them back to the main street.

"My God," Rachel whispered.

"There is no God, Rachel. Not anymore."

Rachel sobbed.

"You'd better get hold of yourself. Nothing attracts more attention than a crying woman."

"You bastard. You cold-blooded bastard."

"Good, get angry. Anger, courage, sometimes one is as good as the other."

They walked between the gray stone walls, a blue stripe

of sky over their heads. By the time they emerged onto the street, Rachel had composed herself, at least on the surface.

"Where are we going?" she asked hoarsely.

"Back to our friendly printer for a refund and some answers."

The door to the old man's print shop was unlocked and slightly ajar. Before Pfifer entered he pressed Rachel against the wall and fixed her with a stare.

"Don't move," he whispered and then pushed the print shop door open.

In the back of his shop, the old man sat stiffly in his chair, behind his counter, and stared at Pfifer blankly. His face looked unnaturally pale in the poor light, his eyes unblinking. Pfifer took a step forward then stopped.

"Rachel, come in and close the door behind you."

In seconds Rachel was by his side.

"Oh, no," she whispered.

"Whoever killed him hates Jews," Pfifer said, staring at the ghastly spectacle before him. "That's the only reason I can think of for doing this, when they could have simply bought whatever information they wanted from him."

Rachel looked at him, unable to speak, only able to tremble. When Pfifer spoke again his voice was cold.

"If I remember correctly, he has an old Volkswagen he keeps parked behind the shop. I don't think he'll mind if we use it."

Pfifer and Rachel sat across from each other in a private compartment. The green countryside flashed unnoticed past their window, as the train rocked gently on the rails. Rachel sat with her arms folded tightly in front of her, eyes cast downward. The fear had ebbed, leaving fatigue behind. Pfifer studied her flaccid expression with some empathy.

"Feeling better?" he asked.

Rachel shook her head.

"You're all right now. Soon, you'll be in Hamburg. I'll get you to the agency there. You'll be safe."

Rachel looked up and then out the window, avoiding his eyes.

"It's not so glamorous when you get right down to it, is it?" he asked.

"No," she answered softly.

"Maybe it's a good thing you found out early. Maybe you can get clear of it, before it owns you."

"And does it own you?"

She turned and looked at him as she asked the question. Pfifer paused before he answered.

"I'm afraid so," he finally said.

"They would have killed us, wouldn't they?"

"Possibly."

"Probably."

Pfifer made a gesture with his hands, palms open.

"Who were they?" Rachel asked.

"That's a very good question. I was wondering if you knew the answer."

"Me? Why do you think I might know?"

"You said you had friends in Amsterdam. Maybe you found a way to contact them? It wouldn't have been easy for you, but you could have done it. Some signal or other to someone along the way? You've been trying to disable me from the beginning. You can't deny that."

"I swear I had nothing to do with it! You have to believe me. The friends I have in Amsterdam are old family friends of my father's. They didn't even know I was coming." Rachel spoke in a nearly desperate tone of voice.

"It doesn't really matter at this point, I suppose."

"Yes, it does matter." Rachel leaned forward to look directly into Pfifer's face. "I didn't set you up."

"If not you, who then?"

"What about Hans? You said yourself he walked a narrow line. Is that how you put it? Perhaps he saw a chance at a profit? What about the men you saw drive past us when we were at breakfast? Maybe they found your 'cobbler'? Maybe they knew about him already, maybe they had done business with him before, just like you have, and were just checking him out. They knew we were in the area. Poor Hans, perhaps he just asked too high a price for his information and was killed for it.''

Pfifer paused for a moment to think. She was right, there were plenty of other possibilities to consider, far more probable, far more consistent. And the fact remained, she had been in just as much danger as he had been in that alley. He just didn't like the way it was beginning to look.

"All right."

"All right, what?" Rachel prompted him.

"So maybe you had nothing to do with it."

"That's a start."

"It doesn't help your brother."

"My brother doesn't have much of a chance now, does he?"

"He didn't have much of a chance to begin with. So his situation isn't significantly different."

Rachel winced. Pfifer immediately regretted the bluntness of his words.

"I do have a plan," he said quickly. "I know where that ship is going, and, as long as I'm not delayed anymore, I still have a shot at it. Your brother still has a chance."

"Martin's dead by now."

"Maybe not. It depends on what he really knows about your father. It depends on how interesting his story is to them. It also depends on how safe they think they are."

"Nice try, but no sale."

Rachel sagged back into her seat. A look of hopelessness came over her. She looked at him steadily, sadly.

"I guess I really blew it," she said.

Pfifer met her gaze. She'd had some bad coaching, he thought. If Joe Bryant had known as much about her as he should have, he should have been able to guess what she might do. If she was the type that tended toward tilting at windmills, he should have withheld his assumptions about Pfifer and his intentions, whether he was right or not in them. Yes, it was Joe's fault, more than anyone's. But Rachel probably wouldn't buy that either. She'd be too loyal to the old hound. Too loyal, and too blinded by that loyalty.

The train suddenly began to slow. Pfifer leaned toward the window so he could see as far ahead as possible.

"We're coming into a station," he said.

"I really thought I was dead. Do you realize that? I thought my life was coming to an end right there in that alley. Do you know what I was thinking about?"

Pfifer looked back at her.

"I wasn't thinking about Martin, or about my father, or about anything else. I was thinking about myself, about what I was going to miss. I feel guilty about it, but it's true. I didn't give a damn about anything or anyone at that instant, just myself."

"Are you shocked to find out you're human? Don't you think we all think along the same lines in that situation? None of us is very noble when our survival is on the line. Some approach the problem differently, Rachel, but the goal is the same. We all just want to keep on living."

"You weren't afraid."

"The hell I wasn't."

"You looked perfectly relaxed, in control of yourself. You made me ashamed of the way I was feeling."

Pfifer shook his head.

"Don't make a hero out of me. It would just be another mistake."

The train came to a complete stop. Pfifer looked out the window and watched the small crowd gather on the landing. They seemed to be eager, but orderly. Germans, Pfifer thought. Some things stayed the same.

He settled back into his seat. He couldn't help but notice Rachel watching him intently.

"If you stopped right now, if you threw in the towel at this point, I wouldn't think any less of you," she said suddenly.

"I would stop, if I could," Pfifer snapped back at her, his patience wearing thin. "I don't have that option, so don't get the wrong idea. I'm not doing this for you."

"Well, I won't give you any more trouble. That's a promise. I'll go along quietly when we get to Hamburg. Just tell me what you want me to do."

There was a note of sincerity in her voice. Pfifer hoped what she said was true. He would be glad to have her off his hands, safe. Mostly he wanted her safe.

The train began to move again. There was a mild series of jerks as the slack in the couplings was taken up.

"If you say so. When we get into the main station in Hamburg, I'll make a call and set up a meeting. They'll take you in, probably to a safe house. Don't be surprised if you are kept there until all of this is over."

"Fine."

They fell silent, but continued to stare at each other from across the compartment, evenly, directly. Pfifer hoped that she had told him the truth.

She made a pretty picture, he had to admit. Francine's makeup was long since gone, and she was more than just a little rumpled, but the clearness in her eyes and the color in her cheeks was genuine. She had made a crossing of sorts. Something within her that had perhaps been there all along, but dormant, had come to the surface, forced its way free. The transformation surprised him.

"Is there something wrong?" Rachel asked. "You're staring at me in a peculiar way."

"No, nothing's wrong."

Rachel smiled at him, then let her head fall back against the cushion of her seat.

"Suddenly, I'm very tired. I think I'll try and get some sleep."

"That sounds like a good idea. I'll wake you before we get into Hamburg."

Rachel nodded and then closed her eyes. Pfifer watched as she quickly drifted off, the smile fading from her face, replaced with the expressionless mask of oblivion. He continued to look at her until he was certain she was asleep, then he settled back uncomfortably and closed his own eyes.

He tried to relax, but the rhythmic, metallic throb of the wheels and rails dominated his consciousness, forbidding sleep. After a brief and fruitless attempt, he opened his eyes and looked out on the broad German plains slipping past beyond the compartment window.

Hamburg would bring safety for Rachel and greater danger for himself. It was that danger he must now think about, not sleep. That danger, and what would need to take place if either he or Martin Stein were to survive.

CHAPTER
Sixteen

Martin Stein looked to the porthole, but it was blackened and he could not see. He could feel the gentle roll of the freighter as it beat forward, and his mind was clear enough to remember where he was. But the fear had a dull edge to it. He could feel its presence, but he was too tired to react to it, too numbed.

Suddenly the cabin door opened and two men entered, both slightly familiar to him, but of course, he had only seen them through the blurred veil of delirium. He knew them and he feared them, but he did not know who they were.

One, the doctor, approached and felt his wrist.

"Martin," the doctor asked softly, "can you speak?"

"Yes," Martin barely whispered.

Immediately the second man stepped forward and pushed the doctor rudely out of the way. He leaned close, his dark bearded face directly in front of Martin's.

"My name is Juan. Can you understand me, Martin?"

"Juan, yes . . ."

"Very good. Now listen very closely, my young friend, for what I am about to ask you will mean the difference between living and dying."

Martin tried to move, but his wrists and legs were bound to the metal framework of his bunk.

"I see you have some strength left," Juan said, starting to smile. "Good, use that strength to save yourself and answer my questions."

Martin tried to spit at Juan, but his mouth was too dry. As he tried, Juan slapped his head viciously to the side and swore.

"Don't be stupid! I can kill you at this instant if I wish. Who would know? Who would care?"

Martin slowly looked back at Juan, his vision now partially blurred. The doctor stepped forward and took his pulse once again.

"Be careful," the doctor warned.

"Our young friend is the one that should be careful," Juan snapped and then turned back to Martin. "Martin, do you want to live?"

"Yes."

"Then tell me why I should not kill you? Tell me what you can trade for your life?"

Juan turned to the doctor. "The drugs," he said.

"You will kill him!"

"Only if he forces me to."

Suddenly, Martin felt the cold point of pain pierce him, and then slowly the room began to darken and he began to drift away from them. Further, further, but not totally.

"Martin," Juan asked, now friendlier. "What would you have to trade for your life? Tell me about your father, Martin. Do you like him?"

"No," Martin heard himself say.

"Why not, Martin? Tell me why not."

"He has betrayed me, he has betrayed them . . ."

"Who, Martin? Who has he betrayed?"

"I can't . . . I can't . . . the network . . ."

Martin Stein was beyond feeling the rude thrust of the stainless steel needle into his veins. He was beyond comprehension in any rational sense. There was only faint light, and dull shadow, and a blur of distant movement about him, none of which he understood.

But there was a voice, a kind and soothing voice that the remnants of his conscious mind, the few spheres not burned to oblivion as of yet, continued to tune to. The tone of the voice questioned him, for the words had ceased to have meaning. The tone of the voice called to him reassuringly but then raised demons from the shadows of his memories.

Horribly and suddenly the demons rose. The sound of jackboots, the flutter of a hated banner. Blood red, black, white, the hooks of a twisted cross. Hands raised to a passing Satan. Flashes of white flame. Legions of marching ghosts.

He saw a face before him. Father. But in the company of demons? No. How could that be? The truth must be perverted. The scene not real but nightmare. Still, the face of his father persists. The demons circle about him, he is in their company.

He had betrayed his father now, just as his father had betrayed him, but there should be peace. Where was the peace now that the scales had been balanced? Was it because now there would be more dying? The innocent along with the guilty? He knew why he had betrayed his father, but suddenly, in perhaps his final, brief moment of lucid thought, he realized his mistake, he realized what horror that betrayal would bring to others, that the pain would not stop, that it would only spread.

Martin wrenched his body at the sound of a hysterical scream, piercing, consuming, his own.

Now only darkness. The demon pictures fade.

*   *   *

The *Baltic Merchant* lay still, held fast to the Hamburg quay. Juan and Lubelski stood on the now-deserted bridge. Juan held the photographs of his two slain men in his hands. As he looked at their blank and lifeless expressions, Juan's anger grew; his anger and his resolve. No simple drunken seaman had done this, he now knew beyond doubt.

"Then there is no question?" Lubelski asked.

"No," Juan said. "There is no question."

"Good," Lubelski said and turned to leave the small radio room they were crowded into. "I would hate to think I had been tricked into identifying the wrong man for the authorities."

"They have gone?"

"Yes."

"Then send your radio man to me immediately."

Lubelski acknowledged Juan's order with a nod of his head and then moved quickly away. Juan sat down beside the transmitter and began to compose the message he would send to Gretchen. It would have to be carefully worded. Gretchen must understand, her listeners must not.

They had stumbled on to much more than they had expected. The possibilities were intoxicating. The diamonds were now almost incidental. What they had learned from Martin Stein would be far more valuable, almost incomprehensibly so. Once Moscow had been informed—and Juan had insisted that he be allowed to do that in person—the ramifications would be felt throughout the KGB. Juan would be instantly prestigious. He would have gained esteem in the eyes of the Kremlin beyond his dreams.

As the anger quelled within him, the excitement grew. Juan wrote rapidly on a pad beside him. There was no need for Gretchen to be told about the revelations Martin Stein had made. No need for her to know about the network or the strange and ironic secret that Juan doubted even the CIA knew. But she must be warned. She must know that she was at risk beyond what they had planned for. For if the CIA had placed an agent this close to them, then they must assume that Gretchen had been under surveillance from the beginning. She must plan for her escape using any means at her disposal . . .

"You sent for me?" a thin-faced man asked from the passageway. Juan looked up, mildly startled.

"Yes. Send this at once, and continue sending it each hour until you receive confirmation. Understand?"

"Yes."

Juan stood up, handed the pad to the radio man and then pushed past him. He heard the key of the transmitter begin its chatter before he had gone a dozen steps down the passageway. He smiled and moved quickly toward Martin Stein's cabin.

Things were beginning to fall into place nicely, he thought. A few precautions, a small amount of luck, and they would be home free.

Reaching Martin's cabin, he knocked firmly on the door and then waited. In a moment it swung open and the frail doctor met his gaze.

"How is he?" Juan asked.

"He still isn't completely stable."

"You must keep him comfortable. Stay with him until further notice. I don't want him left alone."

"I'll do what I can," the doctor said. "But you do realize that the drugs and the interrogation have taken a lot out of him, perhaps too much."

"What exactly are you saying?"

"Nothing. I'm simply trying to tell you that he is weak. He is very weak."

"Then watch him closely. Watch him as if your life depended on it."

The subtle nuance in Juan's voice was immediately understood. The old doctor took a step backward. The lines in his face deepened. Juan glanced past the doctor at the quiet form on the bunk, smiled, then turned away.

"Remember what I said," Juan said back over his shoulder as he walked down the passageway.

Orin Brady lay uncomfortably on the hill. This afternoon his discomfort sprang from two sources: one from his prone body growing numb by degrees, the other from an intense anxiety and anticipation. He watched Gretchen's cottage, half of him hoping that she emerged and walked down the beach to their promised meeting, the other half hoping that she did not. It would be so much easier if she stayed in the cottage, so much safer for them both.

He could hear the lazy roll and muted rumble of the surf pound on the shore; cold thunder on sand. He could also hear the steady throb of his pulse in his ears, as he raised his binoculars and put them to his eyes. He trembled as he brought them into focus.

She came out through the back door as before. Looked over the hillside, moved off down the beach. Orin signaled Josh, left his radio in the grass and hurried up the hill to the footpath. When he reached it he stopped. Carefully, he brushed his clothing off before he went further. As he shook the damp earth from the folds of his pants and jacket he vacillated as to what he should do. He had thought about little else through the night. The conclusions he had come to had been frightening.

When he had failed to tell Long about his first meeting with Gretchen, he had inadvertently put himself in a position in which he would have to choose between warning Gretchen about her surveillance—so that she could escape—or have his career destroyed when she told Long, under questioning, what he had omitted. It was a no-win situation he had only himself to blame for. A deception had been indulged in and now its ramifications suddenly loomed. He had felt the pangs of hopelessness more and more sharply as the night had progressed, realizing that he could not back up or change course, realizing all he could do was go forward and hope there was an escape route for him when the time came.

Satisfied with his appearance, if not with his predicament, Orin moved off down the footpath. He covered the ground quickly, quietly, reaching the spot where the path angled off onto the beach. There he stopped and looked for Gretchen.

At first he could not see her and he swore, venting his impatience. Then, up the beach, he saw her sitting in the sand, low and small against a dune. He moved toward her. As he neared, he could tell she was watching the surf intently.

"What's so interesting?" he asked, slightly out of breath as he reached her.

She sat with her knees pulled up in front of her and didn't look up at him, or even acknowledge his question. Slowly she pointed into the surf where a gnarled piece of driftwood with five twisted branches floated in and out with the advance and retreat of the sea.

Orin's shadow fell across her.

"It looks like a hand," she finally said. "Some horribly twisted hand, reaching out for something, doesn't it?"

"No, not to me. It just looks like driftwood; harmless driftwood."

She looked at him and smiled, but there was a hint of strain in it, or was that just his imagination?

"I was wondering if I would see you today. How is your bird-watching going?"

"I'm afraid I haven't been looking for birds at all today."

"Nor any dark symbolism?"

"No."

"Forgive me, I'm not usually so dreary."

"I didn't think you were. Would you like to walk?"

"Yes."

Gretchen got up and stood beside him. When he turned to go further down the beach, she stopped him with a touch of her hand.

"Let's go this way," Gretchen said and began to walk back toward the cottage. Taken off his guard, Orin fell in beside her.

"So tell me, what does Orin Brady do when he's not watching birds?"

"Nothing too exciting, I'm afraid. I'm a lowly little government employee attached to the American Embassy in London."

"That surprises me. I had you pegged as a rougher type. Perhaps you have potential you've yet to discover."

Orin didn't answer her. He watched her bare feet churn the soft sand with each step. When he looked up they were in sight of the cottage. She slackened her pace, looked at him, then stopped.

"Would you like to come in for a while?" she asked and indicated the cottage with a sidelong glance.

"If you want me to," he answered softly.

Gretchen smiled and led the way.

The dutch door swung open easily. As they entered, Gretchen dropped her shoes just inside and then closed the door behind them. She leaned against it with her back and looked at him for a second. It was almost an appraising look; it made him slightly nervous.

"My mouth seems suddenly dry. You wouldn't have anything to drink would you?" he asked, doing his best to meet her gaze coolly.

"Certainly I do," she answered. "Just sit there on the couch and I'll get it."

She pushed herself away from the door and walked to the back of the cottage. In a moment she returned with two glasses of white wine. She handed him one and then sat beside him.

"You're a complete mystery to me. Do you realize that?" Orin asked, then sampled his wine.

"A mystery?" Gretchen repeated. "I think I like that. I think I like that very much."

They looked at each other. He began to feel the strange magnetism he had felt before. It pulled at him, gradually increasing in strength.

"You really are a beautiful girl."

"So you've told me now for the second time."

"I apologize for yesterday. I really lost my head."

"Don't apologize. I was actually hoping you would have a similar lapse today."

She said it plainly, unashamed. Orin sat his drink on the floor beside hers. She moved slowly closer to him.

The nearer she came, the stronger he felt that invisible undertow. The sensation of losing his footing more and more until there was nothing left to hold him back, nothing to cling to, nothing to do but be suspended in its flow. Tentatively he took her in his arms and kissed her.

She encouraged him gently and his boldness grew. She coaxed him, directed him, until his hunger for her was apparent. Gradually he began to take the lead, the initiative. She responded to his advance, yielded to his touch. Then suddenly she stopped him, pushed him gently away.

"What's wrong?" he asked on the very edge of exasperation.

"Nothing. Just give me a moment."

Gretchen rose from the couch and walked to the window. The beach outside was empty, tranquil. Orin watched her, the tension building within him. He fought for his composure, remaining silently, if impatiently, seated.

"Will you promise me something?" she asked softly, her back to him.

"At this instant, I would promise you almost anything."

"I'm serious."

"So am I."

"Okay. When I ask you to leave, and I will, you won't ask me any questions? You'll go away quickly?"

"If that's what you want."

She said nothing more. She pulled the curtains closed, then turned toward him. Orin watched her in the filtered light as she slipped her sweater over her head and let it fall, then shed her jeans and stood silhouetted in front him.

He got up and undressed clumsily, conscious of her eyes on him. When he came to her he started to speak, but quickly she put her hand to his lips and shook her head. He grasped her fingers gently and pulled them away. Then he brought her hard against him.

CHAPTER
Seventeen

Pfifer did what he could to part a way for them through the crush of the crowd. Rachel stayed close to him as the din of a thousand people, talking, pushing, shoving, enveloped them. Periodically, the public address system of the train station reverberated with a barely intelligible message that only served to add to the confusion. Finally they made their way to a phone booth, took a place in its line and began to wait their turn. Pfifer felt Rachel's hand on his arm as he watched the swarm around them. He was stoic, reserved, but alert.

Under the green vaulted dome of the terminal, waves of sound and motion swept over them and around them. Pfifer could only guess if they were being watched and it put him on edge. There was an uneasy tension in his gut, a particular, anxious tingling. He thought of the crumpled prescription in his pocket and reminded himself to get it refilled as soon as Rachel was safe and he was on his own again.

"Will they come quickly?" Rachel asked as they moved one space closer to the phone.

"Yes, I'm sure they will. They've been looking for us."

"Then we don't have much time together, do we?"

"That should make you happy."

"Yes, it should, shouldn't it," Rachel said and then looked away from him.

"You've had a rough couple of days, but you'll be all right."

"What about you? Will you be all right?"

Pfifer reached down to her and gently turned her face toward him with his hand. The look on her face made him twinge. It was a foreign feeling, one he was only faintly familiar with. It had been so long since he had cared for anyone, so very long since he had dared. He wanted to say something, but he felt far too foolish. Suddenly it was their turn to use the phone.

Pfifer stepped into the booth alone and pulled the door shut. Rachel watched him through the glass as he found the proper coins and dialed his number.

When the call was answered, Pfifer said, "Pisces, Hamburg. I'm with a friend. Instructions?"

There was a brief flurry of activity in the background, then Pfifer heard a familiar voice on the line.

"John? I have to admit we're fairly glad to be hearing from you."

"Hello George. I'm surprised you're in Hamburg personally. Who's minding the store?"

"That's another matter. Where are you?"

"I'm at the main train station. I have someone to bring in."

"I hope you have her chained down in the meantime."

"No, that isn't necessary." Pfifer looked up at Rachel. She still watched him steadily through the door. She hadn't moved.

"Very well then, we'll send a car for her."

"We'll be waiting."

Pfifer hung up the phone, pushed the door open and stepped out of the booth. He drew Rachel to one side as the next man in line pushed past them impatiently.

"It's all set," he told her. "Let's move to the front entrance. There will be a car for you shortly."

Rachel followed him without a word. When they reached the main entrance, they stood quietly out of the flow of people. Rachel stared straight ahead, eyes open but unseeing. Pfifer found himself watching her more than he watched for the special limousine that would be by now en route to meet them.

It had been foolish for her to pursue him. Foolish but undoubtedly courageous. And the fact was, she had done an excellent job of finding him, and of diverting him. If she had been so inclined, she could have taken him out quite easily and quite permanently; an unsettling thought to say the least.

Yes, Rachel was quite a girl, Pfifer thought, a real surprise package.

"You're smiling. Are you that glad to get rid of me?" Rachel asked.

"I was just thinking," Pfifer said and looked down at her.

"What about?"

"When I was a small boy, my father had a favorite game he would play at Christmas and on birthdays. It had to do with surprise packages."

Rachel looked interested but puzzled.

"What he'd do, you see, would be to wrap a gift in several different boxes, one inside the other. You could never guess what the last box contained. That way the gift was always a surprise."

"That's a strange thing to be thinking about."

"Possibly not."

No more than half an hour passed before Pfifer spotted a

dark limousine approaching in the queue of traffic. It bore diplomatic plates and its side windows were tinted heavily. He pointed it out to Rachel.

"This is it then," she said softly.

Pfifer reached into his coat pocket and pulled out a neatly folded piece of paper. He held it out to her.

"What's that?"

"Give this to George Long. It's a shopping list I put together while you were sleeping. He'll know what to do with it."

Rachel took the list.

"You know what this means, don't you?" she asked.

Pfifer shook his head.

"It's the first time you've trusted me."

"I suppose it is."

The limo stopped at the curb a few yards away. The passenger window came down slightly and then went up again. Pfifer recognized the signal.

"They're waiting for you. Go on now."

Rachel looked at him for a long moment. He met her gaze steadily, directly. Finally she said, "Good luck," and moved off toward the waiting limousine.

"And you," Pfifer said under his breath. "And you."

He watched her hurry toward the limousine. She paused to identify herself to the driver before she got in the back. By the time she was inside Pfifer had disappeared into the crowd.

The room was cold, windowless, sparse. A table with three chairs occupied its center. A single bright light was suspended from the ceiling. Rachel waited. She stared at the blank walls and wondered how much longer she would be kept there. With nothing to measure the time by, she grew more and more restless.

She had expected to be questioned when she arrived at the embassy, but they had hardly said a word to her. They had been polite, brief, and cold. She had been brought to this dismal little room and left to pace back and forth unattended. She could only guess at how long she had been there.

On impulse, Rachel walked to the door and put her hand to the brass knob. It was locked. She became angry, then thoughtful, then scared in rapid succession. She trembled. Desperately she struggled to bring her emotions back to center. She told herself that no matter how unpleasant her questioning turned out to be, whenever they got around to it, she was physically safe now. She would survive.

She sat down in one of the straight-backed chairs at the table and buried her face in her hands. When she felt the cold tears begin to track down her cheeks, they caught her by surprise. What was happening to her? The pressure was off now. She was no longer at risk. The risk rested on someone else. She tried to wipe the tears from her eyes, but they continued to come.

She tried to think about Martin, but his face refused to come clear in her mind. The face she visualized was Pfifer's. Again and again—Pfifer. She put her hand to her jaw and felt the spot still tender from his blow. "John Pfifer, you bastard," she said aloud, then smiled in spite of herself. What would he do now?

She considered him, and the two very different sides he had presented to her. On the one hand, he was undoubtedly a cold-blooded killer. On the other, there was that certain thread of vulnerability to him. He had frightened her, hurt her, but also surely saved her life. He had shown brutal strength, but also a temerity toward her. Wistfully, she wondered if he had found her attractive.

As she wiped fresh tears from her eyes, it dawned on her that she had not cried so freely since she had been a child. Tears for a man with no future, from a woman who never cries. Somehow it seemed appropriate. She let the tears continue to flow. She allowed herself to cry for him, for herself, for them all.

More time passed. How much, Rachel neither knew nor cared. She had taken the first steps toward resigning herself to a passive role. She was out of it now. They would either keep her detained in Hamburg or send her home to England. Either way she would be insulated from the events of the next few days, kept far away from any direct action. They would not be so careless as to leave her unguarded. And if she did escape, how could she accomplish anything to help Martin, or Pfifer? No, she had made the grand gesture, she had done what she thought was necessary. It was over now.

She stopped crying. Her face went blank of expression as she began to withdraw back into her defensive shell. She could wait quietly now. Nothing mattered.

After a time, she heard footsteps beyond the door. She listened to them approach. They were heavy, deliberate. She knew it was George Long before he opened the door.

"Mr. Long," Rachel said calmly as he entered the room.

"Rachel, it's good to have you back. You've had us on the edge of our chairs for the last two days."

Two days, Rachel thought, has it only been two days?

"You're looking well, though."

"I'm just fine, Mr. Long. I realize you have some questions for me. Suppose you just ask them and let's be done with it."

"Don't misunderstand me, Rachel. I'm not here to give you the third degree. In fact, I hadn't planned to question you at all. It seems Pat McKintosh and Joe Bryant want to talk with you themselves when you return to England."

Rachel grimaced. That certainly would not be a pleasant meeting. She had no idea what she would tell them. How much she could tell them.

"And when will that be?"

"Soon, but probably not for a few days."

"Then why are you here? You must be particularly unhappy with me."

"I wanted to make sure you were all right, also to give you the opportunity to tell me anything you might wish to."

"As a matter of fact, I did want to see you. John gave me a list." Rachel removed the folded paper from her pocket and handed it to Long. "He said you'd know what to do with this."

"And why would you want to help us now?" Long asked and looked closely at her.

"There's nothing I can say or do at this point to help my brother. I'd say that's up to John now. And he can probably handle it, if anyone can."

Her statement caused Long to hesitate for a moment. Rachel hoped that her face would be as unreadable as his, but she doubted that it was. He was obviously sensitive to the subtle things in people's inflections, and more than a little pride had crept into her voice as she had mentioned Pfifer. He might wonder what that meant. She wondered about it herself.

"I don't suppose you'd care to tell me what went on between you two? If you will pardon my indelicate question?"

The way Long looked at her made her extremely uncomfortable. Finally his eyes dropped to the list.

"It's in code."

"I'm sure that's how he intended to prove the validity of the list to you. He would realize that you wouldn't trust anything I gave you in the clear."

"You're quite right about that."

Long sat down slowly at the table. He spread the list out flat in front of him. His eyebrows rose at several of the items. When he had finished deciphering he looked up at Rachel.

"Did he tell you what he had in mind?"

"Yes."

"I see."

"Tell me something, if you will, Mr. Long. Will you be seeing him personally? If you will, there is something I'd like you to tell him for me. Tell him he hadn't reached the final package."

"Final package?"

"Yes, he'll know what I mean. It has to do with something he told me. It just finally dawned on me what he meant."

Long got up from the table.

"You've had quite an adventure, haven't you, young lady?"

Rachel nodded.

"I'll have you moved to a nicer room."

"Thank you, Mr. Long."

Long left, pulling the door closed behind him. When he had gone, Rachel sat at the table. She felt nothing now but a sense of being shut off, an empty aloneness. She stared at the blank walls and considered their absolute sameness. Pfifer had, indeed, not reached the final package; the final resolution, as far as she was concerned. She wished there were a way they could reach it together.

CHAPTER
Eighteen

It was another hotel; a sloven sister to the one in Rotterdam, but a safe refuge, an anonymous place to be. That was all that mattered.

Pfifer stood at his third floor window, held its stained curtain aside and looked out on the street in front of the hotel. He knew it was too early for there to be much activity. It was dusk still, the neon signs had yet to own the garish glare that would come as the evening deepened, as the waterfront pulled the night around itself like evil pulling a dark hood over its head. Later, the tempo would pick up and he could come and go in its midst unnoticed. Later. But for now he would have to wait.

It was the waiting time that gave him the most trouble, once an operation had begun. In many ways, the waiting challenged him more than the danger. When there was action to deal with, it blocked out everything else. The immediate needs of the moment kept him from thinking, kept him from looking too far into the future. The danger he could face head on. The waiting was faceless, intangible, untenable, and it attacked you wherever it found you vulnerable.

It was a predictable pattern and a tedious one. From the edge of death to the doldrums of boredom and back again. It was a procession down a spiral staircase to hell from which there was no escape. And even to pause would mean destruction beneath the feet of the legions that followed him; to continue, simple fulfillment of his fate.

He stepped away from the window and crossed to the bed. It sagged and squeaked beneath him as he lay down. He closed his eyes and tried to force himself to sleep, but could not. After several moments he simply lay there and stared at the ceiling. He thought about the four men he had killed; four new ghosts to haunt him. He thought about Rachel, who would haunt him in other ways.

He remembered her kiss. The warm feel of her body, the strange new spark of something that had been struck in her sometime during their few hours together. He smiled, but then lost his smile as he realized that spark might kindle a fire in some other man, but not in him. No, thinking about Rachel would do nothing to hold back the cloak of depression. It would not make things easier. Thinking about Rachel would make things more difficult than perhaps they had ever been before.

The activity in the hotel came in waves. Doors slammed and voices echoed. Footsteps creaked up and down the halls. Pfifer listened to each new surge of commotion, never drifting far from consciousness. He lay perfectly still, hoping his body could rest even if his mind would not.

He would see George Long in a few hours' time. If Rachel had been true to her word, Long would have the items on the list. Pfifer would be moved closer to his attempt on the freighter. The danger would be back again, the waiting over.

Pfifer turned on his side. His eyes came to rest on the small bottle of pills he had left on the nightstand beside the bed. They were oval and pale beige in color. He wondered to himself why they looked so different from his originals. The pharmacist he had found near the train station had insisted they should be the same. Who knew? Who cared? What was disturbing was that they weren't working. Another of George Long's tricks? But why? Pfifer closed his eyes again. Perhaps the pain in his stomach would help distract him from more troubling thoughts.

He would concentrate on the pain.

It was dark now. There was a disturbance on the street, angry voices, then laughter, then hurried footsteps. Pfifer sat up and swung his feet to the floor. He checked his watch; it was eight o'clock, a half an hour before his meeting with George Long.

Slowly he got up and began to walk the stiffness from his body. He paused at the window and looked out, but the street was empty again; quiet. Whatever disturbance there had been had run its course. Returning to the bed, he removed the Luger from under his pillow. Methodically, he dropped out the magazine, inspected it, and then rammed it home again. He put the Luger in his belt at the small of his back, then moved toward the door.

The hall was brightly lit as he stepped from his room. Quickly he walked to the elevator and pressed its call button. As he did he glanced to his left and right at the rows of closed doors.

When the elevator came it was occupied by a young man dressed in the clothes of an apprentice seaman. The young seaman clutched a room key in his hand and looked sheepishly at Pfifer as he stepped from the car. Pfifer suppressed a smile and moved past him without comment.

The rendezvous point was several blocks from Pfifer's hotel. It was a short street that ended at a metal railing on the bank of the Elbe. When Pfifer reached the entrance to the street, he took a careful look behind him and then strained to see if he could spot anyone standing at the rail. Satisfied, he went forward. George Long was never early to a meeting. He was always right on time. Pfifer could take a few minutes to check out the immediate area.

The surface of the river danced with reflections from brightly lit cranes, working cargo from the wharves on the opposite bank. After Pfifer had walked the street, flanked by old brick warehouses boarded and deserted, he stopped at the rail and contemplated the scene.

His wait was brief.

Suddenly, the sound of a truck caught Pfifer's attention. As it turned onto the street, its strong headlamps spotlighted him, but he did not turn around. He continued to look out across the river as the truck stopped a few feet behind him and the flood of light went out.

"You're getting damned careless. You know that, don't you?" George Long said as he stepped from the truck and slammed its door.

"You're probably right," Pfifer answered, when Long joined him at the rail.

As always, there was that immediate tension between them, but stronger tonight, because there were questions that Pfifer wanted to ask, questions he knew would go unanswered. Long might lift the veil on the truth a fraction, but he would not expose it completely, not at this stage. Pfifer wondered if the exercise would be worthwhile.

"So how was your little jaunt from Rotterdam?"

"I expect you've heard all about it by now."

"Not a word."

Pfifer smiled to himself.

"It wasn't without its problems."

"Such as."

"There were two men in Rotterdam, from the freighter, a search party . . ."

"I know about that. Unfortunate."

Pfifer studied Long's impassive face. There was no emotion there to be seen, only a mildly inquiring tilt of the head, and that penetrating stare.

"We also had some difficulty after we crossed over, but these were different players, George. They had been following us, but I don't think they were from the freighter. I don't have the faintest idea who they were."

Long nodded, still staring blankly. Pfifer studied his expression carefully for any clue, any indication. There simply was none, but then Long was always unreadable.

"I'll check it out. Is there anything else?"

"Did Rachel give you my list?"

"Yes, I have what you need in the truck. Care to fill me in on your plan?"

"If I didn't, would I still get the equipment?"

"What do you think?"

"I think not." Pfifer paused. Long stared back at him, waiting.

"According to the information I picked up at the safe house," Pfifer began, "the freighter won't sail from Hamburg until day after tomorrow, probably shortly after seven in the morning, providing they stick to the same plan. I'll plant the charges on the freighter tomorrow night, late. Hopefully they won't check her over too thoroughly before they get under way. When I'm sure they've disembarked, I'll go north, pick up a small boat of some sort and intercept them at sea. I would think somewhere near Slyt. I'll get their attention with the first charge and have them put Stein over the side in a boat. It'll either work or it won't."

Long let several seconds pass before he spoke. Pfifer could tell he was less than enthusiastic.

"It's not exactly what I would call a low-profile approach."

"So if I'm caught, I'll speak Yiddish and they'll think I'm Mossad coming to the aid of a fellow Jew."

"Not funny. Besides that, you don't speak Yiddish."

Pfifer turned back to the rail. The cranes and lights and activity continued across the river.

"What happens if they don't stop when you tell them to?"

"That's why I need three charges in progressive strengths. They'll need to believe I'll go all the way."

"You don't see any other way?"

"I've already tried my hand at getting on board. It can't be done successfully. Not with any chance of getting Stein off alive."

"He may already be dead."

"We don't know that for sure, do we?"

"I'll need to show you the equipment."

"Then I take it my plan is approved?"

"With a few modifications. One, you will check in when the charges are in place. Two, you will get my personal authorization before you make your attempt. I think we can give you detailed information on the freighter's position. I can also see you have no trouble getting a boat with the proper speed capabilities and radio equipment. Agreed?"

"Agreed. Show me the charges."

Long stepped away from the rail and shoved his hands deep into his pockets. It was a familiar gesture to Pfifer, it generally meant Long was on the fence about telling him something. In a few seconds, he pulled a set of keys out and tossed them to Pfifer.

"You seem to have an enhanced interest in this all of a sudden. Would you care to tell me why?"

"I just want it over with, George, that's all. The quicker I get Stein off of that freighter the better I'll like it."

Long studied him for a moment. When he spoke it was in an offhanded way.

"As I recall, there is another possibility that would serve our purpose just as well. I trust you haven't forgotten it?"

"I haven't forgotten."

"Very well, then. Your equipment is in the truck. I'll need to brief you on it."

They walked to the truck. It was a small box-type truck

with a roll-up door in the back. Long opened it with a grunt and climbed in. Pfifer followed him.

"There are three charges; limpet mines, actually. Magnetic bases and a firing device actuated by a portable transducer. To set off the mines you simply get within a thousand yards, go through an initial arming sequence which I have written down for you, and, after you've done that, the firing command is fundamental. The first mine will go on a single pulse, the second will go on two pulses, the third on three."

"The charges are numbered so I know which is which?"

"Of course. One more thing, the transducer is trailed in the water from the side of whatever boat you use. You must go slow enough to make sure it is completely submerged. If it isn't, it won't work."

It was all there: the mines, the transducer, a long black cable, a remote keying device, and neatly in a corner a diver's wet suit and tanks. Pfifer ran his hand gently along the edge of one of the mine's crates and looked at Long.

"Is that it?"

"That's it."

Pfifer toyed with keys in his hand.

"Can I drop you anywhere?"

"I have a backup car waiting."

"I would have been surprised if you didn't."

Long climbed out of the truck and turned toward Pfifer.

"Rachel wanted me to give you a message."

Pfifer stared back at Long as stoically as he could.

"She said something about that you hadn't gotten to the last package, whatever that means?"

Pfifer smiled in spite of himself.

"How is she, anyway?"

"She's fine. She's a strong-willed girl. I wouldn't worry about her if I were you."

"Take care of her, George."

Long gave him a troubled, tentative look once again. Then he turned, shoved his hands into his pockets and began to walk away. No good-byes, no good lucks, he simply turned and walked away without a word. Pfifer watched him go and shook his head.

Long was, above all else, a complex man. Predictable in some ways, intractable in others. Pfifer shrugged off his peculiar exit and jumped down. He pulled the rear door of the truck shut once he was on the ground and turned back toward the river.

In the morning he would locate the *Baltic Merchant* and plan the safest approach. He could take his time; he would have all day.

He would also take some precautions. The truck was far too easy to spot, too easy to keep track of. There would be some danger that Pfifer would have to leave the truck at some point. That meant he must stash at least the transducer and the cable and remote keying device. That way if he had to abandon the truck he could double back and retrieve what he needed. He was probably being overcautious, but he would do it just the same.

Somewhere on the outskirts of the city would be best. Possibly an inn where he could have an undisturbed night's rest. He needed that; a few hours of quiet to sort out pieces, rifle through the miscellaneous entanglement of stray details.

Martin Stein, Rachel Stein, Howard Stein, the girl Gretchen; he had been pulled into their lives and their struggle. They had gained power over his life and his expectations. In a very real way they had become a threat to his very existence, but there would be no escape from them. Not until the game was finished; not until it was played to the end.

Long hadn't been fooled. He did have a heightened interest in the situation. He did care about finishing this assignment for perhaps different reasons than ever before.

In the distance the cranes stood motionless; huge, expectant creatures, glowering over the darkness below them. Suddenly their light was extinguished and the river turned black beneath the overcast sky. Pfifer felt a chill and moved toward the cab of the truck.

Pfifer raised the binoculars and centered the *Baltic Merchant* in their field. She was the middle ship in a line of three that were moored to the quay across the channel from him. Her deck cranes were idle. Only a few of the crew wandered about the decks in the morning light. She appeared quite normal; a merchantman waiting for her cargo. Only Pfifer knew better, and he also knew he would have to look very close to see what he was looking for.

He scanned the superstructure more carefully. In a moment he spotted what he had expected. One man, who had been leaning against the bridge wing, turned as if to speak with someone behind him. When he did, for an instant, he exposed the automatic rifle cradled in his arms. Pfifer's view of the freighter was of her stern and port side. He could assume, with no real need to verify it, that there would be another man, on the starboard side, similarly armed, watching the dock.

Pfifer lowered the binoculars as a tug pulling a queue of three barges obstructed his view.

He had been right. He would have to swim the channel with the mines. Using any kind of boat was out. One of the three ships would more than likely be working cargo that night, and the wharves were sure to be flooded with light. Any boat that he tried to use would be easily seen. And there certainly would be enough activity going on to keep the sentries alert. It would mean three trips, underwater both ways, and still some chance that his bubbles would be seen.

Pfifer stood under a bridge beside the truck. Between his position and the channel lay forty yards of open ground. At middistance there was a chain link fence with a barbed wire overhang. A few minutes with some bolt cutters would take care of the fence, but the forty yards of open ground presented an unwelcome problem. If someone was watching that stretch of bank at the right time—or the wrong time, as far as Pfifer was concerned—he would be clearly visible. Even without any sophisticated night scope, in average moonlight they would be able to spot him. It would mean crawling. It would slow him up.

Pfifer turned and got into the truck. Glancing at his watch, he counted the hours. It would be a strenuous night and he had some extra equipment to procure. He drew his sleeve slowly across his forehead, surprised at the amount of perspiration there was, and then started the truck's engine. With two quick manoeuvres he backed the truck between the bridge's supports, turned around and drove away.

CHAPTER
Nineteen

"I'd like very much just to go home," Rachel said, standing rigidly before George Long in his temporary office.

Long looked up from behind the desk and shook his head.

"Your father has been told that we've taken you in for safekeeping. At this point, that's exactly what we've done. Believe me, it's for the best."

"I am a British citizen. You can't hold me against my will."

"One phone call to your government and I can hold you as long as I like. So don't attempt to overplay your hand. It isn't going to work, young lady."

Rachel stared hard at Long, but said no more.

"If it makes you feel better, I've spoken to John, and delivered what he asked for. He should have what he needs to implement his plan. But remember, whatever happens, you will not be involved. That's the way it has to be."

Rachel took a deep breath. The office had a musty, closed-up smell to it. The light green walls and dusty furniture had a decided lack of warmth or style. Suddenly she knew Pfifer was right. They were going to sit on her. She was going to be little more than a prisoner until the situation was resolved. The thought of it made her very angry.

"You have all the cards, don't you, Mr. Long? You've got us all in a neat little package, under control, while you go about your little game. What would you do if my father called off all the bets right now? What would you do if he ended his cooperation with you? What would you do then, and what will you do when I gain control of the purse strings to our little network?"

Long looked down at the papers on his desk. When he spoke it was in a moderated tone of voice. Still firm, but less abrupt.

"You're upset now, Rachel. I can understand that, but you have to remember things aren't always clear-cut." He paused and looked up at her. "They aren't always either right or wrong. There isn't anything else I can or should tell you at this point. You'll just have to wait, like the rest of us, until we hear from John."

"And will you tell me what is happening?"

"I'll tell you what I can."

She studied him and as she did a nagging feeling of distrust gnawed at her. He was lying to her. It was a lie carefully wrapped in silk and protocol, but a lie nonetheless.

"I've decided I don't like you very much, or your precious Agency, Mr. Long. But I suppose we can take that up at another time, can't we? When my brother is either safe, or dead."

Long frowned and then pressed a button on his intercom. He summoned a security guard in a brisk tone of voice.

"Sometime this afternoon you'll be moved to a safe house. The ambassador has had second thoughts about allowing us to keep you here. Please don't do anything foolish. You'll be helping everyone concerned if you simply do as you are told."

Rachel met his gaze coldly. She had a hundred questions she would have liked to ask, but she realized Long would be the wrong person to field them. She tried to control her anger as the security guard, a young marine, entered and took her gently by the arm.

"Remember what I said, Miss Stein," Long called after her as she was led away.

"Oh, I will, Mr. Long. Every word."

The guard took her back to her room and locked her in. Once inside and alone, she looked around herself and let out a long breath. At least this room had a bed and a small barred window. Even though it functioned as a cell, it felt less like one to her. Through her window she could see a steady stream of traffic and pedestrians caught in Hamburg's morning rush. It consoled her to be able to see the world she had been separated from. It helped her believe that her isolation would be brief.

She knew she had been separated from the normal world by more than just the walls of her room. That separation occurred the moment she learned of her father's secret, the moment she took the responsibility for it. It was a fine line, true enough, but she had irrevocably crossed it. Now she realized more fully the ramifications of what she had done. The effect it would have on her life, the grasp it would have on her.

And the secret did grasp her, hold her, restrict her. That was certain enough. She would inherit it and the legacy it represented. She could not turn her back on it. That would mean far too much to far too many innocent people. Innocent people who had no other hope of freedom.

Yes, the trap had been laid for her neatly and well. She had been drawn into the game, fueled by her good intentions, and the highest of ideals. She was held by her empathy for the countless others that depended on her now.

She had traded away her own freedom for theirs, and only now realized it, only now realized what she had really done.

At first her recruiters had been oh so very nice. A person claiming to be a prospective employer had asked to interview her, and to a graduating college student such offers weren't taken lightly. She had happily gone to the office building in Boston that had been identified in an introductory letter. She arrived at the appointed time. Her expectations admittedly high. But the moment the interview had begun, she sensed she was about to be exposed to something quite different from what she had been led to believe.

Mr. Paul was his name—though not his real one, of that Rachel was sure. He was a nondescript little man dressed in a gray pinstripe suit and an artificially benevolent manner. Never once had he tipped his hand, not before he had sounded her out completely.

"So, Miss Stein, if I understand you correctly, you actually grew up in the diamond industry," Mr. Paul said, drumming his fingers lightly on the mahogany desktop.

"That's correct, sir. But I'm confused as to how that fact relates to a job in chemical enginnering. I'm also puzzled why you have asked me so many political questions. I have to admit, this is my first serious job interview, but I am amazed at how far afield our conversation has gone. In fact, I don't recall you even mentioning what kinds of chemicals your company's trying to develop. I can only guess at my qualifications. And you as well, unless you know more about me than I am aware of."

Mr. Paul rose to his feet and looked down on her, the benevolent facade suddenly gone from his face. He walked across his office to a bookshelf and withdrew a bound file from a crowded row of similar files.

"This file, Rachel, if I may call you that, tells a story. It's a story I doubt you know in full. It's a story your father plays a major part in, though. Your father and a number of other very brave people."

"Do you know my father?" Rachel asked, suddenly taken aback.

"I would guess that I know your father better than you do. At least in some areas."

"I'm afraid I'm really confused now."

"If you will give me a chance, I'll explain." Mr. Paul returned to his seat and placed the file in front of himself. Deliberately and slowly he opened it and glanced at the cover sheet before he continued. "Would it surprise you to learn that for over twenty years now your father has been instrumental in helping large numbers of people escape from East Germany?"

"Yes, and I doubt that I would believe it."

Mr. Paul smiled.

"And before we go any further, if we go any further, I would like to know exactly who you are. I suspect you have misrepresented yourself to me, and I can't say I like it."

"I certainly understand your concern, but I am confident, if you will hear me out, you will be glad you came today. And besides, I am here to begin the process of offering you 'employment' of a sort. Shall I continue?"

Rachel stared at the file across the desk from her. Her father's name was printed on it in plainly readable lettering. Her curiosity dictated that she learn what this man had in mind for her and also what he thought her father was involved in. Reluctantly, she nodded her assent.

"Good, you will find out much today, much that would make any daughter very proud of her father."

"Go on, but first I want to know who you are and who you represent."

"I'm from a branch of the federal government. When you leave, and you may leave at any time, I will give you a method of verifying my authority. But for now, just relax and listen; we have a lot of ground to cover.

"To begin with, your father, not too long after he had arrived in England and started his business, was approached by a group of businessmen that had relatives and friends wishing to leave the Soviet-occupied areas of Germany and relocate. Simple enough; at the time immigration was not impossible, thousands crossed freely from east to west—but for certain key people involved in industry deemed important to the Soviets, it was much more difficult. Money was needed to open up the doors, so to speak.

"While the borders were still open, all that was required was a currency readily negotiable and easily hidden for the purpose of bribery. And, for the right price, officials were more than willing to look the other way at poorly forged papers, or in some cases no papers at all. It all worked very smoothly. The businessmen donated cash to your father's business for its expansion and in turn he supplied a source of gems for the businessmen's purposes. Everything was neat and untraceable, and mostly risk-free.

"But of course that changed. After the borders were closed, it became more involved to get people out. It became dangerous to take the diamonds in. In some cases they were found on the couriers and confiscated. For several months extraordinary means were employed to literally smuggle the stones into East Germany. The escape networks slowed to a standstill for lack of funds.

"At that point your father took a bold step. He approached us and negotiated a safe method of delivery for the network's diamonds in exchange for information on the current situations behind the wall.

"I'm here today to tell you that arrangement is still operational today, and although the flow of refugees from behind the wall has slowed to a trickle, it is still a very valuable source of intelligence."

As Rachel listened, she couldn't help but think back at events in her childhood that at the time seemed mysterious to her but that given Paul's explanation made more sense. She had the immediate, instinctive reaction of believing that the bulk of the story was true. It frightened her but it also excited her.

"Why would you tell me this?" she managed to ask.

"Because, in our view, it is time you knew."

"If what you are saying is true, why hasn't my father told me? Why does it fall to you?"

Paul paused and nodded.

"Until now, we weren't sure he hadn't. He probably felt you would be safer if you didn't know, the network would be safer if the spread of knowledge of its existence was kept to a minimum."

"I get the idea, he doesn't know about this little meeting of ours. Am I right?"

"That's why we had to be careful. There's no reason to upset him. We want him to live a very long time, and continue to do exactly what he has been."

Rachel's mind raced ahead.

"This position, you said you were here to offer me, would it have anything to do with rejoining my father's business?"

"Perhaps."

"Why not my brother? Why not Martin?"

"Your brother is a fine young man, I'm sure, but is a bit of a political activist. I'm afraid we can't count on him to remain stable. We feel you would be the most logical choice to continue the work when the time comes. Your father will eventually agree."

"I can't give you any kind of commitment today. You understand. I will have to think about what you have told me. I'll have to try and learn if it is true."

"Why not call Joe Bryant?"

"Joe Bryant?"

"He's one of us, and has been from the very beginning."

Rachel shook her head—Joe Bryant, of course. He was the connecting piece in the puzzle. If she had had doubts, now she did not. Suddenly, she was swept by a curious blend of dread and pride.

"Would you like to learn more, Miss Stein?"

"Yes, Mr. Paul. I believe I would."

The next few months went by quickly. It became a blur of instruction in fieldwork and basic spycraft along with a series of endless interviews. It seemed they needed to take her psychological pulse every few days to make sure she was still on track with their program, to make sure of her loyalty. They were taking a gamble by exposing themselves, that much was obvious, and they were in no place to hedge their bets. What Mr. Paul had said about Martin was painfully true. Martin was less than a bastion of stability, and he always had been.

And so it would come to Rachel, as it must. Rachel would inherit the game.

And now the game had brought her to a pleasant little cell in Hamburg. But, in her mind, it had brought her much further.

Huddled in the alcove in that moldering old alley, she had learned something about herself. She was no martyr. She wanted to live. She wanted to live completely, normally, as a free woman. Free to love a man. But it would be denied her. The game would take preeminence.

Rachel crossed the room and laid down on the bed. She stretched out, folding her hands behind her neck, and stared at the fixture overhead.

"Damn," she said softly.

They went out through the back door of the embassy, an agent at her right and one to the left. She was exposed for only seconds before she was pushed into the car. A third agent drove. No one spoke.

As they drove each of the three men watched a different quadrant. Rachel sat sandwiched in between two of them in the backseat. She had to smile as their heads swiveled back and forth. The humor of the moment, though, seemed lost on all but her.

"Will someone tell me where I'm going?" she asked.

"You'll see quickly enough," the man on her right said.

"Is it far?"

"No, just a few miles, but we have to take precautions. You understand."

They drove in a clockwise pattern, doubling back over their route several times. It took half an hour, by Rachel's estimate, to go perhaps two miles before they came to a block of old two-story houses. They pulled to a stop in front of one with an overgrown yard infiltrated with weeds.

"Let's go," the man to Rachel's right said and pushed open his door.

Rachel followed, catching a quick glance at the weathered brick and bubbled paint on the front of the house as she was hustled in. Then, heeding a warning to watch her step, she mounted a staircase to the second floor. As she climbed she was sandwiched between two of them, the third staying at the base of the stairs near the front door.

The first man entered the door at the top of the stairs and took a quick look through the apartment that was beyond. In a moment he called to them, signaling that it was safe.

"My name is Jack. That's Frank behind you," the agent said as Rachel stepped into the room. "There will be two of us at all times. Look around if you like, relax, but at no time attempt to leave these quarters. We get anything you might need. Understand?"

"I understand you are taking extraordinary precautions."

"We're just following George Long's instructions."

"I don't mean to seem ungrateful. I suppose I should say thank you."

Jack was a dark-haired man with a slightly olive complexion and stocky build. Rachel guessed him to be of Italian descent and probably good in a rough situation. She felt a sense of protection and a mild sense of intimidation at the same time.

"No need for that. No need at all," he said and pulled his coat around himself self-consciously.

She turned and looked at Frank standing in the doorway. Blond and on the slim side, he just stared back at her without comment. Cold, she thought; cold and dangerous.

Jack moved past her and nodded to Frank to follow him into the hall. As they closed the door and conferred in voices too low for Rachel to understand, she took the opportunity to look about her surroundings.

The room was a combination living room and kitchen. It was plain and clean, but had a stale smell to it, unventilated. Rachel stepped to the front window and tried to raise it, but found it jammed shut. She looked out as best she could.

The street was quiet and empty. The car they had come in had already gone. In the near distance, beyond a row of houses, she could see a section of the Elbe. Three houses down at the corner, a street sign was clearly visible. For no particular reason she memorized its name.

The door creaked open. The two agents came back inside.

"Is there anything we can get you?" Jack asked.

"A newspaper," Rachel answered, turning away from the window as she did. "A newspaper would help tremendously."

Jack motioned to Frank, who immediately strode off.

"There's a store of couple a blocks down the street. It'll take just a minute."

"Thank you. I think I'll just freshen up in the meantime."

"Through that door you'll find two bedrooms and a bath. Help yourself."

Rachel found the rearmost bedroom and closed herself in. With a brisk sweep of her hand she pushed aside the curtains over a side window and looked out at a similar window in the house adjacent. She stared at it blankly for several minutes. It was draped and dark, framed with black shutters. She closed her eyes for a moment and then turned her back to it.

When she turned she caught sight of her reflection in the bureau mirror. For an instant she didn't recognize herself. Then, tentatively, she touched the soft curl in her hair and smiled.

She thought of Pfifer. She knew she would be doing that for a long time. There would be nothing she could do to prevent it. For no matter what had happened, or what was about to happen, she knew now that her feelings for him would not change. It was with a sense of deep relief she admitted to herself that she loved him, and though it made no sense, it was as if a cloud had lifted and let a shaft of light penetrate the chill.

The stakes in Rachel's game had suddenly become higher, but her determination to win the deadly contest had grown as well.

CHAPTER
Twenty

Pfifer could feel the heat of the truck's engine at his back as he clutched a pair of bolt cutters in one hand and looked out across the channel. He had taken precautions: his final approach to the bridge had been made without headlights, he had removed the domelight from the cab of the truck so he could open its doors without advertising his presence, he had parked well back out of a direct line of sight. Even so, he felt exposed in the crystal-clear night. Exposed and discouraged by what he saw.

The end ship on the dock was ablaze with floodlamps. A blue-green pool of light reached out from it, deep into the Elbe, illuminating the water under both that ship and the *Baltic Merchant* moored next to her. Pfifer could not imagine it being worse. It meant that if he swam directly across the channel and under those lights, his bubbles would be easily seen. And, even if he made it once, it was highly unlikely he would make it the three times that would be necessary to carry out his plan. Angrily, he dropped the bolt cutters to the ground and studied the situation.

There was only one thing he could do. He would have to swim upriver against the current, then out across to the end of the dock and beneath the freighters. If there was room, he might make it between the freighters and the dock, shortening the distance slightly, but it would be a tight squeeze either way and either way it meant more time in the water than he had planned on.

Would he have enough air in his cylinders to allow him to do the extra swimming? If not, he would have to settle for putting only two of the three charges in place and that would present a second and possibly more serious problem. His plan was desperate enough with three charges. With only two charges in place there would be room for a malfunction, no safety margin. He swore under his breath as he considered it, toyed with the idea of just walking away. No one would blame him, not even George Long. Under the circumstances, it could be very reasonably said that aborting the plan was justified.

But he knew he had something to prove, to himself more than anyone, but something to prove nonetheless, and he had come too far to turn back. Certainly Rachel was part of it, perhaps a compelling part of it. Certainly the thought of Martin Stein was a part of it. But mostly it was for himself. Mostly it was to reaffirm himself with the severest test available. Logic held no relevance in it. It was the undeniable, emotional need that drew him forward and he recognized it for what it was.

Resigned, he picked up the cutters, dropped to the ground, and began the long crawl. He would do it by the numbers and the first item to cut would be a hole in the fence that separated him from the channel.

The ground was sandy and moist, but occasionally sharp rocks gouged his knees and elbows as he went, forcing him to move slowly. It was just as well, he told himself. It was going to be an exhausting exercise. There was no need to burn unnecessary energy. Every ounce of that precious commodity he could conserve would make his chances better.

When he reached the fence, he took a quick look around to see if he was alone. Then, carefully, he raised the cutters and snapped the first link. It parted easily with only a faint click, and, after a few minutes' work, he was able to peel back the mesh, making an opening three feet square. Satisfied, he turned and made his way back to the truck.

After he had stood for a moment to catch his breath, he opened up the truck's rear door and felt in the darkness for the soft, pliant folds of his wet suit. When he had located it he quickly stripped to his swim trunks and began to suit up. The night air was cold on his body. He knew the river would be colder, but he hoped that with the wet suit it would not be numbingly so. He strapped the tanks on his back, careful to adjust the tensions to suit him, and then donned his hood and mask. Finally he picked up the fins and looped them over his arm by their heel straps.

With some effort he pulled one of the crates closer to him and lifted off the top. The flat, gray, pie-shaped mine inside was numbered with a hand-painted numeral one that stood out in stark contrast even in the dim light. He was surprised at the mine's weight as he hefted it out. It caused him to wonder just how big a bang Long had provided him with. All he wanted to do was crack the egg, not break it. He frowned as he turned toward the river with it cradled in his arms.

It was a more difficult crawl with the mine, but he got cleanly through the fence and to the river bank without incident. Once there, he paused for a moment, gave his surroundings one last furtive look, put on his fins, installed his mouthpiece, and then eased slowly into the water. The Elbe closed over him with only the smallest of ripples as he slipped below the surface.

It was cold. The wet suit did little to buffer the harsh grip of that cold at first, but as his body heat warmed the captive layer of water next to him he began to feel much better. The current was not as strong as he had feared, but it would be strong enough to give him trouble if he allowed himself to become overtired. With that in mind, he kicked evenly and steadily, going no faster than he had to.

The light from the dock penetrated the darkness in the river, making a bright globe of translucence just off his left shoulder. He attempted to use it for reference as he swam in the hope that it would keep him from becoming disoriented. When he had cleared the gentle slope of the bank, he let the weight of the mine pull him deeper until he felt he would be safely concealed.

At two-thirds distance, he corrected his direction to allow the current to begin to draw him downriver. He had to experiment with his speed to find the right combination. As he neared the dock and the field of light, he could see the mine out in front of him clearly and the litter-strewn bottom of the river. Behind, his shadow trailed him like some dark ghost, growing sharper and closer as the current pulled him to the light.

He reached the end of the dock in perfect position, swam around the concrete footing and was immediately out of the current. Surprised and momentarily relieved, he continued to kick just enough to maintain his depth.

The crusty black hull of the first freighter looked as though it were pressed firmly into the soft mud on the bottom. The starboard side was jammed tight against camels with little more than eight to ten inches between the hull and the solid concrete wall of the dock. Shaking his head, Pfifer was tempted to swim around the freighter on its outside, but the light was too strong, and, as if to emphasize that point, someone suddenly dropped a bottle over the side from above. It spit little silver bubbles as it descended, its label clearly readable.

He allowed himself to sink lower so he could get a better look into the shadows below. He followed the rudder down, swam between the twin screws. Then, reluctantly, he dove headfirst for the narrow space between the freighter's belly and the muddy bottom.

His clearance diminished as he went forward and deeper. Machinery noises and occasional pounding seemed startlingly close at times from inside the vessel. The heavy mine dragged in the slime underneath him, his tanks scraped unavoidably against the hull above. There was a total darkness in front of him and only a narrow brightness to his left, but gradually the curve of the hull flattened, leaving him enough room to half swim, half crawl.

The hull began to taper and the light improved as he forced himself ahead. Carefully he stayed in the darkest shadows until he came to the freighter's bulbous bow. There he stopped with twenty feet of open, brightly illuminated water separating him from the hull of the *Baltic Merchant* and its concealing darkness beneath.

There was no way to know if anyone was watching at that moment and going to the surface for a look would only ensure his detection if there were. So, keenly aware of the constant stream of bubbles billowing over his head, Pfifer gripped the mine in his hands and swam for it. It would be a pure risk, but at least a brief one.

In a few seconds he crossed from the shadow of one freighter to the shadow of the next and dove straight for the bottom, under the stern of the *Baltic Merchant*.

This mine would be the bow charge.

The *Baltic Merchant* rode higher in the water and her hull was cleaner. It allowed Pfifer to make better time. When he reached the bow, he clamped the charge dead-center, gave it a tug to make sure the magnet would hold, then kicked his way back down under the hull. Without the ballast weight of the mine he had to struggle to stay down. Finally he turned over and swam on his back, using his hands to hold himself away from the hull. He hand-walked the length of the keel in that fashion and then paused near the freighter's huge rudder.

Once again he had come to the light. This time he would likely break the surface as he crossed. He procrastinated to allow himself to gather up his energy. Perhaps he could dive low, pushing off? If he could arc low enough, he might make it. Carefully he pulled his knees to his chest and positioned his fins on the edge of the rudder.

With a violent thrust Pfifer committed himself to the effort. It pushed him deep and fast. Then gracefully he rose, coming closer and closer to the glimmering surface. Just as he thought he had fallen short, his hands slammed against a crusty wall of steel.

He cursed himself for not thinking of wearing gloves when his hands touched the sharp barnacles on the first freighter. He was numb from the cold but he could still feel the sting of salt in each fresh cut as he clawed and kicked his way down. He might improvise something when he got back to the truck, but the damage would be done by then. All he could do now was swim as carefully and as close to the light as he could.

He gave a sigh of relief as he passed between the screws and angled toward the surface. When he was far enough away, he came up completely and swam against the current and across the river.

He stumbled as he walked out of the water. The exhaustion spread throughout his body like a sudden chill. He lay on the soft bank, face in the mud, unable to move. There was a strange tingling sensation in his abdomen. His mind spun dizzily on the very edge of consciousness. He lost track of the time it took before he could push himself up to his hands and knees.

Slowly he crawled away from the river, oblivious to the sand being ground into his wounded hands. He scarcely noticed as he passed through the opening in the fence.

When he reached the truck, he pulled his flippers off and knelt. He wanted to rest, but he did not have the time. Drunkenly, he staggered to his feet, opened the truck and picked up the next mine.

The second trip across took more time. But the results were the same. Pfifer bundled rags into his wet suit to give him something to wrap around his hands for protection, and that helped, but when he returned he lay on the bank for more than an hour before he could move. It was nearly daylight by the time he had recovered and made his way back to the truck.

He sat on the front bumper of the truck and looked at his bloody hands and then at the river. He might have the time to make one last circuit, but did he have the energy? Did he have the oxygen in his tanks? The tingling in his abdomen had become a searing pain. His light-headedness had become acute dizziness. He told himself if he had any common sense at all he would not go back into the water.

But he had one more mine.

He got to his feet and steadied himself for a moment. Slowly he walked around the truck and pulled the final mine from its crate. He nearly dropped it, his hands were so stiff. He swore aloud, then went back to the river, too tired to take the precaution of crawling. He told himself that once the last mine was in place it would not matter how long he took coming back to the truck. All he would have to do would be to put the mine in place. Even if he just swam one way and rested the morning on the other side, at least the third mine would be where it was needed.

He entered the water. He mused that he could no longer feel the cold as the river swallowed him up. He wondered if that was how death felt.

The third mine carried him deeper into the river. He had to kick harder just to keep from touching bottom. He forced himself along, his body growing heavier and stiffer with each exaggerated stroke. At middistance, he had to control the urge to drop the mine and float to the surface. He wanted to quit. His stomach was burning him alive from the inside but he gripped the mine harder until the pain in his hands was as great as the pain in his gut, and he pressed on.

He would have seen the lighter if he had not been so fatigued. He would certainly have heard it. Even in the bad light he should have spotted the small merchant long before it closed on him. But he did not. And the sudden close pass of the hull and cavatating screws frightened him into full alertness. It caused him to reach for his very last reserve of strength to kick himself clear. Clear of the sharp bladed screws and deep into the cold black slit below.

Afterwards he could not remember clearly. He could not recall for sure if he had placed the final mine or not. All he knew was that he had made it back to the truck somehow. His tanks were nowhere to be found. His hands were torn and swollen, the pain in his body paralyzing.

He needed help, and he needed it quickly, but he could not move quickly. His reflexes seemed jumbled. And the pain, the pain was relentless. It consumed him. His body burned with it.

Slowly, tediously, he got himself into the cab of the truck and managed to start it. His hands and feet were heavy and did not seem to respond to his control. His foot slipped off the clutch pedal, causing the truck to jerk and stall. Trembling, it took two more attempts before he got the truck to reverse.

He thought about the bridge supports the instant he hit them. The truck came to an abrupt stop and stalled again, but doggedly he restarted and, amid scraping and grinding, managed to clear the bridge and its obstacles.

He drove a quarter of a mile before he blacked out.

CHAPTER
Twenty-one

The clouds had come. The breeze that filtered through the tall grass on the hill above the cottage was chilled and the smell of rain was in the air. Orin Brady put his binoculars to his eyes and stared at the back of the cottage, but his eyes did not focus. He simply stared for the sake of staring, his mind filled with other pictures.

He was blinded by those pictures. He played them in his mind again and again until they had a dreamlike quality to them. Until they became more than just memory, until they were as fresh and vivid and real as if they were now happening over again. He did not feel the cold, he did not feel the stiffening complaints of his body against the damp earth. All he saw and all he felt was Gretchen.

Her skin was firm and cool to his touch as he pressed her against him, as he caressed her back and hips, as he felt the supple bulge of her breasts. He tasted her kiss, surprised at his hunger for her, then drew her down with him to the floor.

She was ready for him as he laid her gently down. He was less ready for the sudden heat of her when they came together. He gasped, then responded, as she began to stroke his hips with the lightest of touches. Slowly, he rocked her beneath him, moving with the cadence and pace she asked for with her fingertips.

As his excitement grew he forced himself to pause, reluctant to release the moment, preferring to languish in the expectation of it. Gretchen waited patiently, staring up at him with her wide blue eyes until finally, when he felt as if he were about to burst, he gave in in a frenetic surge of energy. Gretchen lay quietly beneath him as he finished.

Fighting off the urge to doze, he pushed himself to the side of her and sat up.

"Please go now," Gretchen said in a whisper barely audible above the muted rumble of the surf.

"I didn't please you, did I?"

"Please, you promised, no questions."

"I'm sorry. I tried very hard to please you."

Gretchen stood. The sight of her standing over him aroused him rapidly. He reached out to her and took her hands in his. Carefully but deliberately he drew them to the sides of his head. She looked down at him for a moment before she understood; then, with an impish smile on her face, she stepped close to him and eagerly guided his new hunger to her.

A light rain began to fall. The radio crackled in Orin's ear.

"Orin? Is anything wrong? You missed your check-in."

"No, sorry Josh, I guess I overlooked it. Everything is fine."

"Do you want Freddy to relieve you? It's almost time anyway."

"No. I'm fine."

The radio made a sound as if Josh were about to transmit more, but then it went quiet. It occurred to Orin that his men might very well be baffled by his behavior the last two days. He wondered how he would sort it all out, how he would manage to cover himself sufficiently to keep his career and if he really wanted to keep his career. As he considered it he frowned and swore aloud at his own stupidity.

The rain fell more heavily. It was a cold rain, an unpleasant rain. Orin adjusted his camouflage hat and turned up his collar, but still he felt its coldness on him.

If George Long learned exactly what had happened, Orin would have no say in what would happen to him. He would be out of the Agency, certainly, and possibly charged as well. It would be far more unpleasant than the cold rain. It would be the end of a way of life, the beginning of a much different one. The thought of it caused him to tremble.

What had happened to his self-control? How stupid could he have been to let Gretchen compromise him so devastatingly? He wasn't some rank amateur. He was supposed to be a professional, a competent and trusted professional. What was it about Gretchen that had made it so easy for her to knock him so thoroughly off-balance?

He had been alone, but that was no excuse. It was a lonely profession. It had been far too long since he had known a woman, even been with someone, but there had been opportunities. He wondered if any of it made any difference now. The answer, he knew, was as much in himself as in Gretchen.

A new sound brought Orin abruptly out of his dazed thoughts. He put the binoculars to his eyes and swept the beach, then looked beyond the shoreline.

A small boat approached. It was headed roughly toward the cottage. Orin watched it and waited to see if it would veer away. When it continued on its course, he picked up his radio and signaled.

"Josh, I've got a small cruiser approaching. Get Freddy down here on the double and tell him to bring a rifle."

"Right!" Josh answered immediately.

Orin watched as the boat bore on toward the shore. He felt an uneasy tension, an apprehension as it neared. Suddenly he wished that it was someone else on the hill at that moment and not him. He questioned whether he would be able to do what would have to be done if what he feared took place—if Gretchen were about to be picked up by her terrorist accomplices. He could not let that happen. She was their only link. He could not let her escape, even though it might solve his problem. If she could not be questioned, she could not reveal his indiscretion. Had she known who he really was, what he was really doing? Would it be possible that she had deceived him, manipulated him, to improve her odds? Whether she had or not, his mistake and subsequent omission had done just that.

He saw Gretchen. She had gone out the front door of the cottage and had begun to cross the open beach. Reluctantly, he got up and started down the hill after her. What would happen now would have to run its own course, he told himself. There would be no time for thinking, only reacting, only duty.

When he reached the cottage he began to run. Ahead of him he could see Gretchen already at the water's edge. The cruiser lay off the shore no more than thirty yards, holding its position in the gentle swells. Two dark-skinned men stood at its controls. One began to wave and shout frantically as he spotted Orin pounding across the sand.

Gretchen turned. Orin could see her face clearly. He called her name.

Then the sharp staccato of an automatic weapon came from the cruiser and the sand erupted just in front of Orin's feet. Violently he jagged to his left and continued to run. All he could see was Gretchen's face. All he wanted to do was to get close to her.

Gretchen stood in disbelief as Orin advanced toward her.

She held her hand up, as if to tell him to stop, as again the automatic weapon began to fire.

This time the aim was far better.

Orin felt the bullets enter his chest, their impact knocking him to the sand. He heard Gretchen scream, felt curiously little pain, and tried to sit up. He met Gretchen's gaze for an instant before she turned away from him and began to lunge into the surf toward the cruiser. From behind him he heard the methodical firing of a rifle.

Gretchen was waist-deep in the surf before Freddy found his mark. When the shell struck her, she stood bolt upright for a fraction of a second before she collapsed backward.

The cold sea lifted her up and as she relaxed into its embrace it pushed her back toward the shore. Orin called to her, but his voice seemed far away. He saw her hand rise above the surface and seem to reach out for him, but then she was lost in the tumble of the waves. Then, as the images faded in his brain, as the numbness spread through his body, they all seemed to get lost in the tumble of the eternal waves.

CHAPTER
Twenty-two

When he woke up the pain was gone. It was the first thing he noticed.

He was in a hospital room; a private room. His hands were bandaged and his face clean-shaven. It was remarkable. Other than some pain in his hands, and a little stiffness, he felt fine again. His head had cleared completely. The dizziness gone.

Pfifer sat up, no problem. He wondered how long he had been unconscious, guessing that it must have been for several days, but that would not explain why his hands had not healed. Even with the bandages he could tell the cuts were still fresh. It confused him. He lay back down slowly and closed his eyes.

Beyond his door someone spoke in a soft voice. Then there was the sound of a chair scraping on the tile floor and the tread of footsteps. Pfifer tensed as he heard the creak of hinges and the sudden increase in background noise. When he opened his eyes he was not surprised to see George Long standing in the doorway.

"Welcome back," Long said and gave an uncharacteristic smile.

"What happened?"

"To begin with, you disobeyed my orders—again. Why didn't you tell me you substituted your prescription? I thought I made our ground rules very clear. That little lapse nearly cost you your life. If we hadn't been keeping an eye on you, you'd be history."

A sudden realization gripped Pfifer. It was a cold grip. He stared at Long, telling himself that he should not be shocked at anything Long might do, but he was repulsed nonetheless.

"So you drugged me? Isn't that a new low, even for you? Why, George? Did you want to kill me?"

"Settle down. If I had wanted to kill you, you would be dead. It was a compound drug; a poison and its antidote mixed in a single capsule. The poison involved stays active in the system somewhat longer than the antidote. It gave us reliable control. If you had been picked up, if you had decided to go over to the other side.... It was necessary."

The anger surged within Pfifer, but he retained his self-control.

"And that makes it acceptable?"

"I'm not here to discuss philosophy, John. I simply wanted to let you know that you are, as of now, out of this operation. You should be returning to the States very shortly."

"And what about Martin Stein?"

Long paused, the smile faded on his face.

"Martin is still in the hands of his kidnappers."

"Then the operation isn't over. Are you aware of the fact I was successful in planting the charges on the freighter?"

Long waved him off.

"You don't understand. The operation is over. We've been blown."

"Blown? How?"

"The girl Gretchen made her surveillance. She was killed in an escape attempt. One of McKintosh's agents was shot as well. But the terrorists that attempted to pick her up from the safe house got away clean. It's very unlikely that the KGB is ignorant of our involvement at this point. They undoubtedly radioed the freighter. That means the main objective of our operation is now a moot point."

It took a moment for it all to sink in. They were writing Martin Stein off. They were writing Howard Stein off with him. And all George Long could do was smile and tell him how cleverly he had tricked him. What was the point to it? What had Long gained that made him so pleased with himself? And where did Pfifer stand now?

"What day is it, George?"

"Sunday. You've only lost a few hours."

Pfifer nodded.

"Rachel. Where is Rachel?"

"She's outside. She wanted to see you. Under the circumstances, I didn't think it would matter. She has to understand now that she's lost her brother." Long studied Pfifer's expression for a moment, then added, "She's quite the girl, isn't she?"

"Yes, as a matter of fact. How's she taking it all?"

"See for yourself."

Long turned and left the room. In a moment, Rachel walked through the door and closed it behind her. She wore a yellow dress. It fit her rather well. Pfifer felt a twinge as he looked at her, and it caught him off-guard.

"Do I look that bad?" she asked.

"No, I'm sorry, I don't know what to say to you."

Rachel looked at him. She seemed composed.

"You don't have to say anything. I know you did the best you could."

Rachel came to his bedside, then reached out and touched his hand. It was a gentle touch, tentative, questioning. Pfifer resisted the urge to take her in his arms. Finally she removed her hand and as she did a troubled expression clouded her face.

"Can I ask you a question?"

"I'm not sure I'll know the answer. There's a lot going on I haven't been told. I'm as confused as you are at the moment, maybe more."

"Do you think Martin is still alive?"

"Probably not."

Pfifer watched helplessly as the tears welled up in Rachel's eyes and her composure evaporated. When she spoke it was with a husky voice.

"I was hoping you would tell me he was still alive, or that you believed he was. I wasn't prepared to accept it until I heard it from you."

"You still haven't heard it from me. Not exactly. I only said probably not."

"Please, don't play games with me. Not now."

"I'm trying not to, Rachel. As I've said before, it all depends on what Martin was willing to tell them. If it was interesting enough, and if he told them before they got too aggressive with him, he could very well be alive."

"That's just it. Martin knows nothing. My father would have never trusted him with any of the information about the network. Martin has nothing to offer but the ransom . . ."

Pfifer stiffened. The pieces suddenly fit together for him. For an instant, he got a glimpse of yet another of the facets of Long's deception. He looked at Rachel and spoke very carefully.

"According to my briefing, Rachel, Martin knows a great deal. Enough to expose the network and cause serious damage."

She stared at him, disbelieving.

"That can't be true . . ."

"And in the beginning you were right in your assumptions about me. Joe Bryant had it figured. If I couldn't get Martin off the freighter alive, I was authorized to kill him."

Rachel wiped her eyes. She stood straighter.

"That doesn't matter now. The important thing is he's still alive," she said. "And I think he can be gotten off that ship. There is a way, there must be."

"Don't do anything stupid. You can't save him, not alone."

"Do I have to do it alone?"

Rachel leaned over the bed and kissed him before he could answer. She kissed him hard, aggressively. He began to react in spite of himself. Reluctantly he pushed her away.

Rachel stood for a second and looked at him. Without another word she reached into her pocket, withdrew a small, tightly folded piece of paper and pressed it into his hand. Then, ignoring his puzzled look, she turned and walked slowly from the room. She did not look back as she closed the door behind her.

Pfifer unfolded the note and read it.

It was an address in a part of Hamburg that he knew. Along with the address, a one-sentence message. "Two men, armed, twenty-four-hour guard. Love."

He crushed the tiny note in his hand and lay back, staring at the ceiling. Did she know what she was asking him to do? Did she understand the risks involved? If he escaped from the hospital—and he was not sure he could even do that—the CIA would be after him in force. George Long would orchestrate a net of agents that he would never evade.

To further suggest that he liberate her from her safe house was only added insanity. He had no papers, no money, no resources—or did he?

Carefully, quietly, Pfifer eased out of his bed and stood. In one corner of his room there was a small closet. He crossed the room to it and pulled its door open. Inside he found his denims, a pullover shirt, and his leather jacket. In the inside pocket of his jacket, he spotted the top edge of his passport and wallet.

He took a step back. His instincts told him all was not right; definitely not right. George Long was no fool. Did he think Pfifer was? Did he think his mind was so drugged, or his feelings for Rachel so strong, that he would overlook so blatant an invitation to slip the traces? Was Rachel involved in the ruse? He swore to himself and stretched his suddenly aching muscles.

Why should he take the bait? Why shouldn't he? What was his alternative? Another mission under Long's control? Elimination by one of Long's fledglings? Why not take the bait? What did he really have to lose?

Pfifer loosened his hospital gown and let it fall to the floor. The sight of his pale, emaciated body stunned him. Why not take the bait, he asked himself again. He was a dead man, anyway. The game was lost. All that was left was one final play to close the hand. He could make that final play and he could do it on his own terms if he was lucky.

Why not?

As he dressed, he ran the situation through his mind. First, he would have to escape from the hospital. If he had guessed right, the security on him would be just enough to look convincing without being too obvious. They would let him get that far. Then he would need transportation, a weapon, and to retrieve the detonator device. They would probably let him get that far as well. Would they let him pursue the freighter? At what point would they close in on him? And would they let him take Rachel, or was that her own variation to the plan?

They might all be looking for him. The CIA, George Long, the terrorists, possibly the KGB, possibly even the German police. Furthermore, they would know approximately where he was headed. The north seacoast would be impassible for him within hours, unless . . .

George Long might sit on the situation. He might cover it up for a short period of time. If he did that, Pfifer might get a shot at it. But why would Long do that? Did he still want the freighter stopped?

Dressed, Pfifer held his hands out in front of him. They were steady. How long did he have? How long before his insides began to burn away? This time they would let him die. This time it would be over.

The clock was running. With each beat the freighter moved further away, his time dwindled. He had to move quickly now, and no mistakes.

Pfifer looked around the room. It was on the first floor. It had a single window covered with a heavy wire mesh. If he could break through it would be a short drop to the ground, but the noise would bring the guard through the door immediately and the mesh looked as if it could take a substantial beating before giving way. No, there was a better way.

He spotted a chair, hefted it, then put it back down. Then he looked at the portable dinner tray. It was fairly heavily built and it was adjustable for height. Pfifer cranked it up so it would match up with a pane on the window. Then he rolled over beside the door and aimed it carefully. After a brief hesitation, he put his foot on the bottom of the tray and gave it a quick shove.

The window cracked and shattered glass fell to the floor as the tray slammed into it. As expected, the guard reacted instantly. He charged into the room as a bull charges a matador's cape. Pfifer had but to administer the coup de grace as he passed, two hands clasped and brought sharply down on the neck. The guard nosed in facedown and limp on the floor. It was too easy.

Pfifer felt the man's pulse. He was still alive. His bulky neck had taken Pfifer's blow well, but if he wasn't truly unconscious, he was a consummate actor. Pfifer felt for his weapon, found a small automatic, then got up, slipped it into his jacket pocket, and stepped over the body to the door. Carefully, he looked out.

The activity in the hall seemed normal. A nurse wheeled a medicine cart nonchalantly toward him, stopped at a room, and went in. Taking a deep breath first, Pfifer stepped into the hall and began to walk. There was an exit sign and an arrow pointing down a side corridor halfway between the nurse's cart and Pfifer's position. He made it just before the nurse emerged from the room.

A door at the end of the corridor led to a parking lot. Beyond the parking lot a small group of people were boarding a bus. Pfifer hurried across the pavement and joined them.

Pfifer parked the rented Volvo station wagon two blocks from the safe house. He made sure the detonator device and his other gear was covered completely in the back and then got out. It was dusk, and it was beginning to get damp as he pulled his coat around himself and started to walk.

It was an old neighborhood. Once it was probably a stylish spot, but now it just looked old, and beaten, and used. One- and two-story houses huddled close together, their ornamental brickwork looking chipped and weathered in the fading light. They looked sad somehow, and foreboding. Pfifer laughed at himself for thinking it so, but quickened his step.

He took notice of the sequence of house numbers as he walked and guessed which one was the safe house long before he reached it. He wanted to pass by it without appearing to be overly interested. He concentrated on the sidewalk, the grass, the curbing—anything—relying on his peripheral vision to tell him what he wanted to know.

The lights were on upstairs, shades drawn. No cars were parked in front. The house next door to the safe house was in complete darkness. He made the end of the block, doubled back down a narrow alley, then leaned up against a fence to think.

Rachel had said there were two men, both armed. Pfifer had seen neither. He couldn't rush them, it was too dangerous. He would have to find a way to split them up, bring them out into the open—a diversion; what?

Perhaps Rachel could help. Pfifer thought of the dark house next door and began to walk. If he could signal her, maybe she would understand what he needed.

The wall behind the adjacent house was slightly taller than Pfifer's head. The gate was iron, spiked at the top, and locked. It seemed that not everyone was cooperating with Long's little charade, if that in fact was what it was. He was very careful as he climbed over and dropped into a garden on the other side.

He half-expected dogs to come barking, or lights to suddenly go on in the darkened house, but neither occurred. He made it to the back door and discovered it quite easy to force open. It had a gridwork of panes, one of which Pfifer broke with a loose stone from a flowerbed, allowing him to reach in and open it from the inside. The shattered glass crunched under his feet as he stepped in and quickly found his way to a staircase leading upstairs.

As he tread softly up the carpeted steps, he tried to listen for any signs that the house might not be as empty as he had assumed. But the house was quiet, and a musty smell told him it had been closed for some time. He followed a hallway from the top of the stairs to what he guessed was the master bedroom. It had a double window, covered with heavy drapes that made the room almost completely dark. It forced him to move slowly across the room, feeling his way with his hands.

The drapes parted easily. Beyond, Pfifer could see into the safe house through its side windows. Careless, he thought, neither one was covered, or perhaps Rachel had already begun to make things easier for him? In either case, he saw both men in the front room; one sat on a couch, the other stood talking with him. But where was she?

Only a few minutes passed before he saw her. She appeared at the rear window dressed in her jeans and a sweater. Pfifer could see her clearly, but she seemed to be looking toward the alley, a troubled expression on her face. Quickly, Pfifer looked about the room he was in, and in the dim light he could see a book of matches on the top of a dresser beside him. He struck one, held it close to the window, moving it back and forth slowly. He struck another before Rachel noticed. When he was certain of her attention, he leaned near the flickering light so she could see his face.

Rachel smiled, held up two fingers to indicate the two guards and then held her palms up for him to wait. Pfifer nodded, blew out the match, and stood in the darkness. She had given it some thought, obviously. He would follow her lead.

He saw her enter the front room and talk to one of the guards. After a brief interchange the man on the couch got up and moved to the door. Pfifer lost sight of him and then lost sight of Rachel as she turned away.

When she reappeared at the window she held up one finger, gave him a cautious look, and motioned him to the front of the safe house. Pfifer struck a third match to acknowledge her, then felt his way back through the dark room and into the hall. In a few careful moments he had made his way downstairs. He paused there, checked the clip in the automatic, slipped it back into his coat pocket, and went out toward the street.

It was nearly dark now. A small sedan passed in the street with its headlights full on just as Pfifer stepped from the house. Watching it go by, he tried to look as nonchalant as possible, as if it were his own house he was leaving. Then, with a quick look up and down the street to make sure it was clear, he moved off.

He had not seen the second guard actually leave the safe house. He could only hope that Rachel had been successful in whatever diversion she had employed. It was up to him now to gain entrance. He was keenly aware that he held both of their lives very much in his hands. He could not count on extricating Rachel with the same ease with which he had escaped from the hospital. The assumption that he could would be far too dangerous for Rachel. No, he would have to believe that his opposition would be real and that it would be deadly.

At the front of the safe house he paused, tried the door cautiously, found it open, and went in.

Inside, there was a short hallway, a door to the right leading into the lower apartment, and a staircase to the left. Pfifer mounted the steps noisily and when he reached the door to the upper level he pounded on it vigorously. His best chance would be a simple ruse. If he did not approach in stealth, perhaps he would gain the seconds he would need to surprise them, perhaps they would not respond quite as quickly. Let them assume, if they would, that he had no inkling of danger or of their purpose. All he would need would be a hesitation, enough uncertainty to allow him to take action first.

At first there was no response. Pfifer pounded again.

"Go away!" a voice finally called from inside.

Pfifer began to speak loudly in German.

"Go away, I said. I don't speak German."

Pfifer continued his routine persistently until, after several moments, he heard the locks begin to come off. In anticipation, he moved closer to the door.

It opened narrowly; an inch, no more. As it did, a sliver of a face appeared to look him over. Pfifer could sense the tension, the uncertainty in the dark eye that peered out at him. Pressing his advantage, he began to speak in a highly agitated voice and point toward the street.

The man caught sight of Pfifer's bandaged hands and let the door open fractionally more. It was enough to let Pfifer see Rachel approaching in the background with a heavy vase in her hands, as well as the thick barrel of the man's revolver.

The man read the subtle change in Pfifer's expression, but it was too late. The instant he glanced behind himself, Pfifer crashed through the door.

Rachel stood over them with the vase poised over her head and a look of near panic on her face as they thrashed at each other on the floor before her. But, unable to find a clear target, she backed away from them helplessly.

Furniture and lamps toppled as they fought. The room became darker by degrees. Pfifer expected to see the flash of the man's gun or feel it crushing his skull at any moment, but apparently it had been jarred loose from his grasp by the sudden impact of Pfifer's charge. It was only minor solace. His stocky foe was strong and his blows seemed to become more accurate as the battle ensued. He was almost convinced that he was overmatched, when he managed to catch the man's guard down and land a direct shot square to the jaw. At that, the man went down hard to his knees. Then he pitched forward in a multicolored shower of pottery shards as Rachel finished the job with a brutal chop of the vase.

Pfifer stood, half dazed, looking at his hands. They were soaked with blood. The next thing he knew, Rachel was in his arms. He held her gently for a few seconds before he spoke.

"Get whatever you need and hurry," he said trying to shake his head clear.

"Right," Rachel answered and pushed herself dutifully away.

"Where the hell is the other one, anyway?"

"I told them I needed some aspirin, he went to get it."

"How long before he's back?"

Rachel glanced at her watch and frowned.

"Anytime."

Pfifer shook his head a final time and pushed her toward the bedroom. She came back quickly with a small case and then together they stepped through the wreckage to the door. Pfifer led as they went down the dark staircase and out.

"I don't see any sign of him," Rachel whispered as they moved along the sidewalk.

"Don't be surprised if you don't," Pfifer said, ignoring her sudden, quizzical look.

"I suppose you'll explain that later?"

"Later."

They reached the Volvo and got under way. Pfifer gripped the wheel and worked the gearshift with some difficulty. As he did, he sensed her staring at the soiled bandages on his hands.

"We'll have to see to those as soon as we can," she said softly.

"They'll do."

He drove quickly but not erratically. He wanted some distance between them and the city. By now, Long would know that he had gone to ground, and, when Rachel's second guard returned to the safe house, he would know he had taken Rachel with him. He could only guess how hot things would get from here on. He could only guess how much further they would let him go. The safest thing he could do was to slip away from them as effectively and as quickly as possible.

In his mind he knew that Long had let him go. He did not know exactly why, and he did not know how deeply Rachel was involved, but he did know what he was going to do. He was going to play straight from the top of the deck, realizing the odds heavily favored the house.

He was going for Martin Stein.

"Would you talk to me?" Rachel suddenly asked.

"The first time I abducted you, you didn't want me to talk."

"Things change."

"So they do."

"You have a plan, don't you?"

"I have part of a plan, Rachel. I'll have to improvise as I go along, as we go along."

Rachel smiled, then turned her face away.

"You have to realize, we don't have much of a chance. The CIA will be on our tail for the duration. They'll catch up to us, or trap us, one way or another, and probably very soon.

"George Long knows what I have in mind for the freighter. We talked about it in Rotterdam. He knows where I intended to rendezvous with them and he has the means to track them—for all I know, the means to track us as well.

"The worst part is, he will be expecting me to follow through. It won't come as any surprise. And that, of course, is exactly what I intend to do. With a very mild modification."

Rachel turned toward him and gave him a long look.

"Why did you come for me?"

"Is it important?"

"It is to me."

"I think you already know part of the answer. The other part, call it a course correction made at whatever price it takes. It's just something I have to do."

"You're one of the most remarkable men I've ever known. Did you know that?"

"I'm perhaps one of the most remarkable fools, but that's ancient history, and what we have to concentrate on is the future, the immediate future, because believe me, that's all there is."

Rachel looked down at the floor, her arms folded loosely in front of her. When she looked up her eyes were moist and her expression cloudy.

"There are some things I should tell you. It will make you angry at me but you deserve to know," she said.

Pfifer looked in his mirror and then back at the road. He waited patiently for Rachel to continue.

"I've made a deal with Long. You were allowed to escape from the hospital."

"Not exactly what I would call a startling revelation."

"You knew? You don't care?"

"You should know that you can't make deals with the devil. What did he promise you, anyway? And what did you promise him?"

"I promised him my cooperation in continuing to run the network after this is over. In exchange, he was to let you finish your assignment, if I could persuade you. And afterward set you free."

Pfifer shook his head. She had offered her very future in exchange for his. Why? Why give everything away? It was more than he could understand. They had so little chance for success—indeed, for survival.

"Is that all of it?"

"Not exactly. I'm afraid getting me out of Long's custody wasn't part of the deal."

Pfifer shook his head. She had double-crossed Long and very well, thank you. No wonder his struggle with her guard had been so difficult. It had been, as he had expected, not part of Long's plan.

"Nice work, Rachel. But you weren't told one very important little item.—They never tell us everything, didn't you know?—Don't ask me to explain it in chemical terms, I'm no chemist, but I do know this. They have me on some sort of medication, some sort of compound. I don't know exactly what it is, but I've had a preview of how it works. When I stop taking the medication, after a day or two, it incapacitates me. I expect the end result is probably fatal."

Rachel looked at him, eyes wide. She had not known.

"Isn't there anything we can do?" she asked.

"Not that I'm aware of. By the time anyone figured out what the compound was and what to do about it, it would be too late."

"Why, in God's name, would they do such a thing to you?"

"George would call it 'reliable control.' This way he knows if I don't do what he says I'm automatically eliminated. As a problem, I solve myself. You see, I deviated from what was expected of me on my last assignment, and this is George's way of covering all the bases."

They reached the autobahn north. Rachel sat stunned in her seat. Pfifer increased their speed. It was nearly an hour before Rachel spoke.

"I've been lied to," she said finally.

"So what else is new."

"I'm not quite sure what to do about it."

"Try helping me."

"How?"

"I managed to get charges in place on the hull of the freighter. I have the equipment necessary to detonate those charges in the back. The problem is knowing exactly where the freighter is. If we can find her, we have a good chance of stopping her. Beyond that it's anybody's ball game."

Pfifer stared straight ahead into the luminous tunnel their headlights were making in the darkness. He had other questions he needed to ask her. He hoped she had the answers.

"I am curious about one thing. Does your father know about your duplicity with the CIA, and is there anyone else involved, the Mossad perhaps?"

Rachel laughed.

"What's so funny?"

"My father knows nothing about my CIA involvement, and he's had a strong dislike for the Mossad for as long as I can remember. He would be absolutely livid if he found out they were involved in any way or even aware of the network in a primary way."

"A Jew, escaped from Nazi Germany, dislikes the Mossad? I suppose it's understandable. The SS would have gone a long way toward putting him off on anybody's intelligence organization or secret police. Still?"

"What are you trying to say?"

"Nothing really, just thinking out loud."

"If you have questions, ask them. I don't want secrets between us, not now."

"I have a basic understanding of what your father has been up to for the last twenty-five years. George Long went to lengths to brief me thoroughly, or so I thought.

"Basically he's been channeling diamonds to the Agency, who in turn has been delivering them to a network inside East Germany. I don't know exactly what this network does, or why it's so important to save."

"The network primarily brings people out of East Germany. The CIA debriefs them for any useful information as part of the deal."

"An escape group?"

"It sounds simple, doesn't it? But it's been my father's lifework. That and his diamond business. It was to be my work as well. Now, who knows. The network will come apart without funding. The KGB can't help but learn of the whole thing. It's all turning to ashes in front of our eyes."

"Maybe it's time it turned to ashes. Maybe that's what George Long had in mind from the beginning."

"That's crazy! Why would the Agency want a valuable source of intelligence, let alone a humanitarian enterprise, exposed to the KGB? What good would that do anyone?"

Rachel was angry. Pfifer did not enjoy seeing her that way, but he had to press her a bit farther. How much did she really know? How many pieces of the puzzle lay about in her mind that for one reason or another she had never connected? He took the next step closer with a deep sense of reluctance. George Long's side game? He felt as if he were on the edges of it, but still he could not see it clearly.

"Let me ask you just a couple of questions about your father, Rachel. Then we can let the matter drop and concentrate on Martin."

"Fair enough."

"How much do you know about the origins of your father's business? Do you know where he got the initial money to set himself up? Do you have an idea who his major stockholders are?"

Rachel stopped and thought.

"All he ever told me about it was that a group of investors had backed him, they apparently had believed in him." Rachel shook her head. "As far as stockholders, he doesn't have any. The business is a sole proprietorship. My father is the only owner."

"Do you know any of the original investors? Where they came from, where they are today?"

"No. I know the diamonds that are cut and fed into the network come from sources all over the world, but their exact names, other than company names, and their identities have never been divulged. If my father knows who they are, he keeps that information to himself."

Pfifer sat up straight.

"You mean that the diamonds he sends in aren't his own, they aren't taken from the profits of his business or pulled out in some other way?"

"Certainly you didn't think he embezzled them, did you? I assure you there is no way that could have been done successfully for the period of time we're talking about. The diamonds are too expensive. Clients are far too careful with keeping track of what they send us and what they get back. It's been his reliability in that area that has helped him build his business as rapidly as he has."

Pfifer drove on in silence. If he had wondered about Rachel before, now he could be certain. She was the one person who was simply what she appeared to be, a sister fighting for the life of her brother. She was obviously holding nothing back.

Her father, on the other hand, seemed to have a few too many secrets. Perhaps that was what George Long had been after. Perhaps that was what this had been all about from the beginning.

Pfifer thought back to the two men he had killed in the alley behind the church, and he thought of the old forger's dead body, so plainly killed in hate. Why couldn't he have seen it sooner? Damn George Long! Someone was paying to pull key people out of East Germany, and they were paying handsomely. It was this shadowy, third faction that Long had been after, and Long had wanted them badly enough to sacrifice Martin Stein, and Rachel, and of course Pfifer himself, in his attempt to get at them. It was a bloody balance sheet so far and the body count would only climb.

"There is one other thing I want to tell you," Rachel said, breaking his train of thought. "I know this isn't the right time to say it, but I love you."

Pfifer lifted his foot from the accelerator and swore under his breath. It was the last thing he had expected her to say, as well as the last thing he was prepared to believe.

"That's an odd reaction to have, after being told someone loves you. Care to explain it?"

"Rachel, I don't have any desire to hurt you in any way, but of all the men on the face of this earth I have the least to offer you. You have a chance to come through this. There's a life for you beyond it. Don't you understand? Let me make it very clear for you. If the terrorists don't kill me and possibly you too, if the CIA doesn't head us off, if we actually do get your brother off that freighter, if we can get past all of that, I'm still a dead man. Whatever drugs the Agency has put in me will see to that."

"I understand perfectly well what you are saying. I know it doesn't even begin to make sense. I've tried to reason my way out of it, but I can't change the way I feel. Logic has nothing to do with it. If you live one more day or a hundred years, it doesn't make any difference.''

''What is it with you people that gives you the capacity for such blind faith? Would you tell me that? What makes you think you have a guarantee on the future?''

She did not answer him. She simply reached out to him and touched him gently on the shoulder. When he looked at her she was smiling.

''I guess you have one more problem now, don't you?'' she said.

CHAPTER
Twenty-three

They sat in the back of the coffeehouse in an ornately carved wooden booth. Along the wall, rows of porcelain figurines stood in legions on long shelves. Pfifer held a large stein cupped in his hands and looked steadily at Rachel across the table from him. She looked back pensively.

"What do we do?" she asked.

"If the freighter got away on schedule, and she has so far, I can estimate their approximate position."

"And then what? Will we try and intercept them off the coast of Denmark?"

"No. We can count on the border being closely watched by the Agency now. Besides, I told George Long I'd make the attempt near Sylt on the North Sea. He'll have his people swarming all over the region before we do anything."

"But my deal? Won't he let us through?"

"You'd better realize, the moment you left the safe house and out from under his thumb, all bets were off. Believe me, what George wants now is to pick us up again, and as fast as possible.''

"What then?''

"What we'll do is go east to Kiel. We'll get a boat and go north in the Baltic and try and catch the freighter as they make their run for home.''

"How will we find them again? Once they're in the open sea, it will be impossible.''

"If they make it to the open sea, you're probably right. But that's where Long will help us.''

Rachel stared at him, bewildered. It was understandable, Pfifer supposed. He decided to tell her, as best he could, what he saw as their only course of action. She had been successful in manipulating George Long, perhaps together they could manage it one more time.

"The *Baltic Merchant* got under way at seven o'clock this morning. She's been headed due north at between twelve and fifteen knots.— That's about as fast as one of those ships can go, and I doubt they'll be wasting any time.— At any rate, it shouldn't be too tough for them to spot her. I'd be surprised if in fact she wasn't already being tracked either by air or radar. But when she passes out of the North Sea and into the Baltic the situation changes. That's the Russians' home turf. Long will have to back off or he'll run the very real risk of a confrontation he has no authorization for. Simply put, once the freighter makes it into the Baltic, she's in the clear.''

"I'm afraid I'm not following you. Isn't that why we should do something before they get to the Baltic?''

"Between Sweden and Denmark there are only five channels she can take to make her entry into the Baltic Sea, but there's no way for anyone to know ahead of time which one of those channels she will use or at what coordinates she will enter the Baltic. Not until the last few hours. By that time Long's options will be limited. It will be the last opportunity for him to know exactly where the freighter is.

"So we're going to run a little side game of our own. We're going to give him a reason to tell us where we can intercept the freighter. I'm going to make it very clear to him that it's the only way he will know where we are, his last chance to pick us up before the Russians gain control of the situation. And make no mistake about it, it is the Russians we're up against on this. Juan and his men are undoubtedly under the control of the KGB. Most of these terrorist operations are run this way. It gives them 'plausible deniability.' "

Rachel shuddered.

Pfifer sat there and drew a long gulp of his hot coffee.

"It's a matter of timing and opportunity. George Long won't like it, but he will do it. He'll get a pilot to crisscross those channels and spot the freighter for us, he'll radio us with the position, and unless I miss my guess he'll be close by when things begin to happen.

"I'm gambling, Rachel. There are a million things that can go wrong, but it's the only thing we can do. How do you feel about it? If you want me to leave you here, I'll understand."

Pfifer set his empty stein on the table. Rachel reached across and touched his hand as he did.

"I guess it's time to place our bet," he said softly.

Slowly but with deliberation Pfifer got up from the booth and moved to the back of the coffeehouse. As he picked up the receiver to the pay phone, near the back door, he paused a moment and listened. The few customers in the coffeehouse were thinly dispersed, their conversations a faint din. Good. Nothing to hear that might be a clue to Long as to where they were. He got hold of the operator; quickly he was rung through.

When Pfifer returned from the telephone, Rachel gave him a questioning glance as he sat down.

"For the moment," he told her, "all we can do is go on

to Kiel, find a place to stay the rest of the night, and locate a boat in the morning. Tomorrow, my darling, is apt to be one very busy day. Let's hope we're up to it.''

In Kiel they found a small guesthouse on the outskirts of the city. A matronly woman took their money and gave them keys and a glance that told them she thought the worst of them but was glad for the business. They followed her upstairs to a tiny room that was almost completely filled with a double bed and a small wardrobe. Then the woman pointed out the bath at the end of the hall and left them to themselves.

"Well," Rachel said. "We certainly shouldn't get lost in here. It reminds me of that packing crate you brought me across the border in.''

"I'll ask her for another room if you want, or separate rooms.''

"No, please, this will be fine.''

Rachel put her small case into the wardrobe and turned to see Pfifer looking at her.

"I'm sorry, Rachel, for this whole thing,'' he said.

"I'm sorry for my brother. I'm not sorry for myself.''

Rachel looked up at the ceiling. The room was lit by a single fixture with a long pull string that fell to the center of the bed. She laughed.

"What's so funny?''

"I was just thinking how convenient that light is to turn on and off,'' Rachel said and lay down on the bed. She looked at Pfifer and casually kicked her shoes onto the floor. "Come lie beside me.''

Pfifer reached behind himself and locked the door. He stood there for a moment and looked at her before he spoke.

"I've warned you. There is absolutely no future to be had with me.''

"Come lie beside me,'' she said again softly.

Pfifer hesitated, then sat on the edge of the bed and removed his shoes. Rachel snapped the light off.

"I was wrong when I told you I was the most remarkable fool. You've got me beat by a mile."

Rachel kicked at him gently, then said, "If you say another word, I'm going to scream."

Pfifer laughed and lay back.

He did not resist her, why should he? If she wanted him, he would give himself to her. It would help him through what he believed were his last few hours, certainly his last night. He needed to make one final intimate connection with his humanity before he lost himself to what would be his unavoidable end. It would give him something to think of, to remember, besides the pain.

She was not expecting him to take the lead. It surprised her, and it pleased her. He gently and deftly removed her clothes and then his own. Then they lay for a long while simply holding each other, gradually exploring.

Rachel responded to him strongly. She caught her breath as he played his hand over her hips, grew impatient, took his hand. He let her guide it to her.

She dug her fingers into the hard muscles of his back as he teased her, tantalized her. Finally he pulled her under him and thrust himself deeply into her. She cried out with the pleasure of it. Her breath came in short gasps as they moved together.

For the moment, there was no world outside their door. No danger, no fear. There was only the bond between them, the filling of a mutual need. The next day would bring what it would. This space in time would belong to them.

The morning poured its golden light through their tiny window and bathed them in its warmth.

Pfifer awoke first. When he opened his eyes, Rachel lay against him in deep sleep. Carefully he pulled the soft blue blanket back so he could see her face.

"Rachel," he said quietly, "wake up. You sleep like a child. Did you know that?"

"I'm not a child," she said, greeting him with sleepy brown eyes.

"I'm very much aware of that."

Rachel drew herself closer to him and kissed him tentatively.

"The dream is over, isn't it?" she asked, sadly.

"I'm afraid so."

"What do you think our chances really are? Are we just going to waste ourselves for nothing? I mean if I knew that Martin was already dead, if I knew there was no hope, it would change everything."

"I'm afraid there's no way to know for sure. I wish you would reconsider what I asked you, though. It would mean something to me, to know that you were safe."

"No. That would be the worst of all. Then I'd never know what happened to either one of you. I couldn't live with that. Besides, you may need my help. I want to be there."

He reached out and traced the line of her jaw with the lightest of touches and then smiled at her.

"If that's what you want."

"It's the only thing I feel I can do. I told you that I loved you. I meant it. I love my brother, too. I can't turn my back on either of you."

"I haven't told you. . . ."

Rachel put her hand to his mouth and stopped him in midsentence.

"You don't have to tell me anything. I know you care for me. I'm not asking for any commitment from you. You don't have to make any promises. All I ask is that you trust me and that if I can help you when the time comes you'll let me."

"It's been a long time since I've trusted anyone. I'm not sure I can just drop all the barriers at will. All I can say is that I'll do the best I can."

"That's all anyone ever does, anyway."

Rachel kissed him again and then sat up in the bed. The blanket fell away from her as she did.

"You know you actually look pretty good with nothing on," Pfifer said as he admired her.

"Well," Rachel said and folded her arms over her breasts in mock embarrassment. "I was beginning to wonder if you just liked me for my personality."

Pfifer caressed her smooth back and felt himself react. Rachel playfully pulled the covers off him.

"Maybe the dream's not quite over?" he said.

"I can see that," she said and let him coax her on top of him.

The yacht broker eyed them suspiciously through his plastic-framed spectacles. He was a rotund little man, his office cluttered with the mementos of his business. A dusty model of a schooner rested on the sill of his salt-spattered window. Beyond, the wharf stretched out, bristled with the masts and rigging of pleasure craft. Photographs covered the walls of the office, every one with a similar theme. In each, the little rotund figure stood beside someone standing beside a boat of some description. Occasionally it would be the same boat with a different new owner, but always it would be the same rotund little man, growing more and more round with each more recent picture.

"If you have such a boat for charter, Herr Schlosser," Pfifer said, "we would like to make the arrangements as soon as possible. We have a limited holiday and would like to make the most of it."

Schlosser glanced at Rachel and smiled.

"Of course the price would have to be fair," Pfifer added.

"Of course," Schlosser said, turning his attention back to Pfifer. "Now, you want a fast cruiser with a fly bridge, radar, and if possible auxiliary tanks?"

"Yes, as I said, we would like to cruise the coastline without having to worry about fuel. Would you have such a craft we could hire?"

"I may. Of course I would have to check with the owner to make sure of the rate. You say you are an experienced yachtsman?"

"Yes, I prefer sail, but for our purposes power would be more convenient. I'm sure you understand."

"Yes, I believe I do," Schlosser answered, clearing his throat. Slowly he pushed himself back from his desk and stood up. "Let me show you what I have and then I can make a call."

"Very well, lead on, Herr Schlosser."

Pfifer and Rachel rose and followed the little man out of his office and down the wharf. They breathed in the salt air and narrowed their eyes against the bright sunlight as they went. Rachel reached for Pfifer's hand and fell into step close beside him.

"Some of these boats are absolutely beautiful," Rachel said quite spontaneously. "I wonder why someone would sell one of them or charter it out?"

'It's not so hard to understand, Rachel. They say the two happiest days in a boat owner's life are the day he buys and the day he sells. Isn't that right, Herr Schlosser?"

The little man laughed. "The gentleman does know something of boats."

Schlosser stopped at the bow of a boat just then and let his hand rest on its prow. It was an older boat, slightly over thirty feet by Pfifer's guess, but just below the waterline, Pfifer could see a thick growth clinging to its hull.

Pfifer shook his head slowly and cast a sidelong glance at Schlosser.

"You must have something else, perhaps in better condition? This one looks as if it's been some time since it's been used. I'd hate to spoil our holiday with a mechanical breakdown."

"I understand," Schlosser said demurely and moved quickly down the wharf. Rachel, waiting until his back was turned, caught Pfifer's attention and made a face at him. He gave her a gentle pinch and pushed her forward.

When they reached the very end of the wharf, Schlosser stopped beside a sleek sports fisher. It had a red fiberglass hull with gleaming white decks and superstructure. Schlosser stroked its stainless steel railing almost affectionately as he began his pitch.

"This is a fine craft. Twin diesel engines, auxiliary tanks that will give you approximately eight hundred miles of range, surface search radar, and the latest ship to shore and shortwave radio. Would you like to go aboard?"

"After you, Herr Schlosser," Pfifer said.

Herr Schlosser's routine was born of long practice. He expertly showed them through the cruiser, pointing out her controls and features in the most attractive way. Pfifer played along, asking questions, some pertinent, some not. In half an hour, Pfifer judged that Schlosser had worked hard enough to earn his sale.

But it would not do to simply acquiesce to whatever Schlosser asked as a price. Pfifer knew the little man would be wary of that. It would take precious time, but in order to convince him that he need not worry about payment there would have to be a period of haggling. It would put his mind at rest. Only men who planned to pay worried about price. Men that could not or would not pay were the easiest of sales.

"And how much would it cost, Herr Schlosser? You have been very careful not to mention that."

"Ah yes," smiled the little man, sensing his timing was right, "shall we return to my office and discuss the details?"

"By all means."

"I can assume, then, that this meets your needs?"

"Approximately."

*   *   *

Pfifer and Rachel sat beside each other on the flying bridge of the cruiser as it churned forward eagerly into the hammered, gray-green expanse of the Baltic. Holding the wheel with one hand and Rachel with the other, Pfifer periodically looked at the compass. Below, they had carefully stowed the equipment. The cruiser's tanks were filled to maximum, and what few provisions they required were on board.

"Do you think you can hold her on a steady course?" Pfifer asked.

"I think so."

"I'll set our radio up so we can establish contact when the time comes."

"Where are we going now?"

"We're headed for coordinates that will put us within reasonable distance of all the possible routes."

Suddenly Rachel slumped in her seat. Pfifer saw her tremble. He drew her closer to him.

"Do you think we'll actually find them?" she asked softly.

"It's possible, yes."

"God help us if we do."

"God help your brother if we don't."

CHAPTER
Twenty-four

Captain Lubelski stood on the bridge wing and looked at the overcast sky. Beneath his feet he could feel a distinct vibration in the deck plates as the *Baltic Merchant* strained forward into the darkening sea. Unconsciously he stroked his jaw with his hand, then stepped back onto the bridge.

Juan waited for him inside, hands clasped behind his back, staring forward through the bridge windows.

"I will have to reduce my speed soon. The weather front will be on us in another hour," Lubelski said to him.

"You will not reduce your speed, Captain. It is now imperative that we reach our rendezvous point as soon as possible."

"We have been at maximum speed for many hours. The longer we continue at this speed, the greater the risk of a breakdown."

"I have confidence in you, Captain."

"You should be aware of the possibilities, nonetheless."

"I am aware of the possibilities, Captain. You must be

277

aware of the realities. We have reason to believe that someone will make an attempt on us before we reach Gydnia.''

"An attempt? What sort of an attempt?"

"I do not know, but the longer we are in the North Sea, the greater our risk. We must proceed with all possible speed. We have no choice. You will do what is required."

Lubelski studied the impassive face of the little terrorist. Except for a very brief reaction to the urgent radio message he had received an hour out of Hamburg, he had remained stoic, unmoved. There must have been some unsettling development in the terrorist's operation. Juan had become noticeably more taciturn. Lubelski wondered what lay ahead for them all. He was filled with anger and dread, in equal parts.

"Yes," Lubelski said after a satisfyingly long pause. "I will do what is required."

"Good."

Lubelski turned away from Juan and stepped to the bridge radar repeater. On its green screen he could make out the coast of Denmark, and, both ahead and behind, he could see large contacts he guessed were probably tankers loaded with North Sea oil. If the weather and visibility failed to cooperate, they would have a busy night of it, trying to thread the needle between them. He did not look forward to it. Especially if they did run into heavy weather. Heavy weather normally made the radar unreliable because of the multitude of spurious echos and interference it brought. Without radar it would be a deadly game indeed.

"Your men should get what rest they can," Lubelski called to Juan. "We may need them as lookouts before the night is over."

The gray sea heaved herself in heavy swells and parted angrily before the onrush of the freighter. Cold white spray swept back over the bow at each impact. Watching, Lubelski sat in his captain's chair and gripped its metal arms as each shudder groaned and rattled through his ship. Madness, he thought, nothing but madness. If he believed there was a God, he would pray to him now.

The bridge had become crowded. There were lookouts on each bridge wing, dressed in rain gear, but most certainly drenched to the skin and blinded by the blast of the sea and spray. Just inside, their reliefs stood ready to rotate with them, the green-tiled deck of the bridge wet from the seawater that dripped from their oilskins.

The helmsman clutched his wheel and struggled to hold the ship on its course. A technician stood at the radar making fine adjustments. Juan braced himself against the chart table. They all looked from one to another with tension in their faces. The experienced were apprehensive because of their knowledge of what could happen and might, the inexperienced simply fearful of the unknown.

"Are you gentlemen enjoying your ride?" Lubelski asked the general group and was answered with nervous laughter.

"It seems this storm came on us quickly," Juan said.

"It's quite common for the North Sea. Storms and fog of some magnitude can catch you off-guard completely. So you try and always be on your guard." Lubelski swiveled to face the technician. "How are you coming with the radar, Stephen?"

"Not well, Captain. It is still intermittent."

"Then we must continue to look sharply. This would be no night for a collision."

Lubelski glanced at Juan. He had become pale and far more nervous since the weather had intensified. Lubelski wished he would go to his cabin. Once he was off the bridge they would be able to reduce their speed. But Juan would not leave the bridge, would not relinquish control for even a moment. The Cuban just stared coldly back at him and braced himself against the roll and pitch of the ship.

Fine spray and a gust of cold air hit them as the bridge

doors slammed open and the lookouts rotated. Several swore under their breath at the sudden flailing of the elements, but at least the air was fresh on the bridge; below decks the ship had been closed up tight. A stale, almost rancid smell overpowered the ventilation system. Pity the poor bastards below, thought Lubelski, they would be huddled like rats in the bilges, aware only of the danger and the discomfort.

Suddenly the port lookout cried out. Lubelski was on his feet instantly, binoculars in hand. He moved like a cat across the slippery deck and plunged into the pelting spray and darkness to take a look for himself. He had no more than put his binoculars to his eyes before he saw dim navigation lights and a huge low shadow dead ahead.

"Hard right rudder!" he shouted.

"Hard right rudder, aye!" the helmsman answered and spun the wheel in a blur.

The freighter protested with a loud groan as she laid over on her port side and fought for a new course against the swells. All on the bridge grasped for whatever they could reach to keep from losing their footing. One lookout was caught out and fell, his head coming to rest hard against the chart table. Unconscious, he slid across the deck in a limp spread eagle, coming to rest against the port bulkhead.

Lubelski continued to look through his binoculars for a few seconds, then called out again. "Rudder amidships!"

The helmsman answered and then announced his new course, his voice noticeably shaken. Gradually the ship righted itself and continued its headlong flight into the void.

Lubelski stepped back onto the bridge, his expression as dark as the night surrounding them. When he spoke there was a solemn timbre to his voice laced with anger.

"She's a big one. A tanker, and she's full," he said. "Thank God she was on a northerly course. We might not have missed her if she had come at us head on."

Lubelski's words were directed at Juan, but they had a

widely disquieting effect. As the *Baltic Merchant* moved close by the still nearly invisible tanker, all eyes watched with a sober reserve until it had slipped behind them and disappeared. Lubelski, struggling with his mounting anger, barked orders for the removal of the fallen lookout, then returned to his captain's chair and sat there, staring into the mist-shrouded sea. Quietly the unconscious lookout was taken below and a replacement summoned to this station.

"Captain," the technician said, "I have the radar working again."

"Very well," Lubelski answered in a flat tone.

The freighter seemed to thrust herself against the sea as they pressed on. At times they went blindly into rain squalls, the radar blanking out totally with the interference, but Lubelski continued to sit stoically in his captain's chair. Juan held his ground at the chart table. The lookouts rotated in and out without comment. The night ground on, a contest of wills between two men and in turn they against the sea.

Lubelski ordered strong coffee for all hands on the bridge every hour. Each time it arrived it was taken eagerly as reinforcement against the tension and cold and fatigue.

As the crew became more tired, eventually, Juan's men were put into service as lookouts. There was some grumbling but it was quickly squelched by Juan, who had become progressively more acrid in mood as the hours passed.

Reinforced by hourly coffee, and kept alert by a common sense of fear, the lookouts did not fail in their task. They passed other ships, but the radar or the lookouts, their awareness undoubtedly heightened by the near miss, detected each of them in time to allow a safe margin. As the weather moderated and the sun broke through in a fiery sunrise, Lubelski recognized it as no minor miracle.

They had survived the mad rush through the storm.

The sea acquiesced into gentle swells and troughs. With the clear weather the mood on the bridge relaxed. The extra personnel were sent below until, of the men on the bridge, only Lubelski and Juan remained without relief.

"You have done well, Captain," Juan said in a hoarse voice that betrayed his weariness.

"We were exceedingly lucky. We cannot count on our luck holding indefinitely."

"At our present speed, when will we reach the Baltic?" Juan asked, ignoring Lubelski's warning.

"At approximately midnight tonight."

"Then we are still on schedule. That is very good."

"You've given me the coordinates for the rendezvous, but you've told me nothing else. Will we be meeting another ship, an aircraft, a submarine? What? I may have to make preparations."

"I suppose it does no harm to tell you. We will be met by a Russian destroyer. They will remove all of my men and our passenger, which should make you very happy."

"As it will you, I am sure."

"I have had a difficult night, I admit that. But the weather has done us a favor. It made it difficult for anyone to keep track of us. I doubt that our position is known at the moment."

"We should hope that it stays that way."

CHAPTER
Twenty-five

They came down from the flying bridge to the lower steering station in the cabin. Rachel held them on course while Pfifer studied his charts.

"You can slow down," Pfifer told her. "If Harry's last position was accurate, we should cross their track somewhere very near here within a half an hour, say by ten-thirty."

"It was amazing the way he found them."

Pfifer smiled. It hadn't surprised him at all. He kept remembering the cove and how nearly invisible it had been from the air the last he'd seen it. If Harry could find that, then a freighter as large as the *Baltic Merchant*, steaming in a narrow straight, would be well within his ability. That Long had chosen Harry Fisher for this particular assignment didn't surprise Pfifer, either. In a way it simply confirmed what he felt Long would do at the final, crucial moment.

"Harry is an amazing fellow when it comes to finding things."

Rachel throttled back and nervously rubbed her eyes.

"Are you all right?" Pfifer asked.

"No, quite frankly, I'm scared to death. I didn't realize this would be happening in the dark."

"It will be harder for them to see us during our little routine and easier for us to get away. Think about it that way."

"What you say is true, of course, but I'm still scared. Who wants to drown in the dark? It's much easier for me to be brave in the daylight."

"You'll be just fine."

"I hope we're both just fine."

The twin diesel engines throbbed steadily as the cruiser slipped smoothly forward on the calm sea. Rachel and Pfifer looked at each other for a moment before either spoke again. It would be so easy, Pfifer thought, to just come around and turn his back on the upcoming confrontation. It would be so easy, if he were any other man but who he was and Rachel any other woman.

"It's either going to work or it won't, Rachel. There's absolutely nothing to be gained by worrying about it."

"How did you get to be such a damned fatalist?"

"Practice."

"I'm not sure it's been good for you."

"You probably have a point." Pfifer turned away from her and snapped on the rear unit. "Let's see if this thing works, shall we?"

The radar screen glowed to life and the transmitter atop the mast began to rotate. Pfifer squinted at the display and adjusted the gain until the picture cleared and he was able to watch the units cursor sweep the empty sea around them.

"Not too shabby," he said. "The range is a little short, but what the hell. It should help us quite a bit. Hold your present course and speed. I'm going to put the transducer to our detonating device over the side and tie it off. Then we'll be ready."

Rachel looked up from her compass and smiled at him.

"Good girl, I'll be right back in."

On deck the night was clear with a partial moon. Pfifer took a deep breath before he began. As he did he became subtly aware of a tightness in his gut. He hoped it was simple apprehension he was feeling and not the first signs that his medication had begun to wear off. He rubbed his stomach for a moment and tried to put it out of his mind as he went to work on the transducer.

He lowered the cylindrical unit over the port side and let fifteen feet of its cord play out. Any more than that and it might strike the prop in a hard turn, or its tether might be severed. Any less and the unit would skip out of the water with only a moderate increase in speed. With it secured to a cleat and double-tied, Pfifer stood back and watched the orange and black device trail just below the surface alongside the cruiser. It would have to do.

Laying out the wires from the transmitter keying box, Pfifer went back into the cabin.

"Do you think that thing is going to work?"

"Yes, I just hope it doesn't work too well."

Rachel turned away from her compass and faced him.

"I don't understand what you mean."

"I just hope that the charges don't cause more damage to the freighter's hull than we're counting on. If any one of those things is a full charge. . . ."

"You got the charges from George Long, didn't you?"

"That's what has me worried."

"I'm not sure I appreciate you telling me that. You two have a strange working relationship. It's sort of like mutual distrust. How have you managed?"

"I guess you'd have to say it didn't work out."

Rachel turned back to her instruments, her face looking suddenly pale in the soft glow of their illumination.

"I suppose not," she said. "How are you feeling, anyway?"

"Questionable. But don't be alarmed. I should be all right for a while yet."

Rachel shook her head slowly. Pfifer could see a glistening in her eyes as she spoke.

"I'll be alarmed if I want to be, damn you. I love you, remember?"

The way she said it moved him. He could not answer immediately. He could only look out on the dark sea and tremble within himself. Of all of them, Rachel had come the greatest distance for the least reward. If she loved him, and he truly believed that she did, she had lost the most, and she would carry the weight of it for the rest of her life. Her brother, the man she loved, and soon her father as well, would have succumbed to the game, leaving her alone to face an uncertain future.

It would soon be over for Pfifer. The long journey from innocence, to the need for revenge, to the realization of what that revenge ultimately cost. It had proven to be a dark tunnel, entered in faith, leading to a blind end, and now finally at its terminus. Yes, it would soon be over, and almost thankfully so.

But there remained the final act, the final gesture against the inevitable. The effort to free Martin Stein would be followed through. The final sequence of events would be enacted, the closing rhythms of a wasted life brought to resolution. Martin Stein would be free or Pfifer would die in the attempt. He would make good on his promise. It would cost him nothing, for nothing remained for him to lose. Or was that true?

Would it be possible for George Long to deny him his goal?

"Damn!" Pfifer said.

"What's wrong?"

"I don't like relying on only one source for our information."

"You're worried about something. Please tell me what it is."

Pfifer hesitated, then went ahead; Rachel deserved to be aware of the possibilities.

"I just wish there had been some way to get an independent position on the freighter. I just can't shake the idea that Long might still have some trick up his sleeve. How do we really know that we are closing with the freighter and not just some trap? For all we know, we could be heading the opposite direction from where we want to go."

"You said Harry Fisher was a friend. You trusted him."

Pfifer met her gaze. She was right. It came down to that.

"Maybe I'm just suffering from a little last-minute uncertainty. Forgive me for that."

"What can we do besides proceed, anyway. It will either be a trap or it won't be, right?"

"Now who's being the fatalist?"

"Maybe you're contagious."

Pfifer smiled, but his smiled faded quickly as he looked down at the radar screen.

"Come left about twenty degrees, Rachel. It looks like we have company."

CHAPTER
Twenty-six

Lubelski was in a dark mood as he looked out over the deck of the *Baltic Merchant* from the bridge. He should, as Juan had suggested, be glad that he was about to be rid of his guests, but he could not shake a vague sense of foreboding. Something was not quite right, and he would not relax until he knew what that something was. He felt a pervading unease, just the whiskers of danger, nothing of substance to define its form.

It was a beautifully clear night. A half-moon silvered the glassy sea and the sky held its stars like diamonds set against an eternity of black. The freighter barely rolled as it thundered forward, a thoroughbred closing on the finishing wire.

Lubelski shifted his weight in his captain's chair. Perhaps he was only tired . . .

"Captain," the radar operator blurted out. "We have a small contact dead ahead. He seems to be turning towards us."

Lubelski spun about and looked at the slight figure hunched over the radar screen. Before he could speak Juan stepped between them.

"How far are we from the rendezvous?" he asked abruptly.

"At least twenty-five miles," Lubelski answered.

"How large a blip is it? Could it be the destroyer?"

"Stephen?" Lubelski said, deferring to his radar operator.

"No sir. It's far too small. It's more than likely some sort of small pleasure craft, or fishing boat."

Juan's expression clouded. He stared hard at Lubelski.

"What do you intend to do, Captain? I do not want that boat to close on us."

"There is very little we can do to stop them if that is what they have in mind. Shall we wait and see what they do?"

Juan shrugged Lubelski off and turned to a ship's telephone.

"I'm going to put some of my men along the side with automatic rifles. I suggest your radioman stand by to signal the destroyer in case we need help."

"There is very little a small boat can do against this freighter," Lubelski said. "And having armed men in plain sight as we pass will only arouse suspicion if the contact is just a simple pleasure craft and its occupants innocuous. Listen to reason, if you will."

"I am not concerned with how much suspicion we arouse at this point, Captain. Nothing is to stand in the way of our rendezvous with the Russian destroyer. For the last time, you will either cooperate without resistance, or you will be sent below."

Juan turned his back on a stunned Lubelski and began to bark orders into the phone. The men on the bridge cast nervous looks at their captain. They had never heard him spoken to in such a manner before. To them his authority had reigned supreme—until the advent of the little Cuban terrorist. Lubelski sensed their growing uncertainty and attempted to regain some semblance of control.

"Where is the contact now, Stephen?" Lubelski asked.

"Still closing, Captain," the radarman answered with a slightly heavy accent on the word *Captain*.

"Let me know immediately if they begin to veer away."

"Yes, sir."

Lubelski spun his captain's chair around again and looked out through the bridge windows. He could see three of Juan's men moving across the deck as they went forward to the bow and crouched down with their rifles at the ready. In the reflection of the window he could see Juan standing behind him, also watching his men's progress.

Juan struck an almost arrogant pose. Chin held high, hands clasped at his back, a condescending expression on his round face. Lubelski's hatred of him seethed as he looked at him. He resented the little terrorist's control over him more than anything he could remember. If it were not for the consequences of such action, he would have ordered his men to overpower the pathetic little beast and introduce him to the very bowels of the cold, black Baltic. But, for now, if he were to survive the ordeal and remain captain of his vessel, he would have to do as he was told. Still, the anger grew perilously within him.

When the bow charge detonated, it was as if the ship had suddenly run aground. Lubelski was lifted from his seat and barely prevented himself from going through the bridge windows by hanging on to the arms of his chair. Juan, a look of sudden terror on his face, fell to the floor as the blast shook the entire ship beneath them.

"All stop!" Lubelski shouted above the chaos.

"No!" Juan screamed from the deck at his feet. "We must continue!"

"Shut up!" Lubelski commanded with a ferocity that left Juan agape. "Unless you want this spot of empty sea to be all of our graves, you will let me do my job! I must know what my damage is."

Alarms were sounded as the *Baltic Merchant* coasted to a

stop in the darkness. Below decks crewmen frantically closed watertight doors and an inspection party was formed to try to determine the extent of the wounds that had been inflicted upon their ship.

On the bridge Juan regained his feet, if not his composure, and tried to spot the men he had sent out on deck. They had vanished with the plume of spray that had enveloped the bow at the moment of the blast. Lubelski watched Juan for his reaction out of the corner of his eye as he received reports from his damage-control personnel.

"My men? Where are my men?"

Lubelski let the question go unanswered.

"They have gone over the side! We must save them, I will need them!"

Lubelski nodded and gave the order for a man-overboard party. But then he ignored Juan, who was teetering on the verge of panic, and continued with the business at hand.

"What caused the blast?" Juan asked, fighting for his self-control.

"At this point we do not know for sure, but whatever it was it was powerful enough to part the steel skin of our bow and flood the forward void."

"Then we are sinking!"

"No, we have the flooding under control."

"Captain," the radarman called out. "That small boat appears to be closing again. He is on a course to intercept."

"Damn!" said Juan, finally coming completely out of his momentary daze. Brusquely he pushed the radarman out of the way so he could see the scope for himself.

Lubelski was about to object, but at that moment a seaman dashed onto the bridge with a message pad clutched in his hand. The perspiration glistened on his forehead, his lips were drawn into a thin pale line.

"Captain," he stammered. "We are receiving radio transmissions from someone who says he has mined our ship. He is making a demand and threatens to sink us."

The bridge became quiet. Lubelski took the message pad and read slowly.

"It seems he wants our passenger," he said matter of factly.

Juan came forward and took the message from Lubelski. As he read, his face colored with rage.

"Never!" he said through clenched teeth. "I will die before I fail in this. Radio the destroyer immediately! We will blow them out of the water!"

"We could all be on the bottom by the time they reach us. No, we must do as we have been asked. It is our only option," Lubelski said as calmly as he could, trying not to elevate Juan's emotional state any further.

"What if there are no other mines attached to this ship?" Juan asked no one in particular, then turned to Lubelski. "We will stall him as long as possible, hold radio silence so he does not realize the destroyer is approaching. The destroyer will be monitoring our transmissions. They will realize the situation and come at all possible speed. We should be able to wait him out."

Lubelski frowned. "You're playing a game with all our lives! Please, do as he has asked. Put this passenger of yours over the side. Your destroyer can just as easily pick him up again when we are safely out of range of whatever detonating device he has. If this madman placed one mine he could have placed many more."

Lubelski could feel the situation slipping away from him. He was overcome with a deep sense of fear for his ship and his men, but apparently Juan viewed the dilemma from a different perspective. Lubelski shook his head in despair.

"Our 'discussion' is over, Captain," Juan suddenly said, his voice much calmer. "We will wait."

The cruiser was dark. Pfifer had made sure that no running lights were visible. The only light inside the cabin was the dim glow from the compass, and even that he had taken care to shield in such a way that only he could see it as he steered a course that would bring him near the freighter's stern. The engines idled quietly. Rachel sat beside him in a padded bucket seat.

"How long will you give them?" Rachel asked.

"Not long. We can't risk them putting divers over the side. Those mines aren't booby-trapped. They could just pull them off and drop them."

"How many mines are there?"

"Only one more that I can count on for sure. Only one more that I would care anything about blowing anyway."

"It's been ten minutes since we radioed them."

Pfifer strained to see the freighter more clearly in the darkness. He thought he could see movement along the main deck, but could not be sure. If they were preparing a surprise for them, he did not want to give them unlimited time. Even concentrated small-arms fire would be a serious problem, if they found the range, and the white decks of the cruiser almost glowed in the bright moonlight. What if the freighter's armory contained something more lethal, a hand-held rocket launcher perhaps? He decided not to worry Rachel with his thoughts.

"They're stalling for some reason. I wish I knew why. Take the wheel for a minute. Let's look at the radar again."

Rachel came and took his place at the wheel. Pfifer snapped on the radar and watched as the green scope came to life. After several minutes, he stood back.

"Anything?" Rachel asked.

"No. It looks like we're still alone, but you can count on the fact they sent out some kind of distress signal. I'd guess we don't have a hell of a lot of time."

"What do we do?"

"We play our trump card, and hope for the best."

Pfifer picked up the transducer's keying device and pressed its button. The second mine was the stern mine. It took two pulses to trip it. The third mine, if there was one, would

take three pulses. Simple, as George Long had said, probably too simple.

They could hear the high-pitched ping as it went out into
the water. It was a curious and innocent little sound, if you
weren't aware of its consequences. Pfifer and Rachel both
looked toward the freighter as they awaited the result.

The explosion boiled the black sea into a stark white burst
of foam. The heavy crump of the detonation could be felt
strongly through the cruiser's deck. Pfifer guessed that the
jolt must have been severe inside the long dark hull of the
freighter. Perhaps now they would take his bluff seriously.

"That should get their attention," Pfifer said.

"If it doesn't sink her," Rachel said under her breath.

She was thinking about it, Pfifer realized. She was
thinking about the death they could be causing by remote
control. Hidden by steel and darkness, but real nonetheless.
He wished he knew the words that would comfort her. But
of course there were no such words. Combat was never
much more than condoned murder. Your soul was scarred by
it indelibly no matter what your rationalization. The best he
could do for them both would be to simply get on with it.

He picked up his microphone and pressed to transmit.

"*Baltic Merchant*, this is Pisces, do you copy, over?"

The acknowledgement came rapidly, the radioman's voice
in a state of near panic.

"We copy, over."

"I wish to speak to Juan personally. I have one more
charge, and it will, I'm afraid, end your capacity to respond. If I am not speaking to Juan in five minutes, I will
detonate it. Do you understand, over?"

"We understand, Pisces. Please wait, over."

Rachel looked at him from her position at the wheel. He
could see the concern in her eyes, even in the dim light.

"What happens if they don't cooperate, John? What do
we do then?"

"Don't go any closer than we are, Rachel. Just circle her

in a clockwise direction." Pfifer picked up the binoculars from a chart table. "I'm going to step outside and take a look."

"You didn't answer my question."

"I'm not sure I know the answer. We just have to wait and see what develops."

Pfifer left the cabin and moved out on deck. As he felt the chill of the night air he unsuccessfully attempted to suppress a shiver. It was almost over, he told himself. Either they would put Martin Stein over the side in a lifeboat and then move off, or they would sit and wait for the coup de grace. It would be show or fold.

Would he have what it took to press that final button? He had intended to put the final mine under the belly of the freighter, near her fuel tanks. If George Long had tampered with the specifications of that final mine, as Pfifer could not help believing he had, then the final charge would obliterate the freighter. There would be few survivors, if any, and Long's problem would be solved. The blast might even be sufficient to take the cruiser with it if they were too close when it went up.

Could he do it? Rachel had asked him that plainly enough. Was the third mine actually in place? How could he be sure? He had been in the throes of Long's drug, and, no matter how he wracked his brain, he could not be sure.

Raising the binoculars to his eyes, Pfifer began to sweep the port side of the freighter.

There were men rushing about the deck of the freighter. Some went forward, some aft. The sounds of their shouts to one another reached Pfifer clearly. It was pandemonium— disorganized, out of control. Surprised that he could not spot any marksmen or evidence that an attempt was being made to spot him visually now that he was under the freighter's radar range, Pfifer lowered his binoculars. What was going on?

"John!" Rachel called from the cabin. "They're trying to raise us on the radio."

Pfifer went in quickly.

"Pisces, this is Juan, come in. Over," a strained voice kept repeating.

"This is Pisces," Pfifer said, putting the microphone to his mouth. "On the following points there is no negotiation. One, within ten minutes, you will put Martin Stein over the side. I expect to see a single lifeboat with only one oarsman. Two, once our transmission is complete you will immediately turn on all topside lights, all of them. Open every porthole and outside hatch. I want to see you lit up like a Christmas tree. Finally, when you have put your lifeboat in the water, I want you to put some turns on that tub of yours and move off. If you do not comply, I will happily sink you. Do you copy? Over."

They waited quietly for Juan's reply. The air noise and static from the radio mixed with the sound of the engines and the slap of the waves against the cruiser's hull. Rachel stood tense at the wheel. Pfifer found himself staring at her.

Lubelski stared at Juan. They had huddled together in the tiny communications room; Juan, the radioman, and Lubelski. When Juan finally spoke, his confidence seemed to have finally returned. He was in charge of himself again. Perhaps it was the acknowledgement by their mysterious foe that he was the force to be reckoned with, perhaps it had simply taken time for him to regain his equilibrium, but he took the lead, he asserted himself once again. Lubelski wondered if it would have been possible for him to do so if his men had witnessed his performance on the bridge moments earlier.

"The latest position on the destroyer?" he asked of Lubelski.

"They should be here within half an hour."

"So, before the transfer could be completed, they will be here to help us?"

"More than likely, but only if they are using their top speed."

"Then perhaps it would be smart to at least appear to be complying with this Pisces. It would give us the time we need." Juan did not wait for anyone to concur with him before he acknowledged Pfifer's demand.

"And who will be the oarsman?" asked Lubelski.

"I will be the oarsman, Captain. Unless of course you are volunteering?"

"No, I am not volunteering. It is your decision."

Juan looked from face to face to those around him. The arrogance had returned and along with it the determination to prove he was worthy. He suddenly laughed loudly.

Lubelski was not surprised at Juan's choice. He realized that the lifeboat would be the safest of all the places to be. Pisces would not direct fire at the lifeboat if retrieving Stein alive was as important to him as it appeared, and if Pisces became impatient and blew the last charge, Juan would be clear of the destruction. No, Lubelski was not surprised, he was sickened.

Then Juan pulled a crumpled sheet of paper from his pocket and handed it to Lubelski. Lubelski glanced down only briefly at the encoded message.

"Unless there is a problem, do not send this, Captain. I still wish to present my information to the KGB personally. Do you understand?"

Lubelski understood all too plainly.

Martin Stein lay on his bunk. Neither asleep or awake, his consciousness came and then vanished at intervals. Everything around him seemed veiled, unclear. His comprehension was as blurred as his vision. The sounds that reached him were meaningless and disjointed. Delirium grasped at him and, all the while, he slipped further and further away.

Then, a sudden, painful brightness startled him. He saw shadows over him, heard strange and angry voices. Then felt himself being lifted up by rough hands, but as they withdrew him from the light, and carried him out and along dark and eerie corridors, he fainted.

He was cold when he awoke, his skin wet from the damp night air. Instinctively, for his instincts were perhaps all he had left, he tried to draw himself into a fetal position for warmth. He was aware of rocking and splashing and of the creaking of oars in their locks.

It was dark again. He trembled uncontrollably.

Pfifer heard a voice over the freighter's loudspeaker. He thought he recognized it as the ship's captain, but he was not sure. He had listened to him for only a moment on the wharf in Rotterdam, and Rotterdam seemed a lifetime ago. It was a strong voice, used to unswerving obedience, but this night it was somehow a sad voice as well. It was the voice of a man who believed his ship would be dying beneath him within moments. It foreshadowed great and catastrophic loss. Pfifer empathized with that voice and with the man.

As the message spread throughout the freighter, the lights began to come on. The cabin lights, the floodlamps on the decks and cranes, every porthole, every light that could be shown was shown, and the freighter glowed brightly in the ink-black sea. It appeared as a shining sentinel, routing the night boldly before it.

No one moved about the decks now. The light had driven them to cover. The only activity centered around a pair of davits where a lifeboat was slowly being lowered to the water. Pfifer focused on the lone occupant, a stocky, bearded man. When the fragile hull touched the sea Pfifer watched as he inexpertly set his oars in their locks and began to pull away. Pfifer knew that man would be Juan.

"Can you see them, Rachel?"

"Yes, but I can't see Martin."

"They must have put him in the lifeboat before the lights came on. Steer for them, but go slowly."

Pfifer lowered his binoculars. Ignoring the pain in his hands, he reached into his pocket for the automatic he had taken from his guard at the hospital, checked its clip, and then replaced it. It was small bore, but at least it had a full clip.

"If something goes wrong, Rachel, I want you to head due north as fast as you can to the coast of Denmark. Don't play heroine. It would only cost you your life."

Rachel looked at him through the open cabin door but did not speak.

The cruiser and the lifeboat closed on each other at a steady rate. Both were illuminated by the glow of the freighter's lights. Juan sat facing them, pushing the oars clumsily in the water. His face was in shadow.

"He's either a very cautious man, a lousy seaman, or both," Pfifer said mostly to himself.

"Can you blame him for being cautious?" Rachel said, surprising Pfifer that she had heard his comment.

"I suppose not."

Pfifer raised his binoculars to look at the freighter. A group of men had begun to gather along the lifelines. None seemed armed; apparently Juan's men had been ordered to stay below. The flooding too must now be under control. They were not moving off as he had ordered, but then the force of the stern charge might have prevented that. Pfifer dropped his binoculars and grasped the butt of the automatic in his pocket.

"Cut your engines, Rachel. Just let them idle. We'll let that fellow pull the last few yards. It will give him something to do with his hands."

Pfifer watched the lifeboat approach. He could see it clearly and he could see that Juan was tiring, his strokes becoming shorter, choppier. Pfifer waited patiently until he was within easy earshot before he spoke.

"Throw me your line, then put your hands over your head."

Juan looked at Pfifer's face carefully as he drifted toward the cruiser. A spark of recognition caused him to grimace.

"So you are Pisces?" he asked.

"Throw me your line—now."

Juan picked up the coiled line at his feet and flung it to Pfifer. Pfifer caught it adroitly and wrapped it around one of the cruiser's cleats with his left hand. He pulled the automatic and held it on Juan with his right.

"Where is Martin Stein?"

"He's in the bottom of the boat, unconscious, but quite alive. You will have to help me lift him over."

The small amount of forward thrust of the cruiser was enough to cause the lifeboat to close against the cruiser's side. Pfifer and Juan looked at each other from no more than six feet away. They studied each other warily but with a certain fascination: mortal enemies at swords' length.

Juan seemed to be in no hurry to make any effort to lift Martin. He seemed to be almost prolonging the proceedings. Pfifer prompted him sharply.

"Can you lift him enough to let me get hold of his arms?"

"Perhaps."

"Try it."

Juan got up from his seat slowly and moved forward in the lifeboat. Stooping, he put his hands under Martin's arms and lifted. As he did Pfifer put the automatic in his belt and leaned over the cruiser's railing.

Pfifer grabbed hold of Martin's wrists and pulled. Juan shoved from underneath. As Martin passed over the rail, Juan suddenly gave one final push. Pfifer was not expecting it, and fought for his footing to keep from dropping Martin heavily on the deck. When he looked back at Juan, his heart sank.

Juan stood there smiling, holding a revolver aimed at Pfifer's chest.

"Now, it would seem, I am giving the orders."

Pfifer eased Martin to the deck and crouched beside him.

"It would seem so," he said.

"Call your helmsman," Juan said and began to step onto the cruiser.

"I'm right here," Rachel said from the cabin doorway. "If you will notice, I have in my hand the detonator to the remaining mine aboard the freighter. If I were you, I would drop the gun and cast off."

Rachel was dead calm. She delivered her ultimatum with an almost practiced ease. Pfifer guessed that she would do exactly what she said she would. He hoped Juan was not foolish enough to call her bluff.

Juan took the sudden turn of events badly. His eyes went wide, his hand shook as he held his gun. His voice trembled with anger.

"I don't believe you would kill so many men. Put the detonator down now, or I will kill this man."

"You are Juan, are you not?"

"Yes, and I will not ask you again to put down that detonator."

"I'm Rachel Stein. That is my brother lying on the deck. I've come much too far to back down, and besides, Jews have special reservations about putting themselves in the hands of their enemies."

"A Jew?" Juan spat the word. "Don't talk to me about that. I know your secret."

Rachel wavered. "What secret? What is it that you think you know? Tell me or I will blow your freighter up this instant!"

Juan shook more violently. He glared at Rachel. Pfifer glanced between them, guessed their resolve to be equal.

But the distance to the freighter was dwindling. Soon they would be within easy rifle shot. Pfifer could see the men along the freighter and hear their voices clearly. The longer Juan waited the stronger his position became, but did he see that, or was he too angry, too blinded by the frustration of the impasse?

"You are no Jew," he shouted. "Your father is no Jew. He is a Nazi, and the network he runs fraught with other Nazis. A very clever man he must have been to fool so many for so long. But the charade has come to an end.

"As I think of it, it was almost perfect. What better thing to do, become one of the hounds instead of the fox."

"But my mother was a Jew," Rachel's voice trailed off weakly. "It must be a lie."

"Then it is your brother that has told the lie. No, Rachel Stein, it is the truth, and when Moscow learns of it they will destroy it all."

The cruiser continued to idle closer to the freighter. Rachel held the detonator delicately in her hands. Juan leveled his gun at Pfifer. Martin Stein began to stir on the deck at Pfifer's feet. Pfifer, mentally marking off the distance between himself and Juan, began to wonder how many times he would be shot during the leap he would have to make.

Faintly at first, then with rapidly increasing strength, they began to hear the drone of aircraft engines. Juan smiled at the sound of them, relaxed, then spoke with a new confidence in his voice.

"If I am not mistaken, that is the sound of a spotter aircraft. I believe you have no choice now but to lay down your arms, so to speak. There is a Russian destroyer on its way here. You must realize now that you have no chance."

"I wouldn't be so sure," Pfifer said. "Spotter aircraft are almost always single-engine affairs. That aircraft has two engines."

The aircraft approached fast and low from the south. When it came into view, Pfifer got a short glimpse of its silhouette before its landing lights came on. It was a seaplane and it literally bore down on them.

Juan, startled by the sudden burst of light, turned to look behind him for an instant. Without so much as a heartbeat's hesitation, Pfifer made his leap.

Juan's gun went off as they made contact. Rachel screamed. The detonator fell to the deck. With all his strength, Pfifer forced Juan back against the cruiser's railing and stripped the gun from his hand. Then, with a sharp chop to Juan's throat, Pfifer watched him collapse to the deck, his windpipe crushed.

Rachel lay on the cabin floor, clutching her shoulder. Pfifer started to go to her, but at that instant, rifle fire opened up from the freighter. He bounded to the flying bridge, realizing that he would draw their fire, also realizing that the thin walls of the cruiser would do little to protect him anyway, and slammed the throttles open.

The seaplane had landed just north of them. Pfifer watched in disbelief as it turned and taxied boldly in their direction. What fool, Pfifer thought, would risk his hide like that? If it were Harry, he must be losing his grip.

The cadence of the rifle fire from the freighter increased as more of Juan's men got into the act. One round shattered the windscreen in front of Pfifer's face, sending sharp fragments flying and causing him to duck involuntarily after the fact. Then, before he had straightened up, the sky turned red and the concussion of a tremendous explosion crushed him into the dash.

He turned and looked behind him, his own hot blood running down his face, and looked where the freighter had been seconds before, but all that remained was a huge ball of flame surrounded by a red and orange sea, while bits and pieces of steel and wood and other more horrible things rained down.

Pfifer's gaze dropped to the deck below him. There he saw Martin Stein leaning against the transom. There was a demonic smile on his face, and Pfifer wondered why, until he saw. Somehow Martin had managed to reach the detonator Rachel had dropped when she was hit. He still held it in his hands, pressing its button again and again.

With numbed senses, Pfifer turned his back on the scene and steered the cruiser toward the seaplane that now bobbed gently, as it waited for them.

Pfifer cut his engines as he swung alongside the seaplane. Almost immediately the seaplane's side hatch opened and Harry Fisher appeared. He grasped the side of the cruiser as it drifted in. His face was stark white at what he had just seen.

Pfifer came down the ladder from the flying bridge and went into the cabin. As gently as he could he lifted Rachel into his arms and brought her out on deck. Martin slumped at the foot of the transom, unconscious again. Juan's body lay along the rail below Harry.

"Am I going to die?" Rachel asked as she looked up at Pfifer.

"Not from this," he said, inspecting the crease in her arm.

"It feels horrible."

"You'll be all right. Now let me help you onto the plane. The quicker you all get away the better."

Rachel stiffened in his arms.

"You're not coming with us?"

"No, but you'll be safe enough with Harry. He'll take you back to England."

Rachel let him help her to her feet and toward the seaplane. She stopped at the hatch and turned to face him.

"Please come with us," she pleaded.

Pfifer took her in his arms and held her, then let her go, and pushed her toward Harry.

"I can't come with you. I plan to at least die a free man. But never doubt that I love you. I'm sorry, that's all I can say. I know it's not enough."

"I'm suppose it will have to be, won't it?" Rachel said, beginning to fade again.

Pfifer looked at Harry and nodded. Harry took Rachel by her good arm and helped her aboard. In a moment he returned to the hatch and helped Pfifer lift Martin Stein's limp body over the rail.

"Take good care of them, Harry. And give my best to George," Pfifer said and then pushed the cruiser adrift.

"You knew, didn't you?"

"I knew you'd be here when the smoke cleared."

"I'm supposed to bring you back."

"Tell George, no thanks. Now get the hell out of here, will you! If we're friends, do just that one thing. Tell Long I had you at gunpoint, or whatever you think will work, but understand Harry, I'm not going back with you, not alive anyway."

Harry fell silent, wavered, was about to speak when he looked past Pfifer, swore aloud and pointed. Pfifer wheeled around and saw a long gray shape approaching fast.

"It's Russian, and he's spotted us!" Harry shouted and then quickly slammed the hatch shut.

Pfifer leaped to the flying bridge and cranked the engines to life. He heard the seaplane engines start behind him as he gunned away. Once the cruiser was at full speed, Pfifer looked back. The seaplane had just become airborne and in a few seconds it was moving away at a rapid speed, low to the water.

"God's speed, Harry," Pfifer said to the wind. "I guess you were a friend after all."

Pfifer looked forward into the darkness and nudged the throttles to make sure they were fully open. He wondered if he would live to make the coast of Denmark, and if he did, what he would do then.

Finally, he simply thought of Rachel and smiled.

CHAPTER
Twenty-seven

Washington's rush hour long past, the bus was only half full as it slogged through the light traffic. Pfifer's eye followed the tall berm of snow, pristine white at its top, dirty brown at its base, as it zigged and zagged roughly parallel to the bus's path. He pulled his collar up and hunched in his seat against the cold, while in his mind he tried to piece together his shattered recollections.

He should have been dead, but somehow they had made a mistake. It must have been a mistake. A miscalculation in the dosage of the antidote they must have put into him in the Hamburg hospital. An oversight by some underling, unaware of the consequences of his omission? It did not matter. The result was that Pfifer did not die, according to the scenario.

He was alive, but he was not free.

After the long run to the coast of Denmark, he had found a beach and grounded the cruiser. Exhausted, he had gone below and collapsed on a bunk, fully expecting he would not live to see the morning. But the morning did come and with it a realization.

He had little money left. He had made no preparations for his fundamental needs, in fact had made no plans at all. It was an ironic joke that had been played on him. Suddenly he was like a captive animal set unexpectedly loose in the wilds to fend for itself. There were no support systems to fall back on; he could not turn to anyone that knew him for help for fear they would tell someone connected with the Agency he was still alive. He was literally in the cold, a loose end.

He could not work legally, for he had no papers that he dared to use. He could not move about easily, for fear they were looking for him. The clandestine world still held him, in limbo, at arm's length, subject to its capricious attention. And so he was almost sorry he was alive, survival being a perverse inconvenience.

He could, of course, turn to the competition for help. The Russians would put him to use, or the Mossad, or any number of other intelligence factions, but that would be to negate his sacrifice, reverse his course correction. The peace he felt within himself would be forfeited. It was true the promise of a quick end in some ways had made it easy to be brave, but now fate was asking him to validate his courage under different terms. The price had gone up, and he would have to reach deep within his newfound determination to make good the debt.

No, Pfifer realized that he had chosen, that the decision was made, and that he would not, could not, withdraw from the consequences.

The bus rumbled to a stop. Pfifer recognized the street and got to his feet. The only passenger to get out, the driver closed the doors behind him as he stepped off and onto the icy sidewalk.

The sun had gone down. The streetlights that glowed over his head made the night sky appear blacker and the snow whiter. Pfifer turned his back as the bus moved away in a dark cloud of diesel exhaust. As he began to walk his breath billowed out visibly in front of him.

He had read nothing in the papers about the kidnapping, or about the loss of the freighter. It did not surprise him. Neither the Russians nor the CIA would want any of the events of the game to be published. The embarrassment would be a two-edged sword, and then there was the network to be considered. The KGB would be aggressive in its efforts to ferret out the players on their end. The CIA might even help them with a few, once the complicity of the Nazis was well known. No, there would be nothing in the papers, it would be kept under wraps, officially termed a nonevent by the KGB, discreetly filed by the CIA. Only the principals in the game would ever know what had taken place.

George Long's apartment building loomed before him. Its many stories were illuminated in a crazy quilt of light patterns, formed by the randomly lit windows. Just inside the entrance, Pfifer could see a desk, manned by a security guard. He looked down at himself, at his soaked trousers and wrinkled black overcoat, wondering if he would be allowed to pass. Then, reluctantly, he felt for the gun deep in his coat pocket. He would not kill to reach George Long, but he would not be stopped.

George Long would know he was alive by now. There would have been a correlation of information from the hospital, from Harry's description of his condition, perhaps even from Rachel. They would realize the drug had not taken hold, and when his body remained unfound the assumption would be automatic that he had survived. But would Long expect Pfifer to seek him out? Would it be just another trap set for him to blunder into blindly? Pfifer thought not. They would assume he would go into hiding and stay there. They would assume he would use his skills to disappear into the normal world, burrow deep, and never surface. The prey would not stalk the hunter, self-preservation would dictate otherwise. They would assume from a basis in logic.

They would be wrong.

Pfifer caught his reflection in the glass door as he entered the apartment building. He barely recognized the stark figure he faintly knew as his own. The beard was mostly grown back, the eyes dark and penetrating, his body gaunt. As the door swung shut behind Pfifer, the security guard at the desk stood immediately and reached for his phone.

"I wouldn't do that if I were you," Pfifer said calmly, lifting the automatic from his pocket.

The guard, a black man of medium build and in his middle years did the sensible thing; he froze. Then, slowly, he raised his hands over his head and stepped back from the desk.

"Whatever you do man, just keep your cool," the guard said, his eyes riveted on the muzzle of Pfifer's automatic.

"Remove your belt and your shoelaces and lay down on the floor."

"Yes sir," the guard answered and quickly assumed the position.

Pfifer bound the guard's hands behind his back with his web belt, used his long shoelaces to secure his feet together and then stuffed a dust cloth he found in one of the desk drawers into his mouth. Satisfied, he shoved the prone, and extremely apprehensive, guard under the desk and admonished him to stay still. Then carefully he stood back and turned.

Rows of mailboxes lined the wall to his left. He went down the columns until he found Long's name, made a mental note as to the number and then moved quickly to the elevators. Methodically he checked his watch as the doors spread open before him. It was a quarter past nine.

Would killing Long be enough? Would it end it, finally, completely, for Rachel, for himself, for them all? Had he come to this as his final alternative? No doubt he would be simply returning in kind what had been planned for him. No doubt there had been times when the act should have been done without thought. Long did stand between Pfifer and any chance for freedom. Long would come after him eventually. The struggle would never be over until he was dead. But, the question remained, would killing Long be enough?

The elevator doors slid open on the appropriate floor, exposing an empty hallway. Pfifer glanced at the closed doors to note which way the numbers ran, then turned to his right. A few doors down he stopped and hesitated. The drone of a television told him what he needed to know.

Pfifer replaced the automatic temporarily in his coat pocket and brought out a set of lock picks. He selected the pair he thought he would need and delicately inserted them. Because of the need to be supremely quiet, it took him several minutes before the handle began to rotate in his hand. Then, when he was ready, he drew the automatic, checked to make sure its safety was off, and leaned hard into the door.

The security chain he was expecting was there and pulled away from the door jamb in an explosion of plaster and wood chips. Recovering his balance quickly, Pfifer closed the damaged door with a thrust of his hand and moved across the room to the back of a large leather chair.

"Have a seat, John," George Long said in a voice that betrayed no fear. "I've been expecting you."

Pfifer rounded Long's chair, warily, his automatic leveled at Long's head.

"You may put that away," Long said. "I am, as you can see, unarmed."

Pfifer continued to stand and hold Long in his sights.

Long met his gaze and turned the television off with its remote control.

"It looks as though you've had a rough couple of months. You should have come in sooner."

"I haven't 'come in,' George."

Long smiled. "Of course, I should have known."

"You knew about Howard Stein from the beginning, didn't you? That he was a Nazi, that the network wasn't what it was supposed to be. Why didn't you tell me?"

"You forget. You'd just let me down on an important assignment. I felt you needed the extra motivation. If you'd known that we'd set Stein and the network up for a fall, you wouldn't have carried out your mission with such dispatch. You are to be congratulated, by the way. You put in a brilliant performance."

Pfifer lowered the automatic fractionally. He should have felt anger, but there was none.

"What purpose did it serve? If you had wanted to burn Howard Stein and the network, why not just let the Russians know? Why do the drill? Start from the beginning, George. A lot of people are dead because of this little operation. I'd be interested in what you have to say."

Long stared at him silently for several minutes, then nodded his head and began. Pfifer knew he would talk, and that he would keep talking, to keep Pfifer from raising his gun, to keep him from pulling the trigger. But Pfifer would only listen as long as he cared to.

"You have to understand something. It was deemed important at Langley that the Agency be free of any possible blame for the loss of the network. Not everyone behind the Iron Curtain involved with the network has Nazi affiliations. As much as we would have preferred, there was no way to be selective as to who would be eliminated once the purge began."

"No blood on Agency hands?"

"Exactly. If the KGB found out on their own what was happening, if we could pull that off some way, we would be in the clear. We would still have credibility with the few contacts that would remain afterward."

Pfifer shook his head slowly; Long continued.

"We've suspected, for some time, more people were

coming over through Stein's network than we were being told. We've also known that the neo-Nazis have been recruiting personnel. It was only a year ago that the connection was made between the escape network Stein funds and the recruiting efforts of the Nazi underground in East Germany. And, if it hadn't been for one disaffected recruit, we still might not know. But that's an entirely different story in itself.

"Access to the escape route Stein's network provided has undoubtedly been an effective incentive for attracting new people to their movement. This is what we were most interested in stopping. This was the apparatus that needed dismantling.

"To get back specifically to Howard Stein, it was arranged that Martin Stein would be briefed as completely as possible on all of the known details of the network and then that he would learn of his father's past Nazi affiliations. —That was easy enough to do. We simply put some incriminating photographs in a place he would be sure to find them.—Then a terrorist group, headed by Juan and infiltrated by one of our agents, was steered to the Steins as a possible, lucrative kidnap victim. We'd had a man in Juan's group for about six months and we knew that Juan was working hand in glove with the Russians and was eager to prove himself to them. We also knew that questioning kidnap victims had become a matter of course in most operations of that type, and that Martin would most likely tell them about his father with little prompting, given the motivation of the knowledge of his father's past.

"We couldn't make it too easy for the Russians, though. They had to believe they had done it on their own. That's where you came in. Half of your function was to provide evidence to the terrorists that someone was eager to get Martin Stein back. They wouldn't know, immediately, if you were CIA, British, or Mossad, and then there was the hoped-for effect of keeping them very interested in finding out just what sort of games the elder Stein had been up to. We had to be sure they would interrogate Martin carefully.

"The second part of your function was to flush out as much of the Nazi underground as you could. We informed Stein about your mission and managed his information in such a way that he would get the idea that your real goal was to kill his son rather than save him.—We were unable to learn his method of communication, but obviously he got the word out through some means.—In this role, I'm afraid you were a bit like the bait on our hook. And an effective one, I might add. The two men that attempted to kill you and Rachel in Germany? They weren't KGB, and they weren't part of Juan's contingent. German intelligence tells us they were recently defected from East Germany. Their high degree of training, made obvious by their ability to follow you, albeit with the clues we were dropping to Stein, is very revealing. It tells us that the Nazis have a serious and capable organization."

Long looked at Pfifer steadily as he talked, his expression almost friendly. Pfifer, both fascinated and repulsed by Long's revelations, could only listen.

"Unfortunately, things did get a bit out of hand for a while. After you eliminated two of Juan's group in Rotterdam, we lost our contact on board the freighter. Don't worry, neither man you killed there was our agent. Ironically, the man Juan left ashore, with instructions to find you and kill you, was our man. He, of course—Miguel is his name— reported to us.

"We knew in Rotterdam, from Miguel, that Martin Stein was still alive and that he had not been questioned yet. —And of course there was the problem of Rachel to consider.—So the decision was made to let you proceed. We were in hopes that you would surface with Rachel under control and turn her back to us. A decision we regretted when we lost contact with you for a period.

"In Hamburg though, we had to hedge our bets. There

was the possibility that Martin Stein could figure out that it was the CIA that had made it possible for him to find out about his father.—Any decent lab would have been able to tell him the photographs were doctored, and that had bothersome potential.—We couldn't very well let the Russians know we had helped set Martin Stein up. That would have spoiled the effect entirely. So, the charges we gave you to plant were not exactly what you had asked for. We had to make sure that Martin never made it to the KGB for a really thorough examination.

"Sorry about that, it must have been quite a surprise when that third charge went off. It was on a timer, by the way. It would have gone off within an hour or so of when it did, anyway."

"So from the very beginning all you had in mind was to burn the network? And you started it all off with a lie? With some phony pictures cooked up just for the purpose?" Pfifer said.

"A lie? Stein is working with the Nazis."

Long paused. Pfifer handled the automatic absentmindedly. He had been the bait, and Rachel with him. He could forgive Long for what he had done to him, he'd given his consent to be used for such things long ago. But he could not forgive him for what he had almost done to Rachel. Rachel had been duped. She had, along with her brother, been led into the throes of a desperate struggle, without knowledge, without consent, to be used as pawns. Were they all that worthless to Long, to the Agency?

"What about Rachel, her brother, Howard Stein? What is to happen to them now?"

"Ah yes, I anticipated that you want a recent report on them. Especially Rachel. I received a dispatch yesterday."

Long turned in his chair and reached for a small drawer in a table beside him. Pfifer leveled the automatic quickly as he did, causing Long to freeze with his arm partially extended.

"Just tell me from memory, George, if you will?"

"Very well," Long said, relaxing slowly back into his chair. "Rachel is running the Company at this point. Martin has been institutionalized.—The drugs that were used on him unfortunately have had a permanent effect.—Howard Stein's health has continued to decline since the incident. His relationship with his daughter is understandably difficult at this point, and he is, for all intents and purposes, under house arrest at his estate while we attempt to unravel his contacts."

"Attempt? Stein isn't cooperating?"

"No."

"Even though he knows that he has been exposed?"

"That's correct. And something more annoying. Apparently the transcript of Martin's interrogation didn't reach the Russians intact. For some reason the radio message that left the freighter, pertaining to what Martin had told them, was not received in total. We must assume he told everything, but our sources indicate much of the network still in place, as if the purge had only gone so far and stopped. Whoever is actually running things from the other side is still in business."

Pfifer stared at Long. It suddenly dawned on him that Rachel's ordeal was not over. As long as Howard Stein lived, as long as the black tendrils of old nightmare reached out for them, as long as there was reason for men to seek to silence a voice that might betray them, she stood in the way of the horror. Too many had hidden too long to simply trust the loyalty of a dying man, a dying man suddenly stripped of the few remnants of happiness he had managed to keep close during the long deception. Stein might choose to go to his grave with the forgiveness of his daughter rather than the cold knowledge he had not given away old participants in a cause that might suddenly have little meaning for him. The Russians would not be the threat. It would be the Nazis, for they were the ones that knew without doubt they were at risk.

"What now, John?" Long asked. "What will you do now?"

"I'm not sure just yet. I'm not sure what I can do."

"Come back in, John. We can use you. Take a long rest if you like, perhaps back up on that old sloop with Harry. You won't survive much longer on your own. Just look at you. You're half starved, tired. You haven't had an easy time of it. It will only get worse. You have no assets."

"No," Pfifer said calmly. "There's no chance of me coming back."

"You've been useful to your country, to the Agency, to me. Why not? In a few more years you could retire from this business in the clear."

"The drugs, George. Remember the drugs? You pumped poison into my veins just as surely as if you had pushed a hypodermic into my flesh. Why? Simply because you needed what? Reliable control? Damn you, George, I'm not even human to you. I'm just an instrument, a game piece, an item in your black bag of tricks. No George, I won't work for you anymore, or anyone else like you. It's finished, forever."

Long lost his pleasant countenance. He stared solemnly at the automatic Pfifer held on him.

"Then you've come to kill me?"

Pfifer looked down on Long. Suddenly the little round man grew ashen as he met Pfifer's stare.

"It would set me free, wouldn't it, George? No one else in the Agency would have your motivation to find me. No one else would know me so well. The advantage would suddenly be mine. Isn't that right, George?"

The panic was in his eyes. Pfifer raised his automatic and held Long's face in its sights for several seconds as he contemplated what he wanted to do.

"What you say is true," Long said faintly. "I won't

argue the point, but before you squeeze that trigger, you'd better read the dispatch I tried to show you. If you care for Rachel.''

Pfifer looked hard at Long; he saw the beads of perspiration beginning to form, the desperation beginning to set in. Rachel. Long would use Rachel as a weapon against him. Rachel was Pfifer's vulnerable point, and Long had been quick to seize upon it. Almost involuntarily the gun in his hand began to lower.

Long slowly reached to the drawer beside him, slid it open, and removed a large envelope. Carefully he extended it to Pfifer. Their eyes locked in a stare as Pfifer took it from him.

Inside, first in a bundle of sheets, was a photocopy of a medical report, Rachel's name clearly printed at its top. The words below began to blur as Pfifer read them.

''Are we now in a position to negotiate?'' Long asked.

''You know what I want,'' Pfifer said, making an effort to hide the anger in his voice. ''What do I have to trade to get it?''

''The names. The names of men involved with Howard Stein. The closer to the top the better. Get me those names and we will hide Rachel where no one will harm her. Where she will be free of it all, where she can safely raise her child, and yours. And it is yours, isn't it, John?''

''And me? What about me, or do I even have to ask?''

''You would come back in. In a few years, if you were productive, you would be allowed to retire and join your family. Think hard before you answer, John. Rachel will not live long enough to deliver her child, the way things stand. The Stein family is as of this moment only a security risk to the Nazis. You know, perhaps as well as any man alive, that no defense can be built around them as long as they remain in place. Someone will get to them.''

Long's words rang in Pfifer's ears. He was right. Someone would get to them. There were a hundred ways it could be done. The miracle was that it had not already been done.

"We will leave immediately for London, together. With luck, by tonight, perhaps we can have what we need. You must confront Stein yourself. He might listen to you, once you point out his options."

Pfifer suddenly raised his automatic. Long stiffened in his chair reflexively.

"I have conditions," Pfifer said.

CHAPTER
Twenty-eight

The snow had turned to a cold rain as Pfifer slogged through the darkness toward the Stein estate. He crossed the tracks of the sentries, filled with water now, bleeding into black splotches, ugly evidence of the presence of Long's soldiers.

But the sentries had been withdrawn tonight, so that Pfifer could make his approach to the house unchallenged. And inside the great old house, only Joe Bryant stood guard, at the door of Stein's study. Upstairs, waiting in the room that once was hers but now could never be again, Rachel.

Pfifer's bare hands were numb in the pockets of his coat. The mantle of snow that had dusted his shoulders and head melted away quickly in the rain, leaving him wet and freezing cold. But he could ignore his physical discomfort, for inside raged a fire. The white-hot flame of hatred and contempt. Contempt for a man that would live a lie for half his life at the ultimate expense of his family. Hatred for the trap George Long had laid for him, precluding his escape.

Deception. Which had been the greater of the two, Howard Stein's—so many years living a charade, behind a shroud of duplicity? Or George Long's? His deception had been designed to trap innocent and guilty alike. For what? The manipulation of the KGB into doing the Agency's dirty work?

The winners and losers hard to identify now. Perhaps they all had lost more than they had gained. Perhaps the convoluted twists of this particularly dirty game had condemned them all.

But Pfifer could not condemn Rachel. He could not condemn his unborn child, and he would be doing both if he did not follow through with Long's bidding. No, Pfifer knew he would be forced to play this game to its end. He knew Long would not move Rachel to safety if there were the possibility she might draw out his prey.

Stein had been told he was coming. He had been given warning that there would be no one else present for his meeting with Pfifer. That and other conditions had been met. There was now but for Pfifer to make good his efforts.

But what could he actually expect to get from Stein? What line of persuasion would give him the information Long wanted? He must understand the risk that Rachel was exposed to, and if her safety wasn't sufficient to break him, what could? What sort of man would hold his flesh and blood to the flame? What could Pfifer do, short of the barbaric, that would open Stein's mouth?

The frozen steel of the automatic lay heavily in the bottom of his right pocket. He grasped it, removing its safety. There was no more time for contemplation. The Stein house towered before him.

A silhouette moved in front of an upstairs window and paused. The curtain parted, emitting a shard of brighter light. Rachel? Would she see the dark figure now approaching so close to the house? Please stay where you are Rachel, until it is done. Then, just a word, a brief word, before our final parting.

The front door was of heavy plank, but it pushed open easily at the turn of its latch. Pfifer closed it behind him solidly and, as he peered down a dim hallway, Joe Bryant stood at middistance, watching him stoically.

"He's waiting for you in here," Bryant said flatly.

"Things haven't turned out as we had hoped, have they, Joe?" Pfifer said as he stopped before Bryant. Bryant shook his head. His sad eyes told Pfifer what his words could not.

"You're unarmed?" Pfifer asked.

Bryant opened his coat showing himself to be so.

"Expect George Long in an hour."

Bryant stepped aside.

Pfifer pushed open the double doors of Stein's study and went in. Bryant pulled them shut behind.

Howard Stein sat in a plain armchair, facing an ornately paned window. He did not turn at first to look at Pfifer, he continued to stare blankly at the patterns of snow and rain beating against the glass. Pfifer stood silently, the droplets from his coat falling softly to the thick rug beneath his feet.

Stein's face was deeply lined, darkly circled. It showed its years and its tribulations. But it remained a proud face. There was that hint of arrogant strength of a man beaten but not destroyed. Testimony to his tenacity and what else? Blind fanaticism? Pfifer could only wonder. Finally Stein turned toward him and examined him in turn with his deep-set eyes.

They stared at each other in silence, neither so much as blinking. Both, condemned men with nothing left to fear, nothing left to lose. They stared at each other, as death might stare at its own reflection on a drowning pool, until finally Stein spoke.

"I would have recognized you," he said. "They would not have had to tell me who you were."

Pfifer stepped forward out of the dim light of the doorway and stopped in front of Stein.

"You must realize why I've come."

Stein simply nodded.

"It has to end, old man."

"Yes," Stein whispered.

"Then you'll tell Long what he needs to know?"

Stein stiffened in his chair. His eyes grew hard and narrowed and Pfifer could sense a sudden anger within him.

"No."

The rain continued to fall against the window, the only sound in the cold room. Once again the stares of the two men locked.

"Do you care for my daughter?" Stein asked.

"Yes."

"And for the child she carries?"

"Believe me, they're the only reason I'm here tonight."

Stein nodded and then smiled faintly.

"I'm beginning to understand. We are much alike."

"I doubt that very much, Herr Stein."

"We are men in a trap. Each caged just as securely as the other. You by George Long and the Central Intelligence Agency, and me by an old madman and a dream that should have died with Hitler and the rest. No, Herr Pfifer, we are much the same. We have each misplaced our loyalty. We each entered into a thing that cost us far more than we planned. We each toe the mark, for different reasons initially, but ironically now for the same reason. It is a strange kinship, is it not?"

A sudden chill ran through Pfifer, a chill to the bone, a chill to his soul.

"Why not simply tell Long what he wants to know and be done with it?" he finally asked. "He'll protect Rachel and the baby."

"No. You don't understand. Telling Long would do no good. He could not strike where he would need to. Your government would never authorize such an operation. The man you would need to eliminate is too highly placed, too well insulated. And as long as this man lives, Rachel will be in danger. Betrayal, you see, is the one unforgivable sin to this man."

"You're saying there's no way out?"

"No, I'm not saying that at all." Stein rose to his feet. He wavered as he did, his strength nearly gone. But he turned to Pfifer and stared at him face to face. "I've seen everything in my life, everything I care about, destroyed. My country, my self-respect, my son . . . Not Rachel, not her as well. Not with your help."

Stein began to walk away from the window to a paneled wall between two tall bookshelves. He paused at the wall, studied the panels for a moment, and then pressed his hand at the seam between two of them. Two narrow doors creaked open as he stepped back. From a shelf inside, he withdrew a black leather pouch and then went to sit at his desk.

"This is something we must do ourselves," Stein said as he emptied the contents of the pouch onto his desk. "I have the means, and you have the skills required."

Pfifer approached the desk. Stein had taken a velvet gem-bag and a small box from the pouch. Stein handed the gem-bag to Pfifer. It was heavy.

"You now have the means to mount whatever operation is necessary. With those diamonds and your skill and no government to tie your hands you can do what is required."

"And you?"

Stein opened the small box that remained on the desk before him. Inside was a single capsule.

"Within ten minutes of your leaving here tonight, I will cease to be a problem. Only one question remains."

"Many questions, Herr Stein. Who is the man you would have me kill, and how does killing him stop this thing from going on? Rachel told me there are others, the ones that send the diamonds . . .''

"Old men, mostly. Frightened old men who would just as soon stop, just as soon forget, if it weren't for this one man. No, Herr Pfifer, killing this man can very well put a stop to it."

Stein paused and stared at Pfifer, the room again falling silent.

A strange kinship, Stein had said, and in a way he was right. Neither he nor Pfifer was free to make his own choices. Both of them had entered a game that had robbed them of that. Pfifer looked steadily at the cold eyes that met and held his gaze. He could never like Stein, he could never forget what he had stood for, the damage his kind had done. But Stein had paid a price and now he was preparing to pay the final price. His life for the freedom of his daughter. His daughter, who was a Jew.

"How do I find him?"

Stein reached into the center drawer of his desk and removed an envelope.

"This letter will tell you all you need to know."

"Rachel?"

"Joe Bryant will be taking her out of the country tonight. A procedure for finding them is in the letter. She will be waiting for you when you return."

Pfifer reached out and took the letter from Howard Stein, then turned. Bryant had entered the room and stood by the door.

"Joe will take you to Rachel now. Good luck, Herr Pfifer."

Stein rose from his desk and stood to the side. In his hand he held the small yellow capsule.

Outside the cold rain had strengthened. Pfifer looked past Stein into the darkness. Through the multipaned window, across the rapidly melting snow, he could see the long dark stain of Howard Stein's shadow as it reached for the darkness beyond.

EPILOGUE

The morning was low and gray as George Long looked out of the window of the parked limousine. Berlin was pale and close in the filtered light. Long considered it in between glances at his watch. It was an appropriate morning to meet with his opposite number from East Berlin. Appropriate for its veils and indistinctness. Distasteful this morning for Long, because he knew all too well what this meeting would be about.

A certain American agent in the hands of the KGB.

They would have him of course, there would have been no way for him to have come out of East Berlin after what he had done.

What price would they extract? How hard should he negotiate to get Pfifer back? Why would they consider giving him back at all? Long grimaced at each question and possibility. All he knew for sure was that a ranking officer in the East German intelligence service had been shot to death with a high-powered rifle as his car had emerged from his country estate. A particularly accurate shot, the reports had it.

Maddening. Dangerous. Confusing. How had he managed it? Only Pfifer was left to say. The only other man who might have known being Stein, whose body lay cold in the ground.

Suddenly it was time and Long pushed open the door of the limousine. Perhaps the Russian could shed some light.

"This may take some time," Long said to his driver. "Wait for me here."

The driver nodded his assent and Long moved off.

The raw cold assaulted him as he walked toward the entrance of the alley. Alleys, warehouses, run-down industrial districts, he had made so many of these meetings in such places, why did this one seem so disturbingly familiar? Perhaps it was only his imagination, only a quirk from a tired mind.

And he was tired. Tired and fatigued but not remorseful. Remorsefulness was reserved for those who did not understand the game in its proper perspective. And if anything, Long prided himself on understanding the game. On this, he had no illusions. No false ideals. Not after so many years.

Shuddering from the cold, Long picked up his pace.

Suddenly, ahead, a dark-coated figure appeared from around a corner. Long, squinting, recognized his man. It was Morozov, the walk was unmistakable, even though he walked facedown, his hat pulled down, his collar up against the chill.

Methodically, unhurriedly, the two men approached.

Long pushed his hands deep into his pockets as he paced off the final few steps. Out of reflex he looked back over his shoulder as he stopped, to see that he had not been followed.

"Morozov . . ." he began to say as he turned.

But then Long abruptly fell silent, for as the dark-coated man looked up and showed his face, it was in fact a familiar face, but the wrong face. A face wearing a smile. A smile to greet the devil with.

About the Author

JAMES UNDERWOOD lives in Connecticut with his wife and children, where he is at work on his second novel. Educated in California, and a veteran of the U.S. Navy, he has traveled widely and enjoyed multiple careers as musician, advertising copywriter and salesman. His other interests are collecting old musical instruments and participating in automobile road racing.

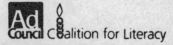